Disintegration of the Atom

Petersburg Winters

Cultural Revolutions: Russia in the Twentieth Century

Series Editor
Boris Wolfson—Amherst College

ACADEMIC
STUDIES
PRESS

Disintegration of the Atom
Petersburg Winters

GEORGY IVANOV

Translated from the Russian,
Edited, Annotated, and with
an Introduction by
JEROME KATSELL and
STANISLAV SHVABRIN

Sections of the initial superseded draft of
Petersburg Winters were prepared with the assistance of
OKSANA WILLIS

Boston
2017

This publication is supported by

AD VERBUM

Translation of this publication and the creation of its layout were carried out with the financial support of the Federal Agency for Press and Mass Communication under the federal target program "Culture of Russia (2012-2018)."

ISBN 978-1-61811-454-9 (hardback) ISBN 978-1-61811-562-1 (paper)
ISBN 978-1-61811-455-6 (electronic)

Cover design by Ivan Grave
On the front cover: *Excavator*, by Mstislav Dobuzhinsky
(from the album "Petrograd in 1921," 1922).
On the back cover: Portrait of Georgy Ivanov by Yuri Annenkov, 1921.

Published by Academic Studies Press in 2016, paperback 2017.
28 Montfern Avenue
Brighton, MA 02135, USA
press@academicstudiespress.com
www.academicstudiespress.com

in memoriam
Vladimir Markov
(1920–2013)

Table of Contents

Acknowledgments

One must be thankful for the growing richness of scholarship that has recently been directed to the life and work of Georgy Vladimirovich Ivanov. Our task as his translators, editors, and interpreters has been greatly enhanced by contemporary scholarship, including but not limited to the analyses and research by Andrey Arieff, Nikolay Bogomolov, Anna Lisa Crone (1946–2009), Jennifer Jean Day (1973–2009), Justin Doherty, Sergey Fedyakin, Roman Gul' (1896–1986), Vadim Kreyd, Alexei Lalo, Francesca Lazzarin, Nikolai Melnikov, Georgy Moseshvili (1955–2008), Kirill Pomerantsev (1906–1991), Andrei Ranchin, Peter Rossbacher (1928–2007), Svetlana Semenova, and Tatjana Senn. Michael A. Green, Professor Emeritus (Program in Russian, University of California, Irvine) assiduously read the first draft of *Petersburg Winters*. We are thankful for his many helpful and precise suggestions. Valuable assistance came from Kirill Tolpygo, Slavic and East European Studies Librarian at The University of North Carolina at Chapel Hill.

One scholar, teacher, mentor, and dearly departed friend we must single out for special praise for his fundamental contribution to the study of Georgy Ivanov. It is Vladimir Markov (Vladimir Fedorovich Markov, 1920–2013, Professor Emeritus with the Department of Slavic Languages and Literatures of the University of California, Los Angeles). Not only did he establish a personal contact with the notoriously difficult and cantankerous Ivanov, but in a serious of groundbreaking publications Markov laid the foundation for an impartial conceptual understanding of this poet and writer's significance for Russian letters and culture. In addition to that Markov should be credited with establishing the subfield of Ivanov studies. He accomplished all this at a time when only a few people were persuaded that Ivanov merited such attention; it should be noted that his contribution to Ivanov studies comprises a mere fraction of his wide-ranging achievement.

Jerome Katsell and Stanislav Shvabrin gratefully dedicate this volume to the memory of Vladimir Markov.

A number of years ago Jerome Katsell and Oksana Willis, with advice and encouragement from Stanislav Shvabrin, set out to redress the dearth of Georgy Ivanov's prose in English. *Petersburg Winters* was translated first in draft. Of its total eighteen chapters, Oksana Willis did first drafts of eight of the first sixteen; Jerome Katsell did likewise, and on his own Chapters XVII and XVIII, which Ivanov added for the final 1952 edition. The initial notes for *Petersburg Winters*, which have now been superseded, were formulated by Katsell and Willis. Unfortunately, Oksana Willis was unable to continue her work on this project. The first draft of and the notes to *Disintegration of the Atom* were the sole work of Jerome Katsell. Stanislav Shvabrin joined the project in 2014. Since that time the initial drafts have been thoroughly revised, and a new introduction written, while the notes have been culled and expanded where needed.

While we are most grateful for all the assistance directly or indirectly proffered by the scholars enumerated here and others, final responsibility for the text remains of course with the translators, editors, and annotators.

On Transliteration, Sources, and Annotation

We have chosen to use a two-tier system of transliteration of Russian names and toponyms. The "service" sections of this volume, such as this preamble, the introduction, and the notes, adhere to a simplified US Library of Congress transliteration system that matches each Russian (Cyrillic) character with its customary English (Latin) counterpart, yet avoids diacritical signs. In the texts of our translations of *Disintegration of the Atom* and *Petersburg Winters*, we have opted for still greater simplicity with the aim of meeting the needs of English speakers who may wish to sound out or pronounce Russian names they encounter in this book. To that end, we signal the presence of the "y" sound found at the beginning of such English words as "young" and "yonder" when it appears before and between Russian vowels: hence the surnames that could be and have been rendered in English as "Esenin," "Evreinov," and "Chebotarevskaia" have invariably been spelled as "Yesenin," "Yevreinov," and "Chebotarevskaya." In those cases where the presence of the accented "o" sound would be obscured by the deceptive correspondence between visually identical Cyrillic and Latin characters, we have used the "yo" combination, hence the spelling of "Fyodor" (not "Fedor") for the first name and "Gumilyov" (not "Gumilev") for the surname.

Whenever supported by precedents in English usage, in the body of our translated texts Russian first names and surnames of foreign origin retain their English or Western spelling (hence "Alexander," not "Aleksandr"; "Hippius," not "Gippius"; and "Wilhelm," not "Vilgelm"). We depart from this practice in those instances where the author deliberately chooses to employ patronymics along with first names: it is for this reason that the reader will find "Alexander Blok" and "Aleksandr Aleksandrovich Blok" for the poet and "Alexandra" and "Aleksandra Fyodorovna" for the empress, for example. Along with those of many first names and surnames ("Dmitry," and not "Dmitrii," "Gorodetsky," and not "Gorodetskii"), the different grammatical endings of Russian toponyms have all been standardized to look identical regardless of the gender of the nouns they modify in the original: hence "Vasilyevsky" and not "Vasil'evskii," "Shpalerny" and not "Shpalernaia." It is useful to recall that much like alphabets, all transliteration systems are mere approximations of the sounds and sound combinations they correspond to in actual speech, and as such they are subject to various spelling conventions and may not altogether eschew occasional incongruities and inconsistencies.

After falling into obscurity, Georgy Ivanov's literary legacy was rediscovered and reevaluated, first in the West and subsequently in the Soviet Union and Russia. His poetry, prose, and critical writings have been republished multiple times, and annotated scholarly editions have long superseded small-run original publications and their reprints. Our translations of *Disintegration of the Atom* and *Petersburg Winters* are based on the versions of these texts established in the three-volume annotated collection of Ivanov's writings compiled by Evgenii Vitkovskii and Vadim Kreyd (see Georgii Ivanov, *Sobranie sochinenii v trekh tomakh* [Moscow: Soglasie, 1994]). Whereas Ivanov did not revise the text of *Disintegration of the Atom* after its publication in 1938, he amended that of *Petersburg Winters* when he republished the memoir in 1952 in such a way that it differed considerably from its initial publication of 1928. Among the most important emendations are the removal of the poem-epigraph from Ivanov's friend-foe Georgy Adamovich, deletion of a number of sections pertaining to Anna Akhmatova (Chapter VI) and the poet and novelist Aleksei Skaldin (Chapter VIII), along with the addition of Chapters XVII and XVIII. Certain fugitive fragments published by Ivanov under the "Petersburg Winters" heading in various émigré outlets were not included in either version of the memoir when it was published as a book in 1928 and 1952 and have not been incorporated in our version of the text. Ivanov's references to "DPs," or "displaced persons" (here citizens of the Soviet Union who found themselves in the American, British, and French-controlled sections of Western Europe in the aftermath of World War II, as was the destiny of this book's dedicatee Vladimir Markov) in Chapter XVIII expand the narrative span of the book from the early 1900s to the 1940s and 1950s. The order in which *Disintegration of the Atom* and *Petersburg Winters* appear here reflects that of the publication of their finalized versions.

Following the lead of our *On the Border of Snow and Melt: Selected Poems of Georgy Ivanov* (Santa Monica: Perceval Press, 2011), the English translations of *Disintegration of the Atom* and *Petersburg Winters* seek to introduce the Anglophone reader to the most significant parts of Ivanov's legacy as a prose writer and memoirist. As translators and annotators of *Disintegration of the Atom*, we have been singularly fortunate to draw on the experience of our predecessors Peter Rossbacher and Alexei Lalo. More expansive and interpretative in their nature and scope, our notes to *Disintegration of the Atom* combine our research with the achievements of our predecessors, while those to *Petersburg Winters* lean heavily on the annotations compiled by Georgy Moseshvili for the aforementioned three-volume collection of Ivanov's writing as well as those by Nikolai Bogomolov (see Georgii Ivanov, *Stikhotvoreniia. Tretii Rim. Peterburgskie zimy* [Moscow: Kniga, 1989]). Our much sparser notes to *Petersburg Winters*, therefore, cannot rival those found in these two editions. We identify the sources of Ivanov's quotations and misquotations, but leave the majority of his references to historical events and characters uncommented, since more often than not interested readers may easily find such background information readily available online or in the editions we have used.

"...Struck by all the horrors of human disillusionment..." Miseries and Splendors of Georgy Ivanov's "Citational" Prose

Among Russia's outstanding lyric poets Georgy Ivanov (1894–1958) remains, and will always be, an uneasy presence. The series of miniatures he composed halfway through and toward the end of his life as he confronted penury, mortality, and oblivion have secured him a place not merely alongside his fellow émigrés Vladislav Khodasevich and Marina Tsvetaeva, but in the all-Russian pantheon that includes the likes of Anna Akhmatova, Osip Mandelstam, and Boris Pasternak. In such books of verse as *Roses* ("Rozy," 1931), and especially *Embarkation for the Island of Cythera* ("Otplytie na ostrov Tsiteru," 1937), *A Portrait Without Likeness* ("Portret bez skhodstva," 1950), *Poems* ("Stikhi," 1958), and *Posthumous Diary* ("Posmertnyi dnevnik," 1958) his growing mastery at distilling despair into austere, indelible idiom stops readers in their tracks, but not—superficially, at least—because they find Ivanov's poems to be life-affirming triumphs of creativity over adversity or chaos. On the contrary, if there should ever be a contest for the thorny wreath of the most morose of Russian lyricists, he would stand a good chance of becoming its laureate. Yet the economy of his form, and his directness in communicating his bitter truths never fail to command attention and reflection, as Ivanov takes it upon himself to draw a line under the imperial period of Russian history (see poems opening with "Nice—there is no Tsar" and "Small enamel cross in his lapel"), when he makes his hero toy with the idea of suicide only to shrink from this prospect in fright ("A bluish cold [A chill at my temple]"), or when he chooses to cast a reproachful parting glance at some of Russia's most enduring myths and aspirations, after holding them up to the disgrace of their fulfillment ("The passage is free at Thermopylae," "Russia is happiness, Russia is light").[1]

One of the most nonchalant of his contemporaries, Ivanov fluttered across the motley but rigidly demarcated landscape of pre-1917 Russian literature with its "strong poets," groups, schools, and movements as it suited him at any given moment. After his departure from Soviet Petrograd to Berlin in 1922, he expended significant effort reinventing himself as a living link between the postrevolutionary dusk of the "Silver Age" of Russian poetry and the younger generation of exiles struggling to make sense of their separation from their homeland. An erstwhile Ego-Futurist and member of the neo-Acmeist "Guild of Poets" (and one-time ardent World War I-era patriot behind the front lines), already at the outset of his career Ivanov chose to treat literature as a game with few hard-and-fast rules apart from those governing the craft of versification. Combined with his weakness for intrigue and manipulation, Ivanov's literary partisanship eventually earned him the reputation of a scurrilous critic as he persisted in waging protracted, public, and ultimately pointless wars with his "rival poet" Khodasevich and Khodasevich's younger protégé and ally Vladimir Sirin (Nabokov). Even though in the circle of the prerevolutionary luminaries Zinaida Hippius and Dmitry Merezhkovsky Ivanov was proclaimed "the first poet of exile"—and despite the influence he enjoyed and shared with his on-and-off friend Georgy Adamovich among the literati aligned with the magazine *Numbers* ("Chisla," 1930–1934)—Ivanov gradually succeeded in alienating all but a few of his closest friends and most forgiving of admirers, withdrawing, as he did, to the company of his second wife, poet, novelist, and memoirist Irina Odoyevtseva (Iraida Heinike, 1895–1990). Predictably enough, what at one point must have seemed a thrilling game of literary vitriol and self-advancement proved impossible to win without incurring significant losses; toward

---

1 The best edition of Ivanov's poetry is Georgii Ivanov, *Stikhotvoreniia* (St. Petersburg: Izdatel'stvo DNK-Progress Pleiada, 2010), ed. Andrei Ar'ev. A representative selection of his mature and late verse can be found in *On the Border of Snow and Melt: Selected Poems of Georgy Ivanov*, introduction by Stanislav Shvabrin; trans. and ed. Jerome Katsell and Stanislav Shvabrin (Santa Monica: Perceval Press, 2011).

the end of his life it fell to Ivanov to document their corrosive effects on the gambler's soul:

> They tell me: "You've won the game!"
> It's all the same. I'm not playing anymore.
> All right, as a poet I will not die,
> Yet as a man I am dying.
>
> ("A Portrait Without Likeness")

It was in that negativity, however, where Ivanov found an equivalent of a guiding light, a way of asserting himself in the face of defeat—and along with it he evolved a sense of poetic irony that helped him cling to some of his dignity:

> I've turned despair into a game—
> What's to sigh and cry about anyway?
> And isn't it amusing, that I'll die
> No later than next week?
>
> I'll die—although I could live on
> Ten or perhaps even twenty years.
> No one took pity. No one helped, either.
> And now it's time to slip away.
>
> ("I've turned despair into a game")

Here must certainly lie one of the secrets of Ivanov's lasting success with modern audiences—or a good deal of it. Unconcerned with—or simply ignorant of—some of the least savory aspects of his literary and extraliterary stance and conduct, his newfound readers sense that under its chillingly crystalline surface Ivanovian despair may actually be hiding a hopeful, affirmative charge. Fittingly, the exegetes of that nihilism of his have forwarded a useful designation of this puzzling, counterintuitive phenomenon. With the aid of a concept adapted from theology, the empathetic students of Ivanov's mature poetry draw our attention to what they designate its "apophaticism": his seemingly illogical ability to derive strength to create from a sense of abandonment and impending doom that should surely have rendered futile any such impulse if Ivanov's poetry truly were as barren of hope as it might appear to a superficial observer.[2] In its essence it is akin to a staunch believer's capacity for affirming God's existence through the negation of everything a supreme deity is not and cannot be, and a theodicean strategy based on this procedure. Thus Ivanov's epitaphs to a Russia that will never rise from its postrevolutionary, post-Civil War ashes seem to have the unexpected and perhaps unintended effect of breathing new life into the very same cultural myths they appear to be demolishing. Despite the prevailing tenor of his mature verse, Ivanov proves to be a "nihilist" who succeeds in becoming "a light-bearer" of a deeply divided culture, in Vladimir Markov's far-reaching formulation.[3]

Attractive and convincing as these hypotheses may appear, first and foremost they concern Ivanov's verse, not prose, and certainly not his legacy as critic and memoirist. But then his most audacious and consequential foray into the realm of artistic prose, *Disintegration of the Atom* (1938), cannot be defined and described in terms customarily reserved for analyses of prose works, be they traditional or unconventional. What is indisputable, however, is the fact that *Disintegration of the Atom*, the graphic nature of its content notwithstanding, represents not only one of the most contentious, but also one of the most elusive texts in the Russian literary canon, and deliberately so. In this compact work Ivanov demonstrated his ability to expand the boundaries of a domain his supporters and detractors agreed on treating as his own—that of a terse versified lyric utterance—to

---

2   Andrey Arieff points out that the earliest substantiation of Ivanovian "apophaticism" was formulated by his younger contemporary, fellow émigré poet, and acquaintance Kirill Pomerantsev (see Andrei Ar'ev, *Zhizn' Georgiia Ivanova. Dokumental'noe povestvovanie* [St. Petersburg: Zvezda, 2009], p. 120).

3   Markov's accessible essay "Georgy Ivanov: Nihilist as Light-Bearer" is both a perfect snapshot of the state of affairs prior to its subject's posthumous rediscovery and reevaluation but also an incisive and thought-provoking comparative analysis of Ivanov's legacy as poet and thinker (see *Bitter Air of Exile: Russian Writers in the West, 1922–1972*, ed. Simon Karlinsky and Alfred Appel, Jr. [Berkeley: University of California Press, 1973], pp. 139–163). It is followed by a selection of Ivanov's poems in Ron Loewinsohn's and Theodore Weiss's versions as well as Brant Basset's translation of an excerpt from the closing chapter of *Petersburg Winters*.

leitmotif-rich first-person prose narrative. At the time of its publication its subject matter provoked resistance not encountered by any other work by Ivanov, a resistance that took the form of an indignant, offended silence.[4]

While literary connoisseurs value Ivanov primarily as a poet, his prose fiction and memoir writing enjoy a considerable popularity. His first experiments with the short story date back to 1914, the installments of his novel *Third Rome* ("Tretii Rim") were serialized in 1929 and 1931, and in 1933 he published a series of fragments united under the title of *The Book of the Last Reign* ("Kniga o polednem tsarstvovanii"), a fictionalized study of the twilight of the Russian Empire. Ivanov the memoirist, author of a range of autobiographical sketches published in émigré literary outlets under the heading of *Chinese Shadows* ("Kitaiskie teni," 1924–1930, collected posthumously) and *Petersburg Winters* ("Peterburgskie zimy," finalized separate edition 1952), has been enjoying a steady popularity as a highly subjective, and highly amusing, chronicler of Russia's literary and artistic scene before, during, and after the turmoil associated with the outbreak of World War I, the Revolution of 1917, the Civil War, and the eventual solidification of the Soviet totalitarian regime.

It is this aspect of Ivanov's controversial but indubitably significant literary legacy that the present translation of *Disintegration of the Atom* and *Petersburg Winters* seeks to bring to the attention of the Anglophone reading audience.

---

4   In his *Russian Literature in Exile: An Experiment in a Historic Survey of Literature Abroad*, Gleb Struve refers to an alleged "conspiracy of silence" that prevented *Disintegration of the Atom* from being reviewed on the pages of the most influential intellectual journals of the emigration (see his *Russkaia literatura v izgnanii: opyt istoricheskogo obzora zarubezhnoi literatury* [New York, Izdatel'stvo imeni Chekhova, 1956], pp. 316–317). For a survey of contemporary reactions to *Disintegration of the Atom*, see Ar'ev, *Zhizn' Georgiia Ivanova*, pp. 247–254.

Disintegration of the Atom

If I did not believe in life, if I were to lose faith in the woman I love, if I were to lose faith in the order of things, even if I were to become convinced, on the contrary, that everything is disorderly, damned, and perhaps devilish chaos, if I were struck even by all the horrors of human disillusionment—still I would want to live, and as long as I have bent to this cup, I will not tear myself from it until I've drunk it all! However, by the age of thirty, I will probably drop the cup, even if I haven't emptied it, and walk away.

—Fyodor Dostoevsky, *The Brothers Karamazov*

Like certain other literary works from the first half of the twentieth century, *Disintegration of the Atom* was composed to shock; unlike the vast majority of such works, it has retained a good deal of its shocking charge until today. This same shocking—or repellent, as it may be alternatively termed—quality, however, accounts for only a fraction of the lasting relevance of this compact prose narrative. Once a contestant for the title of "the Russian Oscar Wilde," Ivanov probably would not mind being proclaimed "the Russian Henry Miller" based on the superficial similarity of their subject matter and the unconventionally blunt—for his time—manner of its presentation,[5] but calling him that would only obscure the fact that in *Disintegration of the Atom* he pursues objectives at once more ambitious and specific. Before these are discussed even briefly, however, it would be useful to take a closer look at the genre nature of this narrative piece.

---

5   In 1955 Ivanov readily acknowledged a certain kinship between Henry Miller and *Disintegration of the Atom*—although the author of *Tropic of Cancer* was unknown to him at the time he wrote his narrative (see Ar'ev, *Zhizn' Georgiia Ivanova*, p. 415). For Alexei Lalo, the surfeit of mostly arid and even repellent sexual references in *Disintegration of the Atom* "appears to be a pioneering attempt at developing [a] new, modern, vocabulary for carnal and corporeal desires in terms recognizable to a contemporary Russian audience" (see his "Exploring the Impetus of Russia's Silver Age: Representations of Sexuality and Eroticism in Aleksandr Kuprin, Ivan Bunin, and Georgii Ivanov," *Toronto Slavic Quarterly*, no. 31 [2010], http://sites.utoronto.ca/tsq/31/lalo31.shtml).

Held together by its nameless protagonist, this agglomeration of themes and leitmotifs, along with all its stylistic lapses (take the incongruent "heartless face," for example), quickly proves to be the result of a well-considered and focused effort, an expertly "literary" work that merely masquerades itself as the cri de coeur of a heartbroken man driven to distraction by his beloved's departure. Compelling as Ivanov's depiction of heartache and rejection may be (few would argue that his protagonist's selfish complaints and misogynistic rants do not amount to a starkly accurate portrayal of the chaotic inner world of a possessive jilted lover on the verge of suicide), soon enough one realizes that Ivanov prompts his reader to take *Disintegration of the Atom* not only literally but also figuratively. One way of defining its genre would be by calling it a parable communicating and illustrating a point that most certainly seemed too delicate to Ivanov to be delivered in direct speech and in his own voice—at that time, at least: as he rushes toward his individual "journey to the end of the night," his Célinian antihero reveals himself to be a modern everyman abandoned not by a tender if perhaps faithless lover, but by God and his faith in that God. The energy released by the force of this same realization, it should be noted, is a spirit that moves most of Ivanov's mature and late poems where he confronts his despair without resorting to the literary ruse of a fictional narrative. By this token *Disintegration of the Atom*, with its unambiguous identification of the traitorous lover with Psyche, a late classical allegory of the human soul in search of a lost union with God, emerges as a periphrastic depiction of the plight of people robbed of their illusions by cataclysms as monumental in their proportion as they were senseless in their cruelty. On this level of abstraction, the fact that Ivanov's antihero happens to be a Russian émigré pinned to the specific backdrop of his Franco-German displacement in a clearly defined historical moment between the two world wars is a detail of lesser importance: this is, for want of a better word, the universal significance of *Disintegration of the Atom*. As such, this work is notable at best, but hardly groundbreaking, much less original or remarkable, notwithstanding the accolades showered upon it by Ivanov's supporters, the mystically inclined Hippius, Merezhkovsky, and those in their orbit. To grasp the true significance of *Disintegration of the Atom* we have no choice but to delve into its peculiarly local, which is to say Russian, set—or garbage pail, as Ivanov would have it—of "accursed" questions. It is at this juncture where a more precise definition of the genre of this coarse metaphysical parable becomes an absolute necessity.

Vladislav Khodasevich, the only contemporary critic who did not dismiss *Disintegration of the Atom* without examining it closely (or chose not to rise to its challenge publicly, as did so many),[6] was the first to point out that it was "an assiduously thought-through, carefully weighed" literary work, that "the contents of the trash can" that Ivanov empties on his pages have been "selected, arranged, and depicted with commendable artistic skill." The same critic (by no means impartial given the long history of the Ivanov-Khodasevich confrontation) was evenhanded enough to point out that many of its "declamatory devices"—its numerous repetitions, refrains, anaphoras, and other rhetorical techniques—effectively render *Disintegration of the Atom* "a [lyric] poem in prose."[7] To put it somewhat differently, the matter that is disintegrating on the pages of this narrative is poetry itself—along with the myth of its soothing, consolatory, and inspirational power. The urgency and portent of this realization for Ivanov and his fellow displaced compatriots who, after all, constituted his immediate "target audience" cannot be overestimated.

---

6   Vladimir Nabokov's dismissal of *Disintegration of the Atom* is highly symptomatic in this respect: "… this little brochure with its dilettantish seeking after God and banal description of *pissoirs* (capable of embarrassing only inexperienced readers) is simply very bad … Georgy Ivanov …, exceptional poet …, should have never, ever 'toyed' with prose" (see Vladimir Nabokov, *Sobranie sochinenii russkogo perioda v piati tomakh* [St. Petersburg, 1999], vol. 5, p. 593). The Nabokov-Ivanov feud became a significant event of Russian émigré letters. Directly or indirectly involving other major literary figures (especially Adamovich, Khodasevich, and Ivanov's wife Odoyevtseva), it left an indelible mark on the work of both parties. Adamovich's and Ivanov's extraliterary conduct inspired Nabokov's story "Lips to Lips" (c. 1931); Ivanov invested considerable energy in trying to become something of a scourge to Nabokov. This feud is the subject of a secondary literature of its own; for thoughtful investigations of the lasting effect of *Disintegration of the Atom* on Nabokov, see Andrei Ar'ev, "Visson: Georgii Ivanov and Vladimir Sirin. Stikhosfera" (*Zvezda*, no. 2 [2006], pp. 201–202) and especially Andrei Babikov, "'Dar' za chertoi stranitsy" (*Zvezda* [2015], pp. 154–155).
7   See Vladislav Khodasevich, "Raspad atoma," in his *Sobranie sochinenii v chetyrekh tomakh* (Moscow: Soglasie, 1996), vol. 2, pp. 414–418.

A carefully wrought "lyric poem in prose," *Disintegration of the Atom* is the perfect, if perhaps radical, realization of the specifications formulated by Ivanov's one-time émigré ally Georgy Adamovich, the critic and theoretician at the head of a short-lived, yet quite consequential literary school universally remembered today as the "Parisian note." While Ivanov never claimed to be a participant in that school (one simple reason for his not doing so may well have been his age—the majority of writers who rallied around *Numbers*, its "bastion," belonged to a younger generation and never had much of a chance to gain a foothold in prerevolutionary culture), his proximity to and direct participation in Adamovich's gravitational pull placed him close to the wellspring of its uniting ethos. Confronted with the necessity to make sense of the loss of their homeland and its culture to a savage tyranny, the adherents to that ethos took it upon themselves to become the closing chapter in the history of a different, all-but-extinct Russian culture. The poetry of the "Parisian note," therefore, became the poetry of last, bitter truths. To express them with a fitting efficacy, the school promulgated a special aesthetics and poetics, that of a short versified utterance stripped of everything inessential, peripheral, or "self-indulgent," such as metaphors, elaborate imagery, and pursuit of beauty and harmony for their own sake ("We will not be asked: / 'Did you sin?' / We will be asked: / 'Did you love?' / Without raising our head, / We will say quietly: / 'We did love. / Love we did. With all our might…'"—so wrote one of the best partakers of that "Parisian" ethos Anatoly Steiger, 1907–1944). Unambiguously—and perhaps understandably—tragic in its outlook, the prevalent emotional strain of the "Parisian note" compelled its participants to regard with suspicion the chief achievement of prerevolutionary—prelapsarian, in terms of émigré cultural eschatology—Russia, the creative legacy of Alexander Pushkin. His exuberance, positively Renaissance inability to dwell on the tragic aspect of the human predicament alone, his celebration of the body, his irreverence and rationalism, the "Parisians" felt and argued, held in itself a promise of a future harmonious Russia that before their very eyes proved to be patently mendacious. It is here where we begin to develop an understanding of the antiliterary (consider his references to Dostoevsky, Goethe, Gogol,

Tolstoy), antipoetic, anti-Pushkinian pathos of *Disintegration of the Atom*, its attempt to demonstrate that the promise of harmony embodied in Pushkin's euphonious verse is little more than a distraction from the inevitable onslaught of what Ivanov's protagonist calls "universal hideousness." In this sense, *Disintegration of the Atom* is an impassioned soliloquy, a bitter reproach thrown in the face of a lost illusion, of a hope and inspiration abandoned forever:

> A lost man walks the streets of an alien town. Like a high tide, the void gradually begins to engulf him. He does not resist it. As he goes away, he mutters to himself: "Pushkinian Russia, why did you deceive us? Pushkinian Russia, why did you betray us?"

Expansive, harmonious poetry in general, and richly nuanced love poetry in particular, was Pushkin's natural idiom. The heartbroken protagonist of *Disintegration of the Atom* realizes to his dismay that the sound of water rumbling in a Parisian *pissoir* is identical to that described by Pushkin in a poem formulating a lover's peaceful resignation in the face of a lost love. Pushkin's poetic equanimity, that cherished gem of Russian cultural heritage, proves of no use to the protagonist dealing with the fallout from his realization that the material rudely tramples the spiritual. The romantic drama at the center of *Disintegration of the Atom* is, of course, a crooked-mirror reflection of the reaction that a personal calamity of similar nature effects in the heart of the Pushkinian protagonist. There is no better way of appreciating this polemical aspect of Ivanov's "lyric poem in prose" than considering it in juxtaposition with that same short poem by Pushkin, the distorted opening line of which provides *Disintegration of the Atom* with the most salient of its refrains. What follows is a literal—not literary—unrhymed English rendition of the Russian original:

> Evening mist lies upon the hills of Georgia,
> The Aragva rumbles before me ...
> I am sad and at my ease; my sorrow is radiant;
> My sorrow is filled with you,
> With you, you alone ... My despondency

Is tormented, disturbed by nothing,

And my heart once more burns and loves—because

Not to love, it cannot.

(1829)

His inability to love and to forgive—and to find in the love poetry of a bygone era a refuge from the inevitable—Ivanov's protagonist blames on his times. Modern man is no longer conditioned to appreciate harmony in art, as art itself has run out of ways to refresh and vivify itself. It is this unsettling suspicion—he calls it "a hunch"—that he is imparting to the world:

> The hunch that art, creativity in the generally accepted sense, is nothing other than the hunt for ever-newer banalities. The hunch that the harmony to which art aspires is nothing other than some sort of supreme banality.

Ivanov's protagonist insists on misquoting the opening line of Pushkin's poem: "evening mist lay upon the hills of Georgia." Hardly noticeable in English, the change in the tense of the verb from present to past creates the most inharmonious aural tautology (cf. "legla ... mgla" and the original "lezhit ... mgla). Modern scholar Justin Doherty credits Ivanov with a masterful use of this aural oxymoron as a trope: "The use of the past tense may ... be read as an attempt by Ivanov to underscore the historical separation of his narrative from Pushkin's text: what in 1829 is represented by Pushkin in the process of happening has become an irreversible fact, had passed into historical time, by 1937."[8] Vladislav Khodasevich, in his response to *Disintegration of the Atom*, saw here an attempt on Ivanov's part to distance himself from his narrator, since as a poet himself he could not have been deaf to this travesty of Pushkinian music. The question as to what the intended effect of this misquotation might have been remains open, what becomes clear from a closer acquaintance with Ivanov's prose is that in it he developed an entire poetics of misquotation. There is every

---

8   See Justin Doherty, "The Pushkin Contexts of Georgii Ivanov's *Disintegration of the Atom*," in *Two Hundred Years of Pushkin*, ed. Joe Andrew and Robert Reid (Amsterdam: Rodopi, 2003), vol. 1, p. 126.

reason to suspect that Ivanov, and not his protagonist, genuinely believed that the contemporary sensibilities had rendered artistic innovation obsolete along with the notion of artistic sovereignty: both in *Disintegration of the Atom* and in his memoirs he freely adjusts the works of others that he cites to fit the needs of his agenda. This is but one of the inevitable consequences of the main idea communicated by Ivanov's poetic prose narrative, the idea that Andrey Arieff defines as follows: "art does not save anybody and must concede its defeat in its sempiternal confrontation with reality."[9] One of the terms of this unconditional capitulation is Ivanov's refusal to admit that in his day and age the pursuit of harmony and artistic innovation is still possible—hence his increasingly adversarial, mocking attitude toward all innovative art in general, and its representative example Futurism in particular (see his passing jibe at an experimental poem by Aleksey Kruchyonykh [Aleksei Eliseevich Kruchenykh, 1886–1968] composed in "transrational language" and his frontal attacks on Futurism in *Petersburg Winters*). Ivanov montages his prose from quoted and misquoted citations, citations well known to him and learned only secondhand (as is the case of his epigraph from Goethe), because, along with his narrator, he does appear to be genuinely convinced that the empty illusion that is art is not worthy of the antiquated sacerdotal attitude to it that used to be prevalent in more naïve, more innocent days. Ivanov seems to have been convinced that it was his calling to shatter all traces of such illusions, and thus to write the last page in the history of Russian poetry. It is hardly surprising, then, that when in 1957 Vladimir Markov queried him about his relationship with and attitude toward the "Parisian note" (by then firmly a part of émigré literary history), Ivanov replied with disarming candor: "the so-called 'Parisian note' can be a footnote to my poetry."[10] Indeed, his approach to the task of verbalizing the notions that united this literary school proved to be most radical, most far-reaching, most uncompromising.

Ivanov, as can be surmised from his writing, made enemies easily. The rumors that *Disintegration of the Atom* was met with a "conspiracy of silence" are not likely to be true to their full extent, but Gleb Struve's

---

9   See Ar'ev, *Zhizn' Georgiia Ivanova*, pp. 5–6.
10 See *Georgij Ivanov, Irina Odojevceva. Briefe an Vladimir Markov: 1955–1958* (Cologne: Böhlau Verlag, 1994), p. 71.

account of them is highly informative of the kind of opposition that Ivanov encountered:

> Rumors went round, clearly improbable ones, that Vladislav Khodasevich was the instigator of the "conspiracy"; he had allegedly addressed to Paul Miliukov a letter in the name of an anonymous "Russian mother." It is true that neither *Contemporary Annals*, nor *Russian Annals*, nor *The Latest News* vouchsafed [*Disintegration of the Atom*] with a review ... Vladimir Zlobin was incensed by the boycott of Ivanov's book and called it very contemporary and for us, people of the thirties of our century, infinitely important.[11]

What may easily escape from a contemporary observer not familiar with the power struggle and politics of émigré intellectual life are the reasons for which *Disintegration of the Atom* would have been met with such a united front of derision and rejection. Ivanov's descriptions alone, no matter how graphic, cannot account for the very possibility of a single literary work running into so much opposition—after all, the Russian emigration was a rather nebulous phenomenon with little or no organization and structure, and enforcing such a comprehensive boycott of a single book would have been difficult indeed. And yet there was something about both Ivanov and his poem in prose that was certain to go against the grain of the attitudes prevalent in the mainstream intellectual life of the diaspora. It was no accident that following the Parisian publication of *Disintegration of the Atom* in 1938, Ivanov ceased to publish his work until 1945, but the reasons for Ivanov's self-imposed exile within exile are best understood within a broader context of his stance as it is represented in his prose works.

---

11 Vladimir Ananevich Zlobin (1894–1967) was a poet and critic closely aligned with Zinaida Gippius and Dmitry Merezhkovsky; Zlobin wrote two complimentary critical essays on *Disintegration of the Atom*. For the quotation, see Struve, *Russkaia literatura v izgnanii*, p. 317.

Petersburg Winters

If *Disintegration of the Atom* is Ivanov's most substantial—and controversial—foray into the realm of fiction, *Petersburg Winters* (first separate publication, Paris, 1928; second, revised and expanded edition, New York, 1952) is his most durable contribution to the Russian canon of the literary autobiography-memoir. As such, it also happens to be his most popular and accessible book; it is entertaining, amusing, and at times genuinely funny. The lion's share of its enduring appeal should no doubt be attributed to Ivanov's virtuosity at establishing a special rapport with those of his readers who know little about literature, but are fascinated with the scintillating and tumultuous period in the history of Russian culture universally known today as its "Silver Age." While Ivanov sprinkles his memoir with quotations (and misquotations) from various poets and writers he depicts, what he is interested in showing in much sharper relief are their personalities. During this period of bold artistic experimentation, when the very notion of art and its boundaries was undergoing a radical reinvention, the desire to turn life into creativity and creativity into life provided a particularly fertile ground for a new aesthetic sensibility known as "life-creation" (German *Lebenskunst-Kunstleben*; Russian *zhiznetvorchestvo*). Armed with his excellent credentials as a participant in that carnivalesque movement, Ivanov the memoirist satisfies his readers' interest in the price his protagonists had to pay for their adherence to a program of "life-creation." Invention, irony, sarcasm, and no small amount of authorial posturing go into action.

On the pages of *Petersburg Winters* Ivanov the lyric poet proves himself to have been as excellent a caricaturist as his protagonists appear to have been exceptionally inspiring sitters. It is impossible, to take one deservedly famous example, not to smile at his unmasking of the leader of the "folk poetry" school Nikolay Klyuyev (Nikolai Alekseevich Kliuev, 1884–1937). In concert with the image of a peasant bard that he carefully devised for himself, Klyuyev—or rather his Ivanovian avatar—went out of his way to pass himself off as a genuine "man of the soil," while remaining the literary equivalent of a cunning social climber (see Chapter VII). In *Petersburg Winters* Ivanov shows himself to be a master of this unmasking technique as again and again he invites his readers to consider, marvel at, and occasionally be disgusted by the extent to which "artists," real talents and fakes alike, were willing to lose themselves in the game of "life-creation." His portrayal of Sergey Gorodetsky, whose amiable façade of a childish poet and leader of innocent literary games masks the potential of a spectacular scoundrel who will align himself with a murderous Bolshevik regime, is another testimony not only to Ivanov's skill, but also to his desire to become a helpful source of information for those who may wish to become his models' arbiters. It is in this and in similar situations where Ivanov the caricaturist crosses the line separating the amusing freak show he depicts from a place where his vantage point as witness becomes a morally higher ground. It is precisely here that Ivanov's readers must remain extra-vigilant to retain their impartiality, no matter how tempting it is to accept his invitation to sit in judgment at a trial where a few genuine martyrs to pure art (Anna Akhmatova and, of course, Nikolay Gumilyov) are separated not only from art's fallen angels (Alexander Blok, Sergey Yesenin, Fyodor Sologub, among others), but also from talented impersonators, nonentities, scoundrels, cheats, and pathetic fools (in whose ranks he lists Ryurik Ivnev, Vladimir Narbut, Larisa Reisner, Nikolay Kulbin, and Velimir Khlebnikov, to mention but a few). Curious borderline cases—the most prominent example being Ivanov's Osip Mandelstam— are to be observed as well.

Not unexpectedly, Ivanov's approach to his task as a memoirist has been encountering considerable resistance since the time when his memoir sketches began to appear in the émigré press in the 1920s. Despite or perhaps thanks to this memoir's genuine popularity with modern readers, today it is not always easy to account for the source of this friction. One may mistake the indignation of those of Ivanov's protagonists who made their dissatisfaction known for the cries of their outsized wounded egos. For instance, when one finds out that Igor Severyanin (Igor' Vasil'evich Lotarev, 1887–1941) was deeply incensed by the way Ivanov had portrayed him, it is tempting, perhaps too tempting, not to see it as a validation of the memoirist's insight. (Severyanin's notoriety as the prerevolutionary king of "life-creation" confirms Ivanov's portrayal of him in the eyes of those who are not willing to take a closer look at the substance behind that appearance—or trouble themselves with discovering Severyanin's subsequent growth into a fine and sadly undervalued major poet.) Why then was Anna Akhmatova, whom Ivanov appears to be showing in the most favorable, flattering light, equally indignant at the liberties Ivanov took with the stories of other people's lives? Why would she, herself a consummate participant in the game of "life-creation," have been so outraged by Ivanov? Saying that Ivanov was not afraid to spill too many beans would be too simplistic an answer to this and similar questions.

The problem with Ivanov's memoir method has nothing to do with the fact that art, like all human endeavors, does not always bring out the best in people, especially when they find themselves under duress—and for practically all of Ivanov's protagonists Russia's descent into authoritarianism proved to be the most exacting test of personal dignity and integrity. This, however, is also true of the memoirist himself, as he repeatedly tries to draw decisive lines under so many artistic careers and lives. On closer inspection, the overtly extraliterary part of Ivanov's memoir-writing agenda is difficult to qualify in any other way than as troubling. For lack of a better designation, this aspect of *Petersburg Winters* may be rather bluntly termed ideological.

Following the lead of the first readers of *Petersburg Winters*, the interpreters of Ivanov's memoirs—and this applies to the entire corpus of his memoir writings of which this book is the kernel—have tended to focus on the imbalance between the number of actual facts and names he uses and the amount of fiction he instills in them. To put it crudely, Ivanov invents a lot—but then so do all memoirists.[12] After examining Ivanov's

---

12 It has become something of a tradition in fore-/afterwords accompanying republications of *Petersburg Winters*, as well as the scholarship devoted to the memoir, to cite an alleged admission Ivanov once made according to another famous memoirist, Nina Berberova: "only one quarter of *Petersburg Winters* was true and the rest had been made up." Scholars and biographers vacillate between thoughtful attempts to separate the wheat of surviving verifiable facts from the chaff of embellishments and blatant lies. Thus Nikolai Bogomolov, after telling the former from the latter, reasonably concludes that the very attempts to find out what is what "stimulates further research" and therefore cannot be altogether useless (see his "Dar dvoinogo zreniia," in *Stikhotvoreniia. Tretii Rim (roman). Peterburgskie zimy (memuary). Kitaiskie teni (literaturnye portrety)*, ed. N. A. Bogomolov [Moscow: Kniga, 1989], p. 517), while Vadim Kreyd

method, Justin Doherty summarizes it as follows: "Ivanov's memoir writings effectively amount to a 'laying bare' of the underlying tendency in all memoir texts towards fictionality or textuality"; according to this scholar, *Petersburg Winters* is "a type of text which asserts not only unique factual knowledge of the subject, but unique understanding; in the memoir texts of Georgii Ivanov… epistemological considerations [take] precedence over the ontological…" Doherty concludes: "Ivanov's memoir texts, like other memoirs but even more so, are really literary fictions in another guise, with their own unique structural organization, thematic resonances, plots and characters, and, not least importantly in the case of Ivanov, their own style."[13] An unbiased evaluation of the "unique understanding" of people, fates, and history Ivanov insists upon having at his disposal requires not only an evolved awareness of the specificity of his memoir technique, but also a good sense of his agenda.

Petersburg Winters certainly is a literary artifact endowed with distinct stylistic characteristics. Likewise, it is an important and major contribution to the literary *topos* known as the "Petersburg text" after Vladimir Toporov's influential study of this enduring and colorful component of Russian cultural mythology. Such an overarching supertext implicates a host of writers, many of them among the most iconic in the history of Russian literature, such as Alexander Pushkin, Anna Akhmatova, Andrey Bely, Alexander Blok, and Osip Mandelstam, as well as monumental triumphalist and apocalyptic myths about the city and its destiny. Somewhat opposed to Toporov's approach is the work of Julie A. Buckler, who treats Petersburg in Russian literature "in terms of a cultural network that cannot be reduced to a single textual structure, [but] as a body of texts that collectively provides a structural analogue for the material city, and not merely as an artistic refraction of it. The geographical, material entity that is Petersburg corresponds to an equally complex structure comprised of diverse literary forms, interrelated in spatial terms,

---

chooses a more lenient approach, stating that "the majority of [Ivanov's] descriptions are truthful and based on facts" (see his *Georgii Ivanov* [Moscow: Molodaia gvardiia, 2007], p. 222).

13 See Justin Doherty, "The Image of Nikolai Gumilev in the Memoir Writings of Georgii Ivanov," *Irish Slavonic Studies* 18 (1997), pp. 87–88.

and modeling specific sites of urban life."[14] Georgy Ivanov's *Petersburg Winters* is apposite to Buckler's expansive definition of Petersburg literature and culture in that it ranges over much of the geographical space of St. Petersburg and incorporates scenes on the Neva River, coursing through the city. The narrative voice takes the reader on a tour of the city, its environs and its people in action, stopping at, to name just a few places, Basseyny Street, Prudki Gardens, Kamennostrovsky Boulevard, Kronstadt, Podyachesky Street, St. Isaac's Cathedral, Tsarskoye Selo, Nikolayevsky Bridge, Senate Square, and Vasilyevsky Island. A willful, sophisticated, and superbly believable reimagining of that cityscape along with its mythical components earns *Petersburg Winters* a place of distinction among the prototypical works in the "Petersburg text" canon.

What sets Ivanov's *Petersburg Winters* apart from the vast majority of the literary monuments constituting and sustaining the continuity of the "Petersburg text" is its author's ambition. When in Chapter XVII Ivanov insists—

> I knew Blok and Gumilyov well. I heard newly completed poems from them, had tea with them, strolled along Petersburg streets with them, breathed the same air with them in August 1921, the month of their mutual—so diverse and equally tragic—deaths... My remarks about them may be incomplete, but there are only two or three people left in Russia who knew them both as well as I did, and in emigration there is no single one...

there should be no mistake: this memoirist wants to be perceived as *the* source of truth pertaining not only to one of the most prominent literary rivalries of the first half of the twentieth century, but to the collapse of the Russian civilization as the pre-1917 world knew it. It is to this end that he constructs his autobiographic double as a source of detachment and excellent moral judgment amid all the insanity that surrounded, but did not affect, him during his years as participant in the artistic life of that

---

14 See Julie A. Buckler, *Mapping St. Petersburg: Imperial Text and Cityscape* (Princeton: Princeton University Press, 2005), p. 5. For Toporov's magisterial study, see V. N. Toporov, *Peterburgskii tekst russkoi literatury: Izbrannye trudy* (St. Petersburg: Iskusstvo-SPB, 2003).

extraordinary epoch. Such credentials are extremely important to Ivanov the memoirist, since it emerges that one of his most cherished ambitions was not simply to explain the reasons for the fall of the Russian Empire and its culture (it is no accident that Ivanov attempted, but failed, to write a fictional—novelistic—account of that same event), but apportion blame for it. It is here where we realize that for all their differences *Disintegration of the Atom* and *Petersburg Winters* are united by a particular theme.

Among those for whom the protagonist of *Disintegration of the Atom* reserves special scorn are the people he calls "Russian snobs":

O, this Russian, this vacillating, glimmering, musical, masturbatory consciousness. Eternally circling around the impossible, like gnats around a candle. The laws of life have intertwined with the laws of dream. Horrific metaphysical freedom and physical barriers at every step. An inexhaustible source of superiority, weakness, inspired failures. O, those strange varieties of our lot who to this day dawdle around the world like lost souls: Anglophiles, Tolstoyans, Russian snobs—the vilest snobs in the world—and various Russian boys, sticky leaves, and that storied Russian type, a knight of the glorious order of the intelligentsia, a scoundrel with a morbidly exaggerated sense of responsibility. He's always on guard; like a hound, he sniffs out injustice everywhere—an ordinary person stands no chance of catching up to him! O, our past and our future, and our current penitent yearning. "But when that child was still alive…" O, that abyss of nostalgia where the wind alone blows, bringing back from over there the terrible "International," and from here to over there—a pitiful, astral, as if singing last rites at Russia's funeral, "Lord, bring back the Tsar…"

(Disintegration of the Atom)

Who are those "Russian snobs," and why should they be "the vilest"? *Petersburg Winters* permits the reader to form a better idea of the phenomenon in question together with its genealogy—as Ivanov understands it. Here as elsewhere, he implicates Russia's thinking class, the entire social stratum responsible for that autumnal flowering of the country's culture that was its "Silver Age," in the horrible end of the civilization that cradled it. Ivanov says as much in Chapter XIV:

> Masquerades, galas, five o'clock teas, mad midnight gatherings. A world of Oscar Wilde-like witticisms, mirror-smooth hair partings, where tie patterns are the only things that change.
>
> It will end horribly. But no one is thinking about the end.
>
> It will end like this. When February 1917 bursts the hothouse mold of a "beautiful and carefree" life, those in whom humanity has not been killed off by that "daily grind," they will rush headlong out into "the fresh air." And the more of that humanity they retain, the more urgent will be their flight, the less of the ability to stay reasonable they will have...

The nameless, faceless "vile Russian snobs" are, of course, a collective image, a purely speculative category. Yet soon enough in this narrative comes a moment when speculation morphs into Ivanov's interpretation of particular people's lives and the sum of their achievements. Some are dealt with in passing—consider Ivanov's characterization of Sergey Bobrov and Vladimir Pyast, for instance—some are selected for special treatment.[15] Such is the sea change suffered at Ivanov's hands by Mikhail Kuzmin (1872–1936).

Russia's first openly gay poet and writer (a detail that Ivanov elects to reference only obliquely, as if not to insult his readers' intelligence—and gain their trust), Kuzmin certainly played a pivotal role in the evolution of cultural attitudes in his homeland. While Ivanov does not deny this, he chooses to interpret Kuzmin's contribution to this process and creative development in a highly biased way. Ivanov (who could not have been unaware of the scope of Kuzmin's achievements—like

---

15 See Ivanov's presentation of one of the founding fathers of the contemporary Russian study of verse, Sergey Bobrov (Sergei Pavlovich Bobrov, 1886–1971)—"the author of *The Lyre of Lyres*, editor-in-chief of the Centrifuge Press, a snob, a Futurist, and a cocaine addict with Cheka links and most certainly a Cheka man himself"—and that of the poet, memoirist, and verse theoretician Vladimir Pyast (Vladimir Alekseevich Piast, 1886–1940)—"a dilettante poet and amateur linguist."

some other creative forces of that generation, after 1917 Kuzmin was to develop into a major artist) deliberately avoids any suggestion that there could have been more to Kuzmin than his pre-World War I literary debut and the essay "Concerning Beautiful Clarity (Remarks on Prose)," his theoretical contribution to the aesthetic experimentation of that period:

> ... In 1909–1910 Kuzmin was completing his novel *Joseph the Magnificent* and the last poems from his *Autumnal Lakes*, the best prose and verse he ever wrote. His writings of that period were quite perfect, especially the prose. It seemed that the poet-dandy, after becoming simply a poet, was coming out onto his genuine, broad pathway.
>
> It seemed that way ...
>
> Kuzmin never came out onto his "genuine" pathway. In 1909–1910 he was finishing his best work. *Clay Pigeons*, the book of poems that followed *Autumnal Lakes*, was a falling off, not a sharp one, but obvious. The same is true of his next novel, *The Dreamers*. The old neckties kept being worn without being replaced by new ones. "Beautiful Clarity" began to look like perilous levity.

Presenting Kuzmin as a poet and writer whose growth was stunted forever by his lack of industry and responsibility, Ivanov fails to mention that 1909–1910 was the time when he, the future memoirist, was among Kuzmin's most ardent admirers and imitators, and not "some" snobs from the Imperial School of Jurisprudence notorious for their gay subculture, in whose company Kuzmin is portrayed in *Petersburg Winters*. Knowing this, it is difficult not to come to the conclusion that by presenting his former role model Kuzmin in such a light Ivanov did not merely assert his creative and intellectual independence, but was exorcising the ghosts of his past. This kind of retrospective exorcism is familiar to readers of literary memoirs and far from unique. Noteworthy is the direction in which Ivanov takes his interpretations.

Chapter XV paints a picture of Petersburg bohemia on the eve of the Empire's downfall, and once again the reader finds Kuzmin in its center:

Kuzmin is singing. From his tuneless, sweet singing, from his languid, strange gaze, from those naïve little words and simpleminded motifs emanates an imperceptible yet deadly poison. The same one protection from which is sought in the prayer by St. Ephrem the Syrian "The Spirit of Idleness…"

Old poison, true poison. At times it seemed that it had evaporated. No, it did not evaporate, it was as potent as ever. And that is exactly why that tuneless singing was so much to everyone's liking—something ever-lasting, potent and overpowering… "The Spirit of Idleness…" Kuzmin has nothing to do with it. Neither do his listeners. He likes it, and they like it, too. This is what they like, and nothing else. Not Blok, nor Sologub, nor Leonid Andreyev—or goodness knows who else. No, right now the power over these human souls, without any doubt, is in these somewhat swarthy hands affectedly pressing the piano keys. Kuzmin has nothing to do with it—if it weren't he, then it would be someone else. And his listeners have nothing to do with it either—it's the times.

Justin Doherty points out that *Petersburg Winters* carries within itself a "distinct moral and spiritual framework,"[16] and Ivanov's portrayal of Kuzmin provides a particularly eloquent example of this artifice at work. Fashioned by Ivanov from easily available biographic material, Kuzmin the Ratcatcher of *Petersburg Winters* becomes one of the propagators of the "spirit of idleness" that enabled the atmosphere in which Russia's disastrous World War I losses were not given their true significance.

Those familiar with the actual background of *Petersburg Winters* could not but be surprised—and dismayed—at the transformation Ivanov seemed to be undergoing on the pages of his memoir. Known to his contemporaries as a quintessential aesthete who authored a collection of "patriotic" poems, *A Monument of Glory* (1915), as someone who painted his lips and wore a haircut especially designed for him by artist Sergey Sudeykin (Sergei [Serge] Iurievich Sudeikin [Soudeikine], 1882–1942), in *Petersburg Winters* Ivanov seized a chance to reinvent himself for posterity as a guardian of traditional morality and spirituality. Small wonder then

---

16   See Doherty, "The Image of Nikolai Gumilev," p. 94.

that those of Ivanov's contemporaries and acquaintances who raised their voices against his mnemonic distortions could not reconcile their knowledge of his opportunism with the brand of Christian piety he was using as his high moral ground to judge others. This is the surface covering more important reasons for Ivanov's rift with his contemporaries and some of his protagonists' prototypes.

Be they genuine or affected, moral and spiritual convictions reside within the realm of individual preferences and as such can only be qualified as the memoirist's sovereign choice (Ivanov's private correspondence, however, complicates all suspicion that he ever underwent any kind of spiritual rebirth later in life). As to Ivanov's choice of his ideological perspective, it deserves to be scrutinized more closely than students of his memoirs have done thus far.

In *Petersburg Winters*, Ivanov's mounting censure of vacuous aestheticism, spiritual idleness, and intellectual snobbery culminates in a series of denunciations directed at that current of Russian cultural and political life he detests with all his might. It is liberalism.

According to Ivanov, in the buildup to World War I and the Revolution liberals failed to grasp the true magnitude of the approaching upheaval, distracted as they were by their dalliances with aestheticism and artistic experimentation. In Chapter XIV he makes no effort to conceal his schadenfreude at the sight of Victor Muizhel (1880–1924), a minor writer of "idealistic," "principled" literature of the "antidecadent" persuasion, who proves himself utterly incapable of service to a new, democratic Russian Republic, a liberal dream-come-true that collapsed as soon as the cynical, well-organized, and ruthless Bolsheviks seized power. For all its insignificance and frankly comic undertones this episode is representative of a major theme running through *Petersburg Winters*, that of the deliberate and methodical denigration of Russian liberalism. It culminates in a "witness" account of the near-totalitarian control liberals once wielded over the country's intellectual life before the Revolution. This is one important thread Ivanov carefully weaves into his explanatory narrative of Sergey Yesenin's career in letters in Chapter XVIII, and it opens with his recounting the details of the peasant poet's audience with Empress Aleksandra Fyodorovna and the repercussions Yesenin was certain to face after those in liberal circles caught wind of it:

> Had it not been for the Revolution, the doors of the majority of Russian publishers, especially the most rich and influential, would have been closed to Yesenin forever. Liberal circles did not forgive a Russian writer such "crimes" as monarchist sentiments. Yesenin could not have misunderstood that and, in all likelihood, deliberately sought to break away. The goals and hopes that compelled him to take such a bold step are unknown. But, of course, Yesenin would not have taken such a risk for nothing. The Revolution, having destroyed those mysterious calculations on Yesenin's part, in a funny way freed him from unavoidable liberal repressions. An amusing metamorphosis occurred: the all-powerful opposition, having overthrown the monarchy, went on from being the opposition to becoming the new power, and unexpectedly became powerless. "The salt of the Russian earth" suddenly lost its taste… Before the Revolution, "Daddy" Milyukov could get any "apostate" "expelled from literature" by placing two or three phone calls from the editorial offices of *Speech*. From there the machine of "public opinion" would work on its own—automatically and mercilessly. But as to Milyukov the Minister, along with all those erstwhile makers of literary fates turned grandees of "the great and bloodless Republic," Yesenin, as the saying goes, didn't give a hoot about them. He knew full well that "the real guys" sat not in the Provisional Government ministries, but at the Durnovo dacha, in Kschessinska's mansion, and in the "Workers, Peasants, and Soldiers Council…" Connections in that sphere opened all doors, obliterated the consequences of not mere foolhardy acts, but of any crime. Through Ryurik Ivnev, Klyuyev, Maxim Gorky, Razumnik Ivanov-Razumnik, and Vladimir Bonch-Bruyevich, Yesenin's connections branched out upwards and rose to the very "heights"—to Mamont Dalsky, Anatoly Lunacharsky, Trotsky … to Lenin himself …

That Paul Milyukov (Pavel Nikolaevich Miliukov, 1859–1943), head of the Constitutional Democratic party and editor-in-chief first of the party organ *Speech* and subsequently of its successor the Parisian Russian weekly

The Latest News, was the most prominent and ambitious of Russian liberals is no revelation; Ivanov's eagerness to present him and those sharing his political convictions as a vindictive quasi-totalitarian clique of oppressors, however, is unsettling. No matter how we define the genre of Ivanov's memoir—even if we follow the lead of Georgy Moseshvili, who insists that *Petersburg Winters* is no memoir at all, but rather a work of fiction[17]— Ivanov's talk of liberal "repressions," of liberals being an "all-powerful opposition" to the tsarist regime, of their ability to have someone "expelled from literature" is no mere hyperbole, no innocuous figure of speech. On a certain level they demonstrate to what extent Ivanov was invested in émigré debates and ideological struggles. A willfully distorted representation of the state of affairs in prerevolutionary Russia, Ivanov's reference to Milyukov sought to cast him as a kingpin of the diaspora's liberal wing and was a reflection of Ivanov's bitter disagreement with his liberal-minded contemporaries and compatriots both in the diaspora and in Russia.

In *Petersburg Winters* similar dubious contentions appear in a specific context and amount to Ivanov's ideological and political statement of purpose. In his memoirs he repeatedly challenges the liberal anti-Bolshevik narrative of Russian culture and its tribulations that was naturally prevalent among the intellectual wing of the diaspora, since by and large it consisted of liberals expelled from their homeland by the Bolsheviks. It is this, essentially reactionary, polemical tendentiousness that endows Ivanov's memoirs with their pathos, their unifying principle; it renders them a considered riposte to a more egalitarian and hopeful vision of Russian history and culture, and their future.

There is no denying Ivanov's mastery at refashioning his material into a hybrid realm of fictionalized history, one populated by seductively believable avatars of actual people. Likewise, it is hardly surprising that this operation could take a serious toll on people's reputations. The most

---

17 See Moseshvili's notes to *Petersburg Winters* in the third volume of Ivanov's collected works (Moscow, 1994). Francesca Lazzarin has recently posited Ivanov's sometimes less than truthful exposition of the facts in *Petersburg Winters* as a constructive principle of his poetics (see her "Fiktivnyi kharakter [psevdo-]memuarnogo teksta kak esteticheskaia programma. Eshche raz o 'Peterburgskikh zimakh' Georgiia Ivanova," *Avtobiografiia*, no. 1 [2012], http://www.avtobiografija.com/issue/view/2).

prominent example of the pernicious effect of Ivanov's methodology is the posthumous legend that clouded the life, art, and death of his older contemporary and one-time mentor Nikolay Gumilyov.

In choosing to present Gumilyov as a paragon of conservative values, a poet-soldier on a lifelong quest for glory, and a man of straightforward religious convictions, Ivanov used both actual and invented traits of Gumilyov's character to enhance his favorable contrast between this paragon and the depraved "snobs." The way this is presented by Ivanov, Gumilyov's participation in a counterrevolutionary plot became a logical extension of his ambition and temperament, his final work of art, one executed in full accordance with the requirements and expectations of "life-creation." As Ivanov interprets it, Gumilyov's disagreement with Alexander Blok takes on the features of a clash of two ethical outlooks: one espoused by a decorated war hero and a monarchist "White Guardsman" and the other followed by a muddle-minded, if highly talented, decadent poet indiscriminate in his liaisons and given to drink and debauchery. For all his insistence on being their close acquaintance, almost a confidant, Ivanov's portraits of Gumilyov and Blok do not attempt to bring his readers any closer to an informed appreciation of their characters, poetry, and aesthetic convictions, the true source of their disagreement. It is highly unlikely that the former took part in any counterrevolutionary conspiracy at all, and the latter never disowned *The Twelve*, but these facts are of little significance to Ivanov, who in his *Petersburg Winters* advances a distinctly idiosyncratic—and, upon closer examination, rather simplistic—version of Russian cultural history. Sinful "idleness," pursuit of the chimera of artistic novelty, liberal posturing and impotence appear to be the true culprits of the tragedy of the Russian revolution, and Ivanov takes it upon himself to communicate this startling truth to his readers.

Such, of course, was the intended effect of *Petersburg Winters*. Behind this elaborate, if far from impenetrable, façade discerning readers will find a deeply personal testimony to Ivanov's inability to put the ghosts of his past to rest, to his desire to be included in the conversation concerning Russia's past, present, and future as befitted his own idea of his insight and worth. Together with vociferous protestations and dismissals, the embarrassed silence that greeted some of his most ambitious forays into fiction and memoir appears to have only strengthened that desire.

Yet the closing pages of *Petersburg Winters* reveal another ambition. As he reflects on the posthumous popularity of Sergey Yesenin, Ivanov can be seen making an attempt to find a new audience, one consisting of those lovers of Russian poetry who grew up in the Soviet Union. Against all expectations, they do not appear to be impervious to the charm of Yesenin's combination of sentimentality, tenderness, and crudeness, that exceptionally potent amalgamation of seemingly disparate emotional strains responsible for his lasting appeal to his ardent admirers. Writing in the 1940s and 1950s from his self-imposed intellectual seclusion and over the heads of émigré compatriots he had alienated, Ivanov was reaching out to readers who might be conditioned to be more receptive to his vitriol, sarcasm, and views. Surprisingly or not, in this respect at least his calculation has proven to be absolutely correct. First members of a new wave of immigration from the Soviet Union who managed to escape to the West during and after World War II, next members of the late Soviet and post-Soviet generations of readers, have been willing not only to enjoy Ivanov's stories of his fabled past, but also to give the benefit of the doubt to his vision of Russian cultural history. The question as to what extent Ivanov's views have contributed to modern Russia's overwhelming distrust of liberal ideas and idealism is open to speculation; it is beyond doubt that the legacy of such conservative writers and thinkers as Ivan Shmelyov (Ivan Sergeevich Shmelev, 1873–1950) and Ivan Ilyin (Ivan Aleksandrovich Il'in, 1882–1954) has been instrumental in justifying a shift away from the liberal values of the late Soviet and post-Soviet years. In the late 1980s and early 1990s, along with those of Shmelyov and Ilyin, Ivanov's name was certainly one of the more visible of the "returned names" (*vozvrashchennye imena*) that commanded the attention of a reading and thinking public eager to internalize the intellectual legacy of the diaspora it had been denied access to for so long. Even though Ivanov's contribution to this process could not have been decisive, negligible it certainly was not.

The slow and uneasy process of the recognition of Ivanov's significance began shortly before his death. Already in 1958, fellow émigré Roman Gul (Roman Borisovich Gul', 1896–1986) laid the foundation for interpreting the author of *Disintegration of the Atom* as the Russian existentialist par excellence, and time has proven the validity and fecundity of this approach to Ivanov.[18]

Writing in 1966, when Ivanov the poet and writer was still largely forgotten, Vladimir Markov defined him as a "citational" (*tsitatnyi*) poet. According to this scholar, although Ivanovian "citationality" (*tsitatnost'*) is a distinct feature of his mature poetic style, the origins of this technique can be traced to a specific point in his career in letters, one marked by the appearance of *Disintegration of the Atom*:

> The beginning of Ivanovian citationality, which burst into such luxuriant bloom during his final period, may be dated more or less exactly. Surprising as it may seem, it begins with his prose, with *Disintegration of the Atom* ... In its time abashed and scandalized Russian Parisian circles silenced this "existential" novella and only the penetrating Zinaida Hippius gave it its due. Now this book is forgotten. Ivanov himself valued *Disintegration of the Atom* very highly, and it truly is his central, "cataclysmic" creation and a key to so much in his creative oeuvre (his later poems not infrequently develop themes first touched upon in *Disintegration of the Atom*). It rests on the interweaving and transposition of motifs and planes, and these motifs are often citational in their nature or origin. Even some of the characters are "cited"—for

---

18 See Roman Gul', "Georgii Ivanov" [introduction], in Georgii Ivanov, *1943–1958. Stikhi* (New York, Izdanie "Novogo zhurnala," 1958), p. 6. Contemporary scholars who have followed in Gul's wake have deepened and widened our notion of Ivanov's relationship with and relation to existentialism. Svetlana Semenova, in her essay "Dva poliusa russkogo ekzistentsial'nogo soznaniia. Proza Georgiia Ivanova i Vladimira Nabokova-Sirina" (*Novyi mir*, no. 9 [1999], pp. 183–205), approaches the protagonist of Ivanov's "[lyric] poem in prose" as a representative of an existential consciousness akin to that of Roquentin's in Sartre's *La Nausée* (1938); Andrei Ranchin, in his "Ekzistentsializm po-russki, ili Samoubiistvo Serebrianogo Veka: 'Raspad atoma' Georgiia Ivanova" (*Neva*, no. 9 [2009], pp. 186–201), interprets Ivanov's narrative as a challenge to the Symbolist artistic worldview. Both Semenova and Ranchin offer stimulating comparative analyses of Ivanov and Vladimir Nabokov.

example, Akaky Akakiyevich here is interwoven with Poprishchin from Gogol's "Diary of a Madman."[19]

Indeed, more than any other work in the Russian literary canon of its time, *Disintegration of the Atom* transforms the peculiarly Ivanovian pathos of cultural, civilizational eschatology into a specific approach to creative novelty and authorial sovereignty. Ivanov interlaced the texture of his "lyric poem in prose" with a patchwork of allusions and citations in which various points of reference intersect to form an intricate web of semantic relationships not only within the text where they surface, but also among themselves. In *Disintegration of the Atom*, the protagonist's musings on the senselessness of life and pointlessness of art find themselves in an uneasy, ambiguous, provocative, but profoundly meaningful proximity with an entire array of Ivanov's constant references. They include, but are not limited to, the Beatitudes of the Blessed from the Gospels of Matthew and Luke, Mikhail Lermontov's contemplation of the Napoleonic myth and Alexander Pushkin's love lyrics and epic verse narratives, Ivan Karamazov's impassioned soliloquy on the brevity of youth, and Osip Mandelstam's reflection on the outcomes of the Russian revolutionary experiment, while the words of a Goethe ballad in Vasily Zhukovsky's rendition are echoed in those of a poem by Nikolay Nekrasov only to acquire a novel significance in the context of Ivanov's "lyric poem in prose." Long before the advent of postmodernism, Ivanov succeeded in

---

19　See Vladimir Markov, "Russkie tsitatnye poety: zametki o poezii P. A. Viazemskogo i Georgiia Ivanova," in his *O svobode v poezii: Stat'i, esse, raznoe* (St. Petersburg: Izdatel'stvo Chernysheva, 1994), p. 226. Tatjana Senn has developed Markov's vision of *Disintegration of the Atom* as a key work (*Schlüsselwerk*) within Ivanov's oeuvre, and as an answer to Aleksandr Blok's review of Ivanov's second poetry collection *The Chamber* ("Gornitsa,"1914). Blok asserted: "You finish your thoughts about the poetry of Georgy Ivanov, having already completely forgotten him, thinking about how nature subtly exacts its revenge on civilization in a variety of ways and with cruelty … Art takes its revenge in the same way, and on civilization too." In response Senn suggests that Ivanov in *Disintegration of the Atom* offers a philosophical, existentialist contemplation of the world in which he attempts to take history out of the equation. There is only the moment (the protagonist is alone in a cheap hotel room with a prostitute), time and space appear to fall away, everything falls away, and there is no longer the possibility of an appeal to art (see her *Georgij Ivanov: die russischen Jahre im literarischen und historischen Kontext* [Munich: Verlag Otto Sagner, 2013], pp. 12, 296–318).

creating a literary text where such a montage of citations and references generates and multiplies levels of significance, while the Ivanovian brand of "gallows humor" presaged some of the most characteristic traits of "black comedy."

Thus by grafting the phrase "sticky leaves" (*kleikie listochki*) onto the stem of his protagonist's sarcastic evocation of "Russian superiority," when he mentions, as if in passing, "Russian boys" before proceeding to define the idealistic, indeed utopian, aspirations of the Russian intelligentsia, Ivanov points his reader in the direction of one well-known Dostoevskian contemplation of *his* protagonist's youthful aspirations and premonitions. As a result of this juxtaposition, the nameless protagonist of Ivanov's narrative instantly morphs into a latter-day incarnation of the Ivan Karamazov of the second part of Dostoevsky's novel. He is the Ivan Karamazov who fulfills his dream of traveling to Europe under a set of unexpected and tragic circumstances prompted by the collapse of the Russia that Dostoevsky knew, to be faced with the utter despair that the Ivan Karamazov of the "sticky leaves" soliloquy from Book 2, Chapter 3, of *The Brothers Karamazov* could only envisage. The Dostoevskian intellectual rationalist encounters his Ivanovian reflection, and the reader of *Disintegration of the Atom* must make sense of the significance of this literary rendezvous—along with a plethora of equally telling literary allusions that surround it. There is every reason to credit the claims of those students of Vladimir Nabokov who suspect that behind the façade of indifference this globally influential master of literary allusion may well have been hiding a desire to engage the author of *Disintegration of the Atom*.[20]

In *Petersburg Winters* this same "citational" technique undergoes a transformation as it becomes integrated into the larger unity of a "fictional memoir" that was Ivanov's final contribution to the game of "life-creation," expostulation of his concept of Russian history, and attempt to reach a

---

20 Aleksandr Dolinin has suggested that in his novella "The Enchanter" (1939), which was a precursor to *Lolita* (1955), Nabokov rises to the challenge contained in *Disintegration of the Atom* and mounts his defense of a Pushkinian vision of the transformative power of harmonious art and its triumph over "universal hideousness" (see his *Istinnaia zhizn' pisatelia Sirina. Raboty o Nabokove* [St. Petersburg: Akademicheskii proekt, 2004], pp. 156–158).

new reading audience. Much like in *Disintegration of the Atom,* the protagonist's seemingly chaotic soliloquizing proves to be a carefully crafted literary construct in the service of a specific authorial vision, the way Ivanov "remembers" and "misremembers" the works of his literary protagonists is calibrated to meet his tripartite objective. As he refuses to be bound by the standards of objectivity he considers limiting at best and pernicious at worst, he selects and transfigures the material he uses in his memoir to present a maximally convincing individual version of Russia's past, present, and future. In this respect, *Petersburg Winters* becomes his final salvo in a creative battle of artistic individualities that was the Russian Silver Age, his most articulate and elaborate attempt to impose his will on the world he sought to order and control by means of his art.

Notwithstanding his numerous protestations that the opposite was true, the sum of Ivanov's career in letters does seem to be speaking to the effect that this believer in the idea that art was dead harbored a fervent hope against hope that his own "hunches" in this area would ultimately be proven wrong. Being given so many opportunities to quit his "game," Ivanov went on playing it to the end, even at a time when most of the indications he could register for the future of his life's work were unambiguously pointing toward irrelevance and oblivion. This last Ivanovian paradox may well be the saving grace he was grasping for all his life.

As translators, editors, annotators, and interpreters of Georgy Ivanov's contentious and influential writings, we see our goal in fostering an informed critical appreciation of *Disintegration of the Atom* and *Petersburg Winters.* It is to this end that we have striven to present our readers with English versions of these Russian texts that reflect the originals with maximal adequacy. We hope that this volume will assist its readers in their evaluation of this poet, writer, and thinker in all his complexity.

Disintegration of the Atom

"Versinke denn! ich könnt'auch sagen: steige!
's ist einerlei…"
***Faust* II**[1]

I breathe. Perhaps this air is poisoned? But it is the only air given to me to breathe. I sense various things, now vaguely and now with tormenting sharpness. Perhaps it's useless talking about them? But is life necessary or unnecessary, do the trees rustle, does evening come on, does rain pour intelligently or foolishly? I experience my surroundings with a mixed feeling of superiority and weakness: the laws of life are tightly intertwined in my consciousness with the laws of dream. It must be thanks to this that the world's perspective is powerfully distorted in my eyes. But this is the only thing I still value, the only thing that separates me from all-consuming universal hideousness.

I live. I walk down the street. I go into a café. It is today's day, it is my unique life. I order a glass of beer and drink it with pleasure. At a neighboring table is an elderly gentleman, a rosette in his lapel. Such reputable old men ought to be eliminated, in my opinion. "You're old. You're reasonable. You're a paterfamilias. You've got life experience. You dog! Take that." The gentleman has a presentable exterior. That is valued. "Presentable"—what nonsense. If it were handsome, pathetic, terrifying, or anything else. No, it is indeed "presentable." In England they say there even exists a profession, false witnesses with a presentable exterior meant to instill trust in judges. And not only trust, that exterior is an inexhaustible source of self-confidence. One of the characteristics of universal hideousness: it is presentable.

✳ ✳ ✳

1

Essentially I'm a happy man. Which is to say, a man who is disposed to be happy. This doesn't occur all that often. I want the most simple, most ordinary things. I want order. It's not my fault that order has been destroyed. I want to have peace in my soul. But the soul is like a stirred-up slop bucket—a herring tail, a dead rat, gnawed leftovers, cigarette butts, they chase each other, now diving into the murky depth, now showing up on the surface. I want fresh air. Sweetish decay—the breath of universal hideousness—it hounds me like terror.

I walk down the street. I think about various things. Lettuce, gloves ... Of those sitting in the corner café, someone will die first, someone last—each one at his precise, down-to-the-second moment. It's dusty, it's warm. This woman is pretty, of course, but she isn't to my liking. She has an elegant dress on, she walks along smiling, but I imagine her naked, lying on the floor with her skull split open with an axe. I think about lechery and repulsion, about sadistic murders, about having lost you forever, about how it's over. "Over"—what a pathetic word. As if, when you take the trouble to think with your hearing, aren't all words equally pathetic and terrifying? The watered-down antidote of sense, it ceases to act surprisingly quickly, and in its wake follows the deaf-and-dumb void of solitude. But what did they understand about the pathetic and the terrifying—they who believed in words and sense, dreamers, children, those underserving darlings of fate!

I think about various things, and through them I incessantly think about God. Sometimes it seems to me that God as incessantly, through a thousand extraneous things, thinks about me. Light waves, orbits, vacillations, gravities, and through them, like a ray, an incessant thought about me. Sometimes I even imagine that my pain is a particle of God's being. That means the stronger my pain is ... A moment of weakness when you want to say aloud "I believe, O Lord..." The sobering up that immediately comes into force after a moment of weakness.

I think about the cross I wore around my neck since childhood as someone would carry a gun in his pocket—in case of danger it should protect, save.[2] About a fatal unavoidable misfire. About the radiance of

2

false miracles that have in turn enchanted and disenchanted the world. And about the only trustworthy miracle—about that inextirpable desire for a miracle that lives in mankind, no matter what. About the tremendous significance of this. About the gleam it casts into every consciousness, especially Russian consciousness.

O, this Russian, this vacillating, glimmering, musical, masturbatory consciousness. Eternally circling around the impossible, like gnats around a candle. The laws of life have intertwined with the laws of dream. Horrific metaphysical freedom and physical barriers at every step. An inexhaustible source of superiority, weakness, inspired failures. O, those strange varieties of our lot who to this day dawdle around the world like lost souls: Anglophiles, Tolstoyans, Russian snobs—the vilest snobs in the world— and various Russian boys, sticky leaves,[3] and that storied Russian type, a knight of the glorious order of the intelligentsia, a scoundrel with a morbidly exaggerated sense of responsibility.[4] He's always on guard; like a hound, he sniffs out injustice everywhere—an ordinary person stands no chance of catching up to him! O, our past and our future, and our current penitent yearning. "But when that child was still alive."[5] O, that abyss of nostalgia where the wind alone blows, bringing back from over there the terrible "International," and from here to over there—a pitiful, astral, as if singing last rites at Russia's funeral, "Lord, bring back the Tsar..."[6]

I walk down the street, think about God, peer into women's faces. Here's a pretty one, she's to my liking. I imagine her washing herself down there. Legs spread apart, knees slightly bent. Stockings slide off her knees; eyes turn velvety dark somewhere in their very depths; an innocent, birdlike expression on her face. I think about how an average French woman, as a rule, does a good job washing herself down there, yet rarely washes her feet. Why bother? After all she always does it in stockings, very often without taking her shoes off. I think about France in general. About the nineteenth century that has lingered here. About the cute little violets along the Madeleine, the baguettes soaking in *pissoirs*, the adolescents on their way to their first Holy

Communion, the chestnut trees, the spreading of gonorrhea, the silvery chill of the "Ave Maria." About Armistice Day in 1918. Paris went wild. Women slept with whomever came along. Soldiers climbed up lamp poles, cock-a-doodle-dooing like roosters. Everyone danced, everyone got drunk. No one heard how the voice of the new century said: "Woe to the Victors."

I think about war. About it being an accelerated—as if in cinematography—life, condensed down to its extract. That the war, all by itself, had nothing to do with the misfortunes that befell the world. A push that hastened the inevitable, no more. To a dangerously sick patient everything is dangerous, so the old order started to crumble at the first push. The patient ate a cucumber and croaked. The world war was that cucumber. I think about the banality of such meditations and simultaneously sense, like warmth or light, the pacifying caress of banality. I think about the epoch decomposing before my eyes. About the two basic species of women: either prostitutes or those taking pride in refraining from prostitution. About inhumane universal allure and animate universal hideousness. About nature, about how stupidly the classic writers portray it. About multifarious nasty things that people do to each other. About pity. About the little child who asked Farther Christmas for new eyes for his blind sister. About the way Gogol died: how they would shave him, threaten him with the Last Judgment, treat him with leeches, force him to sit in a bathtub. I recall the old lullaby: "Tomcat Purr had a wicked stepmother." I again return to the thought that I am a man disposed to be happy. I wanted the most ordinary thing—love.

From my masculine point of view ... Then again, a point of view can only be a masculine one. A feminine point of view doesn't exist. A woman, by herself, does not exist. She is a body and reflected light. And now you absorbed my light and left. And all my light left me.

For now we are skimming across life's surface. Peripherally. Along the ocean's blue waves.[7] The appearance of harmony and order. Filth, tenderness, sadness. Now we'll dive. Your hand, my unknown friend.

* * *

The heart stops beating. The lungs refuse to breathe. Torment similar to rapture. Everything is unreal except for the unreal; everything is senseless except for senselessness. Man simultaneously loses and gains sight. Such symmetry and such disorder. A part that has become larger than the whole—the part is everything, the whole nothing. A conjecture that the clarity and completeness of the world are a mere reflection of the chaos in the mind of a quiet madman. A conjecture that books, art, are the same as descriptions of feats and travels intended for those who will never travel anywhere and will not perform any feats. A conjecture that enormous spiritual life expands and burns out in the atom, in a man outwardly utterly unremarkable, yet chosen, unique, and unrepeatable. A revelation that the first person you meet on the street is this unique, chosen, and unrepeatable one. A multitude of contradictory conjectures that seem to confirm in a new key the eternal, intangible truth. Secret dreams. "Tell me what you dream in secret and I'll tell you who you are." "All right, I'll attempt to tell, but will you make out my words? Everything is smoothly walled up; not even one bubble will break through to life's surface. The atom, a dot, a deaf-and-dumb genius, and under his feet a deep subsurface layer, the essence of life, the sedimentary coal of decomposed epochs. A world record of solitude." "Go on then, answer, tell us what you dream about in secret there, at the very bottom of your solitude?"

The history of my soul and the history of the world. They are intertwined like life and dream. They have grown together and through each other. Like a backdrop, like a tragic underpainting, behind them stands modern life. Having embraced, merged, and intertwined, they rush off into the void at the terrifying speed of darkness, behind which, not even trying to catch up with it, light lazily moves along.

Fanfares. Morning. A splendid curtain. No curtain at all. But the desire for durability, solidity is so powerful that I feel the touch of its thick stitched silk. Blue-eyed craftswomen have been weaving it from morning till night. One of them was a bride-to-be ... It wasn't woven anywhere. Go on. Don't look.

A dead rat lies in a garbage pail, among cigarette butts shaken out of ashtrays, next to the cotton ball with which the bride-to-be washed herself down there for the last time. The rat had been wrapped in a piece of newspaper, but it came open in the pail and swam up—it is still possible to read snatches of news from the day before yesterday. Three days ago these snatches were still news, the butt emitted smoke in a mouth, the rat was alive, the virginal hymen was intact. Now all of this is mixing up, losing color, disappearing, falling apart, flying off into the void, rushing away with the terrifying speed of darkness, while the light, not even trying to catch up to it, moves along in its wake like a tortoise.

A safety razor, catching on a bloated cigarette butt, reflects a sunray that gleams rainbow-like through the slops and focuses it on the muzzle of the rat. Its teeth are bared; pus shows on their sharp edges. How could it happen that such an old, experienced, careful, God-fearing rat did not protect itself and ate poison? How could a Minister who signed the Treaty of Versailles get caught in old age stealing because of some girl? A presentable exterior, a collar starched rock-stiff, the Commander's Cross, "Germany Must Pay!"—and in confirmation of this axiom a firm flourish of a gold pen on historic parchment. But suddenly some girl, her stockings, knees, warm tender breath, warm rosy vagina—and out with the Treaty of Versailles, the Commander's Cross—a disgraced old man dies on a prison bunk. His unattractive, respectable widow muffles herself in crepe, moves to the provinces for good, their children are ashamed of their father's name, his colleagues in the Senate shake their bald pates in sad reproach. But the culprit of all this filth and nonsense has already preempted her, preempted her long ago, preempted her at that moment when the bedroom door closed behind him, the key clinked, his past disappeared, and all that remained was that girl on a wide bed, a counterfeit promissory note, bliss, disgrace, death. Having preempted his fate, he is now flying in icy space, and the eternal darkness ruffles the tails of his foppish, old-fashioned coat. Ahead of him fly cigarette butts and historic treaties, combed-out hairs and blossomed-out universal ideas; behind him fly other hairs, treaties, cigarette butts, ideas, spittle. If the darkness does finally carry him to the foot of the Throne, he won't say to God: "Germany Must Pay!" "O last belated love, thou art..."—he'll murmur in confusion.[8]

***

Copulation with a dead girl-child. The body was quite soft, only some-what cold, as if after a swim. With exertion, with special enjoyment. She lay there as if asleep. I didn't do anything evil to her. On the contrary, in those several spasmodic moments life still continued around—if not for—her. A star burnt pale in the window, the jasmine bloom was about to fade. Semen trickled back out; I wiped it with my handkerchief. I lit my cigarette from a fat wax candle. Go on. Don't look.[9]

You were taking away my light, leaving me in darkness. All of the world's delight was concentrated in you alone, you and only you. And I painfully regretted that when you are old, sick, unattractive, that when you die in anguish, I will not be by your side, will not lie to you that you are getting better, will not hold you by the hand. I ought to have been glad not to be subjected to this torture at least. Meanwhile there hid the main, perhaps the only, constituent that constituted love. My horror at the mere thought of this had always been the lodestar of my life. And now you are long gone, yet this star still shines as it used to in my window.

I am in a forest. Terrifying, fairytale-like, snowy landscape of an utterly uncomprehending, disturbed, doomed soul. Glass jars with cancerous tumors: a gastrointestinal tract, a liver, a throat, a uterus, a breast. Pale miscarried fetuses in greenish alcohol. In 1920 in Petersburg that alcohol would be sold as a drink—appropriately enough, it was called "Fetus Juice." Vomit, sputum, smelly mucus crawling down your bowels. Carrion. Human carrion. Stunning similarity of the smell of cheese to that of foot sweat.

Christmas at the North Pole. Radiance and snow. The purest shroud of winter, covering life.

Evening. July. People walk down the street. People of the thirties of the twentieth century. The sky begins to turn dark, the stars will be out soon. The stars of the thirties of the twentieth century. One can describe today's evening, Paris, the street, the play of shadows and light in the cirrus clouds high above, the play of fear and hope in the lonely human soul. One can do this cleverly, artfully, vividly, plausibly. But what one cannot do anymore is create a miracle—the lie of art cannot be palmed off as truth. Not that long ago one could still pull it off. But now ...

What one could pull off yesterday has become impossible, unachievable today. One cannot believe in the appearance of a new Werther, whose example will suddenly set off the crackle of enthusiastic gunshots of enchanted, enthralled suicides all over Europe.[10] One cannot imagine how a contemporary man, after leafing through a notebook of poems, would brush away tears that come all by themselves and look up at the sky, a sky like this evening's sky, with aching hope. Impossible. So impossible that it is hard to believe that it was possible some time ago. The new iron laws that are stretching the world as if it were rawhide are unfamiliar with the consolation of art. Moreover, these soulless, fair laws—still uncertain, already irreversible, they are being born in the new world or are giving birth to it—they have a reverse power: while a new inspired consolation cannot be created, one can no longer be consoled by the old one. Even today there are people still capable of crying over the fate of Anna Karenina. The soil they are still standing on is disappearing along with them, the same soil into which was laid the foundation of the theater where Anna, radiant in her torment and beauty, leaned on the velvet railing of her loge, suffering her disgrace. This radiance almost does not reach us.

Maybe it touches us only a little with its faded slanted rays—either as a last glimmer of something that has been lost or as a confirmation that the loss is irreparable. Soon everything will turn dim forever. What will remain is the play of intelligence and talent, a piece of diverting reading not requiring us to believe it or instilling any belief. Like *The Three Musketeers*. Something Tolstoy himself sensed earlier than anybody, an unavoidable line, a frontier, beyond which—absolutely no consolation in created beauty, not a single tear shed over a created fate.

*** * ***

I want the most simple, most ordinary things. I want tears, I want consolation. I want to look up at the sky with aching hope. I want to write you an insulting, heavenly, filthy, most tender and long farewell letter in the world. I want to call you an angel, bitch, to wish you happiness and to bless you, and to say also that wherever you may be, wherever you hide yourself, my blood like a myriad of unforgiving, never leaving particles will swirl about you. I want to forget, to rest, to get on a train and go to Russia, to drink beer and eat crayfish on a warm evening on a rocking barge on the Neva. I want to overcome this revolting feeling of numbness: people have no faces, words have no sound, nothing makes any sense. I want to shatter it no matter how. I simply want to catch my breath, to gulp some air. But there isn't any air.

For a moment the bright light and hubbub of the café give the illusion of freedom: you have dodged, you have jumped out, your peril has floated past. If you have twenty francs to spare you can go for a walk with a pale and pretty street girl who is slowly walking down the sidewalk and stops upon encountering a man's glance. If you nod to her right now, the illusion will solidify, grow stronger, turn pink with a patina of life, like an apparition that has had a drink of blood, stretch to ten, twelve, twenty minutes.

Woman. Flesh. An instrument by means of which a man produces that sole note from the divine scale he is permitted to hear. A light bulb shines under the ceiling. Her face is thrown back on the pillow. One might think she is my fiancée. One might think I got the girl drunk and am hastily raping her like a panting thief. One might think nothing, shuddering, listening intently, hearing amazing things, anticipating that moment when woe and happiness, good and evil, life and death cross their orbits as during an eclipse, prepare to unite into one, when the horrifying greenish light of life-death, happiness-torment will gush from the perished past, from your extinguished pupils.

✳ ✳ ✳

The history of my soul and the history of the world. They have intertwined and grown into each other. Modernity is behind them like a tragic backdrop. The semen, which could not fertilize anything, trickled back out;

I wiped it with my handkerchief. All the same, while this lasted, life still trembled here.

The history of my soul. I want to incarnate it, but only know how to disincarnate. I envy the writer refining his style, the artist mixing his paints, the musician engrossed in sounds, all of those people who have yet to go extinct on earth, belonging to that sensitive-heartless, farsighted-nearsighted, all-familiar, already good-for-nothing breed, those people who believe that a plastic reflection of life is a victory over it. All that's needed is talent, that special artistic vein throbbing in the mind, the fingers, the ear; all one needs to do is to take a little from make-believe, a bit from actuality, a bit from sadness, a bit from filth, flatten it all like children do when they level sand with a toy shovel, decorate it with stylistics and imagination, like a confectionary cake with glaze, and one's job is done, all is saved, the absurdity of life, the futility of suffering, solitude, torment, sticky nauseating terror—they all are transfigured by the harmony of art.

I know the price of it all and all the same I envy them: they are blessed. Blessed are the sleeping, blessed are the dead. Blessed is the expert before a painting by Rembrandt, piously convinced that the play of shadows and light on the face of an old woman is a universal rapture before which the old woman herself is a nonentity, a speck of dust, a zero. Blessed are the aesthetes. Blessed are the balletomanes. Blessed are Stravinsky's listeners and Stravinsky himself. Blessed are the shadows of the departing world, those seeing its last, sweet, mendacious dreams that for so long have been lulling mankind to sleep. In departing this life, having already departed it, they carry away with them an enormous imaginary richness. What will we be left with?[11]

With the conviction that the old woman is infinitely more important than Rembrandt. With the confusion as to what we are to do with this old woman. With the torturous desire to save and comfort her. With the clear understanding that no one can be saved or comforted by anything. With the feeling that only through a chaos of contradictions can one break through to the truth. That this advance is possible only through distortion. That one cannot lean on reality itself: a photograph lies and every human document is patently counterfeit. That everything average, classical, appeasing is inconceivable, impossible. That a sense of proportion slips like an eel from the hands of anyone who strives to capture it, and that this elusiveness is the last of its remaining creative attributes. That when it is finally seized, what the seizer is holding in his hands is base vulgarity. "...In seinen Armen das Kind war tot..."[12] That everyone around has got a dead child on his hands. That he who wants to make his way through the chaos of contradictions to eternal truth, or at least a pale reflection of it, has only one path left to him: to pass above life—like an acrobat performing a high-wire act—above an unsightly, disheveled, contradictory shorthand transcript of life.

A photograph lies. A human document is counterfeit. Once I lost my way in the Berlin Polizeipräsidium building and accidentally found myself in that corridor.[13] The walls were festooned with photographs. There were dozens of them, all depicting the same thing. How those suicides or crime victims were discovered by the police. A young German hangs by his suspenders, the shoes he had taken off for comfort lie next to an upended chair. An old woman—a large blot on her chest the form of which is reminiscent of a rooster—a thick glob of blood from her slit throat. A fat, naked prostitute with her stomach ripped open. An artist who shot himself from hunger or unhappy love, or from both combined. Under a smashed skull a splendid artistic bow, on an easel next to it some kind of branches and clouds, the unfinished daubery of holy art. Bulging eyes, swollen, bitten-through tongues, vile poses, revolting wounds—and taken altogether, all of this is unvaried, academic, not scary. Not a single twist of an intestine that has slithered out of a ripped-open stomach, not a single grimace, not a single bruise has escaped the camera lens, but the main thing has, the main thing is missing. I look and don't see anything that would stir me, force my soul to shudder. I make an effort—nothing. And suddenly the thought of you, that you are breathing here on earth, suddenly in my memory as if it were real, your beguiling, heartless face.

And immediately I see and hear everything—all the grief, all the torment, all the futile entreaties, all the words said before dying. How that old woman wheezed with her throat slit, how that prostitute tried to beat off the sadist as she was getting caught in her own intestines, how—as if it were me—that talentless, hungry artist lay dying. How the lamp burned on. How the dawn lit up. How the alarm clock banged. How the minute hand approached five. How, unable to resolve, having resolved, he licked his lips all over. How he squeezed the revolver in his awkward, sweaty palm. How the icy barrel touched his burning mouth. How he hated them, those staying alive, and how he envied them.

I would like to go out to the seashore, lie on the sand, close my eyes, sense the breath of God on my face. I would like to begin from afar—with a blue dress, with a quarrel, with a hazy wintry day. "Evening mist lay upon the hills of Georgia"—I would like to talk to life using approximately such words.[14]

Life no longer understands that language. The soul has not yet learned another. This is harmony's sick way of atrophying in the soul. Perhaps when it has completely atrophied, fallen off like a dry scab, the soul will feel the primordial lightness anew. But the transition is slow and torturous. The soul is terrified. It seems to her that every single thing that used to vivify her is flaking away. It seems to her that she herself is flaking away. She cannot be silent and she has forgotten how to speak. So she is grunting convulsively like a deaf-and-dumb woman, pulling ugly grimaces. "Evening mist lay upon the hills of Georgia"—she wants to utter in a resounding, triumphant voice, singing glory to the Creator and herself. Yet with revulsion similar to enjoyment she is muttering obscene curse words she saw scribbled on the metaphysical fence, some sort of "dyr bu shchyl ubeshchur."[15]

A blue dress, a quarrel, a hazy wintry day. A thousand other dresses, quarrels, days. A thousand sensations that run through the soul of every person unnoticed. A few of them that have become naturalized, entered literature, usage, spoken language. And those that remain, those countless sensations that have not yet found literary expression, have not yet broken away from the innermost transrational nucleus. But that does not make them any less trivial: thousands of unincarnated banalities that patiently await their Tolstoy. The hunch that art, creativity in the generally accepted sense, is nothing other than the hunt for ever-newer banalities. The hunch that the harmony to which art aspires is nothing other than some sort of supreme banality. The hunch that the true path of the soul coils somewhere on the side—it goes into a spin, a spin as it pierces universal hideousness.

I want to speak about my soul in simple, convincing words. I know there are no such words. I want to tell the story of how I loved you, how I was dying, how I died, how a cross was placed above my grave, and how time and worms turned that cross into rot. I want to gather up a handful of that dust, look up at the sky for the last time and blow on my palm with relief. I want different, equally unrealizable things—once again to breathe in the smell of the hair on the back of your head and yet again extract from the chaos of rhythms that unique rhythm from which, like a cliff from a blast, universal hideousness will collapse. I want to tell the story of a man who lay on a messy bed and thought, thought, thought—how to save himself, how to right things—and could not think up anything. The story of how he nodded off, how he woke up, how he remembered everything at once, how he said out loud, as if talking about some other person: "He was no Caesar. All he had was this love. But it encompassed everything—power, the crown, immortality. And now it came crashing down, he has been stripped of his honor, his shoulder straps have been ripped off." I want to explain in simple convincing words a myriad of magical, inimitable things—blue dress, quarrel, hazy wintry day. And I also want to caution the world against a terrible enemy, pity. I want to shout out so that everyone hears: people, brothers, firmly take everyone else's hands and swear to be pitiless to each other. Otherwise pity—the chief enemy of order—will pounce and tear you to pieces.

For the last time I want to summon from the void your face, your body, your tenderness, your heartlessness, to gather the mixed, putrefied matter that used to be yours and mine, into a handful of dust in my palm, and to blow on it with relief. But pity once again gets everything confused, once again gets in my way. I again see the fog of a strange town. A beggar turns the handle of a barrel organ; a little monkey, shivering from the cold, walks along the circle of gapers with a saucer. The gloomy gapers stand under their umbrellas and reluctantly toss the odd coin. Will it buy us a place to sleep out the night, where we could pull something over ourselves as we lie in each other's embrace until morning?

This appeared to me in the midst of a noisy ball—with champagne, music, laughter, the rustle of silk, the smell of perfumes.[16] It was one of your happiest days. You radiated youth, charm, heartlessness. You were enjoying yourself, you triumphed over life. I glanced at you, smiling, surrounded by people. And I saw the little monkey, the fog, the umbrellas, solitude, penury. And caustic pity, as if an unbearable dazzle, made me lower my eyes.

A shiver that summons pity. A shiver that unavoidably turns into a feeling of revenge. For the deaf child, for a senseless life, for humiliations, for shoes with rents in their soles. To take revenge on a prospering world any excuse will do. "Anyone who has a heart" knows this.[17] That almost mechanical shift from dismayed pity to another, "now-you-just-hold-on" form of powerlessness. Even the little creatures were agitated, they whispered together, took a long time composing "A Protest-Pamphlet": "You, Who Torture Cats." They asked if it could be published in the newspapers so everyone could read it.

The little creatures were inseparable from us. They ate from our dishes and slept in our bed. The main ones among them were two Razmakhaychiks.

Razmakhaychik Green Eyes was good-natured, affectionate, he did not do any harm to anyone. Gray Eyes, when he grew some, turned out to have a temper. On occasion he could even bite. They were found under a metro bench, in an empty box for dates. A note was pinned to the box: "Razmakhaychiks, or Razmakhays, or Razmakhaytses. Of Australian origin. Require love, food, and walks in the Bois de Boulogne."[18]

There were other little creatures as well: Golubchik, Zhukhla, Freuhstuck, Kitaychik, silly Tsutik, who answered all questions the same way—"Tsutik it is." Then there was old, outwardly rude, yet most tender in her soul Khamka, possessor of a short fish tail. Somewhere to the side, rejected by the group, loitered, instilling hostility and fear, dismal Von Klopp.

The little creatures had their routine, habits, philosophy, honor, their views on life. They had their own creature-land, the borders of which were washed by dream as if by an ocean. The land was expansive and not completely explored. It was known that its south was inhabited by camels, and a white horse came to wash and trim them on Fridays. In the far north always stood an illuminated spruce and Christmas was eternal.

The little creatures expressed themselves in a mixed language. It had proper Australian words refashioned from ordinary ones according to the Australian style. For example, in letters they would address each other as "osthonored" and inscribe envelopes "To His High-Chinned Excellency." They loved dancing, ice cream, long walks, silk bows, holidays, and name days. The way they saw life was as follows: "What does a year consist of?"— "Three hundred sixty-five holidays."—"And a month?"—"Thirty name days."

Those little creatures were adorable. They tried to adorn our life the best they could. They didn't ask for ice cream when they knew there wasn't any money. Even when they were very sad, they danced and celebrated name days. They would turn away, and tried not to listen when they heard something bad. "Hey, little creatures, little creatures"—the terrifying Von Klopp would whisper to them from his crack at nighttime—"Life is passing, winter is approaching. You will be buried under the snow, you will freeze, you will die, little creatures—you who love life so much." But they pressed themselves against each other more tightly, stopped their little ears, and replied calmly, with dignity: "That doesn't consume us."[19]

A man wanders about the streets, thinks various things and peers into other people's windows. His imagination works separately from him. He doesn't notice its work. He sits in a café, drinks beer and reads the paper. Debate in the Chamber of Deputies. Motorcars on Installment. He snoozes and dreams nonsense. Ink spilled onto the tablecloth. A fish swam past—the ink disappeared. He should close the door, but the key won't fit in the keyhole. English Public Opinion. A Cyclone. It turns out the fish is the key and that's why it didn't fit. The sleeper suddenly awakens. No fish, no public opinion.

Sitting in a café, slouching along the streets, peering into other people's windows is, after all, better consolation than Anna Karenina or some Madame Bovary or other. Following lovebirds who sit cuddling over unfinished coffee, then roam the streets, and, finally, after a furtive look over their shoulders, enter a cheap hotel, is the same thing, if not greater, than the most perfect poems about love. "The little foot taps along, the golden ringlet tosses."[20] Here it is, the little foot that taps along the asphalt of a Montmartre sidewalk, here is the golden ringlet that flashes and disappears behind the glass door of the hotel. This is today's day, this is the trembling, flittering instant of my unrepeatable life—surely, these two things cannot be compared—this is superior to all poems taken together. The tapping of the foot fell silent, the ringlet flashed and disappeared behind the door. I'll stand here, I'll wait. There, a first-story window lit up. There, a curtain went down.

The lackey got his one-franc tip and left them alone. Little lamp below the ceiling, motley wallpaper, white enamel bidet. Perhaps this is the first time. Perhaps this is the most blessed love in the world. Perhaps Napoleon waged war and the *Titanic* sank solely so that tonight these two could lie in bed next to each other. On top of the blanket, on top of the rock-solid bed sheet, a hasty, awkward, immortal embrace. Knees spread wide apart, hose sliding; hair scattered on the pillow, face delightfully distorted. O, make it last, make it last. Hurry, hurry.

"Wait. Do you know what this is? This is our unrepeatable life. Sometime, in a hundred years, they'll write a long poem about us, but it will all be resounding rhymes and falsehood. The truth is here. The truth is this day, this hour, this flitting instant. No one ever spread your knees, and here I am, in this bright light, on this white, pressed bed sheet, unceremoniously spreading them apart. You are ashamed and in pain. Every drop of your pain and shame enters with its full weight into my unaccountable triumph."

Who are these two? O, it does not make any difference. They are gone now. All there is left is a radiance trembling outside while this is lasting. Only tension, rotation, combustion, the blessed rebirth of the sacred meaning of life. The icy pinnacle of universal delight, illuminated by a volley of fire. Seminal vesicles, ovaries, broken hymen, bird cherry blossom, knees spread apart, swoon, stars, saliva, bed sheet, veins a-tremble, smithereens, smithereens, uh … uh … uh … The sole note accessible to man, its horrific ringing. O, make it last, make it last; hurry, hurry. Last spasms. Hot semen flows down toward the contracting, vibrating uterus. Desire described a complete circle along a spiral thrown deep into eternity and has now returned back to the void. "It was so beautiful that it cannot end with death," the young Tolstoy writes down after his wedding night.

A man sits in a café. An ordinary little man, a zero. One of those about whom they write after a catastrophe: ten dead, twenty-six injured. He's not a trust director, not an inventor, not a Lindbergh,[21] not a Chaplin,[22] not a Montherlant.[23] He finished the newspaper and now knows the mood of English public opinion. He is done with his coffee and calls over the *garçon* to pay his bill. He thinks distractedly about what to do next: go to the cinema or put aside money for a lottery ticket. He is calm, he is peacefully disposed, he is asleep and dreams nonsense. And suddenly he sees before him the black hole of his solitude. His heart stops beating, his lungs refuse to breathe. A torment similar to rapture.

The atom is motionless. It is asleep. Everything is smoothly walled up, not a single bubble can break through to the surface of life. But if you poke it. Stir its sleepy essence. Hitch it, shake it, split it. Send a million volts through the soul, and then plunge it into ice. To learn loving someone more than yourself, only to see a hole of solitude, a black icy hole.

A man, a little man, a zero stares ahead distractedly. He sees a black void, and in it, like a fugitive lightning bolt, the unattainable essence of life. Thousands of nameless, unanswerable questions, illuminated for a moment by a fugitive fire only to be at once swallowed by darkness.

Consciousness, trembling, exhausted, seeks an answer. There is no answer to anything. Life poses questions and does not answer them. Love poses ... God posed to man—by man—a question, but gave no answer. And man is condemned only to ask, does not know how to answer anything. Failure's eternal synonym—answer. How many beautiful questions have been posed throughout the history of the world, and what kind of answers have been given to them ...

There are two billion inhabitants of this earthly globe. Each person is complicated by his own torturous, unrepeatable, identical, good-for-nothing, tedious complexity. Each, like an atom in its nucleus, is enclosed by an impenetrable armor of solitude. Two billion inhabitants of earth—two billion exceptions to the rule. But the same goes for the rule itself. Everyone is revolting. Everyone is unhappy. No one can change anything or understand anything. My brother Goethe, my brother the concierge, neither of you knows what you are doing and what life is doing to you.

A dot, an atom, through whose soul fly millions of volts. Now they will split it. Now the immobile impotence will resolve into terrifying explosive potency. Now, now. Already the earth has started trembling. Already something has creaked in the pilings of the Eiffel Tower. A sandstorm has whirled its turbid streams in the desert. The ocean drowns ships. Trains fly off slopes. Everything rips, crawls apart, melts, comes to dust—Paris, the street, time, your image, my love.

The man, the little man, the zero sits with fixed gaze. The lackey walks up and makes change. The man draws his breath and rises. He lights a cigarette, he walks down the street. His heart has not yet burst—here it is beating in his chest as before. Universal hideousness has not come crashing down—here it is, like a cliff, it shores up the world as before.

A blue dress, a quarrel, a hazy wintry day. A desire to speak, a longing to sing— about one's love, about one's soul. Devastate oneself, choke on simple, convincing words, words that don't exist ...

How did our love begin? As banality, banality. As all things beautiful, it began as banality. Probably all there is to harmony is banality. Probably it is senseless to repine against it. Probably there is one and only one path for everyone—to walk above life like an acrobat does, using the tormenting feeling of the tightrope of life. The elusive feeling that arises from final physical intimacy, final inaccessibility, soul-rending tenderness, the loss of all this forever, forever. Day breaks outside the window. Desire has made a full circle and gone into the earth. A child has been conceived. Why is a child needed? There is no immortality. Immortality cannot not be. Why do I need immortality, if I am so lonely?

Daybreak outside the window. On the rumpled bed sheet in my arms lies all of the world's innocent delight and the bewildered question what was it that was being done to it. This delight is divine, it is inhuman. What is man to do with this delight's inhuman radiance? Man—wrinkles, bags under the eyes, calcium in both soul and blood, man—is above all doubt in his divine right to do evil. "A human being begins from sorrow," as some poet has put it.[24] As if anyone ever argued with that. A human being begins from sorrow. Tomorrow life begins. The Volga flows into the Caspian Sea.[25] Dyr bu shchyl ubeshchur.

This day, this hour, this fleeting minute. Thousands of same such days and minutes, identical, unrepeatable. These cirrus clouds of a Parisian sunset fading before my eyes. Thousands of such same sunsets over contemporaneity, over the future, over the perished centuries. Thousands of eyes, looking with the same hope into the very same glowing void. The eternal sigh of universal delight: I am fading away, I am burning out, I am no more. "Evening mist lay upon the hills of Georgia." And here it is, lying in the same way on Montmartre's hill. On the roofs, on the street crossing, on the café sign, on the semicircle of the *pissoir*, where, with an alarming noise exactly like that of the Aragva, the water rumbles.

Opposite the *pissoir* a small bench. On that bench an old man in rags. He is smoking a butt he picked up from the sidewalk. He has an indifferent sleepy look. But it is an act. All alert, he watches the people walking into the *pissoir*, where on a patch of newspaper lies a chunk of bread bloated from urine. Here is a thick-necked worker undoing his pants on the go. Planting his feet wide apart, he urinates above the bun. A blessed twitch in the soul of the lousy old sod. Now, after a quick look over the shoulder, hastily he will wrap the soaked newspaper with its snatches of yesterday's news still readable and will carry this bun home. Now, now—he will chomp it, wash it down with red wine as he will be imagining to the smallest detail the thick-necked worker, the boy in yellow shoes, all, all of those who saturated this half-kilo of *gros pain* with their tart, warm urine. Now, now. A torment similar to rapture, a blessed twitch. As he walks away, he mumbles something on the go. Perhaps his deaf-and-dumb soul struggles to bellow in its own way "Upon the hills of Georgia…"

Sunsets, thousands of sunsets. Over Russia, over America, over the future, over the perished centuries. The wounded Pushkin props himself with his elbow in the snow and a red sunset gushes into his face. Sunset in the morgue, in the operating room, over the ocean, over the Alps, in a slatted camp latrine: all shades of yellow and brown, commas on the walls, a complex stench broken by freshness drafting through the cracks. A new recruit, a rosy stripling, holds the door shut with one hand, while hurriedly masturbating with the other. A choke, a muffled scream, and he comes. About a half-glass in all, covering his fingers in sticky warmth and scaring away the flies, it splashes into the brown mess below. The stripling's face turns gray. He pulls up his pants sluggishly. He didn't manage to imagine the fiancée he left behind in his village. Of course, he will get killed in the war, maybe already this year.

Sunset over Le Temple. Sunset over Lubyanka.[26] Sunset on the day the war was declared and on Armistice Day: everyone danced, everyone got drunk, no one heard how the voice said: "Woe to the Victors."[27] Sunset in the room where you and I once lived: the blue dress lay on this chair.

※ ※ ※

The early Petersburg sunset has long faded. Akaky Akakiyevich trudges home from his job to Obukhov bridge.[28] Has his overcoat already been stolen? Or is he only dreaming about a new overcoat? Lost Russian man stands on a foreign street, in front of a foreign window, and his masturbatory conscience imagines every sigh, every spasm, every fold in the bed sheet, every little trembling vein. Has the woman already betrayed him, already dissolved without a trace in the cirrus clouds of the evening sky? Or is he only anticipating a meeting with her? What does it matter anyway?

The sunset has long faded. The job has long ended. In the attic near Obukhov bridge warm beer gurgles, tobacco smoke swirls. "He was a Titular Counselor—she a general's daughter," ingratiatingly, tenderly sighs the velvety guitar.[29] The attic chancellery myth is blossoming, this myth being a self-defense and counterweight to the icy myth of Pushkinian clarity. This myth is sulfuric acid, a secret dream—it will disfigure, corrode, corrupt this clarity.

Akaky Akakiyevich gets his wages, copies out documents, saves money for an overcoat, dines, and drinks tea. But all this is only surface, dream, nonsense, endlessly removed from the essence of things. The dot, the soul, is motionless and so small that it cannot be made out with the most powerful microscope. But inside it, under the impenetrable nucleus of solitude, lie endless absurd complexity—a horrific explosive force—secret longings, caustic as sulfuric acid. The atom is motionless. It is fast asleep. He dreams of his job and Obukhov bridge. But if you stir him, hitch, split ...

A general's daughter, Psyche, a cute little angel all in muslin, runs into His Excellency's study, and the ink rat, the little man, the zero, the servile shadow in a hand-me-down frock coat, he greets her with a deep bow. That is all. Psyche will whisper "bonjour, papa," kiss the general's ruddy cheek, flash a smile, her muslin will rustle before she flutters off. And no one knows, no one guesses, what an illusion all this is, a dream, vanity ...

With his head clouded by the boredom of life and beer, to the insinuating murmur of a guitar, Akaky Akakiyevich abandons vanity and surface and descends into the essence of things. Secret longings envelop the image of Psyche and little by little his greedy thought transforms into her desired flesh. Obstacles, so insurmountable in daytime, fall by themselves. He slides soundlessly across the empty sleeping city; unnoticed by anyone he enters His Excellency's dark chambers; like an inaudible shadow, between statues and mirrors, along parquet and carpets, he steals to the cute little angel's very bedroom. He opens the door, stops at the threshold, and sees "a paradise of the kind which does not exist even in heaven." He sees her white little undergarment casually spread on the armchair, sees her sleepy little face on a pillow; sees the little bench onto which she places her little foot of a morning as she pulls her white-as-snow stocking over that little foot. He was a Titular Counselor—she a general's daughter. And now … Nothing, nothing, silence…[30]

To the murmur of a guitar, clouded by secret longings, by his insistent, enflamed, directed-for-long-hours-and-long-years-at-one-spot imagination, he materializes Psyche, forces her to come to his attic, to lie on his bed. And she comes, lies down, raises her muslin hem, spreads her naked satin-smooth delicate knees. He was a Titular Counselor—she a general's daughter. Upon encountering her he would greet her with a servile bow, not daring to raise his eyes from his patched boots. And now, spreading her delicate knees wide apart, smiling the innocent smile of a cute little angel, she obediently waits until he gets his fill ravishing her to his heart's content, to the gills, to the gills.

"Show all your splendor, Peter's city, and stand erect," Pushkin exclaims impishly, in defiance of premonition, and who is not to be found on his Don Juan's list. "Nothing, nothing, silence," mumbles Gogol, his eyes upturned into the void as he masturbates under his cold bed sheet.[31]

"Show all your splendor and stand erect." On the surface of life, in the clear rays of the sun, even if it is setting, that seems to do it. After all, Paris stands erect to this day. On this warm summer evening it is magnificent. Chestnut trees, motorcars, midinettes in cute summer dresses. The magic of streetlights suddenly coming to life around the ugliest statues in the world. A scattering of flowers on street stands. Sacré Coeur against a darkening sky. Despite a premonition, the soul clings to life. Here she is in light cirrus clouds. "I am fading away, I am burning out, I am no more." And exactly like that of the Aragva, the muffled water solemnly, sadly rumbles in the *pissoir.*

But the sunset quickly darkens and night haze still more quickly seizes the man. This haze makes him follow itself to such a depth that, after he returns to the surface, he no longer recognizes it. But he will not return anyway. In the black happiness, ever deeper into which coils— going into a spin, a spin—the soul, whatever for would it need its long-ago-shaken unshakability and its long-disfigured comeliness? Peter will be ripped out of his coffin and left leaning up against the wall of the Peter and Paul Cathedral with a cigarette butt stuck in his teeth to the accompaniment of Red Army soldiers' guffawing, and so what, the Peter and Paul Cathedral will not plummet underground. D'Anthès will kill Pushkin, but Ivan Sergeyevich Turgenev will most politely shake d'An-thès's hand, and so what, Turgenev's hand won't wither away. And none of all this is any concern of ours at the very bottom of our souls. Our iden-tical, different, deaf-and-dumb souls, they have sensed a common goal, and going into a spin, a spin, through appearance and surface they coil toward it. Our revolting, unhappy, solitary souls have united into one and going into a spin, a spin through universal hideousness as they try their best to rip their way to God.

A pale, pretty street girl slows her pace upon encountering a man's glance. If you explain that you don't like her to wear stockings while doing it, she will eagerly wash her feet in anticipation of a little extra. A bit puffy from the hot water, their cute little toenails clipped short, the naïve feet of a street girl, unaccustomed as they are to someone looking at them, someone kissing them, someone pressing his hot forehead to them, these feet will turn into the delicate feet of Psyche.

The heart stops beating. The lungs refuse to breathe. The snow-white stocking has been pulled off Psyche's delicate leg. As her knee, ankle, tender childlike heel slowly, slowly bared—years flew past. An eternity passed before her dainty toes showed ... And now everything is fulfilled.

Nothing more to wait for, nothing more to dream about, nothing to live for. Nothing more left. Only the cute little angel's naked feet pressed to ossified lips and the only witness—God. He was a Titular Counselor—she a general's daughter. And now, now . . .

Cold-as-ice bed sheet. Night's turbid glow in the window. A sharp birdlike profile, pressed back into the pillows. O, make it last, make it last; hurry, hurry. Everything has been attained, but the soul is not yet sated to the end and shudders that it won't become completely sated. Before time is up, before the night is over, before the cock crows and the atom, after a tremor, explodes into myriads of particles—what else can be done? How else can you penetrate deeper into your triumph, into the essence of things, what else can you use to poke into it, to hitch onto it, split it? Hold on, Psyche; stay awhile, darling. You think this is it? The highest point, the end, the limit? No, you won't get away with it.

Silence and night. The naked childlike toes are pressed to ossified lips. They smell of innocence, tenderness, and rose water. But no, no—you won't get away with it. That spin, the spin of greedy passion coils upward, through appearance and surface, as it rapturously strives to discern in the angelic flesh a shameful essence kindred to itself. "Won't you tell me, through your innocence and rose water, what your ivory feet smell of, Psyche? In the very essence of things, what do they smell of—answer me. Of the same smell as mine do, my cute little angel, the same, darling. You won't get away with it, no!"

And Psyche knows: there is no getting away with it. Her little feet tremble in the prehensile greedy palms, and, as they tremble, they give up the last thing she possesses—that which is most sacred, most cherished because most shameful: the lightest, ephemeral yet all the same indestructible by any loveliness, any innocence, any social inequality, odor. The exact same that I give out, o my darling; the exact same that give out my most plebian feet, o my little institute girl, my cute little angel, my blue blood. This means there is no difference whatsoever between us and there is no reason for you to find me disgusting: I kissed your aristocratic little feet, I traded my soul for them, and now why don't you go bow down and kiss my rotten socks. "He was a Titular Counselor—she a general's daughter." What am I to do with you now, Psyche? Kill you? It's all the same—even dead you will be coming to me now.

A lost man walks the streets of an alien town. Like a high tide, the void gradually begins to engulf him. He does not resist it. As he goes away, he mutters to himself: "Pushkinian Russia, why did you deceive us? Pushkinian Russia, why did you betray us?"

Silence and night. Complete silence, absolute night. The thought that everything is ending forever overflows the man with quiet triumph. He senses, he knows for sure that this is not so. But while this second lasts, he does not want to resist it. Already not belonging to life, yet not swept up by the void—he permits himself to be lulled by a vague mellifluous lie, as if it were music or the incoming tide.

Already not belonging to life, yet not swept up by the void ... On the very brink. He swings on a spider's thread. The entire weight of the world is weighing on him, but he knows: as long as this second lasts, the spider's thread will not break, it will endure everything. He stares at one dot, an infinitely small dot, but as long as this second lasts, the entire essence of life is concentrated there. The dot, the atom, millions of volts fly through it, and as they do, they melt to smithereens, to smithereens, the nucleus of solitude.

... A spiral was thrown deep into eternity. Through it flew everything: cigarette butts, sunsets, immortal poems, pared fingernails, dirt from under those fingernails. Universal ideas, blood spilt for them, blood from murder and intercourse, hemorrhoidal blood, blood from suppurating ulcers. Bird cherry blossom, stars, innocence, sewage pipes, cancerous tumors, beatitudes, irony, Alpine snow. The minister who signed the Treaty of Versailles flew past singing to himself "Germany must pay"—pus congealed on his sharp teeth, rat poison glowing in his stomach. Catching up to his overcoat, Akaky Akakiyevich rushed by, with his birdlike profile, wearing canvas drawers smeared with the semen of a masturbator. All the hopes, all the spasms, all the mercy, all the mercilessness, all the bodily moisture, all the smelly soft tissue, all the deaf-and-dumb triumph ... And thousands of other things. A man who in a dream sees himself playing a game of tennis in a white shirt and swimming in the Crimea as he is eaten alive by lice in Solovki.[32] Varieties of lice: body lice, head lice, and special subcutaneous ones, treated only with sulfur-mercury ointment. The sulfur-mercury ointment, pills against obesity, *globuli vaginales* against pregnancy, an ice drift on the Neva, sunset on the Lido and all descriptions of sunsets and ice drifts—in the useless books by literary classics. In the incessant motley stream flashed a blue dress, a quarrel, a hazy wintry day. A spiral was thrown deep into eternity. Shattered to smithereens, melted universal hideousness convulsed and vibrated as it rushed into the void. There, on the very brink, right at the target, everything coalesced into one again. Through rotation, shudder, and glimmer, some features came through. The meaning of life? God? No, it was the same: that dear, heartless, irrevocably lost face of yours.

If the little creatures could know in what an important official letter I am using their Australian language, they would of course be very proud. I would be already long dead and they would still be celebrating, dancing away and clapping their little hands.

"Ost Honored Mister Commissar. Voluntarily, in a not particularly sober mind, but with a strong, very strong presence of mind, I conclude the celebration of my name day. Myself being a part of universal hideousness, I see no point in blaming it for anything. I would also like to add, paraphrasing the words of the newly wed Tolstoy: 'It was so senseless that it cannot end with death.' With astonishing, irresistible clarity I understand this now. But—once again switching to the Australian language—'This does not consume you, Your High-Chinned Excellency.'"[33]

24 February 1937

Petersburg Winters

They say that at the last moment a drowning man forgets his fear and stops gasping for air. He suddenly feels at ease, free and blissful. And, as he loses consciousness, he sinks to the bottom with a smile.

By 1920 Petersburg was already drowning almost blissfully.

People feared hunger until it established itself "for sure and for the long run" and then stopped noticing it. The same went for executions by firing squads.

"So how did you manage to get home last night after the ballet?"

"Everything went fine, thank you. Even my fur coat didn't get snatched. Though I was forced to freeze in the courtyard for a half hour or so. There was a search of apartment 8. No one was allowed on the stairs until they were done."

"Did they grab anyone?"

"Young Perfilyev and some student or other; he was staying the night with them."

"They're going to shoot him, right?"

"Right…"

"Anyhow, Spesivtseva was enchanting…"

"Yes, but she's got a ways to go to be a Karsavina."

"Well then, Pyotr Petrovich, stop by and see us…"

Two Petersburgers met, got conversing about life's trifles, and then went their separate ways. "Ballet … Fur coat … Young Perfilyev and some student or other … You know what, they handed out herring at our co-op today … They're going to shoot him … Right…"

Two citizens of the Northern Commune calmly discuss quotidian matters:

> One citizen calls out to another citizen:
> "Hey, citizen, what's in today's dinner pot?
> Did you sign up to eat, citizen, or not?"

They talk so calmly not from heartlessness, but from habit. Everyone has the same odds: it's the student today, tomorrow it's you.

> Today, citizen, I slept badly—
> I traded my soul for kerosene.[1]

Now *that* was something some people did worry about: how do I trade my soul for kerosene, yet keep a bit of it for myself? So some hatched plots, others prayed, and some traversed the entire city by foot, be it overflowing with a thaw or covered in sheets of ice, to see Giselle—the embodiment of eternal love, an angel personified—flutter out to the delicate thunder of music, against a moonlit background of rustling and sumptuous paper roses…

Only to catch a glimpse, to sigh, and then walk back again at night, across the entire city.

> Golden sparks above checkpoint fires,
> Steamy ice floes over the Neva …
> … And a stray bullet over the Neva
> Seeks out your poor heart… [2]

Well, perhaps it won't reach mine today. Why bother now?

* * *

Petersburg Side, Plutalov Street. A place so remote that even the Red police doesn't bother to come here. Otherwise some local speculator would not be brazen enough to nail up a sign advertising his trade. But the sign's right there in black and white: "Dog Mete Sold Heer."

V. lives on Plutalov Street. He occupies a room with a kitchen in a grimy six-story building.

V. is a former writer. Fifteen years ago or so he would publish something or other, and at some point even "made quite a splash." Nowadays he writes "for himself," meaning he writes nothing, only pretends.

In moments of frankness he confesses: "The hell with literature: living it up is the main thing."

He is a strange man. His scribbling lacks talent, and yet "there's something in him." He is incredibly tall, with a scruffy black beard and the bulging eyes of a thug, but he speaks with the cloying intonation of a monk. Sometimes he spends weeks on end burying himself in books from morning till night in his "apartment," which is furnished with random bric-a-brac he takes for antique. Sometimes he disappears for months, nobody knowing where he goes.

"So where have you been, V.?"

A sly grin: "Well, I made a quick trip to Mount Athos."

"Why on earth did you go to Mount Athos?"

The same sly grin: "Simply had to go, that's all. And the trip didn't go badly either. Pity though my knapsack got stolen, together with all my treasures: a bottle of Old Regime *zubrovka*—how would I love to treat you to some of it now!—and some holy relics too..."

Another half-year goes by, and the same story: "Where did you disappear?"

"Well, I had to stop by a certain monastery in the Caucasus..."

I once decided to spend a night at the place of this same aesthete of seminarian stock with the looks of an operatic villain, and here is how it came about.

I had stayed late with friends on the Petersburg Side, but now had to go to the very end of Basseyny Street where I lived. When I was getting ready to leave I realized it was a quarter to eleven, and if I were to go home, I was sure to run into a patrol and wind up in detention, because in addition to failing to obtain a night pass, I did not even have an ordinary laborer's identification papers on me. A night in jail is an unpleasant business, and then there was the question of how the next morning would play out, they could let me go, or they could send me to the Cheka. To exclaim in the manner of Osip Mandelstam (who, by the way, was terrified of policemen):

> I have no need of a night pass,
> I have no fear of sentries—[3]

would not have been very rational. There was nowhere to sleep at my friends' place where I had lost track of time. This is when I remembered that V. lived nearby.

There was no heavy hanging lock on the door—that meant that he was home. No one answered my knock, however. Could he have gone out? I knocked louder. There was a sound of steps and then V's voice:

"What are you doing trying to break in so early? Get lost. I won't let you in till twelve anyway."

Having decided that these words could not possibly be addressed to me, I knocked again and gave my name.

V. opened at once. "My dear fellow! Fancy seeing you here! Would you like to warm up?" He pushed a full shot glass toward me.

V. had evidently "warmed" himself while getting ready for bed. The collar of his *kosovorotka* unbuttoned, his face was red and eyes glistened. That, however, was his usual state—halfway between drunk and sober. His perpetual "just a bit tipsy."

Upon finding out my intention to sleep over, V. began to fret somehow.

"If it's inconvenient for you, just tell me and I'll leave."

"Not at all, my dear fellow, not at all! Very convenient, very pleasant. It's just that..." His eyes began to dart about again: "But how about you—will it be convenient for you?"

"Don't worry about me."

"Sure, sure, but will you be comfortable? Do you sleep soundly?"

"Very. And besides I'm extremely tired. I've been on my feet all day. I'm about ready to drop."

"Well, well." V. visibly brightened up. "You see, I'm expecting a visitor here ... A book lover ... A neighbor ... Coming to sort through some books ... So I was afraid we might bother you."

I put V.'s mind at rest by saying that no one or nothing would bother me. Ignoring my objections, he put me in his bed that stood behind a tattered damask curtain.

"Not to worry, not to worry—you'll be more comfortable here, and I'll feel more at ease myself. I'll sleep on my little couch—I've got a fine little couch here."

V.'s bed was wide and soft ... In the other corner of the room V. puttered about with his books, his teaspoon tinkling in his glass now and then. The book-loving neighbor was not coming ...

... I woke up. A quiet conversation was taking place behind the curtain. An unfamiliar, insinuating, and squeaky voice led the way. Only occasionally would V. interpose something or other.

"So you've turned away from God all right. Turned away, right, that's all very well. It's just that it's not enough to turn away from God, my friends. But first you must serve *Him*. Don't you go thinking that *He* will accept you right away, will start helping you barely after you've torn the cross away from around your neck!"

"But how do we go about serving *Him*? Should we build churches in *His* honor? Sing hymns in *His* praise?"

"Right, build churches, sing hymns, and hold *Him* and *Him* alone in your heart. The main thing is to hold *Him* in your heart. Now that's when *He* will help you.

"So what will happen when *He* comes to help?"

"You will have everything, mark my words, everything. Bread rolls of all sorts, hams, sprats, vodka galore, anything you want. And not for money, not even at the old prices. Everything for nothing, eat what you want, drink what you want, all of it free and forever—only you must hold *Him* in your heart."

Cautiously I raised myself up and peeked through a tear in the bed curtain. V. was seated at a round table. In front of him with his back to me sat some figure in a short sheepskin coat. On his skull there was a large bald spot surrounded by sparse, light hair. He was bent forward, his neck pulled into his shoulders ...

"... right, hold *Him* in your heart." The speaker grew quiet for a moment. "Well all right now, for starters, like you and I agreed, that'll be five grand..."

"What, five already? Yesterday it was three!"

"Five grand," repeated the old man. "I won't manage on less. And now take this note here. You'll need to copy it, you know. And not on a type-writer, in longhand. Toil in *His* glory!"

With a sigh, V. began to count out the money. The little old man hid it away, but not before counting it carefully.

"Well, time to go. My dead folks must be getting worried about me—I've been away for two nights already. All these things to do, things to do…"

"Aren't you afraid at the cemetery?"

"What's to be afraid of? On the contrary, I quite like the company."

"Aren't you disgusted?"

"What do you mean, 'disgusted'? Of course, if someone's maggoty and cuddles up to you … But those who've been out there for a long time have pretty well dried. What's to be disgusted by in that? Among them dames you get some real nice ones…"

"Enough of you already! I won't sleep a wink after all your stories."

The old man giggled.

"A scaredy-cat, aren't you! And you want to become our Minister! A Senator would be about right for you when our time comes, heh-heh … All right, now don't you go forgetting—the main thing is to hold *Him* in your heart."

"Are you asleep, G. V.?" called out my host after he had seen off his guest.

I didn't reply. "He's asleep all right," muttered V. For a long time after that he busied himself with opening and closing something, jingled his keys, shuffled papers, and sighed. At long last he lay down, put out the light and began to snuffle, and to the sound of his snuffling I too fell asleep. In the morning when I was leaving, V. was still sleeping the heavy, deep sleep of the drunkard.

✳ ✳ ✳

"Copy this prayer and send it to nine of your acquaintances. If you don't do it, great misfortune will befall you…"

Then came the prayer: "Morning Star, well of mercy, strength, wind, fire, procreation, and hope..."

"What a strange prayer! After all, the Morning Star is the star of Lucifer. Strange! Could this be the same prayer that the little old man, that devil worshipper, ordered V. to copy—remember, I told you about it?"

Six months later this conversation took place at Nikolay Gumilyov's apartment on Preobrazhensky Street. As he sat next to a small round stove, he was stirring coal embers with his son's toy saber.

"What a strange prayer! It may well be that it was V. who sent it to me, since he, as you say, dabbles in the demonic. But it's stupid for someone who knows who I am to be sending me such stuff. What kind of an Orthodox Christian would I be if I were to copy it and send it around?"

"It's stupid to be sending it around at all. Why would anyone bother to recopy it?"

"Well, there are those who will. First, the majority wouldn't even make out what it's all about—they'd think it's simply some sort of a hymn. And those who will make it out will probably copy it anyway, being superstitious as they are. After all, the majority is more likely to be superstitious than true believers."

"You mean they'll copy it out of fear that something bad will happen to them?"

"Right."

"What nonsense!"

Gumilyov tapped a Russian cigarette on his tortoise-shell cigarette case.

"Not as much nonsense as you think. These threats, believe me, are not empty words."

"Misfortune must now befall you then?"

"It must. Misfortune will be directed at me for this, of that I have no doubt. Don't smile—I say this in all seriousness. Someone has deliberately sent me a challenge—and I, as a Christian, deliberately accept it. I don't know from where the attack will come, or what sort of weapon my adversary will use, but if there is anything of which I'm certain, it is that my weapon—the cross and the prayer—is stronger. And therefore I am serene."

"Astonishing—first there was V. and that shriveled old man of his, now this prayer, and now your words. As if we were in some kind of fifteenth century! I never thought anything like this existed."

"But here you are, it does. One can live one's whole life without knowing anything about it, and that's the best. But it's easy, by chance—like your sleeping over at V.'s place—to touch something, some kind of a spider web stretched across the whole world—and you're not free anymore, you've got yourself caught, and you have to make some sort of effort to untangle yourself. If you don't, you could be lost. And, take note of this, before that night you spent at V.'s you had lived and never came across anything like that. But you came across it once, and immediately this hymn turns up, and then our conversation, and all this is bound to be turning up from now on. Someone *there* is interested in you. Perhaps they sent me this scrap of paper so that you read it. Or maybe it's the other way around, I am the one who's being hunted, and you've got nothing to do with it."

"You're frightening me," I laughed.

"Don't be frightened, my friend—one must never be frightened. On the other hand, one mustn't be trifling with such things either. But let's drop this conversation, enough. Let's go for a walk…"

✳ ✳ ✳

Sparse but heavy snowflakes are falling. Brownish snowdrifts rim the sidewalk, and muddy dirt squelches under our feet …

… Into the yellow fog of Petersburg winter,
Into the yellow snow clinging to the flagstones.[4]

Come to think of it, this is not winter anymore, rather mid-March. Hands still freeze without gloves, but one can breathe easily—it is spring.

A crow flies heavily above the bare branches of Prudki Gardens. Street urchins peddle cigarettes at the corner of Grechesky Prospect.

"How much for ten of them?"

"Three hundred." "You must be joking!"

"At your service, citizen—I'd sell them for two hundred."

"His are fake, take mine—two hundred fifty!"

The stench of a sulfur match follows, then comes the greenish smoke of a cigarette. Even a cigarette lit in this increasingly warm air already has a particularly "vernal" taste.

"Where shall we go?"

Gumilyov brushes snow from his frozen fur coat and adjusts his Finnish hat with earflaps.

"Are you in a rush? Then let's walk as far as the Lavra. I want to stop at the shoemaker's."

"With pleasure. But why this idea to repair your soles at the Lavra when you've got a shoemaker on your landing?"

"Well, my fellow at the Lavra is not a simple shoemaker, and that's why I go to him. He's a most clever old man. A church reader—he knows the Holy Scripture as well as any archbishop, can talk about Pushkin. I'm going to bring Lerner to meet him—let them have a little talk."[5]

"Is he some kind of a general in hiding or a professor?"

"Oh, no—he's a Volga peasant who only learned to write when he was thirty. But he's an extremely intelligent fellow—and a hilarious one. A bit like Klyuyev, only sharper. You'll see for yourself."

We walked the length of Old Nevsky Prospect and, having passed the Lavra, turned into some lane. A wooden fence, a yard covered in snow, then an entryway, a small stairway, and finally a narrow door with a knocker. A barefoot girl answered the door: "Are you here for Ilya Nazarych? Yes, he's at home."

Nimbly wielding an awl in the light of an oil lamp, there sat an old man in a dirty blouse, his prickly eyes gleaming from behind iron-rimmed glasses.

"You'll have to excuse my saying this, Nikolay Stepanych," the old man goes on, "But Pushkin, Aleksandr Sergeyevich, did not love Russia one bit. He had no interest in Russia whatsoever. He's got a German soul, that's the thing. And if you really want to know, he only loved his wife and Peter."

"Peter who?"

"Peter the First, 'the Great' as they call him. And why 'great'? That's all because of his being German too, and not a Russian."

"Aren't you going a bit far, Ilya Nazarych? Pushkin's a German, Peter the Great is a German. Who's Russian then?"

"Russian?" The old man hammered flat a bump on the spread sole of a boot. "Heh, heh … Who's Russian…" (Where did I hear this creaky voice and that snickering? I did hear it somewhere, didn't I?). "Russian? How shall I put it … Take, for example, our Saint Petersburg, the city of Saint Peter, heh, heh … Who built it? 'Peter,' you'll say. But it wasn't Peter standing up to his neck in the swamp knocking in pilings. Peter's bones are lying on gold in a cathedral. But those thousands and thousands whose bones are rotting away right here—he stomped his foot—underneath us, whose souls weren't given last rites, souls useless to either God or the Devil, to this very day those souls wander in the night all across that Saint Petersburg of ours, they curse your Peter and all of us along with him—those are Russian bones, Russian souls." He bent over the boot again. "It's hard to work for you Mr. Gumilyov. You strut about with your back straight and keep bashing up your welts. There's no way to put the sole back in place."

"Must be my cavalryman's gait."

"Maybe it is a cavalryman's, but you'll have to excuse my saying this, you're pigeon-toed."

"But just the same, Ilya Nazarych, why would Pushkin be German?"

The little old man began to snicker again. "Why don't I answer you with a verse or two—

I love you, Peter's creation,
I love your austere, graceful aspect,
The Neva's stately flow,
Its embankment of granite.[6]

"Well, what do you think? 'I love!' What's that he's loving? Peter's creation. It behooves a Russian to hate it, but this one goes: 'I love.' A regular German! The imperial state, that's what he loves! 'The flow!' The same granite we hauled on our backs, the granite that crushed our bones! What do you say to that?"

"I also love it, and yet I'm Russian."

"Well, in good time they'll figure out if you're a Russian or not … They are ready, your boots. Are you paying cash or will settle it later with some flour? Flour? Fine. I'll wrap them for you right away."

The shoemaker shuffled out.

"An amusing old fellow."

"Quite. A bit touched in the head though."

"Could be. But very smart. Did you hear him reason with me? He would fit perfectly with a religious-philosophical society rather than mending boots. And isn't his room cozy? Look—cleanliness, books all in order. What is he writing? Let's have a look."

Gumilyov turned the cover of a penny notebook. The following was carefully traced on the first page: "Morning Star, well of mercy, strength, wind…"

"Here are your boots, my good sir."

Gumilyov turned around with the notebook in his hand:

"What is this, Ilya Nazarovych?"

The old man looked up from under his glasses and shrugged his shoulders.

"That's so one doesn't have to fumble about in strangers' things."

"So, that means you sent this to me?"

"So it would seem it was me, doesn't it?"

"Whatever for?"

"It says there what for—copy and send it out."

"And do you understand for whom the prayer is intended?"

The shoemaker frowned.

"I haven't any time, citizens, unfortunately, I have no time. Here are your boots. And now would you be kind enough to pay me for the work—come to think of it, I can't wait for the flour. And, my good sir, if you need more help in the shoe repair department, look for another shoemaker. I'm leaving for my village…"

Where did I hear that voice? Yes, that's it!

"Leaving, aren't you? The dead folks must be getting worried?" I said softly.

The old man looked at me derisively.

"And why would they be getting worried, young man? They've nothing to worry about in the ground. More likely the living should be worried. Citizens, I remain your humble servant."

✳ ✳ ✳

A year later, to the thunderous accompaniment of Kronstadt cannons, I was walking down Kamennostrovsky Boulevard.[7] Someone called my name. It was V.—he looked mangy and had lost weight.

"What's happened to you?"

"I've been in the Shpalerny lockup. Got caught in an ambush."

"But where?"

"Well, alcohol's to blame. There was a certain shoemaker who would get it for me now and then. So I dropped by his place—and, wouldn't you know it, they had an ambush ready. Three months they held me…"

"The shoemaker? The one from the Lavra, Ilya Nazarych?"

"Oh, I see now—you're not such a deep sleeper after all. True, it was Ilya Nazarych. But how come you know his name and address?"

"Not only do I know his address, but I've been to his place and wouldn't mind dropping by again, for a quick chat. Would you care to come along?"

V. smiled a crooked smile.

"That would be a bit difficult: he was executed by firing squad back in December. All because of his alcohol. It's really too bad—he sold great alcohol, from Estonia, and didn't charge that much."

II

In the summer of 1910 during the school break I read an announcement about a new book in *The Maurycy Wolff Publishing Chronicle*. It was called *The Impressionists' Studio*.

It cost two rubles.

It had a surprisingly large number of pages and its contents seemed tempting: a monodrama by Nikolay Yevreinov, poetry by Velimir Khlebnikov, something by David Burlyuk, something by Vladimir Burlyuk, and then something or other Assyrian by some woman, complete with her own drawings in seven colors.

So I ordered that *Studio* book. They told me later at Wolff's that I was one of three buyers. I ordered it, and so did some young lady from Kherson and also a certain Mr. Petukhov from Semipalatinsk. Not a single copy was sold in Petersburg or Moscow. It was only the three of us who were willing to part with our long-treasured two rubles, not counting shipping costs, for the pleasure of reading the brothers Burlyuk with Assyrian illustrations in seven colors.

Only us: me, the young lady from Kherson, and Mr. Petukhov. Three out of one hundred and sixty million.

O, Rus! *O, rus!*[8]

But all this was explained to me at Wolff's later. At that time, ordering the book, I even experienced a certain anxiety: would I really get it or could it be sold out?

The exterior of *The Impressionists' Studio* did not disappoint. The book had a large, elongated shape, and its brownish-lily cover depicted something incomprehensible, could be a woman, could be a house. The Assyrian drawings were not that bad either, although seven colors turned out to be an exaggeration. There were only two of them, those same two, brownish and lily. The content itself evinced such "total audaciousness" that it shook me to the core. Consumed by envy, I read and reread the poem about a deer run down by hunters:

And suddenly he grew a mane,
And sharpened lion's claw,
And carelessly, and playfully,
He demonstrated the art of touching.[9]

Or those subsequently famous "Laughaniks"—"o, laugh laughingly, laughaniks, laughers ho, laughing so."[10]

Not that I was all that taken with them: Konstantin Balmont and Valery Bryusov were much closer to my heart. But how could one not envy such daring and innovation?

Nikolay Kulbin, the author of the introductory piece and editor of *The Studio*, stressed all that was extremely new, bold, and beautiful in it with such zest that there could be no doubt about it whatsoever.

I reread his article reverently.

Then again I hungrily went through the monodrama. "A revolution in the dramatic arts," this is how it was touted right then and there.

Then "Laughaniks."

Then the monodrama once more ...

It was only natural then that two weeks later, I took a registered mail package containing about ten brownish and lily poems of indeterminate meter to the post office, with an accompanying letter addressed to the editor Kulbin.

Having sent it off, I began to wait for a reply. A certain amount of experience suggested to me that it would not be coming soon, and when it did come, the news would hardly delight me. Yet contrary to my previous experience, a reply came at once. And what a reply!

On a sheet of rough paper, also brownish and lily, there stood the following:

Dear Friend. The submitted is a masterpiece. Goes straight into the upcoming issue. I greet and embrace you.

No, this could not be more different from *Grainfield* that would subject one to two months of "doubts and hopes" only to return one's manuscripts with the unvaryingly repulsive note: "Dear Sir, We regret to inform you..."

✳ ✳ ✳

The school break ended, and I returned to Petersburg. Kulbin, the publisher of *The Studio*, invited me to come over to his place immediately after my arrival. Needless to say, I was dying to do it. Becoming acquainted with the influential publisher of a trailblazing almanac, meeting people like the Burlyuks and Borisyak ... Was it not the literary life, the novelty, and what could possibly be better? To my regret, there was a little "but" that greatly embarrassed me. How could I go to meet my "impressionists"? If I did, my shame would come out right away: I was a sixteen-year-old wearing a cadet uniform with a brocaded red collar. The age was not such a big problem—I could always throw in a few extra years ... But what about my military school uniform?

I pictured Kulbin as a longhaired gentleman of an inspired disposition, pale and pensive. OK, suppose I write to him that I am coming, and he is expecting me. Here I am, climbing to the sixth story to his poetic mezzanine all hung with brownish paintings and strewn with lily-colored manuscripts. I ring the bell. He looks at me, baffled. "Surely, young man, you've made a mistake, the colonel's apartment is on the third floor. He's got a son who is a cadet…"

But let's just suppose, everything comes out right. I mean he wrote that my poems are masterpieces, and the poems are the thing after all, not my age or my military school uniform. Just the same, suppose we go out on the street. He says: "Dear friend, look, today the sun is absolutely violet…" And what if at that moment some general is walking toward us? And instead of agreeing—"Yes, you're right, like a violet," or responding tastefully: "Violet? I would say, it's sort of greenish"—I would have to stand at attention (three ceremonial steps: a heel turn, hup-two). And what if he proposes: "Shall we step into a restaurant, have a chat over a bottle of wine?" "Excuse me, but I'm only allowed to enter a pastry shop." And once inside I immediately have to run over to the nearest officer: "Lieutenant, Sir, may I be allowed to sit?"

After thinking it over a long while, I decide to wait until my older brother goes to the country, so that I can go to Kulbin's place in my brother's civilian suit. I have already tried it on in secret; it is a little baggy and I have to turn up the pant legs, but altogether it's not bad. Meanwhile I send off a notebook of new poems to Kulbin with a note saying I'm sick and that I will come when I'm feeling better.

It was Monday, but I was at home, "to hide out," as we would say at my military school, from some sort of written test. It was about two in the afternoon. I looked out the window sadly: better that I not go out during school hours. Suppose here comes some general: "Cadet, why aren't you at your military school? Let me see your pass." I would be in so much trouble.

… Some general seen out my window crossed the street, looked about, and turned down a corner, right in the direction of our entryway. He was a dried-out, little old man with a severe mien, a military doctor wearing spectacles and a greatcoat with crimson-colored lining. I moved back from the window and sat down to work on my unfinished verses. But the rhyme wouldn't sneak up on me for some reason …

Suddenly my brother, the one on whose suit I was counting on, ran into my room with a worried look: "I think they've nabbed you this time—a doctor's come by from your military school to check how sick you really are!"

With understandable confusion, I entered the parlor. The very same dry little old general sat there, the one who crossed the street.

"I came by to get acquainted," he said, stretching out both hands to me, "I am Kulbin, editor of *The Impressionists' Studio.*"

✳ ✳ ✳

A brightly polished copper plate:

> Nikolay Kulbin
> Medical Doctor
> Visiting Hours ...

And a little higher up, pinned to the red upholstery of the door, there hangs a piece of orange cardboard:

> The Club for the Equal-Acting.
> Assoc-Art-Poet-Futuro-Cubo
> Of Impressionists

This is a large, respectable-looking apartment. A waiting room with heavy furniture—slip covers, chandeliers, candelabra, a bronzed bear holding a dish filled with dusty visiting cards. On the table there is an old issue of *Grainfield*; on the walls there are yellowing group portraits: "Military Medical Academy, Class of 1879," "Yaroslavl, 1891." Everything as it ought to be.

However, mixed in among issues of *Grainfield* and brochures advertising the Yessentuki Resort there lies a copy of *Pomade* by Aleksey Kruchyonykh, wrapped in gilded paper like a Christmas cracker, the *Zasakhare-Kry* almanac, and the *ouvrage*-exposé *The Secret Vices of Academicians.* And on the walls, among the group photos, there hang paintings.

Paintings quite inappropriate for a doctor's waiting room: crimson, brownish, green, and lily-colored ones. Over there—a gray cone against an orange background, here—a yellow cube set off in pale blue, between them something mottled, multihued, and across all that array are the words: "Astrakhan … Herring…" All these works are by Kulbin himself. The office is decorated with gifts from his friends and like-minded members of the "Assoc-Art-Poet-Futuro-Cubo" club.

At a large desk in the office, in the soft light of a lamp, there sit two figures. Puffing away at a dainty fragrant cigarette, his hands in the pockets of a soft, gray double-breasted jacket, a doctor in gold-rimmed sparkly spectacles converses with a patient.

That the person seated opposite is a patient can be recognized right away. And it would hardly be a mistake to conclude that he is mentally ill.

He appears to be yellow and emaciated; he has a savage look in his eyes; his hair is disheveled. He speaks with a stutter, twitching at every word; his head trembles on his long, skinny neck. He takes a cigarette but can't light up straight away, because his hands are shaking so much. He gets it lit, then throws it away, grabs a new one, only to throw it away, too.

Sometimes he jerkily whispers something. The doctor, his glasses sparkling, nods his gray head and makes some sort of notations with his pencil. He must be making notes on the course of the illness. He must be writing out a prescription.

But have a listen to their conversation.

"Excellent," says the doctor. "Existence has the form of a triangle. Consequently, the soul is triangular as well."

"Y-y-yes," the "patient" confirms with a twitch. "T-t-triangular a-a-and r-r-rect-t-tangular."

"Quite right," nods the doctor. "So let's write it down, then. The soul— thought—is a triangle. Death—the womb—a circle."

"N-n-no," the "patient" is upset. "N-n-no … Better write this: w-w-womb-um—t-t-tree-um."

"But, my dear fellow, you're getting carried away. Why a tree? Isn't our goal to formulate everything as precisely as possible?"

"T-t-tree-um," insists the "patient." "T-t-tree-um." His head begins to shake even more violently. "T-t-tree-um—w-w-womb-um."

"Very well, very well, don't be upset, my dear fellow. If you want a tree let's have a tree. Let's proceed. Life. Death. What then? Creation?"

"Creation—abomination!" interjects the "patient," beaming.

The doctor is also beaming. "Witty! Brilliant! Deep! 'Abomination'! Bravo, bravo! But it's not a formula. Let's find a formula. What would you say to the word 'vessel'?"

This is the founding father of Russian Futurism Nikolay Kulbin and "the most inspired poet of the world" "Velimir" Khlebnikov. They are putting together the philosophical theses providing the foundation for a new movement. But this picture may change at any moment: Khlebnikov may have a horrible epileptic fit and his interlocutor may need to recall his other skill—that of a doctor.

This respectable apartment, these group portraits hanging on the walls, these epaulets of a general, these gold-rimmed spectacles, the unhurried demeanor of the graying professor—this is all spectral.

State Councilor Kulbin lived in this apartment several years ago. He received patients, gave lectures, wrote scientific papers—he did everything one is expected to do, he lived as one is expected to live. In his spare time he dabbled in painting and went to exhibitions. Of free time he had precious little, however. Paintings he had begun lay about for months without being finished. One of them is still hanging over there in that dark passageway. It's a *nature morte*—a jug, two apples, and a fish. It is painstakingly, carefully depicted, since State Councilor Kulbin was imitating the Flemish masters. But one cold January day Kulbin set off as usual for the hospital or the Military Medical Academy, but never came back. Another person with his look and his gait, wearing his uniform greatcoat and spectacles came to the apartment and opened the door with his French key.

Between ten in the morning and seven in the evening, Doctor of Medicine and State Councilor Kulbin lost what had been his soul somewhere in the back alleys of snow-covered Petersburg.

Here is his story in his own words:

"I was crossing a bridge—felt like stretching my legs. I thought about things, patients, lectures ... My new galoshes, I remember, still squeaked loudly. I wasn't in the least worried about anything, nor in any particular mood. And then right near Troitsky Square there was a horse on its side, and a coachman beating it, trying to get it to stand. He beat it in the eyes, the eyes ... But it couldn't get up, only twitched. And at that very moment the lamps on Kamennoostrovsky Boulevard burst into light. It hadn't even grown completely dark, and suddenly the lamps burst forth. You know how magnificent it is?"

"Well?"

"That's all. Nothing more. At that moment something turned over inside me. As if I was completely perishing and was saved by a miracle. So I was standing there and for some reason took off my hat. And I thought to myself: 'You old fool, what did you kill fifty years of your life for? A policeman came running over to me. 'Your Excellency, Your Excellency ... ' He got me into a cab. Since then..."

Since then everything at the apartment on Kirpichny Boulevard is topsy-turvy. Kruchyonykh is on the phone at three in the morning demanding money. Homeless Futurists spend the night sleeping in the dining room.

How I love pregnant men,
When they gather at Pushkin's monument.[11]

In the morning David Burlyuk's booming bass resounds from the bathroom. His brother, Vladimir, a delicate creature, demands breakfast in bed: he is not feeling well and needs to rest a little longer. A well-dressed maid serves him "coffee" on a silver tray—a decanter of vodka and a gherkin ...

How I love pregnant men ...
N. I. could really use twenty-five rubles ...
Creation—abomination ...
Assoc-Art-Poet-Futuro-Cubo ...

Kulbin feels marvelously well in the middle of this muddle. Fifty years "killed" leading the life of a placid, orderly professor. Who knows how much life is left? This way, at least, every minute of what's left will not be lost.

"You old fool ... Fifty years of life ... But it's all right, all right—we'll catch up."

Repeating these words, Kulbin chuckles strangely. He tugs at his little beard, his eyes sparkle from under his gilded glasses.

"There was so much that could have been done, so much to experience! But it's all right, all right."

A strange chuckle, a strange glance. There is something agonizing in all that.

Here my interlocutor who wears a general's double-breasted jacket turns around abruptly and inquires with suspicious tactfulness:

"Do you think I'm insane?"

✳ ✳ ✳

Nothing came of my Futurism. I lost my taste for composing lily-hued "masterpieces" fairly quickly. I made new literary acquaintances that I found more "congenial" for me than the company of Kruchyonykh and the Burlyuks. I was seeing Kulbin more and more rarely, only in passing, by chance. So I was quite surprised when in January 1913 I received an urgent invitation, written on familiar brownish-green paper, to come over in the evening.

I did. Why would I not go? Judging by Kulbin's note, there was to be a gathering, possibly a performance or a lecture by invitation only. I was the sole person invited from "right-wing circles"—an honor vouchsafed to me as a sign of our "old friendship." To decline such an honor would have been imprudent. After all, if there were to be a "private gathering" at Kulbin's place, that meant that there would be something worth seeing. And then that intriguing postscript: "This invitation is to be presented on entering."

The elegant young man who met me at the entryway did not ask for any invitation, however. He shook my hand in a most well-mannered way and introduced himself: "Benedict Livshits." At that time this was a famous name. It had associations with an officially confiscated book, a slew of rows at literary disputes, fights, and blank shots fired at the public attending his readings. In contrast with such a reputation it was amusing to discover him to have refined society manners and an elegant coat. Clicking his heels yet again, he ushered me into the hall.

... A large room, chock-full of people. Most of them are unknown to me. Some young men, their faces painted with geometrical patterns, some animated young women. A disheveled poetic heap of hair here, a licked-straight hair parting there; someone flashes a blue blouse and someone else sports sable wraps. Mixed company indeed.

On a pedestal there sits Kulbin. I do not recognize him at first. Arms crossed on his chest, his face is strangely pale because it is thickly powdered. He wears a wide bloody-red loose-fitting chlamys and has a golden band on his forehead.

... The Military Medical Academy ... Emperor Nicholas's Hospital ... The attending physician stands at attention: "Your Excellency, Sir..."

... Kulbin sits on his gilded pedestal motionless like an idol. Before him stands Kruchyonykh with a thick wax candle in his hands and mumbles something incomprehensible in a hysterical whisper. Then suddenly he squeals, wails, and drops to the floor. Those standing in the front row rush to help him up. But he immediately jumps to his feet, his face distorted in exultation.

"It has come to pass, it has come to pass!" he squeals like a holy fool. "Here he is ... he's assumed power, he's the Master ... Futurist ... the Tsar of the Revolution!" The entire hall howls, applauds and stomps. Khlebnikov writhes in a fit. Kruchyonykh's falsetto outshouts everyone: "He's ascended the Throne ... Master ... Tsar..."

Kulbin continues to sit still, his arms crossed, his head slightly bowed. A silent nonsensical smile spreads across the face of this powdered idol ...... I sought out my greatcoat in a pile of others—there the dog-fur collars belonging to the Futurist fraternity were mixed with other people's beaver collars, all in disarray. My gloves could not be found anywhere—to hell with those gloves. I needed to get out of there, quick ...

The respectable door with the red upholstery softly shut after me. The respectable copper plate softly glowed with its carefully engraved letters:

Doctor of Medicine
Visiting Hours ...
Ear, Nose, & Throat

"You old fool, what did you kill fifty years of your life for?"

"It's all right, all right—we'll catch up."

"Do you think I'm insane?"

After that evening I stopped going to Kulbin's, and frankly he never invited me again. Perhaps upon encountering him I did not quite manage to hide the awkwardness I felt after his "coronation." From time to time I continued to meet him here and there. He would be the same as always—respectable, serious, with gleaming spectacles and epaulets. Then the war broke out ... Then in the beginning of summer in 1917, on a clear, cheerful, sunny day, some acquaintance who ran into me on Nevsky informed me:

"Do you know? Kulbin has died."

"From what?"

"From fright."

"How do you mean?"

"Just like that. He was walking down the street. A truck full of soldiers comes toward him. They saw he was a general. They grabbed him and took him to the Duma. They held him there for half an hour and, of course, let him go with apologies. He went straight home and took to his bed. He lay there two days and then gave up his soul to the Lord. And there was nothing wrong with him—he had an excellent heart, too. He just got very frightened. Poor devil!"

It is customarily assumed that Igor Severyanin's all-Russian fame began with Tolstoy's famous quip concerning the worthlessness of Russian poetry.[12] It is true that in support of his opinion, Tolstoy quoted Severyanin: "Drive a corkscrew into a springy cork, and ladies' glances won't be timid." Indeed, thanks to it the name of this future idol of the stage and editorial offices (alas, this future proved to be evanescent) flashed by on the pages of newspapers (up to that moment it had been fated to be confined to mail boxes marked: "regrettably rejected"). Genuine fame, however, came to him later, and, in essence, it was completely "legitimate": first Fyodor Sologub took an interest in him, later so did Valery Bryusov, and then they both "promoted" him widely.

It was the spring of 1911. I was seventeen. I had published several poems in two or three journals and had made the literary acquaintance of Mikhail Kuzmin, Sergey Gorodetsky, and Alexander Blok. I was brimming over with literature and poems.

I had not heard Severyanin's name before. However, once I was going through the offerings in Wolff's "poetical" bookstall and I opened a brochure of about sixteen pages (I no longer remember the title) with a complicated subtitle: such-and-such notebook, such-and-such issue, such-and-such volume. On the backside of the book all the volumes and notebooks being prepared for publication were listed; somehow there were too many. It was also announced there that Igor Severyanin, Podyachesky Street, house number so-and-so, receives young poets and poetesses on Thursdays, publishers on Wednesdays, female admirers on Tuesdays, and so on. All the days of the week were accounted for, all hours indicated precisely, as if in a clinic. I read several of the poems. They "pierced" right through me. Naturally their lack of taste hit you right between the eyes, even such inexperienced ones as mine (it was only a month since I had been told that one did not get enthused about Dmitry Tsenzor). But, and I will say it again, they pierced right through me. With what, I simply do not know. With that same thing, it seems, that a year later, also by chance, they pierced Fyodor Sologub.

Tempted as I was, I could not bring myself to attend a reception on Podyachesky Street. How should I carry myself, what should I say? Should I go as a young poet? There was something humiliating about that. As an admirer? Same thing, even if one forgot about one's manly nature, since only female admirers were indicated in the announcement. So I found a way out: assuming a respectable look, I set out for Severyanin's place during the hours reserved for publishers. In point of fact, I was getting ready to become a publisher at the earliest possible date—that is, of my own book (I had seventy-five rubles, with which I had persuaded my older sister to part, in a safe place).

As I rode from Kamenoostrovsky to Podyachesky, there was still one other circumstance that perplexed me. There could be no doubt that someone who receives visitors of different categories each day, whose poems are filled with lobsters, automobiles, and French phrases should be a brilliant high-society man. Will I become flustered when I arrive at the Podyachesky Palace with my cabby and nag, when a haughty servant in violet livery leads me into the blindingly bright study, when Igor Severyanin himself appears and begins speaking to me in French with an astonishingly good accent?

Yet the die had already been cast, the horse cab hired, too late to retreat ...

Igor Severyanin lived in apartment number 13. The inhabitant played no part in the selection of that fateful number. The management, for understandable reasons, had given this number to the smallest, dampest, and dirtiest apartment in the whole building. The entryway was through the backyard. Cats scattered every which-way on the filthy stairs. On a business card tacked to the apartment door stood a signature with a grand flourish above the first "e": "Igor Severyanin."[13] I rang the bell. A tiny old woman, her hands soaked in foam, opened the door. "Are you 'ere for Igor Vasilyevich? Wait a moment and I'll tell 'im." She went behind a curtain and began to whisper. I looked around. This was not a living room but rather a kitchen. Something was boiling and smoking on the stove. The table was overflowing with unwashed dishes. Something was dripping on me: I was standing under a clothesline with laundry for drying hanging from it ...

"The prince of violets and lilacs" greeted me, covering his neck with the palm of his hand: he was not wearing a collar. The little room containing a bookshelf, pathetic furniture, and some sort of decadent picture on the wall was in exemplary order. For its owner this seemed as much of an embarrassment as it did for me. He had not yet acquired the habit of receiving visitors.

After a silence, and quite a long one, he began to say something about a dacha and that it was hot in the city. Only after that did we proceed to discuss poetry. Severyanin suggested that I read some of mine. Then he began to read his. His manner of reading was the same as the poems themselves—revolting and endearing at once. He sang them as if following some kind of operatic motif, always the same one. But it seemed to go with his poems. His voice was sonorous, his appearance rather fetching: tall, prominent facial features, dark wavy hair. We sat for quite a long time, no one disturbed us, no other "publisher" made an appearance. When it was time to part, we did so as if we were practically friends. Soon afterwards we really did become friends.

I became a frequent guest on Podyachesky Street. Though completely new to me, the life of literary bohemia attracted and flattered me. I have mentioned that I had already made some literary acquaintances. But taking tea at Mikhail Kuzmin's or engaging Alexander Blok in deferential monthly conversation was not exactly the same as going to the "Vienna," the "Cherepennikovs," or "Davidkis," participating in "poeso-evenings" in Ligov or on the Vyborg Side, wearing a red bow around my neck instead of a tie. I started sporting that bow at Igor's suggestion, and, certainly not daring to put it on at home, I would tie it on Podyachesky. Boisterous poeso-evenings and boisterous drinking bouts alternated with "editorial" meetings at Severyanin's apartment. Quite a few poets grouped themselves around Igor. Three were given the high privilege of being part of his "Directorate." They were— myself, Konstantin Olimpov (son of Konstantin Fofanov, he was a clearly insane, if not altogether untalented, lad of about sixteen), and then Graal Arelsky—Stepan Stepanovich Petrov, according to his passport—a student past his prime, he was perfectly balanced and perfectly untalented.

The "Directorate" decided to act, to storm the barricades of glory and to create a literary revolution. Pulling together a ruble and a half each, we put out the Manifesto of Ego-Futurism. It was written in simple and clear language, and remarkably enough the theses followed each other point by point. One of them I still remember: "The prism of style equals the restoration of the spectrum of thought…"By the way, that Manifesto was reprinted by quite a few newspapers, and the majority of them commented on it and argued with it in complete seriousness.

✶ ✶ ✶

One day, a genuine publisher turned up on Podyachesky Street, although it did not seem to have happened at the appointed hour. It was true that he had yet to publish anything, but after reading our Manifesto, he decided to put his purse at the disposal of "the restorers of the spectrum of thought." That purse of his was not exactly bursting with money, and therefore, to meet the needs of our editorial enterprise, Ivan Vasilyevich Ignatyev's gold fob-watch frequently had to travel to the pawn shop. For all it was worth, the weekly *Petersburg Town Crier* was now at our disposal; when it closed down due to being completely unprofitable, we still retained an almanac of the same title. Poems were called "poesas," publications—"editions," the editor—"Director." For the summer season, another newspaper was at the service of the Ego-Futurists—but alas, it bore the vulgar name of *The Nizhny-Novgorod Dweller*. It came out in the city of the same name during its Fair and was full of prices, trade balances, and articles about the sale of fish to Persia. Some uncle of Ignatyev's was not averse to the sublime and published whatever his nephew would send him. We took great advantage of this. I recall publishing there a big article proving that Maurice Maeterlinck was a vulgarian, and a talentless one at that ... Needless to say, we were never paid any honoraria.

In a small wooden "private residence" on the corner of Degtyarny and Rozhdestvensky streets, in the editorial office of the *Petersburg Town Crier*, from time to time took place "poeso-holidays," the news of which, for their "shock value," were reported by special communiqués to the editorial offices of various newspapers. These booklets were called "vergettes" (vergé being a variety of paper), and they were compiled exceedingly seductively and pompously. A dinner menu was attached as well, and it featured pineapple in champagne, Crème de Violette, and filets of young nightingales. In reality, of course, it was a bit simpler. Although half a bottle of Crème de Violette (bottled by Cusimier and sold at Yeliseyev's) did decorate the table, it was a symbol of poetry and elegance more than anything else. Vodka and house wine, however, were served in such quantities that both the guests and the Directorate often found themselves in a state of utter irresponsiveness. Completely wild things occurred there sometimes. Thus one time a certain Pyotr Larionov—this possessor of the strange position of the head of the Tsarskoselsky Poultry Farm was seduced by Futurism at the age of forty-five—walked out of Ignatyev's place with a half-shaven head (he had sported a full head of poetic hair), face painted like that of a Red Indian, and sporting an ace of diamonds on his back.[14]

This very Ignatyev, who appeared to be the most normal of people— his round and rosy cheeks were typical of a middling merchant—died a truly horrific death. The day after his wedding, after paying visits to his relatives, he threw himself on his wife in broad daylight with a razor. She managed to escape. He then cut his own throat.

My friendship with Igor Severyanin—both conventional and literary— did not last too long. I went over to "The Guild of Poets" and established more "fitting," and therefore infinitely more durable, ties. I found it difficult, however, to part ways with Severyanin himself. I even attempted to bring him closer to Gumilyov and to have him enter "The Guild," which, of course, was nonsense. We went our separate ways (two or three later meetings do not count), when Severyanin was at the zenith of his fame. The Bureau of Press Clippings would send him as many as fifty clippings a day, and quite frequently they were feuilletons filled with either rapture or rage (which, in essence, comes down to the same thing as far as "the technology of fame" is concerned). The print runs of his books were unheard-of for poetry; the enormous hall of the City Duma could not accommodate all those wanting to attend his "poeso-evenings." Unexpectedly, all his dreams came true: thousands of female admirers, flowers, motorcars, champagne, triumphant tours across Russia … It was a truly genuine, if perhaps somewhat histrionic, fame. Igor Severyanin did not manage to hold onto it, just as he had not managed to hold onto the authentic charm that had been in his early poems. It would be better not to mention what he writes these days.

IV

The classic description of Petersburg almost always begins with fog.

Fog occurs in many cities, but Petersburg fog is special. For us, of course. A foreigner, going out on the street will huddle up: "brrr … damned climate…"

> We huddle up too. And yet—
> … we won't trade anything for this magnificent,
> Granite city of glory and sorrow;
> This vast, gleaming ice,
> These black solemn gardens.[15]

And this fog—the soul of these "ice and gardens."

"Neva's stately flow, embankment of granite," Peter standing on a cliff, Nevsky Prospect, those same Pushkinian iambs—all that is this city's mere appearance, its outerwear. The fog, however, is its soul.

There, in that yellow twilight Akaky Akakiyevich is robbed of his greatcoat; Raskolnikov goes to kill the old hag; Innokenty Annensky, decked out in a beaver collar and starched plastron, collapses with a dull pain in his heart onto the dirty steps of Tsarskoye Selo Railway Station, directly—

> Into the yellow fog of Petersburg winter,
> Into the yellow snow clinging to the flagstones—
> the ones he "loved so painfully."

All this, however, is common knowledge.

On Nevsky Prospect—hubbub, carriages, the glow of curving street lamps, the headlights of the *Voisin* type, the cab drivers' shouts "out of the way," "sables on the shoulders and a face behind a veil," military uniforms, radiant shop windows. This is a splendid European street—not Rue Royale, perhaps, but certainly on a par with Unter den Linden. Even the fog here is not "quite the same"—it is Europeanized and neutralized. Could it be that that "same" Petersburg fog does not even exist anymore?

No, it does, right here, two steps away. Two steps from this radiance and liveliness lies an empty street, dim streetlamps, and the fog.

Strange people wander about in the fog.

Take a turn around the corner on Maly Konyushenny. Walk past two or three houses and then—

Walls are painted gray,
A green sign: "Tailor."[16]

Come to think of it, the sign is not green. By order of the city police chief, all main streets signs must maintain "respectable uniformity." The police chief must have read a little too much of Kurbatov.[17]

The tailor's sign is black with gold letters. Its imposing appearance does not correspond to its owner's rank—this tailor is small fry. In order not to frighten the customers away, there's a note on the glass door that softens the solemn coldness of the sign: "Alterations, Styling, Ironing at Lowest Prices." Alongside it a yellowing business card:

Nikolay Karlovich Ts.,
Independent Artist,
Not Graduated from the St. Petersburg Conservatory.

"Is Nikolay Karlovich home?"

Without raising his shaggy head from something brown and greasy, something that is being altered or refashioned, the tailor gloomily replies:

"He's sleeping."

"Sleeping"—this means that he is at home. What else should he doing at home, if not sleeping after yesterday's bender and gathering strength for today's?

It is a half-dark large room with the drawn curtains. In the twilight a piano can be made out, a covered chandelier, and a table with a pile of papers. In a corner on a bed someone is snoring away ...

"Nikolay Karlovich!"

The napping fellow turns over heavily, forcing all the mattress springs to creak.

"Whatta ya need? Go to hell! What time is it?"

"It's late." (Early it certainly is not—it is four in the afternoon.) "Get up."

The tousled head rises with difficulty from the pillow. The arms come free from under a fur coat. In a voice that is hoarse but pleasant and lordly, he speaks with a slight French lilt to his r's:

"Be so kind, *mon chevalier*, if it will not indispose you, as to turn on the electricity in order that I may see your noble features."

The impression of the room changes in the light.

In the twilight it looked lovely, even respectable. A high ceiling, an open grand piano, "the vestiges of inspiration's labor" … But in the light…The floor is littered with cigarette butts, matches, and scraps of paper. There are piles of old newspapers, empty bottles, and tins from canned food.

A short three-kopeck candle has been affixed with its own burnt-down dribble directly onto the piano's top. Another one, burnt down, has melted into an intricate stalactite spread out across a mother-of-pearl insignia: "Bechstein." On the walls, amid the traces of dampness, a charcoal has traced the ugly outlines of Adam and Eve picking fruit (extremely lifelike), tomcats with lifted tails, devils. The bed is a chaos of motley rags. A bottle with some vodka left at the bottom rests on the nightstand.

The owner, the independent artist "not graduated from the Conservatory," looks fat and bloated, and he hasn't had a shave in a long time. The expression on his face is a mixture of after-binge nausea and irony. Yet there are faint traces of respectability in his manner of extending his arm, in his putting on his pince-nez with barely responsive fingers, and in his way of lighting a long cigarette.

"Very sweet of you, my dear Marquis, that you've come to visit this old drunkard. I beg you to take a seat … So, brother, do you want some vodka?"

✳ ✳ ✳

If there is such a thing as a special Petersburg fog, then the most "special" of it all is to be found at nighttime on Vasilyevsky Island …

At the intersection of Bolshoy, Maly, and Sredny avenues there are beer halls. All along the Vasilyevsky Island "lines" there are fog, gloom, and silence. Yet the shafts of electric lights flood the intersections, where drunken palaver accompanies the words of "The Little Chinese Girl" pouring from a hoarse megaphone:

> After tea, at my leisure,
> Where the Amur River flows,
> I espied a little Chinese girl …

Some of the beer halls are remarkable.

Germans built them back in the 1880s, anticipating a respectable and easygoing clientele—other Germans. Solid small marble tables, full-size beer mugs, glazed coasters beneath them with engraved sayings like: "Morgenstunde hat Gold im Munde." Scenes from *Faust* are depicted on Dutch tiles, and crockery for gala occasions is held in a glass cabinet. It has been put away under lock and key long ago: the good old clients are long gone, and proper German has not been heard here for a long time. Now a days the dregs of Petersburg bohemia gravitate toward all these "Edelweiss" and "Rhein" entitled establishments …

The raucous tune of "The Little Chinese Girl" squeals and wheezes. Scribblings are scratched all across the surfaces of mirrored walls that glisten with an unwashed sheen as greasy white foam slithers along thick glass.

"Hey, waiter! A couple more beers! Warm ones!"

Warm beer "gets you there" quicker. Only "showoffs" drink their beer cold.

> Little Chinese Girl, Little Chinese Girl,
> Little Chinese Girl of mine …

By nine in the evening, the Edelweiss is full. Officially they "conduct business" until midnight, but customers hang around until one in the morning. Then it is time to move on to the Dominic on Nevsky Prospect, since it stays open until three … And at four in the morning, cabmen's tearooms begin to open on Sennoy Square—there you can get fried eggs with scraps to wash down alcohol from a battered teakettle that sits on a filthy brown tablecloth. This is known as drinking "with transfers" ...

... Little Chinese Girl ... Little Chinese Girl ...

Almost all the tables are taken. Three have been pulled over next to each other under a dusty, artificial palm tree in the corner. This corner is the poetical-literary-musical one. Ts. presides there. Endless conversations are under way.

Here is Sh., a poet, an eternal student—he is gangly, dark, as though he has been burnt; he wears a long-hanging, faded frockcoat. He is extremely knowledgeable and half-crazy. His "voyage with transfers" starts in the morning—instead of coffee he takes a glass of vodka and a couple of sprats. He is already blind drunk and mumbles something or other about Nietzsche. G.—also a poet, and also drunk—gags and interrupts him:

"Romanticism, romanticism ... Novalis, *The Blue Flower*."

Some other people are present as well. Also poets—or musicians or philosophers—who can tell? M. is louder than any one—an actor who isn't a drunkard, and not even a drunk—he is simply pretending. Why is he pretending? Everyone knows that he will slip away from the Dominic and will go straight home, to his bed. After all, there is going to be a rehearsal tomorrow, and God forbid he misses it. And he does not even like drinking one bit, and it is a shame to waste the money—and yet he finds it necessary to pay not only for himself, but for others too. Why on earth does he do this?

Out of honor. You might say that this is a strange kind of honor. And yet here you are ...

M. loudly clinks glasses and spills some on purpose while loudly proposing a senseless toast. He gesticulates, beats himself in the chest, and weeps..."Let's drink to Art ... We'll build a luminous palace ... Where have you gone, my youth?!"

Drunks of the genuine kind clink their mugs and drink. They know that M. is faking it, that he does not have any "shattered hopes" that need washing away with alcohol, and that he is simply a clown and a vulgarian. But they could care less with whom to drink, or to whose nonsense to listen. It is all the same, and has been for a long while. Everything in the world is rubbish, nonsense, gibberish. "Hey, waiter! A couple more!"

… Little Chinese Girl—Little Chinese Girl … Romanticism … Blue distances … Thus Spake Zarathustra …

Ts.'s voice—hoarse and imperious—suddenly drowns out all else:

"If the soul is immortal … Right … And it is … Then God will ask me … Up there … 'Nikolay, did you do anything of worth? Why don't you play something for me?' I'll play for Him … Right … I'll play 'Chizhik' for Him![18] And I'll be … in my rights, won't I?"

His fist crashes down on the table with a terrible blow. "I will, don't you think?"

"You will … You will…" shout drunken voices. "Right on, Ts.! Way to go! Play 'Chizhik' for Him. And here another one to…"

M. is ecstatic and wants to kiss everyone.

✳ ✳ ✳

When one comes across various circles within "bohemia," one makes a strange discovery.

One meets talented and subtle people most of all among its refuse.

Why would this be the case? It may well be that the very nature of art abjures moderation. "Either you make it or you disappear." People disappear immeasurably more often. But between the highest circles and the refuse there is a blood bond. "He disappeared." But he could have made it, and perhaps he could have become someone more important than others. No such luck, something got in the way—not much "strength of character," and no willpower. And the opposite of "making it" occurs—a "disappearance" takes place. And your average "clean and respectable" fellow never, ever had a chance, because his nature was completely different.

In this awareness of a link between themselves and a higher world, and over the head of the respectable world, lies the pride of the refuse. Needless to say, that pride is pathetic.

Ts. began brilliantly.

"At our Conservatoire there was this boy Ts."—the frail old general César Cui would recall—"What a divine talent he had! Had he lived he would have turned our idea of music upside down. Such talent, such range!"

"But Ts. isn't dead! Not long ago Jurgenson published some romance or other of his. Very talented, true, however..."

Cui would only shake his head. "'A romance?' 'Talented'? No, this isn't that Ts., it can't be him. That one, had he lived, he would have shown everyone..."

Since Ts. has not died or has not "turned our idea of music upside down," there was only one thing left for him to do—to become a drunkard.

... A room at the tailor's on Konyushenny. Two guttering candle stubs. The high ceiling shimmers in the twilight. The grand piano stands open.

The shabby walls, the damp spots, the cigarette butts and empty bottles are not visible. The room appears to be vacant and solemn. The flame of the candle stubs flickers.

This flickering light renders invisible another feature of Ts.'s face that is so striking in the "dead, pitiless light of day": the puffiness of sleepless nights, cheeks long unshaven, the acrid, hopeless "little grin" of a man sinking to the bottom. It has grown younger, this face, and changed. The eyes gaze penetratingly and intently at the tattered musical manuscript ...

Ts. plays two or three chords, then swipes the sheets of music from their stand.

"To hell with it! I'll play it as is."

"As is" means to improvise. There are all kinds of improvisations, but what Ts. is doing is unlike anything else.

First of all, there's "rinsing the teeth"—as he himself calls this prelude of his. Something like musical scales played by a diligent female student, except there's something not right in the scales, some sort of worm in the apple. Little by little, unnoticed, separate tones blend into an inaudible, even monotonous, noise. A minute goes by, three, five—the noise grows, becomes heavy and turns into a crashing thunder. Quite an improvisation. It is like the banging of a thousand wooden spoons on a drum. What kind of music is that?

Hush! Don't interrupt, and listen carefully. Do you hear? Not yet? Well ... Can you hear it now?

… Among the thousand wooden spoons, there is a silvery one. And it is striking against a thin resonating glass …

Do you hear?

It is barely audible, it is rather felt than heard. But it exists, and its thin, light sound penetrates, gives meaning to and transforms that wooden rumble. And the rumble is no longer wooden—it fades away, retreats, and grows weaker …

Without taking his fingers off the keyboard, Ts. turns toward his listeners. His face has grown flushed, his eyes crazed. He outshouts the music:

"The cannibals retreat, clicking their teeth. They didn't manage to gobble up the gorgeous Englishman!"

Don't pay any attention to that wild "clarification." Listen, listen …

… The noise has disappeared. A pure, surprising, not-to-be emulated melody triumphs. Better close your eyes. Close your eyes and listen to this triumph of sounds. Neither Konyushenny, nor the melting candle stubs, nor the beer-splashed grand piano exist any longer. The moment has arrived when:

All vanishes—and there remains only
Space, the stars, and the singer.[19]

Listen! Soon everything will come apart, the piano lid will be slammed down, and a hoarse, deep voice will sound out:

"All right, enough of this nonsense!"

"What a lovely piece you played, N. K. Why don't you write it down?"

"Write it down?" He pulls a silly-fake grin. "Write it down? I've given it a try, and more than once. *It's not amenable* to be written down…"

And indeed, why bother? It is audible anyway. "Those who have ears can hear," Ts. stretches out like a church deacon. Then he affectedly bows low:

"Allow me to inquire, Viscount. Which do you find more pleasurable, sitting in the rabbit hole of an old drunkard or heading out to that rather well known establishment, Edelweiss?

Once, when the war had already begun, I stopped by in passing to see Ts., and was surprised.

Smoothly combed, cleanly shaven—he was carefully tightening an "artistic" bow on his snow-white blouse. A morning coat ... perfectly pressed trousers ... the smell of eau de cologne ... What kind of a miracle is this?

Ts. smiled.

"Are you dazzled by the shimmer of my outfit, Signore? Do you think it's appropriate for an old souse? Has he gone off his rocker? Did he receive an inheritance? Is he off to propose marriage?"

"Really, N. K., where are you going all dressed up like that?"

Ts. clicked his tongue: "Do you know what happens to those who know too much? However, if you don't mind, I can take you along with me. I promise—there will be a most curious spectacle ... and quite a good dinner. Really, let's go—you won't regret it."

"Where?"

He made a serious face.

"To the St. Petersburg Society of Beyond-Audible Music. Yes, that's right, *beyond-audible*! You haven't heard that term before? No wonder. This discovery is being kept secret for the time being."

He substituted his high-flown tone for an ordinary one. "Let's go, you won't be sorry. There's sure to be champagne. No use explaining, you'll see for yourself."

I did not have anything to do that evening. So I went.

... We came in through the darkened entryway of some mansion. The butler, silently bowing low, removed our fur coats. Just as silently, a servant led us through some sparsely, but expensively furnished rooms. I became uncomfortable: I am showing up at a strange home, uninvited by anyone there, and to top it off, in a gray suit ...

"Nonsense," Ts. says to that. "No one cares about jackets here. You have to reach higher—here they look for the spiritual essence of the person ... That's right, that's the kind of people we are dealing with here ... Of course, they're staring at the book without being able to read anything from it—but that's a 'common human' trait, at the very least here they're guided by good intentions..."

There were about twenty people in the large, dimly lit dining room. Several ladies in black dresses, several men in starched plastrons.

The others were dressed somewhat simpler, but also had the look of presentable and cultured people.

Ts. was greeted with quiet applause. In a dignified manner he bowed, shook some hands, all of this silently, as if in the movies. "They're deaf and dumb," he whispered to me. "They're, all of them, deaf and dumb. Don't speak loudly, it upsets them when they're getting ready to listen. Not to the sound of the voice, of course, but to gestures, lip movements. They're a nervous bunch. Sit over there. It's about to start."

… The servant clicked off the lights. The lamps went dark. A disk a half-yard wide in diameter burst out in pale-gray light. This pale light barely illuminated a tall instrument resembling a piano and the corpulent figure of Ts. behind it. Everything else was submerged in darkness. Complete silence reigned.

And then Ts. struck the keys with all his might. Instead of the thunder of music, only muffled banging could be heard. But the disk burst into bright-orange, then deep blue light, and then sped through all the nuances of red, from pale-rose to crimson …

So that is what it is, beyond-audible music!

The soundless keys crackled dryly under the powerful blows of Ts.'s fingers. Orange, deep-blue, red, green—they all swept by on the disk in a wild cacophony of colors.

And suddenly … There could be heard in the hall some sort of snuffling, a rustling, a rumble. The deaf and dumb listeners had begun *to pick up the tune.*

At first it sounded out shyly and quietly and then with ever greater intensity. The unstructured noise, similar to grumbling, rose higher, becoming more and more discordant. It became not merely a snorting, but a bark, a bleating, a shout, a wailing, and a wheezing that filled the entire room …

The disk flickered and flickered. When it flashed particularly brightly, the listeners would become visible. Expressions somewhere between blessedness and horror were on all their faces. Some were bawling, making strange movements with their mouths, others fell over holding their heads in their hands, others shook with their whole bodies, and still others threw their arms about as if conducting an orchestra …

… The deaf and dumb doorman, having gotten a twenty-kopeck piece from me, started to mumble horribly in gratitude. While I was getting dressed, Ts. caught up to me in the lobby.

"Leaving? Did you become frightened? What kind of nonsense is that? I'll play two or three more pieces, and then we'll have dinner, the whole family together. Really, why don't you stay over? They serve magnificent food here. If you're unable to listen, why don't you sit somewhere in another room?"

I begged off with a headache, and then my head had begun to hurt in earnest. Ts. shook his shoulders:

"All right, goodbye then. You really should stay. The cognac here is first class. So you didn't like my little music even one bit? And by the way, do you know what I played for them and what they were keeping time to? Believe or not, they're getting ready for a concert—they're learning the sheet music for the Ninth Symphony."

V

The calling card read: "Boris Konstantinovich Pronin, Doctor of Aesthetics, *Honoris Causa*." However, if the servant presented this card to you, you would not have time to read the big title. The "Doctor of Aesthetics," joyful and radiant, would already be embracing you. A hug and several juicy, random kisses were as natural a form of greeting for Pronin as a handshake would have been for someone less exalted.

After showering the host with kisses and throwing his hat on the table, his gloves in a corner, scarf on a bookshelf, Pronin would begin laying out yet another new plan of his, the realization of which would require either your money or your efforts or your participation. Pronin never showed up without some plan or other, not because he did not want to visit his acquaintance—he was sociable to a fault—but he simply did not have the time. He always had some project, and it was understood to be urgent. The project would be occupying all his time and thoughts. When it stopped obsessing him, another project would come along automatically. Where was there any time for visits to friends?

Pronin was on informal terms with everyone. "Hi!," he would embrace someone he would chance to meet at the entryway of the Stray Dog.

"Why do I never see you anymore? How's life? Come right in, all *our people* (a wide gesture made in space) are already here…"

The visitor is stunned, flattered—he is a lawyer or engineer who finds himself among the Petersburg Artistic Society for the first time (that was the official name of the Stray Dog at the time), and looks about anxiously. No one knows him and probably he has been mistaken for another. By now, however, Pronin has flown off somewhere.

If you ask him: "Who was that you just welcomed?"

"Who?" he would ask with a broad smile. "The Devil knows. Some bum!"

That was the answer you were most likely to get. In the lexicon of our "Doctor of Aesthetics," the word "bum" carried no insult. He hugged everyone he met, not out of any sort of calculation, but simply from an abundance of feeling.

As soon as he showed up with a project, Pronin would deluge his interlocutor with verbiage. Any attempt to object, interrupt, or ask a question was hopeless. "Understand … You know … I swear … Prodigious … Unbelievable … Three days … Meyerhold … City mayor … Ida Rubenstein … Verhaeren … Total cost … Sudeykin … Prodigious …" Those words would come flying out of his perpetually smiling mouth like green peas. It was rare that someone was not stunned into compliance, especially the first time around.

The "prodigious" undertaking would, of course, not pan out. It was because of some "trifle," it went without saying. Pronin would not get discouraged. The next time all difficulties would be anticipated. "Prodigious … Unbelievable … Brilliant … Richard Strauss."

Having grown wise through experience, the target of Pronin's grooming is understandably coy.

"But didn't you say the last time that everything would work out as well?"

"My God, what sort of person is this?" reads the expression on Pronin's face. "He doesn't want to understand the simplest thing. The last time everything fell apart because of his intrigues. Now he's with us. You'll see, this time everything will work out amazingly…"

And again someone signs a check with a sigh or is off to petition a ministry, or writes a play, or, to the extent of their abilities, gets involved in the work of the idle machine known as the activities of Boris Pronin.

⁎ ⁎ ⁎

That machine, however, did not remain altogether idle; a few bits of grain would eventually be ground in its mill supposedly designed to grind hundreds of pounds. "Something" would finally get done, or, as Pronin would say, "would get churned out."

In this fashion first the House of Interludes, then the Stray Dog, and then finally the Comedians' Repose would get "churned out." Not bad really, especially if one remained in the dark about how much energy— both Pronin's and that of others—got wasted in the process.

Pronin bustled about the arrangements for the Comedians' Repose. The "machine" was running at full capacity. Workers demanded money, but there was not any; some military institution sent a few soldiers to clean the premises, since it turned out that that institution had legal rights to it, and the water that was running down all the walls was not the biggest problem, it was the fact that it was pouring out of all the newly constructed fireplaces. That was worse because how can you dry walls without functioning fireplaces?

Pumps were brought in to get out the water. Wet fire logs would be replaced with new ones, but water from the Moyka, at the corner of which the Comedians' Repose was situated, would flood the building again. Pronin, disheveled, without his jacket despite the cold weather (he was always taking off his jacket when he got excited, no matter where he happened to be), wearing a snow-white cambric shirt, his tie to one side, his face smeared with soot and paint, screaming, making phone calls, shooing off the soldiers, assuring the stone masons (he would cross his heart), that tomorrow ("tomorrow" had been going on for six months), they would be paid, and all the while he grabbed the kerosene pump and soaked the firewood that refused to catch fire.

He would greet enthusiastically those who would stop by and take them on a tour of his holdings:

"This," Pronin would nod toward a dirty room with vaulted ceiling, its walls covered in brown damp patches, and a porridge of lime and dirt instead of a floor, "this is the Venetian Hall. Maestro Sergey Sudeykin will decorate it. It will be in black and gold. Over there will be the variety stage. There won't be any vulgar chairs, only velvet backless benches…"

"But those will be uncomfortable, won't they?"

"Incredibly uncomfortable! Those benches will be low, slanting, *Venetian*. But that's the whole point: *our* regulars will be sitting back there on chairs. But the benches here will be built on purpose for the bourgeois—each place will go for ten rubles ... Over here will be a Montmartre bistro. The frescoes will be by Boris Grigoriyev—they will be amazing. See here, the gas is already hooked up. It will be just like in Paris."

A pathetic *gasolier* sticks out of the wall. All over the ceilings there are traces of the electricians' work, but this is the only light fixture within the entire premises.

"It had to be specially installed." Pronin proudly gives it a tap. "It cost us seven hundred rubles to get it connected. Look at it now, though—such chic, just like in Paris. The bourgeois will light their cigarettes, wowed."

"And what goes in here?"

Pronin himself has yet to decide what should go between the bistro and Venice—but this he does not want you to know.

"In here? Well, a little nook, we'll throw on some fabric, a rug, put in a wide sofa…"

"And this room reminds me of a spa."

"A spa?" Pronin screws up his eye. "A spa. Inspired! Incredible! Right in here we'll have an oriental spa. Tomorrow I'll have them break that pool down. We'll fill it up with water—we've got plenty of that here! Colorful walls … Stained glass … A swan swimming in the pool … Light from above…"

"Well, it'll be tricky to put in an overhead light…"

"Not at all—we'll break a hole in the ceiling."

"You mean you'll break through all six stories?"

"And what's the big deal? I'll rent all the apartments and break through the ceilings … On the other hand, maybe I am getting a little carried away in my fantasy…"

"Boris Konstantinovich!" The boy who is hanging the wallpaper comes running in. His face expresses worry and excitement. "Water!"

"Oh, damn it!" And with his face expressing as much worry and excitement as that of his helper, Pronin runs off to the Venetian Hall, from where one can hear the muffled splashing of water flooding the floor …

* * *

It is unlikely that Pronin would voluntarily have come up with the idea of forsaking his old haunt in the cellar on Mikhaylovsky Square to engage in his "dynamite-explosive" activity at the corner of the Moyka and the Field of Mars. the Stray Dog had become a part of his soul, if not his entire soul. Business was going well, which is to say that the landlord—a malleable fellow—dutifully waited for the rent he was owed, while in the meantime taking advantage of the right to enter his own property and the honorary title of a "Friend of the Stray Dog" in lieu of interest. The restaurateur, an Italian called Francesco Tanni, would also patiently sell his sour wine and second-rate cognac on credit, finding consolation in the fact that his little restaurant, previously empty, became the head-quarters of Petersburg bohemia. The majority of the new customers also paid their bills only on extraordinary occasions—most of the time they dined on credit.

That same Francesco Tanni's was where improvised feasts would often be thrown. Thus one day upon waking up in the morning Pronin decided it would be his name day today. It had to be celebrated. But it was too late to telephone people and send out notes. What Pronin did was this: he began to stroll along the sunny side of Nevsky Prospect, inviting over every acquaintance he chanced upon. Acquaintances he had aplenty. At the appointed hour some sixty people desiring to honor the "dear name-day boy" had squeezed into the small and cramped quarters of Francesco's. Tables were moved together; sour Cabernet, cloudy Chablis, and the not particularly delicate but exceptionally strong cognac produced by the mysterious French house Prima all went into action. The same was true of Chianti, naturally. The "name-day boy" drank, his "friends" drank, and the owner, the respectable, gray-haired Italian who resembled a famous violinist, followed suit. Finally came the call "everything eaten, everything drunk," time to close the restaurant. Pronin was handed the bill. He unfolded it with fingers that would not obey his will.

"This ... What is this?"

"The bill, Boris Konstantinovich, Sir."

"And this?" A finger performs several pirouettes in the air, like a bird looking for a place to settle, and then starts pecking at the bill's total.

"Two hundred rubles, Sir…"

A flash of surprise and horror animates the blissful face of the "name-day boy." He remains silent for a minute, then exclaims pathetically:

"Scoundrels! So who is going to pay now?!"

No, of his own accord Pronin would hardly have parted with Mikhaylovsky Square. The idea of trading the modest rooms of the Stray Dog, with its straw stools and a hoop for a lampshade, for the Venetian halls and medieval chapels of the Comedians' Repose was instilled in him by Vera Aleksandrovna.

The portrait of that "Vera Aleksandrovna," or "Verochka" from the Comedians' Repose, was to be drawn by none other than Konstantin Somov.

Somov—no matter how coldly the strict guardians of artistic fashion may smile when they read this—Somov is the most astonishing portrait painter of his era, that tragic and ravishing sunset of "Imperial Petersburg."

I imagine this never-painted canvas thus: dark hair, a mere half an hour ago meticulously curled at Delacroix's, is already a bit mussed. The plunging décolleté of her bodice slips off one shoulder—her breast is scarcely hidden. The bodice itself is black, and it sharply wedges into the velvet crimson of her skirt. Her plump arms are strangely white, as if someone sprinkled white powder on them; they are helplessly and awkwardly pressed to her chest on the side of her heart. In her entire posture, there is some kind of helplessness, some kind of perplexed splendor. And there is also something old-fashioned about all this: the pleats of her Parisian dress lie like crinoline, her large curls remind one of a wig.

Gray squinting eyes, small smiling mouth. And in that smile there lurks some kind of treachery…

***

Not long before the war, Émile Verhaeren came to Petersburg. As is our custom, he was fêted, and, as is our custom as well, the festivities turned out to be a little ridiculous, and perhaps even slighting to our famous guest. This is not to suggest that the organizers' intentions were anything but good, that their efforts were not zealous enough. Somehow it just happened, all by itself, that everything went not the way it was supposed to go. The banquet hardly began, yet everyone—the organizers, the guests, and, it seemed, Verhaeren himself—sensed it. Several speeches in a lofty style extolling "our dear teacher" were accompanied by the clanging of knives and barking; then suddenly for no rhyme or reason came a "hurrah!" from the far end of the table where the junior literary brethren had already managed to get soused. The "catering" provided by the Maly Yaroslavets Restaurant amounted to sweaty waiters wearing cotton gloves and an excessive number of bottles of not a particularly decent wine ... In a word, it would have been better had this banquet never taken place at all ...

I knew, or at least recognized, almost everyone in attendance, to be sure. This is why I was surprised to see sitting next to Verhaeren some lady completely unknown to me. She was extravagantly and showily dressed; diamonds sparkled in her ears, her gray eyes squinted, and a smile flitted across her small lips ...

Who is she? I turned to my neighbor, who did not know. I asked someone else—the same answer. Verhaeren did not bother to listen to the welcoming speeches where every third word was "chaos" and every fifth "cosmos"; animatedly and obligingly, he conversed with this unknown lady while wrinkling up his nose in the manner of an old man.

Who could she be, after all? At that very moment, Pronin, the famous Pronin—"Doctor of Aesthetics," Director of the Stray Dog—happened to pass by. His tuxedo vest was already unbuttoned, pure bliss lit his face, and the neck of a champagne bottle rested in each hand.

"Boris, who is this lady?"

The omnipresent "Doctor of Aesthetics" just shrugged his shoulders.

"I don't know. Nobody else does either. She came on her own and sat down next to Verhaeren on her own..."

Then he added, as if immersed in deep thought:

"Maybe it's his wife or (a blissful smile) ... or ... his niece."

In all likelihood, Pronin soon got a chance to ascertain how wrong he was concerning the identity of the mysterious lady. Be that as it may, when a half-year later another poetic guest—Paul Fort—arrived in Petersburg, Pronin, when introducing him to Vera Aleksandrovna, presented her as:

"Voilà la maîtresse du Chien…"

He meant to say "the lady in charge of the Stray Dog." By that time Vera Aleksandrovna had already become the wife of our rudderless and merry "Doctor of Aesthetics."

* * *

When we have gotten to know each other better, I hear Vera Aleksandrovna confess to the following:

"Like Andersen's *Undine*, I would agree to any sort of torture—to suffer pain at every step as if walking on nails—only to have power, power over people…"

"Do you mean power over their souls or … well, like a police chief or the tsar?"

"Ah! Any kind I can get. I'd settle for just a tiny bit of power to start with. Even the power of a police chief will do. Even that much power is a terrible force, you only have to know how to take advantage of it…"

"You should go to Mexico, Vera Aleksandrovna, there it's possible—women can get elected governor there."

But she pays no attention.

"Power," she draws out the word as if weighing it. "Power … over people's souls? But any kind of power is over the soul. To have power over someone means to degrade him. Degrade him and elevate yourself. The greater the denigration, the more elevated the degrader…"

She laughs.

"Why are you looking at me like that? I didn't make it up by myself. I read it somewhere in Balzac. Or maybe it was in Huysmans."

And mysteriously, as if imparting a secret, she reveals:

"Power equals money. More than anything in this world I want money."

"Everyone does, Vera Aleksandrovna," I answer her in the same mysterious whisper.

She stomps her foot.

"Stop! Do you think I want it *that way*? And by the way ... do you know who my childhood heroine was?"

"Lucrezia Borgia?"

"No, it was Thérèse Humbert."

And, to the accompaniment of "her high heel hammering against the parquet," she declares:

"The sweetest thing in the world is to torment people."

The dark blue cups on the lacquered table are jumping up and down from the tapping of her French high heel on the floor. A small, plump, white-as-powder arm offers me a plate with a slice of fruitcake on it...

"Of course, I'm joking. I'm a most ordinary woman. Even to become an actress I never had enough will. Not to mention..."

Her gray eyes squint coldly; a smile appears on her painted lips. And in that smile there is some sort of cunning ...

Having married Pronin and become "la mâitresse du Chien," Vera Aleksandrovna immediately began to redo, change, and expand everything in the Stray Dog. And, of course, by the third month she got bored.

And who would not get bored? The Stray Dog was a tiny cellar, funded with a few twenty-five-ruble notes collected from acquaintances. It became crowded when forty people squeezed in, but if sixty came one simply could not turn around. There was no set program, Pronin always did things impromptu. "Fedya" (i.e., Shalyapin) has promised to come and sing ... If Shalyapin doesn't show up, well ... we'll make Mishka (Pronin's mutt) dance a quadrille. "We'll cook up something," one way or another. Rickety tables and straw stools stood in the main hall, there were no waiters—the visitors themselves would go to the buffet. Most of those visitors were "our kind of crowd"—poets, actors, and artists, who very much liked such a routine and did not want to change anything ... In a word, Vera Aleksandrovna had nothing to do at the Stray Dog. After her unsuccessful attempt to introduce some elegant improvements, after quarrelling with everyone on whom the honorary title "Friend of the Stray Dog" had been bestowed, and having grown bored with a role that was too modest for her and her Parisian dresses, Vera Aleksandrovna, as Pronin put it, decided to "wring the doggy's neck." At night sleepless bums from Petersburg's bohemia stopped waking up the yard keeper stationed at the gate on the corner of Mikhaylovsky Square and Italyansky Street, and the ventilator duct—to strike fear into "bourgeois" visitors who had wandered into the Stray Dog, it displayed a menacing sign "Don't Touch: Death"— had stopped humming in the narrow stairwell of the third yard entryway.

The huge basement that had been leased on the Field of Mars was not meant to resurrect the Stray Dog, but to create something grandiose, unprecedented, astonishing. The hostess of this future "grandiose and unprecedented" marvel moved into an apartment right above. The apartment was huge as well, with enormous windows and unusually high ceilings. It was terribly cold in there. Several floors above, in Leonid Andreyev's apartment, stoves were stoked day and night, everything was wrapped in rugs and curtains, yet all the same breath came out of people's mouths in a puff of steam. That is how cold it was in that house. In Vera Aleksandrovna's apartment there were no rugs or curtains, firewood was often in short supply, and many of the windows were not even caulked. From morning till night the deafening banging of the stonemasons' hammers was coming from downstairs; from morning till night the incessant doorbell ringing of the people wanting to collect payments for the bills the couple could not settle resounded at the entrances to both the front and back stairways. Pronin slept out the cold and boredom, having buried himself under every fur coat he could find, while Vera Aleksandrovna, all curled and painted, spent hours upon hours seated in front of a freezing mirror and dreamt of who knows what—of the future Comedians' Repose (this was to be the name of the new cabaret) or of power over people's souls . . .

To escape the cold, she muffled herself in her wide and fluffy sables. Those same sables, however, every once in a while had to go to the pawnshop, and then she would wrap herself in blankets.

✳ ✳ ✳

"Why, Vera Aleksandrovna, are you bored here too?"

"A lot."

"And do you feel crowded?"

"Yes."

"So tell me, are you still going to rebuild and expand the place?"

"I've already rented the basement next door. In summer I'll have them break down the wall, so that the Venetian Hall is followed by a gallery. In that gallery . . .

She waves her hand.

"I don't know, maybe I won't be rebuilding or expanding, after all, or I'll leave it all to Boris, let him do whatever he wants. I'll go traveling somewhere..."

And then, raising her penciled eyebrows high:

"I've had it. I'm bored..."

The interior of the Comedians' Repose was splendid. The dirty basement with its gutted walls had indeed been transformed into some sort of "magic kingdom." A dim light coming from underneath lacy masks illuminated a hall decorated black-red-and-golden by Sergey Sudeykin; the Bistro turned out to be covered with Boris Grigoriyev's marvelous Parisian frescoes, and the adjacent hall was decorated by Alexander Yakovlev. Antique furniture, brocade, wooden statues from ancient churches, small stairwells, nooks, mysterious corridors, all of this was astonishingly well designed and executed. Vera Aleksandrovna, wearing silks and diamonds, would triumphantly greet the guests: "Well, how do you like it?" Pronin beamed. Decked-out in a tuxedo, Pronin would take the guests on tours around the various marvels of the Comedians' Repose. When explaining something especially passionately, he would, as was his old habit, grab the lapels of his tuxedo to throw it off. But all he did was to grab them and then immediately let his hands drop. The place was not the same, the time was not the same—what would have seemed completely natural at the Stray Dog would be quite indecent here.

After their initial delight, the old regulars from the Stray Dog were somewhat put off by the air about the new cellar, to which they were unaccustomed. In the Stray Dog one could sit wherever one liked, guests themselves fetched their food and drinks from the buffet and set their plates wherever they fancied ... Down here it transpired that all the seats in the main hall where the stage was installed had been numbered, reserved for somebody over the phone and paid for handsomely, whereas the so-called Esteemed Members of the Petrograd Artistic Society were expected to watch the performance from another room. But even in that room, before you could sit down, a waiter with a napkin would come flying over to you, and upon finding out that you did not "desire" anything, he would practically slap his starched napkin on the nose of the "unworthy" guest ...

... Tamara Karsavina smiles, alluring Olga Sudeykina dances her charming polka. The red-black and golden walls shimmer. Music, applause, the popping of corks, the clinking of glasses ... Suddenly the flabby and drunk composer Tsybulsky gets up and staggers forward with a glass in his hand: "I r-request the floor..."

"May God rest our 'Doggy's' soul in peace, Ladies and Gentlemen," he begins, tripping over his tongue. "I feel sorry for the dearly departed ... Boris ... Yes, you, Boris, did you have to make all this fuss? Did you have to invite—he nods at the tuxedoes in the first rows—all these pharmacists, all this scum..."

✳ ✳ ✳

All in all, it turned out to be "aesthetical," quite "aesthetical," but nevertheless just a restaurant. The public was pleased. The public paid a nice cover charge, drank champagne, and watched Nikolay Yevreinov's performances in costumes by Sergey Sudeykin.

Well, what could go wrong if the public came and drank their champagne?

And I was reminded: "More than anything I want money..."

However, all of a sudden the Comedians' Repose, along with the upstairs apartment, all that glazed pottery from the West India Company, and all those dresses with plunging necklines turned out to be distrained property. It turned out that the Comedians' Repose not only did not pay for itself, but ran at a terrible loss. All of its patrons refused to come to its aid, and within a week it was to be auctioned off.

"How is this possible?" I asked.

Vera Aleksandrovna raised her eyebrows wearily:

"That's the way it is. I don't know. There wasn't enough money. I kept signing promissory notes…"

But a few days later she greeted me happily. A new patron of the arts had been found. For the time being, the Comedians' Repose would close down for repairs, and to prepare a new program …

She stood in the medieval hallway, the one decorated by Alexander Yakovlev, leaning on the wooden statue of some saint, holding in her small, pudgy, strangely white hand an ancient knife recently delivered by an antique dealer.

"Lucrezia Borgia!" I joked.

She burst into laughter.

"Aha, I see, you remember that conversation! No-no, not Lucrezia … I'm Thérèse. Here, read this."

I opened the document.

"What is it?"

"The contract with the new patron. He has committed to pay me the whole time the Comedians' Repose is closed, monthly…" She named some large sum.

"Only when it's closed?"

She laughed broadly:

"Oh my God, how naïve you are! Don't you see, there's no expiration date. I can leave the Comedians' Repose closed my whole life, and he'll keep paying me…"

"How did he come to sign such a thing?"

She pursed her lips ceremoniously:

"Oh, he's a very sweet man, a friend of my father's. He signed this without reading…"

✳ ✳ ✳

I do not know whether the "sweet man" protested or whether Vera Aleksandrovna fancied playing the hostess once again, but the Comedians' Repose opened all the same. In the summer of 1917, there—at the very same "artistic" table—sat Alexander Kolchak, Boris Savinkov, and Leon Trotsky, so that Vera Aleksandrovna ended up looking like a veritable Lucrezia in their company.

She was very animated, and very lovely in those days. It seemed she was no longer "bored" and that some new "grandiosities" and "possibilities" began to appear to her again. I concluded this from her outward appearance; she did not enter into conversation with me since she had far more interesting interlocutors to entertain.

The "soul" that the Comedians' Repose lacked during the days of its flowering came to dwell there for a short time right before its demise. Those who frequented it at the end of 1917 and the beginning of 1918 are unlikely to forget those evenings.

Cold. Half-darkness. No reserved tables, no cigars in mouths, no well-fed faces. The luxuriousness of the furniture and the walls had faded considerably. The electricity was not working, but here and there fat wax candles guttered ...

A rehearsal of *The Green Parrot* is underway. What an inspired idea to put on *such* a play in *such* an atmosphere, don't you think? Schnitzler's dialogues sound eerily "convincing" for the viewers and the actors alike. Vera Aleksandrovna, pale, without jewelry, listens with her arms crossed on her chest. It was she who thought up the idea of putting on *The Green Parrot*.

Cold. Half-darkness. Shots heard from the street ... Suddenly there is stomping behind the wall and banging of rifle butts against the closed gate. Ten or so Red Army men under the command of an ugly woman festooned with ammunition pour into the Venetian Room.

"Citizens, your papers!"

They are pacified with the display of some sort of document signed by Anatoly Lunacharsky. They exit, grumbling: "Just you wait, we'll get you..." And once again guttering candles, poems by Anna Akhmatova or Charles Baudelaire, music by Claude Debussy or Arthur Lurie ...

... The Comedians' Repose was not shut down—it perished, broke apart, and turned to dust indeed. Dampness, no longer held back by the heat of the fireplaces, came into its own. The gilding peeled off, the carpets began to rot, the furniture came apart. Huge hungry rats began to run about with no fear of people, the grand piano became damp, and the stage curtain ripped ...

Once, during a thaw, some pipes burst, and water from the Moyka, the old enemy of those ravaged walls, flooded them.

... In the Comedians' Repose stands

Stagnant, unpumped water.
Do you know? Have you been there?
Never, really?[20]

VI

"La Rotonde." Usual evening hubbub. I look for an empty table. Suddenly, my eyes meet with eyes that once were well-known to me (Petersburg, snow, 1913 ...), gray Russian eyes. It is S., the wife of a famous artist.

"You here! Since when?"

A smile—a distracted "Petersburg" smile: "It's been a month since leaving Russia."

"From Petersburg?"

"From Petersburg."

S. is a friend of Anna Akhmatova. Naturally, one of my first questions is: "How is Akhmatova?"

"Anya? She's still living at the same place on the Fontanka, near the Summer Garden. She doesn't go out much, only to church. She writes, of course. Does she publish? No, she doesn't think about that. How can you publish these days..."

... On the Fontanka. Near the Summer Garden ...

1922. Autumn. I'm leaving for abroad the day after tomorrow. I'm going to Akhmatova's to bid my farewell. The Summer Garden already rustles autumnally. Engineers' Castle glows red in the sunset. How deserted it all is! How disturbing! Farewell, Petersburg!

Akhmatova extends her hand to me. "I'm here passing the night away," she says. "Are you leaving for abroad?"

Her delicate profile is outlined in the darkening window. Her shoulders are wrapped in the storied dark shawl with large roses on it:

O Phaedra, a pseudoclassical shawl
Slides down from your shoulders.[21]

"Are you leaving for abroad? Convey my regards to Paris."

"And you, Anna Andreyevna, you're not planning to leave?"

"No. I won't leave Russia."

"But it's getting more difficult to live here."

"Yes, more difficult."

"It may become completely unbearable."

"What can one do?"

"You won't be leaving?"

"I'm not going to leave."

... No, she is not even thinking about publishing—where would she publish now ... She doesn't go out much—only to church ... Her health? It's becoming worse, true. And life is such that she is forced to do everything for herself. She ought to travel south, to Italy. But where would she get the money? And if she had it ...

"She won't be leaving?"

"She won't."

"You know." The gray eyes look at me almost strictly. "You know, Anya was walking once along Mokhovoy Street carrying a sack. I think she was carrying some flour. She got tired and stopped to rest. Winter. She was dressed poorly. Some woman or other walked by ... She gave Anya a kopeck. 'Take it, for the love of Christ.' Anya hid that kopeck behind her icons. She has been treasuring it ever since..."

1911. "The Tower"—Vyacheslav Ivanov's apartment—is hosting one of its literary Wednesdays. All the crème de la crème of poetic Petersburg gathers here. Poems are read here in a circle, and the "wise man of Tavrichesky Street," squinting from under his pince-nez and throwing back his golden mane, hands out his verdicts. For the most part they are politely lethal. The cruelty of the verdict is mitigated by only one feature—it is impossible to disagree with its caustic precision. Ivanov's praises, on the contrary, are extremely meager. The slightest of approvals is a rarity.

Poems are read in a circle. Celebrities and beginners, they all read. The turn comes round to a young lady, thin and dusky.

It is Gumilyov's wife. She "writes too." Well, of course, wives of writers always write, wives of artists busy themselves with paints, wives of musicians play an instrument. It seems that this dark and dusky Anna Andreyevna is not altogether without ability. While still a young lady she wrote:

> And for whom will these pale lips
> Become a fatal potion?
> A Black man behind her, haughty and crude,
> Peers out cunningly.[22]

Sweet, don't you think? It's beyond understanding why Gumilyov becomes so irritated when his wife is spoken about as a poet.

And Gumilyov truly does become irritated. He too looks at her poems as the whim of "a poet's wife." And that whim is not to his taste. When her poems are praised, he smiles derisively. "You like it? I'm so happy. My wife does lovely embroidery as well."

"Anna Andreyevna, will you read us some?"

Condescending smiles spread across the faces of the "genuine ones" present. Gumilyov pulls a dissatisfied grimace and taps a cigarette against his cigarette case.

"I will."

Two spots show on her dusky cheeks. Her eyes look forward bewildered and haughty. Her voice trembles slightly.

"I will."

> My breast turned helplessly cold,
> But my steps were light,
> On my right hand I put
> The glove from my left hand.[23]

An indifferent-amiable smile appears on the faces. Certainly not serious stuff, but pleasing, don't you think? Gumilyov throws away an unfinished cigarette. The two spots stand out even sharper on Akhmatova's cheeks ...

What will Vyacheslav Ivanov say? Probably nothing. He will be silent for a bit, then make note of some technical peculiarity. After all, his devastating verdicts are for serious poems of genuine poets. And here we have ... Why insult someone for no reason?

Vyacheslav Ivanov remains silent for a moment. Then he rises, walks up to Akhmatova, kisses her hand.

"Anna Andreyevna, I congratulate you and welcome you. This poem is an event in Russian poetry."

✳ ✳ ✳

Arkady Rumanov's study is appointed with amazing Alexander I-era furniture, and it is here where hangs a large canvas by Nathan Altman, whose portraiture has recently become fashionable: it was Rumanov who started this fashion, having paid this up-and-coming artist a "fantastic" sum of money for the portrait.

Several shades of green. The kind of green that is poisonously cold. It is not even malachite—rather a bronze vitriol. Disturbing green corners and rhombuses flood the sharp contours of the drawing. They were supposed to depict trees, foliage, but not only do they not resemble them, but, on the contrary, they seem in some way hostile:

> ... in the ocean of primordial gloom,
> No clouds and no green grass,
> Only cubes, and rhombs, and angles,
> And sinister metallic ringing.[24]

The color of caustic vitriol; the malevolent ringing of brass. They constitute the background of Altman's painting.

Against this background a woman is seated—very slender, tall, and pale. Her collarbones protrude sharply. Her black bangs look as if lacquered; they cover her forehead to the brows. She has swarthy-pale cheeks, and a pale-red mouth. Her thin nostrils are translucent. Her eyes are in dark circles; they peer coldly and motionlessly ahead—as if not registering their surroundings.

Only cubes, and rhombs, and angles—

—and all the features of her face, and all the lines of her figure are angles. An angular mouth, the angular bend of her spine, the angles of her fingers, the angles of her elbows. Even her raised slender, long legs are at an angle. Can there be such women in real life? This is the whimsy of the artist! No—this is the very much alive Akhmatova. You don't believe me? Come to the Stray Dog some time after hours, around four in the morning.

> Yes, I loved them, those nocturnal gatherings:
> Frosted glasses on a small table,
> Pungent, delicate steam above black coffee,
> The heavy winter heat of a red-hot fireplace,
> The caustic gaiety of a literary jest,
> And a friend's first glance, helpless and terrifying.[25]

Four or five in the morning. Tobacco smoke, empty bottles. And hour ago all was joyful and loud—someone sang silly couplets to their own accompaniment, someone demanded more wine. Now all those revelers have either gone or are nodding off. The cellar is almost silent.

Very few are still seated at the little tables in the middle of the hall. There are more in the corners, next to gaudily painted walls, under boarded-up windows.

> The little windows boarded shut forever,
> What's out there—hoarfrost or storm?[26]

Isn't it all the same whatever is out there on the street, in Petersburg, in the world? Your head is going round from the wine you've drunk, the smoke clouds your vision. Conversations are carried out in a half-whisper.

Here many chains have come unbound;
This underground hall will preserve everything—
Including the words uttered in the night
That certain people would not utter in the morning.[27]

And suddenly—deafening, crazy music. Those dozing shudder. Shot glasses jump on the tables. The besotted musician bangs the piano keys with all his might. First he bangs them and then breaks off and plays something else that is quiet and sad. His face is red, sweaty. Tears roll down from his blissfully stunned eyes onto the liqueur-splattered keys.

Five o'clock in the morning. The Stray Dog.

Akhmatova sits by the fireplace. She sips black coffee and smokes a thin cigarette. How pale she is!

Yes, she is very pale—from fatigue, from the wine, from the stark electric light. The edges of her lips are downturned. Her collarbones protrude sharply. Her eyes peer coldly and motionlessly ahead, as if not registering their surroundings.

Here we are all sinners or harlots,
How joyless we are together.
Flowers and birds on the walls,
Languish among clouds.[28]

But—

… in the sea of primordial gloom,
No clouds and no green grass.

Grass, clouds, life, laughter—it was all left on the other side of the "little windows boarded shut forever." Here can only be found:

The caustic gaiety of a literary jest,
And a friend's first glance, helpless and terrifying …

This gaiety is too caustic. These glances are too terrible.

Akhmatova is never by herself. There are friends, admirers, those in love with her, and some ladies in big hats with made-up eyes. Two years have passed since that memorable evening at Vyacheslav Ivanov's when she read her poems in a breaking voice. She is an all-Russian celebrity now. Her fame keeps growing.

The cigarette in her slender hand trails smoke. Her shoulders, wrapped in a shawl, shudder when she coughs.

"Are you cold, have you gotten a chill?"

"No, I'm perfectly healthy."

"But you are coughing."

"Oh, that?" A tired smile. "That's not a chill, it's consumption."

And, as she turns away from her alarmed interlocutor, she engages someone else:

"I never knew what happy love is…"

… She was carrying a sack … She got tired and stopped to rest … Some woman or other …

… Young men in tuxedos reverentially hang on to Akhmatova's every word. Enraptured eyes follow her every move.

… Anya hid that kopeck behind her icons. She has been treasuring it ever since … The Gumilyovs have a house in Tsarskoye Selo. From the outside it looks like the majority of Tsarskoye Selo houses. Two stories, flaking plaster, wild grapevines crawling up the wall. But the indoors is warm, spacious, and comfortable. The old parquet squeaks, large bushes of azaleas glow rosily in the glass-enclosed dining room, the stoves are stoked hot. The library has large couches and bookshelves to the ceiling… There are many rooms, sundry little offices here and there with piles of soft pillows; all this is dimly lit, and the ineluctable scent of books, old walls, perfumes and dust hangs all over …

Suddenly the silence is pierced by a shrill screech. The curved-beaked cockatoo is angry in his cage. The very same one as in the poem:

And now I've become a plaything—
Like my rosy friend the cockatoo.[29]

"Rosy friend" flaps his wings and seethes with anger.

"Masha, a cloth over his cage, please…"

At home, and very rarely at that, you can catch a glimpse of a completely different Akhmatova.

The Gumilyovs are holding their last reception. It is the end of May. Everyone is leaving for somewhere.

"I'm so glad," says Akhmatova, "that we are not going abroad this year. The last time in Paris I almost died of boredom."

"Boredom? In Paris?"

"Well, yes. Kolya traipsed around some exotic museums for days at a time. I can't abide exotica. Museums give me migraine. You are all by yourself, and you sometimes get bored. I even got myself a tortoise. The tortoise crawls around, I look at it. At least it's a distraction."

"Anya," Gumilyov interrupts her in an annoyed tone. "You're forgetting that in Paris we went to theaters and restaurants almost every day."

"Every evening would be stretching it a bit," Akhmatova teases him. "Two times altogether."

She laughs like a little girl.

"How different you now look from your Altman portrait."

She shrugs her shoulders derisively.

"Much obliged. I do hope I don't look like that."

"You dislike it that much?"

"As a portrait? To be sure! Who likes to see oneself as a green mummy?"

"But sometimes the likeness seems stunning."

She laughs again:

"You're saying insolent things to me." She opens an album. "And how about here—would you call that a likeness?"

It is a photograph taken some time before the wedding. A joyful, girlish face …

"What a haughty look you have here."

"Yes! I was very haughty then, but nowadays I've grown more amenable…"

"Did you derive your haughtiness from your poems?"

"Oh, no, what poems? Swimming. I swim like a fish, you know."

The same house, the same dining room. Akhmatova pours tea into the same cups and offers it to the same guests. But their faces are somehow more sallow as if they had aged in the course of two years, their voices quieter. There is some sort of shadow on everything, on both their faces and their conversations.

And the hostess does not look either like the decadent dame in the Altman portrait or like the young girl who is haughty because she swims "like a fish." Now there is something of a nun about her.

"Two Corps have perished in Augustów Forest."

"There's no weaponry and no food supplies…"

"Two of Z.'s sons have been killed."

"They say we'll soon run out of bread."

Gumilyov is gone—he is at the front.

"Read some poems, Anna Andreyevna."

"The poems I write these days tend to be tedious."

And she reads "The Lullaby":

… Sleep my quiet little boy,
I am a bad mother.
Rarely does the news reach
Our porch.
They've given a little white cross
To your father,
There was grief, there will be grief,
Grief without end.
May St. George
Preserve your father.[30]

Two more years go by. I have two or three chance encounters with Akhmatova. She is more and more unlike her former self. She looks more and more like a nun. Only the shawl on her shoulders is as in the old days—dark with red roses. "A pseudoclassical shawl." What kind of pseudoclassical shawl is that anyway? It is a plain peasant woman's kerchief thrown over her shoulders to keep them from freezing.

Still another year passes by. There is an evening to honor Pushkin. A strange celebration—some wear evening jackets, others are in sheepskin coats—in an unheated hall. Alexander Blok is on stage speaking about Pushkin. He speaks indistinctly and with agitation. Akhmatova is standing in a corner. She is wearing an old-fashioned silk dress with a high waist. Bone thin, her face looks pitiful—and magnificent. She stands alone. Men come up to her and kiss her hand. More often than not they approach silently. What can anyone say to someone like *that*? You cannot say "how are you," can you?

… Another half year passes. Smolensky Cemetery. Blok's coffin is covered in flowers. Two more weeks, and a memorial service in Kazan Cathedral in memory of the recently executed Gumilyov …

Yes, I loved them, those nocturnal gatherings,

Frosted glasses on low tables …
Incense. Tear-stained faces. Choirboys.
… The caustic gaiety of a literary jest,
And a friend's first glance …

VII

A poster is pinned up in the elevator cabin: a devil with a laughing mug, green little eyes, and a lilac tail. Right below runs an inscription:

You are requested not to smoke poisonous green stuff (tobacco)

Who is requesting it? The homeowner?

No. The poster was hung by a third-floor tenant, Sergey Gorodetsky.

And where does he come off giving orders? The elevator is not his apartment after all.

Oh, come on … so he gives orders. Who's going to stop him?

Sergey Mitrofanovich Gorodetsky is such a fine fellow, so agreeable. Even if the homeowner wanted to bring something to his attention, how would he go about it? So he would go: "To my regret, I'm going to have to request that you…" But Gorodetsky, not hearing him out, would slap him on the shoulder: "How are you doing, my dear man? How's your precious health? How are the wife and kids?"

He adores children. He draws little pictures for them—just like the one in the elevator: "Little Devil in the Furnace," "Nine Mice and Pussy Cat Manya." He makes scary eyes, a horned goat with his fingers, and improvises poems right on the spot.

"What's your name?"

"Petya."

"Okay then, listen:

Once upon a time there lived a boy named Petya,
There are many Petyas in this world.
Only that Petya of mine
Was completely different …

His eyes are bright, his gaze direct and "heartfelt." His hair is ruddy blond and curly. He speaks in a singsong voice. He is not all that handsome, but more pleasant than any good-looking fellow on account of "an appealing exterior," and that "exterior" of his is not a deceptive one: he really is a fine fellow. He is ready to be of service or help to anyone. If he meets a simple old woman on the street carrying a sack, he would say: "Granny, let me give you a hand!" He does not walk past a beggar without giving him something. A child comes his way—he has a lollypop at the ready, he always carries them in his pocket …

Here he helped someone, there he made a joke, smiled at someone, and now he goes on his way whistling or humming a tune. His eyes shine, his white teeth shine. Even his Finnish fur hat with its earflaps looks so winning on his thrown-back head.

✳ ✳ ✳

"You are requested not to smoke poisonous green stuff." At the same time, though, Gorodetsky has set aside a little nook for incorrigible smokers. When their addiction gets the best of them that is where they retreat.

There, provided they do their duty to tightly close the doors, they can "poison" themselves to their hearts' content at the window that opens wide onto the back stairwell. The walls of the nook have been decorated with an edifying story: "The Persistent Tobacco Smoker and What Befell Him." He has done a really talented job. Say what you like, but what a talented creature this Gorodetsky fellow is! Whatever he puts his hand to is done with talent. And he does it all on the fly, with a joke, a smile, in passing ... This is the way he began to write poems too, as a joke, and then became a celebrity just like that. One night he went to bed an unknown twenty-year old student, the next morning his collection *Yar* came out and he woke up famous. Was there anyone who did not know these lines by heart before a month was out?

> Moans, chimes, chimes on chimes,
> Moans-chimes, chimes-dreams,
> High and steep cliffs,
> Steeply sloping greenery ...

... The Gorodetskys receive guests each Tuesday evening. A line quickly forms at the entrance to the smokers' nook. This is where they light up, hastily gulp some smoke, and, having made room for others, they go back into the parlor. A large round table occupies the middle of the room. There are roses in a crystal cylinder, melon marmalade, and steaming teacups of Gardner porcelain. Surrounded by literary ladies, Gorodetsky's wife, "The Nymph," her somewhat heavyweight beauty glowing, pours tea with her plump little fingers. Why would Gorodetsky, the despiser of any kind of "classical rot," call his wife "The Nymph"? And why a nymph? She is more like Ceres ... But the nickname firmly stuck to Anna Aleksandrovna, especially after one of Gorodetsky's books came out with the dedication: "To you—my Nymph."

Along the canary-colored walls of the drawing room poets have been sat down in two rows.

In two rows. Below guests sit on ottomans. Their life-sized portraits are hung on the walls, all painted by the host.

If you make Gorodetsky's acquaintance and begin to frequent his place, and you are a poet, then he will definitely draw your portrait. It would be a bit gaudy, but quite the likeness, and rather "nice." And without doubt it will be done on burlap.

Gorodetsky always paints on burlap—it is his invention. It is cheap, and has a "simple-folk" feel to it, which is so close to his heart. And although simple people do not use burlap for painting, Gorodetsky sincerely believes that by depicting Max Voloshin on burlap wearing a frockcoat with a chrysanthemum in his lapel, he gets much closer to the "authentic native element" than if he depicted the same thing on canvas.

On the one hand, there is this "native element," on the other hand— Italy. Those daubed square chunks of burlap—it really looks like a mosaic, don't you think?

This passion for Italy has recently been inculcated into Gorodetsky by his new friend Nikolay Gumilyov, from whom he has become inseparable. After "a restaurant conversation over a bottle of wine" about Italy, Goro- detsky, who an hour before had been totally indifferent, "fell in love" with the country with all his signature ardor. Due to this same ardor, after having fallen in love with Italy he could not sit still in Petersburg another minute without seeing it in person—with his own eyes, immediately.

And it came to be that within a week Gorodetsky was already strolling about Venice, shaking his curls and making a horned goat with his fingers at the Italian kids. Not bad—he liked it.

✳ ✳ ✳

The burlap portraits shone with a whole spectrum of colors. Their real-life models were sitting along the walls, and they looked more humdrum, naturally. They would be divided into mere guests and honored guests. The former wore jackets with collars and expressed themselves in "the dead language of the intelligentsia." The latter sang out their "o's" and were dressed in *poddyovkas* and *kosovorotkas.*

With all the inconstancy of his views and tastes, Gorodetsky had one unchanging "aspiration": his passion for the folksy "Russian spirit" of the *lubok* style … It did not matter what he "sang the praises" of at various times in a variety of empty, sonorous, and chattering stanzas. Their *lubok* essence always remained the same—no better, and no worse. "Presentation of the Tsar" did not differ from the "Ode to Budyonny," and his descriptions of Venice gave off a hint of a "Tea Room of the Russian People"...[31]

A natural outgrowth of Gorodetsky's enthusiasm for the "Russian spirit" was his striving to discover talent from among the people and to surround himself with it.

It would seem that there was nothing amiss if a well-known and influential Petersburg writer went out to meet beginners in so friendly and openly accepting a manner. Even more so in the early days, when those beginners "from the village" had the least experience and were the most helpless. Quite the opposite—what could be better?

But it turned out badly. Very badly indeed.

This is what would happen. Sergey Yesenin arrives in Petersburg. He is sixteen, shy, and is raving about poetry. His dream is to become "a real writer." He came in bast shoes, but with the firm conviction to throw off all his "country drabness." Next thing you know, he has already put his "all" into it, got himself a "three-piece suit," in order not to look different from the "town folk," "the learned ones." But he understands that the main difference is not in the way he is dressed, though he tries to destroy that difference with the entire might of his sixteen-year-old "vigor." Of course, that kind of feverish fervor is not without its dangers—wiping things out with too much zeal, one may lose all of one's originality and freshness. In such cases the help of a well-disposed and experienced older comrade is indispensable. Beyond such professional help there is another requirement: a friendly hand reaching out to one who is lost in circumstances completely foreign to him.

It goes without saying that Yesenin—and in general "all Yesenins"— having felt the chill of the traditional Petersburg "cold shoulder," were happy to run across Gorodetsky.

After a month of tramping around with a notebook of poems from one writer to another, the neophyte country poet would become abashed and disappointed.

Writers are "stiff," indifferent people; they regard him as they would an ordinary new recruit to the literary infantry—so many of them go to and fro around here, with their notebooks in tow. Alexander Blok's cool approval ... Zinaida Hippius casts a stern look at him through her lorgnette ... Fyodor Sologub's carping analysis: "This line here is not bad, the rest is too green..." And to all those niggardly complements they all add this same constant refrain: study, study. Work, work, work ...

And then suddenly you make the acquaintance of Gorodetsky—so warmhearted, tender, sweet, such a "kindred spirit." And after one conversation with that "kindred spirit"—you experience a complete "reevaluation of all values." The village upstart, as does each and every beginner, is convinced, of course, that "the world underappreciates him," but it's unlikely that before his conversation with the "kindred spirit" he understood to what extent this pitiless world is deaf and blind. It turns out he's a genius, decidedly so. And not simply a genius, but a "folk" genius, and that's higher than ordinary. And much simpler, too. All those tricks with diligent work, it's for the intelligentsia, for those inferior beings. The calling of a folk genius is to "reveal the elemental." That's what it is. It turns out one doesn't need to shake off all that "provincial dust," because it is the "elemental" indeed. Get all that "dead learning" out of your head as soon as possible, jump back into your bast shoes, slip on your *poddyovka* again, grab your squeezebox, and burst into some rakish ditty.

With each season Gorodetsky's "folk school" grew with the addition of newly "seduced peasant lads," and in their midst such compliments as "inspired," "above and beyond Pushkin," and so forth were given out as ordinary praise. Gorodetsky also organized free-admission evenings—or "galas," as one might call them. There—

... Everything was very simple, everything was very nice...[32]

A portrait of Aleksey Koltsov is displayed on stage, shadowed by a tin sickle and wooden pitchforks. Below are two stacks of rye (quite ragged from frequent use), and a towel with cross-stitch embroidery. The background is decorated with a *plakhta* taken from Gorodetsky's study. In this way the "intelligentsia indifference" of the stage is toned down and a mood is created that is close to "the elemental." It appears that in order to bring the audience closer to the surroundings of a Russian village, the usual call bell has been dispensed with. In its place there's something not quite a gong, and not quite a tambourine. Something with jingle bells on it ... In ordinary times it hangs in the study, by the tiled stove.

Gorodetsky comes out onto the stage and strikes the tambourine. He looks exalted, beaming, pleasantly preoccupied. His curls are all ruffled. He's wearing a sky-blue or "scarlet" *kosovorotka* ... The attentive eye may make out behind the *kosovorotka* the outline of a stiff plastron—it means that after the show Gorodetsky must drive over to an elegant club where "Nymph" likes to dine, and that the show shirt is put on over starched linen and the black bowtie of a tuxedo to facilitate a quick change.

Gorodetsky strikes his "tympanum" and calls for attention. The light goes off. Only the stage with the stacks and Koltsov are in the bright light of the projectors.

Sergey Yesenin.

The green *plakhta* with crimson patterns is thrown off. Out steps Yesenin.

He is also wearing a *kosovorotka*—it is pink and silky. He also has on a gold sash with wide, velvet trousers. His hair is curled, his cheeks are rouged. In his hands he's holding—God help us!—a bunch of paper cornflowers.

He comes out—hands on hips, elbows out, swaying in a particularly "waggish" manner. He must have rehearsed this entrance a number of times. His smile is roguish, and ... lost. This smile most likely has been rehearsed too. But his embarrassment is stronger all the same. After coming out on stage he is silent and casts about, disturbed ...

"Go for it, Seryozha"—Gorodetsky's words of encouragement are heard from behind the *plakhta*. "Go for it, why be shy?"

Why be shy indeed ...

Yesenin screws up his courage. His voice begins to sound more confident. His rowdy smile grows wider. I saw Yesenin half a year ago, before he met Gorodetsky. He has changed, there is no doubt about it. His poems have really changed too ...

... *Ladas, Lels, gusli-samogudy, struny-samozvony* ... It's doubtful Yesenin had heard about these *samogudy* and *Ladas* earlier. Sometimes an inappropriate, "dirty" word pops up among the others. He certainly knew such words earlier, but because of his "inexperience" he supposed, one would think, that not only were they not fit for putting in poems, but were also unsuitable for conversation. Now, however, he shouts them out with gusto, and looks around at the audience, as if saying: "How's that? How do you like that?"

Sergey Klychkov ...

Klychkov, dressed up as a village peddler from a choir, comes forward. He drawls when he reads, like operatic blind men. He's got the same *Ladas* and *guslis*, only his are more wooden, less catchy than Yesenin's. It was not long ago that he too carried himself more modestly, writing more simply and better. Now, thanks to his mentor, he has "found himself." Had it not been for that, he could have completely perished preparing himself for the university and practicing his Latin ...

Nikolay Klyuyev ...

Klyuyev hurriedly primps his *poddyovka* in front of the dressing-room mirror and fixes the spots of rouge on his cheeks. His eyes are thick with eyeliner, like a ballerina's. Wrinkles around his intelligent, cold eyes (Klyuyev is about forty) spread into a fake, sweet, dim-witted smile.

"Nikolay Vasilyevich, hurry!"

"I am coming already ... ," he replies with his drawl and crosses himself devoutly. "Coming ... It's just that I'm all afraid, little brother. Well, it's do or die for me ... God bless me..." Klyuyev is not in the least "afraid"—he is a man who has been around and knows his worth. This is how he gets into the character of a "simple-minded peasant."

Dignifiedly he floats out onto the stage, dignifiedly bows low to the "honest folk," and then starts out as a devout man would, drawing out his "o's":

O, Sweet Bird, Bird of Paradise,
Fluffing your golden feathers...[33]

As it happened, Gorodetsky overlooked the only real poet in this genre. He read Klyuyev's manuscripts and did not pay them any attention. Klyuyev was discovered by the "soulless" Valery Bryusov.

However, having arrived in Petersburg, Klyuyev immediately fell under the influence of Gorodetsky and completely made his own the role of a *travesti en paysan*.

"Well, Nikolay Vasilyevich, how are you settling in Petersburg?"

"Praise be to God, our Patroness has not abandoned us, sinners though we are. I've got myself a little cell of a room—who am I to be needing much? Stop in, my son, you'll make me happy. I live on Morskoy Street, just around the corner."

So one day I stopped by at Klyuyev's. The cell turned out to be a room in the Hôtel de France with a wall-to-wall carpet and a wide Turkish ottoman. Klyuyev sat on the ottoman, wearing a high collar and a tie, while reading Heinrich Heine in the original.

"Yes, I can make out a few of them foreign words." He had noticed my astonished glance. "A few of them I do. It's just that they don't touch my heart. Our nightingales' voices trill sweeter, oh so much sweeter ... But what's wrong with me?" Suddenly he becomes agitated. "How am I treating such a valued guest? Sit, my son, sit down, my dove. What treats should I be treating you to? I don't drink tea, nor do I smoke tobacco, and I haven't got any honey cookies put away for you. But you know what? (he winks) If you're not in a hurry, you and I can sup together. There's a little tavern close by. The owner is a good man, even if he's French. Right here, around the corner. They call him Albert."

I was not in a hurry.

"Well, all right then, that's marvelous—I'll go change right now."

"Why are you going to change your clothes?"

"You must be kidding, really—how can I go like this? The dogs will howl from laughter. Wait a minute, I'll be back in a flash."

He came out from behind a screen wearing a *poddyovka*, oiled boots, and a crimson-colored shirt.

"There we are, much better!"

"But they won't let you into the restaurant in that getup."

"We're not trying to enter a public dining room. How can we peasants be among ladies and gentlemen? Everyone should know his place. We're not going to a public room, but to a little cell of a room, a private room set aside. They'll not turn us simple folk away from there..."

✳ ✳ ✳

The audience applauds. The audience is satisfied. Gorodetsky beams.

He is genuinely happy, this sweet, pleasant, courteous, gifted man. He's happy from the bottom of his heart that everything went so well and that everyone liked it so much, and most of all he himself, Gorodetsky. He joyfully casts his clear, open gaze about the hall, claps someone on the shoulder, shakes someone's hand, then embraces someone else ...

Accidents do occasionally occur, of course. Sologub, for example, when taking his leave, might grumble old-man style: "And where's your master of ceremonies?"

"Who do you mean, Fyodor Kuzmich?"

"Why, Leifert the costumier! You rented your bast shoes from him, right?"

But what does Sologub know about "folk art" anyway?

In Soviet days Gumilyov would often sigh:

"Too bad Gorodetsky's not here."

"He's with the Whites, seems like."

"Yes. Somewhere in the south. That, probably, is for the best. If he got stuck here, he'd be shot for sure."

"But they don't shoot us, do they?"

"We're another kettle of fish. Gorodetsky's too much of a child: gullible, excitable ... and simpleminded. He'd start to agitate, throw the truth in the faces of the Bolsheviks; he'd get caught with some jingles ... They'd have shot him for sure. Thank God he's with the Whites. But sometimes I really miss him, the joy that just poured out of him."

And he added with a smile:

"In essence, our entire friendship was that of an adult with a child. Me—the adult, serious and boring. But the way Gorodetsky lives—he lives exactly the way he would if he were playing a game of tag. It must be that this is what attracted us to each other, the fact that we were so different.

✳ ✳ ✳

In the spring of 1920 Gorodetsky came to Petersburg. He came with a brand-new Party ticket in his pocket, making way for the Communist Larisa Reisner. Her husband, the well-known Fyodor Raskolnikov, Commissar of the Baltic Fleet, captured Gorodetsky along with an OSVAG train where he was working.[34]

... This time displayed on stage is not Koltsov, but Lenin, and not pitchforks, but a hammer across a sickle. And Gorodetsky is no longer sporting a *kosovorotka,* but a rather "revolutionary" trench coat.

Reisner gave the opening remarks. "Who of us can cast a stone at him? Who of us doesn't have hands dirtied by the ink of *Speech*?[35] He lost his way, now he's ours. Let's forget the past..."

After Reisner came Gorodetsky. He tossed his locks back, surveyed the audience with his sweet, kind gray eyes, and proceeded to read poems about The Third International.

Gumilyov, shrugging his shoulders, said:

"True, how can anyone cast a stone at him? We were the first to encourage this lack of responsibility in him; in fact this is what we loved him for. It wasn't for his poems, right? So that's why he goes on playing tag now ... There's only one thing"—he adds—"I don't care for that childishness of his anymore. I've lost my taste for it. We'd be better off to live with ordinary, not-so-amusing people ... who can actually answer for themselves."

Prior to my departure for abroad, in the fall of 1922 I was in Moscow. In a tobacco shop someone patted me on the shoulder. Gorodetsky.

He looked the same as before. He looked at you just as sweetly, and smiled as before.

"And just look at me"—his smile spreads out and becomes childlike—"Who would have thought that I'd become a tobacco smoker in my old age ... Tell me, is *La Bayadère* a good brand of cigarettes?"

As he collected his change, he turned to me again, as if he suddenly remembered. Now his gray eyes peered out sadly and "soulfully":

"And poor Gumilyov! How unfortunate..."

I kept my silence.

VIII

At seven in the morning the faces of those who still lingered at the Stray Dog began to take on the look of the dead. Bright electric lights, gaudily daubed walls, leftovers and empty bottles on tables and on the floor. A drunken poet is reading poems that no one is listening to; a drunken musician with uncertain steps approaches the piano piled high with cigarette butts and bangs the keys to play a funeral march, or a polka, or both at the same time. The drowsy cloakroom attendant is asleep, having forgotten about the fur coats entrusted to his care. Boris Pronin, the director of the Stray Dog, is sitting on the snow-strewn steps in the narrow stairwell of the exit. He pets his shaggy, nasty mutt Mushka and cries bitterly:

"Mushka, Mushka—why did you eat your puppies?"

The faces look like those of the dead. Some patrons sleep, others pretend to be lively. But what kind of liveliness can this be?

Someone has turned off the electricity in the hall. Only the refreshment bar area has light, and a narrow, gray band of sunrise has crept through the open door from the street and onto the stairs where Pronin is weeping. In this twilight a man emerges from a corner and, swaying on his feet, starts walking over to me. He approaches. He looks. He seems to have red hair and a heavy, intent stare. I don't know who he is. I'm seeing him for the first time.

"You're sitting alone, and I'm alone. Let's sit together."

"Let's," I say.

"Drunk?"

"Not at all."

"Well, I'm drunk. But who cares. It's even a good thing. But you, if you're not drunk, why are you sitting here? Are you waiting for the tram?"

"I'm waiting for the train to Gatchina."

"The train ... To Gatchina ...," he repeats dreamily. "Gatchina ... The train approaches ... Snow. It's white. No. It's blue. Everything is covered in snow. The sun is rising. A flash, it's painful to look ... Some sort of dairy maids trudge along ... Steam. The trees are in hoarfrost..."

He yawns.

"But you know what, it's all nonsense. There too it stinks like soot, just like it does here. And why is it, please tell me, that you live in Gatchina?"

I said that I'm not drunk at all. But that's not true. I'm a little tipsy. I have no idea who my interlocutor is. And what business is it of his where I live. But, since I'm not completely sober, his question doesn't at all surprise me. I don't answer with "I live there because I like it" or "the air is drier there," I tell him the truth. I have moved to Gatchina because I'm in love, and the one I'm in love with lives there. My interlocutor listens silently, puffing on his short pipe. He doesn't interrupt me, and I talk, repeating the things he has just been saying to me, about the snow and the rising sun. Well all right—I am a little drunk. There's nothing wrong with that, in fact it's perfectly fine. I'm blabbering on to a stranger who silently puffs on his short pipe. He doesn't interrupt me and I blabber everything to this man about whom I know only that he smokes a pipe, right up to what "she told me last night," right up to the love poems composed the day before yesterday:

> A golden sunset. Snows
> Drowned in amber.
> Gatchina is dear to me,
> As it was in days gone by…[36]

I blab out everything. Then I become uncomfortable. I cut short a phrase without finishing. The man with the pipe is silent. Then he begins to speak deliberately:

"The best thing is to kill yourself at dawn. Of course, if you don't use poison. Poison is horrible to drink in the morning, your whole being goes into spasm. That's just the way man is made. You've decided to die. In order to die you have to swallow a shot glass full of the right liquid or take a capsule. But you're one thing and your stomach is another. It doesn't want to die. It resists. It doesn't want to swallow strychnine, it prefers coffee with cream … But shooting oneself at dawn is quite easy, and I would go as far as to say, fun."

"Is hanging oneself fun too?" I'm propping up the conversation.

"Hanging yourself can't be done for fun," he answers seriously. "Hanging yourself must be done triumphantly. Of course, it's no fun if you do it in a rush, using your own suspenders like an apprentice who has been caught stealing ... But just imagine you do everything slowly and methodically. The silk rope has been well soaped. A hook has been firmly driven into the ceiling. The noose is carefully tied. One can read a prayer, smoke a last cigarette, and drink one's last gulp of cognac. The executioner's hurrying: 'Enough of this nonsense—time to get to work.' You don't argue—it's useless. You put on the noose. 'How wonderful life is. I don't want this!' That's your stomach, your lungs, your muscles that are resisting ... But your brain, the executioner, is merciless. 'Cut it out!' Smack! The stool is kicked out from beneath your legs and rolls into a corner. Farewell, Mr. Lozina-Lozinsky! Farewell, failed poet Lyubyar!"

At this point I become uncomfortable. I know that Lyubyar is the pseudonym of a poet who attempted to kill himself several times unsuccessfully and has finally recently succeeded. I have read his poems, some nonsensical, some lucid, even too lucid, with a certain hint of insanity. They were talented poems, nevertheless. The mention of his name makes me uncomfortable. Why disturb the memory of the deceased? I say it out loud.

"That's a prejudice," my interlocutor yawns. "Why can we speak disparagingly about Pyotr Petrovich while he's alive, and not say anything after he's gone. Nonsense. And then..."

He doesn't finish saying what "then."

"Well, it's time I was going, and the same for you, Mr. Inamorato. Why don't you get a cab, then board a train—the sun, the snow ... Sweet is her sleep..."

Do not awaken her in the dim morn
Warm her drowsiness with a kiss...[37]

"However, this doesn't pertain to your case. Annensky didn't take all those kisses for the real thing. He knew what they meant..."

"So what do they mean?" I ask, looking around for my fur coat. He is silent. I don't repeat the question. There are several cabs at the entryway. My interlocutor gets the first one.

"Well, good-bye."

"Hold on!" He stops the cabman who was about to head out. "Listen, perhaps you can give me a call at some point? Here's my card. I'll be most happy, most happy … And about those kisses, Anennsky, take my word for it, he knew and always remembered all about them—the bared cute little teeth, eyes leaked out of their sockets, cute little cheeks disintegrating … Get going!"

The freezing horse pulls the sleigh friskily away. I look at his visiting card:

A. Lyubyar …
Lozina-Lozinsky …
Such-and-such street …

✳ ✳ ✳

Some two months later I received an invitation from the Bronze Horseman Society to a meeting honoring the memory of the poet Lyubyar. This time (three weeks or so after our meeting) the previously unsuccessful suicide managed to pull it off.

The evening gathering was awkward. A group of about thirty assembled in Professor S.'s huge and modernized study. First there was someone's boring talk. Then Mikhail Lozinsky read poems by Lyubyar. As always he read wonderfully, but after the reading there was a stupid mix-up with some student who proposed to express condolences "to the brother of the deceased and magnificent reader of his works," who, in actual fact, only shared the dearly departed's last name, but had never seen him in person. The professor host, trying to smooth things over … released Lidiya Yavorskaya to read some sonnets of her own composition, dedicated to various poets. As Yavorskaya, with all the pathos of an actress, finished reciting a sonnet dedicated to Kuzmin:

… and naked youths,
Forgetting their shyness, retire to an alcove …[38]

someone whistled. The professor blushed beetroot. A still greater embarrassment reigned supreme.

Tea was served. Everyone drank in silence, silently munching on petits fours. One young man, desirous of amusing the company, got it into his head to sing Armenian couplets, to his own accompaniment on the piano—

And so in Tiflis I had
A certain friend,
A lovely fellow,
Only very stupid.

—Larisa Reisner, practically a girl then, after enduring it for some time, got up, stamped her foot and shrieked out that all this was disgusting, unworthy, that she had come for an evening in honor of a poet's memory, but was being treated to vulgarities.

Everyone got their hats and hurried to get out of there. The host, purple with confusion, accompanied his guests to the door. His venerable beard was shaking and his hands trembled.

Needless to say, the evening was an outrageous bust. But as I walked home and crossed Troitsky Bridge, I remembered my recent nighttime interlocutor's little grin and thought that perhaps that hapless man would be content with just such a wake.

IX

The feud between Petersburg and Moscow had gone on for centuries. Petersburgers ridiculed "the Dog Run" and "Dead Passageway," Muscovites reproached Petersburgers for their primness, which they deemed uncharacteristic of the "Russian soul." The residents of both cities feuded with each other, and so did the artists in both capitals.

In 1919, the era of fascination with electrification and other great undertakings, one poet proposed to the Soviet government a project to unite both capitals into one. The project was simple. It required forbidding construction of new homes in Moscow and Petersburg anywhere else but along the Nikolayevsky Railway line. According to the calculations of the inventor, within ten years both cities would be united into one, "Petroscow" with the central thoroughfare, Kuz-nevsky Mos-pect. The project did not come to life because of a trifle: nothing was built in Petersburg or in Moscow—everything was destroyed. And it was a pity! Perhaps such unification would have brought to an end two centuries of bickering.

The *lubok*-like, but luxuriant blossoming of Moscow in the days of Symbolism came to end—the magazine *Libra* closed down.

The members of "the Triumphant Reaction" founded the Petersburg-based *Apollo*, and Georgy Chulkov danced a cannibal's dance over the corps of his enemy (see his "Concerning *Libra*"). Jobless Moscow "luminaries" from among the second-raters willy-nilly began to call upon colleagues in Petersburg. Some were simply looking to make a paycheck, others wanted to "destroy the enemy from within," to engage in conspiracies and establish new literary schools.

Once I chanced to be at one such a conspiratorial gathering.

K., a young man who wrote poems, drew me aside somewhere and furtively told me that Boris Sadovsky very much wanted to make my acquaintance. I was flattered. I was about eighteen and had not been especially spoiled by fame. It was true that several days ago in the Stray Dog a gentleman of bourgeois appearance introduced himself to me as my passionate admirer, but when in reply to his remark, "You are so young, and already so famous," I told him with false modesty that "Well, I'm not that famous," he exclaimed with fervor, "Come now, who doesn't know *Vyacheslav* Ivanov!"

And so I was flattered and answered that I, in my turn, would be very glad to meet Sadovsky. K. nodded happily. "That's marvelous. Come to his place tomorrow evening, I'll let him know."

A cabman drove me to a gloomy house on Kolomensky Street. The shabby sign over the entryway proclaimed "furnished rooms," called either "Toulon" or "Marseilles" or some such. There was something Mediterranean about it in any event. I warily climbed the gloomy staircase. A barefoot bellhop was carrying a steaming samovar. I asked him about Sadovsky. "Please follow me, I'm bringing the samovar to His Excellency."

He bumped the door open with his knee without knocking and entered the room, enveloping me, who was following him, in the heat.

Thus, preceded by the bellhop with the samovar, for the first time—"isn't it significant!"—I entered the quarters of a poet who had named one of his books after that tea-making contraption:

> If only I could finish with this burdensome life
> Beside my dear samovar,
> Taking my china cup,
> A quiet death from carbon monoxide.[39]

✽ ✽ ✽

I had pictured this meeting somewhat differently to myself. I thought I would be greeted by a respectable looking gentleman whose whole appearance was imprinted with his profession, that of a Symbolist poet. Something, you know, in the style of Georgy Chulkov or Ivan Rukavishnikov. He would arise from a deep armchair, put away a volume of Maeterlinck, and, having thrown back a poetical lock of hair, extend his hand to me. "Hello. I'm glad. You are one of the few who has succeeded in glancing under the veil of Isis…"

… Twenty poets were rubbing shoulders in a long and narrow "hotel room," all of them from among the greenest of youths. I knew some, others I was seeing for the first time. Thick tobacco smoke obscured faces and objects. There was a terrible racket. A thin, balding man with a yellowed lecherous face sat lounging on the bed. His tiny poisonous eyes winked, his hand banged a guitar with bravado. He sang in a tremulous falsetto:

> The soldiers of the Russian Tsar
> Will gladly sacrifice themselves …
> Not for money, not for pay,
> But for the honor of their native land.

He wore an unbuttoned nobleman's full-dress uniform with shiny buttons and a sky-blue silk *kosovorotka.* His small gouty foot wildly beat out the rhythm.

I stood bewildered—had I fallen into the wrong place? And even if it's the right one, should I leave? But my acquaintance K. had already noticed me and said something to the guitar player. The poisonous eyes bore into me with curiosity. The singing stopped.

"Ivanov!" The host bellowed nasally, putting the stress on the "o." "Welcome, Ivanov. Do you drink vodka? The caviar has been gobbled up, you shouldn't have come late! You can catch up now though—we'll be warming some punch."

He made a gesture of invitation in the direction of a table that was crowded with every imaginable type of bottle, and started singing once more:

Hey there, vodka,
Hussar's aunty!
Hey there, hot punch,
Hussar's wifey!

"Sing along, lads!" he suddenly shouted, sounding exactly like a rooster now. "Drink up, Russian Nobility! Hurrah! God is on our side!"

I looked around. "The Russian Nobility" was plastered, as was the host. They heated up the punch, spilling hot alcohol onto the rug; they read poems, sang, drank, gulped down the punch, shouted "hurrah," and hugged each other. I didn't remain sober for very long either. "Ivanov's not drinking. Give him a goblet of White Eagle!" ordered Sadovsky. There was no way to get out of it. A tea glass filled with some horrible concoction immediately altered my mood. The company seemed to be extra sweet, and the bossy-friendly tone of the host completely natural.

… The tobacco smoke got ever stronger. Glasses fell from hands still more frequently, smashing to smithereens. As if in a dream, I remember the arrogantly wooden features of Nicholas I looking at me from all the walls, and Sadovsky's dress uniform stained with wine, his dry, yellowed finger, raised toward my face, and his didactic whisper:

"Inebriation is the intercourse of our astral substance with the music (stress on the "i") of the universe…"

✳ ✳ ✳

The same room. The same voice … The same penetrating, poisonous little eyes below his bald forehead. But his room is respectably neat, and Sadovsky's falsetto sounds prim, ingratiating. In his long draped coat he looks more like a psalm reader than a debauched hussar.

On the walls, on the table, and by the bed, everywhere hang portraits of Nicholas I. About ten of them. On horseback, in profile, in a winter coat, on horseback again. I look at them surprised.

"That valiant man of courage," explains Sadovsky, "was the greatest of all rulers, not only in Russia, but throughout the entire globe. Take his little boy, though," he trades his high-flown tone for an old-woman's babble, "his little sonny-boy was an insignificant goose. Such an ugly horror he perpetrated, set free all those louts. And one of them bumped him off…"

Among the portraits of the Russian Tsars, beginning with Mikhail Fyodorovich, hung and placed in every corner of the room, there was none of Alexander II.

"There's no room for him in nobleman Sadovsky's home."

"But you haven't been in Petersburg very long. Why do you always bring these portraits along with you?"

"Yes, I bring them."

"Wherever you might go?"

"Even to Siberia. I take them all when I'm traveling for some time, let's say for about two months. If I go for a week, I take only Nikolay Pavlovich, Alexander the Blessed, Catherine-our-Little-Mother, and Peter. And Elizaveta Petrovna, she comes too. True, she was a so-so tsarina, but she had a comely shape. Like a merchant's wife! That I like very much!"

Sadovsky sets forth his "ideas" while boring into his interlocutor with his sharp eyes: is he taking this seriously? I've already been told that his love of serfdom and nobility are an act, and I don't take them seriously.

His sharp eyes look out penetratingly and cunningly. "The sacred mission of the upper class…" He breaks off without finishing the phrase. "The hell with all that. Let's talk about poetry!"

"Let's."

* * *

Boris Sadovsky was a weak poet. As a matter of fact, he was no poet at all. He had only one quality required of a Russian poet—laziness. It was laziness that prevented him from pursuing his real calling, that of a literary critic.

If Sadovsky is still remembered for his pale and competent poems, his articles have been forgotten by everyone. Unfairly forgotten. Sadovsky's two little books, *Winter Crop* and *Ice Drift*, are worth more than many a "respectable" work of criticism.

It was not without reason that Sadovsky's literary enemies called him the "guard dog of *Libra*." When someone complied a list of his curses, some of them not fit to print, it occupied a half page in eight-point brevier.

But behind his swearing lay a sharp mind and a thorough, consummate understanding of poetry. Beyond the polemics, personal grudges, a nobleman's eccentricities, all that "blessed memory of Nicholas I," there were quite remarkable pages.

By the way, Sadovsky's career illustrates how dangerous it is for a writer to hold himself in proud isolation. To sit in one's corner and write poems isn't all that bad. But Sadovsky, when his coincidental and unfirm connection to the Moscow "decadents" was sundered, attempted "to swim against the current," offering up "a free voice" from his "farmstead Borisovka, also known as Sadovsky." For that he got eaten alive.

The publication of *Winter Crop* and *Ice Drift* was met with universal booing. To his misfortune, Sadovsky wittily couched his remarks concerning poetry in the Prussian style, comparing Briusov to Wilhelm, Gumilyov to the Crown Prince, and calling the rest their "lieutenants." "Gumilyov is spilling his blood at the front, and we will not allow…" Sergey Auslender pounded his chest in "letters to the editor." "We will not allow…" Sergey Gorodetsky pounded his chest in turn. It was a time of war and things went badly for Sadovsky. That anti-Gumilyovian "slander" prevented everyone from reading, or at least appreciating, his remarkable article on Mikhail Lermontov, to mention but one example, which may well be the best one ever written:

" … This collection of Lermontov's narrative poems is in essence a stack of inspired drafts that failed to become fair copies due to his death…"

✳ ✳ ✳

In Sadovsky's entourage there was another amusing figure, another "former Muscovite," the poet Alexander Tinyakov-Odinoky. At Sadovsky's court he was something of a valet or an aide-de-camp.

"Aleksandr Ivanovich, my dear fellow, won't you fetch some cigarettes." Tinyakov would bring the cigarettes. "Aleksandr Ivanovich, some beer!" "Aleksandr Ivanovich, where was it that Kant said such-and-such?" Tinyakov would answer without so much as a stumble.

He was a man of frightening appearance, ragged, overgrown with hair, walking about in worn-out shoes—and extremely erudite. He had studied everything, from cuneiform writing to hypnosis. His hobbyhorse was the Talmud, which he had studied with incredible thoroughness, and which he interpreted somewhat peculiarly. When he was sober he was meek, with a beaten-down and sad appearance. When drunk, and he was almost always drunk, he would become enterprising.

The Stray Dog. A gentleman and a lady are sitting at a table, casual visitors both. In the jargon of the Stray Dog they both qualified as "pharmacists." They had paid the three-ruble entrance fee and are observing the "bohemians" with eyes wide open.

Tinyakov walks past them with an unsteady gait. He stops. He fixes his blurry eyes on them. He sits at their table without asking. He takes the lady's glass, pours some wine and drinks.

The "pharmacists" are surprised but do not protest. "Bohemian mores … Rather interesting…"

Tinyakov pours himself some more wine. "Gonna read some poems, want me to?"

"Bohemian mores … A poet … How interesting … Yes, please do, we're so glad…"

Tinyakov reads, hiccupping as he goes:

It's my delight, spit-wad spit that I am,
To float by in the gutter,
Pressing up along the slippery side…[40]

"Well now … How'd you like it? How else, you liked it very much! And did you get it? And what did you get? Go on now, tell me in your own words…"

The gentleman wavers: "Well … these poems … you say … that you are a spit-wad … and…"

A tremendous smash of the fist on the table. The bottle flies onto the floor. The lady jumps up, frightened to death. Tinyakov shouts in an savage voice:

"Ha! I'm a spit-wad! I'm a spit-wad! Then you're a…"

In 1920 this same Tinyakov unexpectedly turned up in Petersburg. He looked as he always did: dirty, rumpled, unshaven. No one was interested in where he came from and what he did. One time he came as a guest to the writer G. They talked about this and that and then turned to politics. Tinyakov asked G. what he thought of the Bolsheviks. The writer unburdened his thoughts without any shyness.

"Ah, so that's how it is," said Tinyakov. "That means that you are an adversary of workers-and-peasants power! I didn't expect this! Even if we're friends, there's going to have to be a search of your place." And he pulled out of his pocket a mandate from some provincial Cheka office …

In 1916 I was in Moscow and had breakfast with Sadovsky at the Prague. Sadovsky was, as he put it, "treating" me. Breakfast was splendid, the bill rather substantial. When they brought the change, Sadovsky counted it, hid it, felt around in his pocket, and produced two five-kopeck copper coins. "Hey, lackey!" he threw the five-kopeck coins on the table. "Here, get yourself some vodka!" "We thank you humbly, Boris Aleksandrovich." The lackey bowed obsequiously, as if he had received an out-of-this-world tip. I was astounded. "Spoiled bunch," Sadovsky growled. "During the reign of Catherine-our-Little-Mother you could buy a calf for a ten-kopeck piece…"

He slowly donned his soiled greatcoat. One lackey gave him his cane, another his scarf, and a third his aristocratic peaked cap.

A few days later I strolled into the Prague alone. I was waited on by the same lackey. "Dare I ask, if Boris Aleksandrovich is not well—I haven't seen him in quite some time?" "No, he's healthy." "Well, thank God, he's such a fine gentleman." "Well, it seems, he doesn't spoil you with his tips?" The lackey broke into a grin. "Are you talking about the ten kopecks?

Sometimes it's ten kopecks, and sometimes His Excellency leaves twenty-five rubles ... Can't complain, such a fine gentleman ..."

X

In the autumn of 1910 a young man emerged from the third-class carriage of a train arriving from abroad. No one met him, he had no baggage—he had lost his only suitcase en route.

The traveler was dressed strangely. He wore a broad shabby cape, an alpine hat, bright ruddy shoes, unpolished and worn. A Scottish plaid was thrown over his left arm, his right hand clutched a sandwich ...

Just like that, sandwich in hand, he made his way over to the exit. Petersburg greeted him with hostility: a light cold rain over the Obvodny canal wafted impecuniousness. A policeman in oilskin below a muted sky in a gloomy recess along Izmaylovsky Avenue demanded the traveler's permit to reside in Petersburg.

The traveler was named Osip Emilyevich Mandelstam. In the suitcase he had lost in Eydkunen, apart from his toothbrush and a volume of Henri Bergson, there was a ruffled notebook of poems. The only substantial loss, however, was the toothbrush. His poems and Bergson's writings Mandelstam had committed to memory.

" ... At your age I earned my own bread!"

Ruffled eyebrows loom threateningly over the birdlike little face. Splattering, the plate of soup jumps to the middle of the table. Napkin flies into corner ...

Father is in a bad mood. He's always in a bad mood, Mandelstam's father. He's a failed businessman, consumptive, set-upon, forever fantasizing. He is constantly hopeful that his leather business will go well. Yet these hopes of his are constantly dashed: no luck, this didn't turn out, that went bust ...

His mother is a heavyset, anemic, goodhearted, helpless woman who sneaks her son a ruble she has secretly withheld from the household budget. His dried-out ninety-year-old grandma, trifocals on her nose, is hunched over the Bible: she's counting out the time until the coming of the Messiah ...

In winter it's a dark Petersburg apartment, in summer—a sullen dacha. Both winter and summer meals are taken in menacing silence, conversations are in whispers. Fear of a knock, fear of the telephone's ring. The bailiff's shadow is polite and implacable, the smoke of dark-brown sealing wax ... Mother's tears: "What are we to do?" Father is like a Leyden jar, touch him and he may explode and kill you ...

The hanging lamp sheds a sullen light. You don't feel like drinking your tea. "What are we to do?" The promissory note has been referred to the court ...

A pregnant silence. Grandma's hoarse whisper from the next room. She's hunched over the Bible: terrible, incomprehensible ancient Hebrew words.

And yet we pull through somehow. The bailiff removed the seals. They've agreed to reissue the promissory note. New hope all over again: it seems the export of butter will go well ...

But everyone knows nothing will get better, that it's all untrue, shaky, and will end in something dreadful, in a heart attack, suicide, poverty.

... The skinny, swarthy, unattractive adolescent finally breaks away from tedious tea-drinking and goes to his room to read *The Critique of Pure Reason*. It's difficult to read. The Kuno Fischer, however, is tossed under the table—to hell with Kuno Fischer.

It's still difficult to follow Kant "with one's head," but Mandelstam's whole being is already absorbing that Kantian "marvelous chill." There's a little noise in his head, and it is also "marvelous": the sweetest way to read, not with one's mind, but with premonition ...

He puts the book away and goes over to the window. On deserted Kamennoostrovsky streetlamps are burning. In the frosty air, winter stars. How spacious is the Petersburg expanse, the world, the cosmos ...

"Osip, go to bed. Father will get mad again."

"Oh, right away, Mama."

... Fog in his head. Kant ... Music ... Life ... Death ... His heart starts pounding ... His lips begin to move.

Your image, tortured and tremulous,
I could not sense it in the mist.
"Dear Lord!" I said by mistake,
Not meaning to say it.

God's name, like a large bird,
Flew from my chest—
In front the thick mist swirls,
And an empty cage behind...[41]

***

Mandelstam is the most easily amused creature in the universe.

No matter where he is, no matter what he's doing—just give him a wink and all his seriousness melts away. A minute ago he was having an important and learned conversation with a no less important and learned interlocutor, and suddenly:

"Ha, ha, ha, ha..."

He laughs himself to the point of suffocating. His face becomes red, his eyes fill with tears. His interlocutor is surprised and shocked. What's happening to this young man who has been reasoning so cleverly, so insightfully? Could he be sick?

Oh no, he's not sick. On second thought—why shouldn't he be sick? After all, that would be a more plausible explanation for his laughter than its actual cause: someone sneezed, a fly landed on someone's bald pate...

"Why bother writing humorous stories?" Mandelstam sincerely wonders. "Really, *everything* is funny as it is."

Once Mandelstam and I were walking along Sergiyevsky Street, past the house where two years ago he lived with his aunt and uncle, after being "temporarily" cursed and thrown out by his father (it happened often). I visited him several times in that exile of his. Mandelstam was living there incomparably better than at home. His uncle and aunt coddled him extravagantly. His aunt, cheerful, rosy, round like a balloon, overfed him with something greasy and tasty, as his thin and bald uncle kept treating him to good cigarettes and cognac, while stuffing his pocket with five-ruble notes. Mandelstam also loved them most sincerely.

"Wonderful old codgers, sweet old things..."

We were walking past the house of those "wonderful old codgers." I noticed a white "to let" signs on the windows of their apartment.

"Have your relatives moved somewhere? Where are they living now?"

"Living? Ha ... ha ... ha ... No, not here ... Ha ... ha ... ha ... Yes, they've moved."

I am surprised.

"So, they've moved, what's funny about that?"

His face turns bright red.

"What's funny? Ha ... ha ... Just ask me, *where* they've moved!"

Chocking with laughter, he clarifies:

"Last year ... Off they went ... From cholera ... They moved to the other world!"

And, absolving himself from his unseemly cheerfulness, he says:

"It's shameful to laugh ... They were so wonderful ... But it's so funny—both of them, cholera ... And you ... you go asking 'Where they've mo ... ' Ha ... ha ... ha ... Mo ... Moved!"

He is giggly—but sensitive, too.

After talking to Mandelstam for an hour, it's impossible not to offend him, the same way it's impossible not to get him laughing. It often happens that one and the same thing will first make him laugh, and then later offend him. Or the other way around.

But then this proclivity toward experiencing slights, be they real or imagined, with particular sharpness, is a trait "common to poets." Next comes the ability to make fun of those slights—and of oneself.

Mandelstam took offense at not being handsome, well-off, at people not listening to his poems and at their laughing at how impassioned he was ...

The reader may ask: "Well, what about Byron?" He was handsome, famous, and rich, but then he still had a slight limp. Oh, only tiny, barely detectable. But it may well be that all of "Byronism" stemmed from this slight limp ...

Indeed, this is a trait "common to poets." It is just that the evil fairy who controls the fate of poets somehow took a "special interest" in Mandelstam. She gave him the most pure, most "angelic" gift and cast him out into the world quite naked, defenseless, maladjusted ... Fend for yourself as best you can.

And fend for himself he did:

For us—abandoned in space,
Fated to die, as we are—
There is no need to grieve for magnificent constancy
And loyalty![42]

The poems, composed in Switzerland or Heidelberg by a Russian student who surprised the local inhabitants with his funny-looking checkered plaid, his sparse red side whiskers, and his habit of walking about somewhere in the park during school hours, mumbling under his nose in a monotone (that's how his poems were composed), those poems, the manuscript of which had been lost along with the Bergson and his toothbrush, appeared in the November issue of *Apollo*.

A body given to me—what shall I do with it,
so one and so my own?
For the quiet joy breathing and living,
tell me whom am I to thank?
I am the gardener, I am the flower too,
I'm not lonely in the prison of the world.[43]

Upon reading this and several other "swaying" misty poems signed with a name unfamiliar to me, I experienced a tremor in my heart:

"Why wasn't it I who wrote this?"

That kind of "poetic envy" is a most characteristic feeling. Gumilyov considered it to be the most accurate among judgments in defining the "weight" of others' poems. If "why not I" has stirred within you, it means that the poems are "genuine."

The poems were astonishing. Indeed, astonishing. First and foremost, they *astonished*.

At that time I very much "respected" *Apollo*, perhaps even to excess. I had not yet published there myself, and I regarded all who had as some sort of initiates. Up until that November issue of 1910, I sincerely considered everything published in the poetry section of that magazine *poetry*. But the issue that contained Mandelstam's poems for the first time led me into "fatal apprehension." The issue looked somehow special, unlike previous ones. And that was not to the issue's credit . . .

For the first time, the shimmer of the "Silver-Bowed One" appeared to me somewhat . . . tinny.

> . . . My breath and my warmth
> Have already lain on the windowpanes of eternity . . . [44]

The poems signed with an unknown name, "O. Mandelstam," glimmered, shone, turned cold like stars in water. And that "celestial" proximity all too vividly revealed the true nature of its surroundings—the printer's ink and high-quality vergé paper.

About two weeks later, in his Tsarskoye Selo dining room, Gumilyov, smiling condescendingly (he always smiled condescendingly), introduced us:

"Mandelstam. Georgy Ivanov."

So that's what he looks like—Mandelstam!

On his puny body (his suit, it went without saying, was checkered, and the pant knees, it went without saying, were stretched beyond the limit, which in no way interfered with his evident dandyism: the silk breast pocket handkerchief, the tie, all askew, but polka-dotted, etc.), on his puny little body sits an incongruously large head. Perhaps it isn't really that large, but looks that way when thrown back so exaggeratedly on his overly thin neck; his soft orange-red luxuriant hair tumbles about and stands on end (and in the midst of it a bald spot—and quite a large one), and his protruding ears stick way out … And in addition to all this the wispy tufts of his Chichikovian sideburns! And that head of his seems incongruously large.

His eyes squint, the eyelids half-closed so that one can't see the eyes. His movements are strangely lacking in freedom. He offers his hand and immediately withdraws it. He nods, and within a second stands even more ramrod straight than before. As if he's on a string.

He started speaking to me for some unknown reason in French, assiduously rolling his r's. On one overly "Parisian" "r" he somehow tripped up. He tripped up, grew silent, blushed a thick crimson shade, and again stood ramrod straight with even more hauteur …

What happened was this: not knowing me at all, not having exchanged even one coherent phrase with me, Mandelstam had already taken offense at me. Whatever for? Because he hadn't pronounced something quite right, or hadn't extended his hand in a particular way—and I may have observed this and, to myself, surely had thought something about it …

A quarter of an hour later, however, at tea he was laughing at some nonsense I said in passing until his eyes filled with tears. It was something about the cabman who took me somewhere, some sort of nonsense. He laughed like a child, burying his face in a napkin and gasping for air.

When I first heard Mandelstam reading his poems, I was surprised again.

I had plenty of opportunity to accustom myself to strange styles of recitation. All poets read "uniquely," one with a slight lisp, another with a bit of wailing. Without the least surprise I had listened to Igor Severyanin's "chasonnette-like" reading, to Gorodetsky's roar, and to Georgy Chulkov's funeral dirge. Nonetheless Mandelstam's reading bowled me over.

He too sang and wailed a bit. Keeping time to his singing, he also shook his head, burdened as it was with those ears and side whiskers, and made some kind of flutters with his hands. In conjunction with his appearance this singing of his should have seemed very funny. However, it did not.

Quite the opposite: Mandelstam's reading, for all its absurdity, was somehow bewitching. He sang along and wailed, swaying his head on his thin neck, and I felt some sort of chill, terror, agitation, as if in the presence of the supernatural. Such a pure manifestation of the whole essence of poetry was in that reading, as in that man (in everything, in everything—even in those checkered trousers of his), that I had never seen in my life.

And yet again I had to be surprised on the first day of our acquaintance. Having finished reading, Mandelstam raised his eyelids, slowly, like an ostrich. His red, lashless eyelids hid beaming, piercing, splendid eyes.

✴ ✴ ✴

"Above the yellow of government buildings" the sphere of the frosty sun glows without emitting any warmth. Cabmen transport their riders, ministers are ensconced in sumptuous offices, washerwomen pound icy laundry, and officers of the Horse Guards breakfast at the Bear. But what does all this regimen of tsarist Petersburg have to do with him, Mandelstam, someone who does indeed appear to have dropped on the Petersburg pavement from some planet Mars? He's got no money. His protruding ears are freezing.

> A row of motorcars flies into the fog,
> A self-regarding modest pedestrian,
> Eccentric Eugene, ashamed of his poverty,
> Breathes in gasoline, and curses his fate...[45]

Well all right, this is an occupation as good as any other—sauntering along the sidewalk, breathing in gasoline while being ashamed of one's poverty! Moreover, because—

> ... If he so desires, a poet finds
> Happiness even in wet asphalt...[46]

Soon after he returned from abroad (his parents' home had become "no place to be"), Mandelstam began to live independently.

Mandelstam and independent life!

Yet he managed somehow. At the price of long conversations and complicated exchanges of a pile of clean laundry for a still greater one of unwashed clothes—from the strong, reddened hands of washerwomen were extracted the dazzlingly colored motley shirts in which Mandelstam loved to shine. By some sort of miracle petty tailors, by nature not inclined to ready outfits on credit, were persuaded, sighing and shaking their heads, to make him large-checkered suits to fit his absurd physique. That, and having some pocket money, was the most complicated part of his independent existence. An apartment and a table were easily obtained: sympathetic retired colonels and kind-hearted elderly Jews who rented apartments without bothering their tenants too much existed in prerevolutionary Petersburg … Pocket money was necessary for tobacco and black coffee: in order to write a five-stanza poem, Mandelstam required on average eight hours, and in the course of that time he destroyed no less than fifty cigarettes and a half-pound of coffee.

If there was positively no money, there remained one last way out, tedious but surefire. One could slide under the frozen top of a cab as if into an abyss. "Off you go…"

Nothing to pay with. But one must pay. That means someone, somewhere will pay. And most likely he who pays the cabman, will find a three-ruble note for the passenger as well …

… The frost-covered cabman shambles off in an "unknown direction." Other cabmen flicker by, knowing where they are going, with fares that have apartments and liquid bank accounts. In the store windows of Yeliseyev's shadows of pineapples and wine bottles flash by, and the ghost of a lobster curls its red, lacy tail on the ice. Reserved seats for the international cars to Berlin, Paris, and Italy are being sold on the corner of Konyushenny Street and Nevsky Prospect … Women made bright red from the frost wrap themselves in their sables; behind the windows of flower shops one can see piles of cut roses. And all of this is so ephemeral … an appearance …

In reality there's his greatcoat, knocked about by the wind, his room from which he's being evicted, the cabman—it's not known who will pay him—his unpretty face with ears turning purple from the cold, real and imagined insults, the imagined ones often sting worse than the real ones ... And on and on, but there is a singular, pathetic consolation:

> ... If he so desires, a poet finds,
> Happiness even in wet asphalt ...

" ... Why write comical things. I don't understand, really everything is already so *funny*..."

One time Mandelstam had to travel without delay to Warsaw. He was in love (hopelessly, it goes without saying). And on the results of his journey hung (or it seemed to him it did) "his entire fate." It was wartime, but he demonstrated unheard of energy and arranged for all the needed passes and permissions. But in all his running around he forgot one "trifle," money for the trip.

He had to be in Warsaw—"absolutely or I'll die"—by a certain time. And here he was, without money and faced with the complete impossibility of getting any. I ran into him in the doorway of some editorial office where his "magnificent gift" was "highly valued," but of course he was not given an advance. He said then:

"I've only now understood that one can die right in front of everyone's eyes and no one will even turn around..."

He landed in Warsaw anyhow. Dearly departed Nikolay Wrangel took him in his hospital train. In Warsaw his "fate" underwent a kind of catastrophe—he fought a duel, unsuccessfully, of course. Having rested up in the hospital, he returned to Petersburg. The day after his return I ran into him at the Stray Dog. Chocking with laughter, he read a quatrain he's just written:

> Don't feel low,
> Get on the tram,
> So empty,
> So Number Eight...[47]

✳ ✳ ✳

When "October" arrived and "the failures of all countries" were promised palaces, grand meals, and every sort of success, Mandelstam wound up "on that side" with the Bolsheviks. Put more exactly, he wound up in the vicinity of the Bolsheviks. He didn't join the Party (out of timidity, most likely: "If the Whites come, they'll hang me"), and he did not become some People's Commissar's deputy. He hung around somewhere, flattered someone, shook hands here and there—shook hands he should not have shaken, and obtained certain advantages in exchange for that. This was, of course, not entirely right, but not so terrible either, if one thinks what a little "bird of God" Mandelstam was (and hungry, helpless and alone all at the same time). Among "the Russian literati"—many of whom were far from being "birds of God" like Mandelstam—he would not be the only one compelled to draw an elegiac sigh—

> I shook such dirty hands,
> I agreed to such things[48]

—upon recalling themselves in the years 1919–1920 and Smolny, "The Astoria," "The White Corridor" of the Kremlin ...

... The year is 1918. Wilhelm von Mirbach has not been assassinated yet. The Soviet government is still a coalition of Bolsheviks and Left Socialist Revolutionaries. So here we are: at some expropriated Moscow grand house a "coalition" drinking bash is underway. I can't depict that or a similar bash for one simple reason: I never went to any. But it's not hard to imagine one: intelligentsia-type clipped beards and gold-rimmed spectacles mixed with leather jackets. Soviet ladies. "Here's to sweet women, charming women..." "Baby-Doll..." "The International." Lots of people, lots of drink, plenty of grub. And right there, among all those spectacles and "Baby-Dolls," "The International," the vodka and the caviar, stands Mandelstam. The "bird of God" has latched on to that caviar, to those heated and brightly lit rooms, to the "money exchange bill" that Olga Kameneva will issue him tomorrow, if he manages to flatter her cleverly today. Everyone is drunk. Mandelstam is also tipsy. He's only a bit tipsy because he doesn't like to drink. He's more after the pastry, the caviar, and a bit of ham ...

A Soviet drinking bash, of course, is also hilarious, and like any gathering of people it is also "individualized" by the Soviet manners of the "charming women" and by the "powerful International" and by who knows what else. "The coalition" is drinking; Mandelstam eats caviar and pastry. Kameneva smiles at his clever flattery and says: "Come around and see my secretary tomorrow." "Baby-Doll" speaks loudly. It's warm. Everything's all right. Everything's pleasant. Everything's amusing. And ... no need to drink a lot, perhaps one shot glass and then one more ...

But suddenly the smile on Mandelstam's face grows pale, droops, and looks perplexed ... What's that about? Has he drunk too much? Or did the ash of the delicious cigarette provided by the host burn through the cloth of his newly tailored suit, one procured after so many difficulties?

Or perhaps his teeth, his unfortunate teeth that constantly ache since he can't pluck up the courage to go to the dentist who is certain to start drilling into them, have those teeth begun smarting from all the sugar and candies?

No, it's something else.

A confounded smile on his face and an unfinished biscuit in his hand, Mandelstam is staring at a young man in a leather jacket seated not far away. Mandelstam knows him. This is Yakov Blumkin, a Left Socialist Revolutionary. Mandelstam knows and fears him, the way he fears all leather jackets, naturally. He definitely prefers Anatoly Lunacharsky's softly glinting glasses or Kameneva's immaculately perfumed and mani-cured little hands. Leather jackets frighten him, but this Blumkin guy especially so. He's a Cheka guy through and through, a mass executioner, a frightful, horrible man ... Usually Mandelstam tries to give him a wide berth, avoiding all eye contact. Right now, though, he is staring at him without averting his eyes, and with such a strange, pathetic, confounded look. What is the matter?

Blumkin has had too much to drink. But you can't say that he looks completely drunk. His movements are heavy, but confident. He's laying out a piece of paper on the table in front of him—some sort of list; he makes it smooth with the palm of his hand, slowly rereads, slowly goes over it with a pencil, making some kind of notations. Then, with the same heaviness and confidence, he takes from the pocket of his leather jacket a stack of some blank forms ...

"Blumkin, what are you busy with over there? Drink to the Revolution!"

With some difficulty, in a voice that is as heavy yet confident, the man responds:

"Hold on. I've got some blanks to fill out—counterrevolutionaries, you know ... Sidorov? Ah, I remember. To be shot. Petrov? Who's this Petrov? Well, what difference does this make, to be shot as well..."

This is what Mandelstam is looking at, this is what he is listening to, that homeless "bird of God" that flittered in here to get warmed up, to peck at some caviar, and to weasel out some "money exchange bill" or other.

What he is hearing and seeing is this:

" ... Sidorov? Ah, I remember, to be shot..."

... The blank forms are already signed by Felix Dzerzhinsky. In advance. The proper stamp is attached. "Mr. Golden Heart" trusts his coworkers "totally." All that is needed is to write in the last names and ... So that's why the drunken Chekist's pencil heavily, but confidently, hovers over the stack of blank forms now.

" ... Petrov? Who's this Petrov? Well, all the same..."

And Mandelstam, who quivers at the sight of a dentist's drill as if it were a guillotine, suddenly jumps up, runs over to Blumkin, grabs the blank forms, and tears them to bits.

Next, before Blumkin or anyone else comes to their senses, Mandelstam runs headlong out of the room, rolls down the stairs, and runs on and on without a hat, without a coat, into the night streets of Moscow, through the snow, along the railroad tracks, all the time with one and only one thought: "I'm dead, I'm dead, I'm dead..." He spends the whole night wandering about Moscow in terrible agitation. Perhaps it was thanks to that agitation that he, who would catch tonsillitis from a mere draft, in this case, after being out in the frost all night without his coat, didn't even come down with a cold. "What were you thinking about?" I asked him. "Nothing at all. I read some poems, my own, others'. Smoked. When dawn started to come up and the Kremlin became a little rosy, I sat down on a bench near the Moscow river and began to cry…"

He sat on a bench and began to cry. Then he got up and dragged himself into that same slightly rosy Kremlin, to Kameneva.

Kameneva, of course, was still asleep, so he had to wait. At 10:00 am Kameneva awoke and was informed Mandelstam was waiting to see her. She came out, clasped her hands and said:

"Go into the washroom, comb your hair, clean yourself up! I'll give you Lev Borisovich's greatcoat. I can't take you to Comrade Dzerzhinsky looking like that."

And Mandelstam "got himself cleaned up" in Comrade Kamenev's washroom, poured Comrade Kamenev's eau de cologne over his head, retied his tie, and polished his shoes. Then he drank tea with Kameneva. They drank in silence.

> She was silent, and he was silent.
> And what is there to talk about, my friend?[49]

Then they set out by car.

Dzerzhinsky took them in immediately. He heard out Kameneva, paying close attention. He heard her out, tugging at his small beard.

He got up. He extended his hand to Mandelstam.

"I thank you, comrade. You acted as any honest citizen should have acted in your place." Then Dzerzhinsky spoke into the telephone. "Immediately arrest Comrade Blumkin and assemble the board of the All-Union Extraordinary Committee to review his case." And once again, to Mandelstam, who was shaking with a tremor of happiness:

"Blumkin will face the firing squad this very day."

"C-c-comrade…" Mandelstam began, but his tongue would not obey him, and Kameneva was already pulling him by the sleeve out of the office. So he never got a chance to articulate what he wanted to articulate: a request to arrest Blumkin, exile him someplace (oh, how terrible it would be if Blumkin were to stay in Moscow—what would Mandelstam's life be like?). But…"if it's possible," don't make him face the firing squad.

But Kameneva had already led him out of the office, taken him home, pushed some money into his hands, and ordered him to stay at home some two days and not to show his face "until this whole affair dies down…"

Mandelstam was not destined to fulfill this advice. Blumkin was arrested at noon. At 2:00 pm he appeared before "the most severe revolutionary court," yet at 5:00 pm some well-wisher called Mandelstam on the phone and told him: "Blumkin is at large and looking for you all over town."

Only several days later after he got to Georgia could Mandelstam draw a sigh of relief. How he managed to get there—God only knows. But get there he did, and that was where he drew a sigh of relief. Relief, however, was rather relative: taken for a Bolshevik spy, he was jailed.

Several months later Blumkin was in "more serious" hot water than signing execution orders in a drunken state: he assassinated Count von Mirbach. Out of caution, Mandelstam let the events "blow over": who knew how it might still turn out? But everything went swimmingly—the Left Socialist Revolutionaries wound up in various jails, and Blumkin, sentenced to death by firing squad in absentia, disappeared. Mandelstam began to get ready to go to Moscow. He didn't have any money, and that "energy of horror," that carried him like a miracle from Moscow to Georgia left him too. But no fear, he managed. He was helped by friends, Georgian poets. They got busy and managed to secure for Mandelstam … an official deportation order from Georgia.

The first person who crossed Mandelstam's path when he had just arrived and had stopped to look at "what and how" in the poets' café was … Blumkin. Mandelstam fainted. The owners of the café, the Imaginists, persuaded Blumkin to put away his Mauser.[50] Blumkin's rage, however, had cooled anyway after two years: when Mandelstam fled from him to Petersburg practically the same night, Blumkin did not chase after him …

XI

Two narrow rooms with windows near the ceiling as in a basement. But this is not a basement: on the contrary, it's the sixth floor. If one gets on one's toes, or better yet stands on a chair, one can see the snow-covered Tauride Garden down below.

The rooms are small. The furniture is mismatched. On the walls hang reproductions of Botticelli: sad and tender angel-children against the backdrop of a mellow landscape, half-Edenic, half-earthly. Many books. If one glances at their spines, one notices the collection is motley. Saints' lives, Giacomo Casanova's *Memoirs*, Rainer Maria Rilke and François Rabelais, Nikolay Leskov and Oscar Wilde. A volume of Aristophanes in the original lies open on the desk. In the corner, in front of darkened icons, hangs a blue "archbishop's" sanctuary lamp. One senses the mixed smell of perfume, tobacco, and burnt candlewick. The room is hotly heated. The winter sun shines very bright.

Such are Mikhail Kuzmin's rooms in Vyacheslav Ivanov's apartment.

First comes the drawing room, next the bedroom. Kuzmin gets up around ten and works in the bedroom at a bureau, the same type merchants use to add their accounts. He works standing. One falls asleep when seated, he insists. Most of the time, he writes without making corrections. He'll scrawl out several pages, chew on the back end of his pen, then fill up more pages without a break and with almost no alterations.

While Kuzmin works, visitors begin to assemble in his "drawing room." There are some well-groomed civilians, some cadets. One sports the green cuffs of the Imperial School of Jurisprudence and the red ones worn by the students of the Imperial Lyceum.

These are aesthetes, admirers of the "Petersburg Wilde," the name they've bestowed on Kuzmin.

While the *maître* is at work, the aesthetes chatter in low voices.

"Right now I'm rereading Leconte de Lisle," says one of them, "It's so splendid."

Another one, not so literary, squints his eyes distractedly:

"Quel est ce comte, André?"

"Villiers de L'Isle-Adam, my darling," injects sarcastically a third.

But the literary aesthete doesn't sense the sarcasm. He shrugs his shoulders indifferently:

"Connais pas…"

" … such geniuses as Leonardo da Vinci…"

" … Leonardo, Leonardo, what's this about your Leonardo? If Akim Volynsky hadn't written a book about him, no one would remember him. Now take Klever…"

" … And Petka caused an uproar again at the Bear. Have you heard?" injects the completely unenlightened aesthete, who has grown tired of learned conversations. "He got plastered, told them to bring a bowl, and he put a lobster in it…" Those conversing about Leonardo look at him disapprovingly: he is screaming his head off about some nonsense or other. "What would the *maître* say?"

The *maître* is actually interested.

"You don't say, Georgie? Got plastered again! Ha, ha! Put a lobster in a bowl! Ha, ha! And then what? What happened next? He wanted to fight? What a daredevil! Did he get away without a police report? Well, thank God for that! He'll get it just the same from his cavalry captain. Will he stop by? Is he resting at home? We should visit the poor fellow…"

Kuzmin returns to his bureau. The maid brings tea. Munching on English cookies and smoking Egyptian cigarettes, the aesthetes carry on with their chatter.

" … Rodgers was enthralling yesterday…"

The evening of the same day. Vyacheslav Ivanov is entertaining some guests. His vaulted hall filled with antique Italian furniture, "the Sage of Tauride Street" is conducting a grave conversation concerning some rare and erudite topic. This is not a "Wednesday," when all of literary Petersburg gathers in this drawing room; several chosen "initiates" have come together to talk over "the mysteries of art" inaccessible to mere mortals.

Kuzmin is not here. But that is quite natural. What would he do with himself among these gray-bearded professors?

But wait—Vyacheslav Ivanov has already twice sent someone to inquire "has Mikhail Aleksandrovich returned yet?" Finally Kuzmin enters. A cigarette between his teeth, the smell of perfume about him and a dandified suit complete the look of someone distracted and frivolous. What is there for him to do here?

"How wonderful that you've come, my dear friend," says Vyacheslav Ivanov. "We've had a bit of an argument here concerning an interesting philological topic. My claims appear unconvincing to the professor. I'm counting on your erudition..."

When I became acquainted with Kuzmin in 1909, he had recently shaved his beard. If this fact concerned someone else, there would not be any need to mention the beard. But in Kuzmin's biography a shaved beard, the cut of his suit, the kind of perfume he wore, or the restaurant where he had breakfast are facts of the first importance. Milestones, so to speak. By such "milestones" one can trace the entire "trajectory" of his career in letters.

So, Kuzmin has recently shaved his beard. To be more exact, he has ceased to be interested in his outward appearance, stopped changing his multihued waistcoats daily and manicuring his hands. He has stopped sealing his letters with orange sealing wax with the imprint of his coat of arms and perfuming them with sickly-sweet Astrée. In short, the apostle of Petersburg aesthetes, the ideal dandy from the sunny side of Nevsky Prospect has become indifferent to both dandyism and aestheticism.

He has stopped. But the elegantly cut suits are not gone, the smell of Astrée has yet to waft away from the crackling paper. And these not-exactly-fashionable suits, this crackling paper, they have suddenly acquired a "charm" they formerly lacked—the legitimate, modest, and collateral charm of things "about the man."

They ceased to be (or appear to be) the goal and have acquired a certain glamor.

Marquises, beauty spots, the eighteenth century, stylized libertinism, the feats of Alexander the Great, lotuses, the Nile, Nubians, the eighteenth century and marquises once again—everything that Kuzmin had written about until that time ceased to interest him along with his neckties and colored sealing wax. But he kept wearing those neckties. Having abandoned recherché subjects, Kuzmin moved on to ordinary ones. But his language, his manner and his light touch remained. And, having ceased to be the goal—they have acquired glamor.

… In 1909–1910 Kuzmin was completing his novel *Joseph the Magnificent* and the last poems from his *Autumnal Lakes*, the best prose and verse he ever wrote. His writings of that period were quite perfect, especially the prose. It seemed that the poet-dandy, after becoming simply a poet, was coming out onto his genuine, broad pathway.

It seemed that way …

Kuzmin never came out onto his "genuine" pathway. In 1909–1910 he was finishing his best work. *Clay Pigeons*, the book of poems that followed *Autumnal Lakes*, was a falling off, not a sharp one, but obvious. The same is true of his next novel, *The Dreamers*. The old neckties kept being worn without being replaced by new ones. "Beautiful Clarity" began to look like perilous levity.[51] Elegant carelessness quickly turned into sloppiness. Having freed himself from his former "aesthetic" content, Kuzmin's writings, with each new work, became ever more definitely idle chatter without any content whatsoever. "Zinaida Petrovna is worthless and nasty, she's full of intrigues and ruins everything. She's got a long nose she's always busy powdering. But then Lieutenant Vanechka is like an angel…"—now there's a subject for a novella or even a novel. And upon proving to be treacherous, "Beautiful Clarity" keeps lending ever more deadly, photographic shades to the vacuous "chatter" of uninteresting characters …

How did it ever come to pass?

I repeat myself: the shaved beard, the kind of perfume he wore or the restaurant where he had breakfast—those are the facts of the first importance for his biography. Such is his "feminine" nature: there trifles are allotted an equal place with important matters, sometimes even more so. The fate of such writers is completely dependent on the "air" they breathe, regardless of how talented they might be. Even if they are as talented as Kuzmin.

In the beginning Kuzmin landed in a brilliant milieu, one could not have dreamed up anything better for him. He moved into Vyacheslav Ivanov's apartment, and all the best of Kuzmin's work was written under the "tutelage" of this connoisseur, arbiter, and *friend* of poetry who was perhaps unique in the history of Russian literature. He himself was a cold, heavy, bookish poet, but someone else's poems, someone else's gift Vyacheslav Ivanov could understand and direct like no one else.

Life at Vyacheslav Ivanov's was exactly what Kuzmin needed. He began to write with more self-confidence, the "sound" of his poetry was becoming ever purer.

But then came a cooling of their relationship, and Kuzmin moved out from Ivanov's. He was by nature incapable of living alone, and within a short time he was surrounded by new company, also literary. He was living again under the same roof with a different writer. Kuzmin could not live alone—he needed "air" in order to breathe. And now the air has been found. And Kuzmin breathes it as freely as he breathed the air of Ivanov's "Tower."

Now he is under the tutelage of a lady writer, N., the author of *The Wrath of Dionysus*—he lives at her place.[52] Now it is she who is giving him literary advice. The aesthetical-minded jurisprudence students and cadets have followed their *maître* all the way to the hospitable salons of this salon lady writer, and they are quite content. Here it's much jollier than on Tauride Street. Kuzmin is content as well—there's no "boss" over him, no one is "directing" him, no one is "counting on his erudition" when he's feeling lazy after a good dinner and not in the mood for intellectual conversations. Here, behind his back and to his face, they call him a genius and greet his every word with rapturous "wows" . . .

" . . . Mikhail Alekseyevich, you are the Russian Balzac!"

" . . . Kuzmin, he is a marquis come to us from the depths of time . . ."

" . . . He earned his philosophy through suffering . . ."

The author of *The Wrath of Dionysus,* the famous lady writer, beguiles her new "ally":

"You are subtle. You are sensitive. Those Decadents forced you to sunder your talent. Forget what they foisted upon you . . . Be your true self."

Forgetting is not so hard. Becoming "one's true self" is so pleasant. Writing without sundering one's talent is so easy. Nowadays one doesn't even bother making corrections—there isn't as much as a mere slip of the pen.

And the main thing—no intellectualizing, no underground currents: "Zinaida Petrovna is worthless and nasty and keeps powdering her nose. But then Lieutenant Vanechka is an angel…"

Two times two—four,
Two plus three—five,
That is all we can do,
All we can know…[53]

" … *Charmant, charmant*…"
" … He earned his philosophy through suffering…"

✳ ✳ ✳

"What do you think, should I put these poems into the book?" I ask Kuzmin.

Kuzmin looks at me, surprised.

"Why not include them? Why did you write them then, anyway? If you wrote them, they should be included."

He "includes" everything he's ever written. He writes, by the way, whatever comes into his head. Sonnet-acrostics, narrative poems, ballet scenarios. On one page there are verses about a Sibyl who appeared to the poet (although they are dedicated to N., which somewhat softens their self-important tone), and on the next we read:

How joyful spring in April,
How captivating to us;
At the beginning of next week,
We'll go to have our photograph taken at Boason's.[54]

He really was getting ready to have his photograph taken. At breakfast at Albert's they began talking about this project, the rhyme "spring/Boason's" popped up, and soon enough an entire "verselet" followed. When he came home, Kuzmin wrote the whole thing carefully into his notebook. As he gathered material for a new collection of poems, he didn't forget to include that one either.

" ... Why not include it? If you wrote it, it should be included ..."

He composes his poems on the go. "I was coming to see you, and voila, I've composed something along the way." He writes music in the same room where his sister's children are playing. He doesn't need bass keys on the piano: as it is, the children bang on them with all their might. While they're at it, using the higher octaves at the keyboard's opposite end, Kuzmin is working out a new "ditty," concocting his "cute little music stirred with poison."

When he writes his prose, he goes straight away for the fair copy. "Why should I rewrite when my handwriting is neat?"

O, sisters Gravity and Tenderness—your features are identical ...[55]

O, sisters "beautiful clarity" and "perilous levity"—your features are also identical, to the inattentive, not wishing to be attentive, eyes ...

As for Kuzmin himself—what an intricate life, what a strange fate!

" ... Kuzmin walks about in oiled boots and a *poddyovka* ..."

" ... Kuzmin receives guests in a silk kimono while cooling himself with a fan ..."

" ... He is an Old Believer from the Volga region ..."

" ... He's a Jew ..."

" ... He worked as an apprentice in a flour warehouse ..."

" ... He was educated by Jesuits in Italy ..."

" ... Kuzmin has extraordinary eyes ..."

" ... Kuzmin is a freak ..."

All this gossiping contains a good deal of nonsense, but the most outrageous nonsense contains a drop of truth. Silk waistcoats and coach drivers' *poddyovkas*, Old Belief and Jewish blood, Italy and the Volga— they are all fragments of a motley mosaic that is the biography of Mikhail Alekseyevich Kuzmin.

The same goes for his almost freakish and charming looks. Short stature, swarthy skin, curly, flattened across the temples and the bald spot, sparse locks of deliberately lubricated hair—and those huge, extraordinary "Byzantine" eyes. Kuzmin's life played out strangely. He took up literature as he was approaching thirty. Before that he occupied himself with music, but not for long. And before that?

Earlier he had had a life, one that began very early, a passionate, tense, and unsettled life. He ran away from home at sixteen, wandered about Russia, spent nights on his knees before icons, then there was atheism and the verge of suicide. And once more religion, monasteries, dreams of taking vows. Innumerable pursuits, disappointments, infatuations. Then books, books, books—Italian, French, Greek. Finally came the first glimmer of spiritual contentment—in an obscure Italian monastery, in conversations with a simple-hearted canon. Along came the first thoughts concerning art—music ...

✳ ✳ ✳

Kuzmin was getting ready to be a composer; he had studied under Nikolay Rimsky-Korsakov. He didn't graduate from the conservatory, but did not give up music. It was in fact his musical pursuits to which he owed his rapid literary fame or perhaps his whole career.

The music critic Vyacheslav Karatygin heard Kuzmin play somewhere and was captivated. Kuzmin entered the Petersburg poetic circle in the capacity of a musician, and it was only there that his true calling was discerned.

The person who "taught" Kuzmin to write poems was Valery Bryusov.

"Look, you constantly search for words for your music," Bryusov tried to convince him, "and you can't find appropriate ones. Yet other people find them effortlessly—they take the first to come along, someone like Dmitry Rathaus, and they're satisfied. You, however, can't find them. Why? That's because for you words are no less important. That means you need to write them yourself."

"Goodness, Valery Yakovlevich, how would I go about writing them? I don't know how. I can't rhyme."

So Bryusov taught the thirty-year-old beginner "how to rhyme." The student turned out to be able.

By the way, on the subject of Kuzmin's music. This is how he defined it: "it's not music-music—it's cute little music, but there's poison in it."

An exact definition.

Imagine a Petersburg drawing room. Ladies and young people, lorgnettes raised to the eyes, solicitous smiles. "Mikhail Alekseyevich, play something." Kuzmin is coy like a woman: "Really, I don't know…" "Please, please!" Still playing coy, Kuzmin walks up to the grand piano. The way he touches the keys is also somehow feminine. He turns about with a smile: "What should I play? I don't remember, I've forgotten my sheet music…"

> Darling child, don't reach for a rose in spring,
> You can pluck it in summer too…[56]

Not rolling his "r's" and whispering under his breath along with the tune, Kuzmin sings like an old woman, accompanying his singing with something sweetly melancholic. He has no singing voice. Empty, slightly silly words; empty, slightly silly music à la the eighteenth century. Not music-music, but cute little music. Close your eyes—can't you see a provincial aristocratic old lady surrounded by her grandchildren who remembers her youth and the old, sentimental romances?

> If we had known in our youth,
> How quickly the days of love fly by,
> We would not have missed anything,
> Catching bliss here and there…[57]

Not music-music—cute little music. But there's poison in it.

Now we no longer find Kuzmin in a salon; he sings and plays for an audience of connoisseurs. Vyacheslav Karatygin. Émile Medtner. Eugene Braudo. They listen attentively to this strange "wonder." Is it imitative?—To say the least. Trite?—Certainly. Lightweight?—No question. Yet …

"Mikhail Alekseyevich, more, sing some more…"

His unsteady voice cracks, his silly-sentimental "verselets" float along on a primitivist melody, his unsophisticated rhymes effortlessly find each other:

> Mommy-dear told me:
> Run away from evil love,
> Its sting is dangerous,
> It pricks stronger than a needle.

I obey my mommy-dear,
I'll take her advice,
But can a girl live
An indifferent life at sixteen?[58]

Kuzmin's literary fate has been odd as well.

After 1905 the tastes of Russia's "advanced" public began to change. People grew weary of all manner of "intrepid experimentation." After the thunder bursts of the first years of Symbolism, one longed for simplicity, levity, and the ordinary human voice.

Kuzmin could not have appeared at a better moment.

The first poem of his first book began with lines that sounded at the time like a revelation:

Where shall I find a style to catch a stroll,
Chablis on ice, a crispy toasted roll…[59]

That was exactly the thing. Everyone had grown tired of high style, everyone longed for the "Beautiful Clarity" that Kuzmin had proclaimed.

In those days few names inspired more attention and hope than that of Kuzmin. It was true not only of his readers, but of those people whose approval was hard won: Vyacheslav Ivanov, Innokenty Annensky. For the cream of the poetic youth of the day Kuzmin's name was the most cherished.

His early things are still captivating even now. This is true even today, after the charm of their novelty has passed and all the shortcomings of this poetry have come to the fore. Reread *Nets* and *Autumnal Lakes*, the first three volumes of his stories, and *The Chimes of Love*. For all their "peculiarities," they are a part of the splendid heritage of Russian literature. And I believe they will remain so.

But:

" … Why should I rewrite when my handwriting is neat?"

" … Why not include it? If you wrote it, it should be included…"

" … He earned his philosophy through suffering…"

" … Early next week we'll go to have our photograph taken at Boason's…"

"Beautiful clarity—perilous levity."

Kuzmin possessed everything needed to become a remarkable writer. Only one thing was missing—determination. "Everywhere the wind blows."

At first the wind blew in the direction of the boulevard novel, then back to stylization, then toward Mayakovsky, then somewhere else altogether. For the destiny of Russian literature this "change of winds" had long ceased to matter.

XII

A Vasilyevsky Island landlady, the widow of an official, wavers as to whether she should rent a room to Gumilyov:

"You are a respectable gentleman, no question about that … I can tell a gentleman when I see one, thank you very much … So you say you own a house in Tsarskoye Selo? Right, right. You want to rent a room, so you'll be able to sleep over when you come to town? Right, right. The way the trains run nowadays is torture, that I understand. I believe you, Sir, I understand you; I can tell a gentleman, thank you very much, when I see one … A tenant like yourself is most suitable for me. Only that … Would you like me to give you an address, not far from here, right on Tuchkov Lane—they have rooms for rent as well. Take a look, maybe they'll be to your liking…"

"But why would I go look there? I like your place."

The widow smiles prissily:

"And I like you too, Sir. Thank you very much, I see who I'm dealing with. A house of his own … A quiet, educated tenant…"

"Well, then, what's the problem? Let's shake on it. I'll move in tomorrow."

The widow is silent for a moment.

"Right here, on Tuchkov. It's around the corner. Nice, bright rooms. The wife of a lieutenant colonel is renting them. Go take a look, Sir, you'll like 'em … But I apologize—I'm afraid…"

"And what are you afraid of?"

"Well you said yourself that you're one of them poets. Sorry, but everyone knows what kind of folk go and become them poets ... Me being an old woman, my peace is dearer to me. Do go and talk, Sir, to the general's widow..."

As hurtful as it is, one must acknowledge that out of the mouth of that old woman came life's wisdom. The "folk" that went and became "them poets" weren't "quite right" indeed—they were odd, crazy, restless ...

✳ ✳ ✳

The poet Vladimir Narbut went for his shaves to Molle, the most expensive barber in Petersburg.

"Why do you go there? So much money, and the way they shave is somehow odd."

"Ho-ho," Narbut smiles with his whole mouth. "Ho-ho, it really is on the expensive side. *Ein, zwei, drei*—a drop of lotion here, a splash of eau-de-cologne there, and you're out three rubles. And the way they shave you—*ein, zwei, drei*—much too fast. Zip one cheek, zip the other. It's scary, like they're going to cut off your nose."

"So why do you go there?"

Narbut's pockmarked face spreads even wider.

"Ho-ho! They all speak French there."

"So?"

"I like to listen to it. Like music, beautiful and incomprehensible..."

That Narbut was a strange man.

In 1910 a book of his poems came out. It had real talent. Its themes were straightforward: thunderstorm, evening, morning, bird cherry blossom, first snow. But the poems wafted freshness and quick wit—a "Gift from God."

Lots of things in that book were inept, sometimes crude, sometimes provincial in its aestheticism (this last could be forgiven by the fact that the majority of the poems bore the imprimatur of some godforsaken corner of Voronezh province), much of it was simply immature—yet all the same that little book brought attention to itself, and in *Russian Thought* and *Apollo* Valery Bryusov and Nikolay Gumilyov reviewed it very sympathetically. Once they got interested in the poems, they got interested in the author—where is he, what's he like? It turned out that Narbut was the brother of the well-known artist Georgy Narbut. They addressed their queries to the artist. He shook his head.

"My kid brother? He's all right, a capable fellow. Only don't hope for too much—nothing will come of it. He drinks like a fish, and he's a hooligan to boot..."

"But where is he?"

"He's in Saratov province, got a little estate there. He's probably drinking—he's always on a binge in the fall after the crop's been sold."

"Do you think he might come to Petersburg?"

"He will, don't you worry. Especially now that you've been so complimentary to him in your *Apollo*. You'll get to meet him ... And you'll be sorry to have made his acquaintance..."

That conversation took place in November. And in January the secretary of *Apollo* was summoned as a witness in court proceedings concerning a member of *Apollo*'s editorial team, a certain "gentleman Vladimir Narbut." Narbut had finally made it to Petersburg, and during his first night there was detained "for insulting a policeman carrying out his official duties." That night on his way from Davydka's to some other dive, egged on by the spongers who were accompanying him, he tried to climb onto the back of one of the Klodt horses on Anichkov Bridge and inflicted grievous injuries on a policeman who stopped him ...

Narbut came to Petersburg not only to ride a cast-iron stallion, to pay off his appropriate court-imposed fine, and to make literary acquaintances. He had another, more serious goal: to astound and rock Petersburg and Russian literature.

When someone said something flattering about Narbut's earlier poems, he would only smile in a mysterious and condescending manner: just wait and see what's coming. Soon, first in one place and then in another, some news flashed in the literary chronicle: Vladimir Narbut is publishing a new book, *Hallelujah*. It is well known that the importance a poet gives to the appearance of his book is proportionately opposite to the impression made by this same event on the reader. Valery Bryusov reckoned that he was read by about a thousand people throughout Russia. No one would accuse Bryusov of lowering this number out of modesty. And this count was done at the height of Bryusov's all-Russian fame and his readers' interest in him. So what could a beginner expect? It was a long way indeed from encouraging reviews in *Apollo* and *Russian Thought* to a fame comparable to that of, say, Leonid Andreyev. For all his presumptuousness, Narbut understood this. But since he really wanted fame, and waiting by the seashore for the weather to clear wasn't his style, and he was not in the habit of accepting only a little, he decided to push things forward.

The printing press of the Holy Synod, where the manuscript of *Hallelujah* had been submitted to be typeset, refused to produce it "in view of its secular content." The content, it is true, was "secular"—half the words in the poems were obscene.

Narbut needed the Synod printing press because he wanted to print the book in a Church Slavonic typeface. And not just any Church Slavonic typeface, but a special kind. Other printing houses did not have it. There was no other way—the special typeface had to be bought. The suitable paper could not be found in Petersburg either—it was ordered from Paris. Narbut generously tipped printers and typesetters, paid them overtime, and even hired some sort of specialist in Church Slavonic orthography ... This typographical masterpiece was ready in three weeks: it was produced on light-blue paper with red capital letters, and provided—here Narbut's Saratov origins made themselves known—with a portrait of the author a chrysanthemum in his buttonhole and his signature with a wild flourish ...

To celebrate this occasion, Narbut threw a feast in the "Vienna," the grandeur of which was unparalleled even by the standards of that "literary" restaurant. Close to four in the morning, Boris Sadovsky emptied all six bullets from his "bulldog" into the mirror in a shootout with "the ghost of Faddey Bulgarin"; the maître d'hôtel got nearly thrown out the window—he barely escaped when they were getting ready to toss him out using a tablecloth. Sipping some infernal concoction from a beer mug, Narbut accepted congratulations, his frockcoat soaked in liqueurs, his tie askew, and a garland of acorns on the back of his head. Gorodetsky (he was the one who brought the garland of acorns) fussed over the "star of the evening" more actively than anyone. They had already drunk to their eternal friendship, and Gorodetsky, pounding himself on the chest, prophesied:

"You … you … I believe it … I see it … you will be the second … Koltsov."

Unsatisfied, Narbut shook his head.

"K-koltsov? I don't wanna…"

"What?" Gorodetsky was horrified. "You don't want to be another Koltsov? Then who? Nikitin?"

Narbut frowned his pockmarked, brow-less forehead. His tiny shifty eyes glinted cunningly.

"No … Gabriele d'Annunzio…"

*** *** ***

Hallelujah did not bring Narbut the fame of Gabriele d'Annunzio. The book was confiscated and burned by court order.

I don't know if this failure affected Narbut or whether his entire supply of ingenuity was expended on *Hallelujah*.

… Narbut doesn't drink … Narbut spends hours on end in the Public Library … Narbut is attending the university … For those acquainted with the author of *Hallelujah* all this seemed improbable. But it was true. Narbut "went respectable."

I would run into him quite often here and there during his "quiet" period. Two or three conversations stayed with me. I did not suppose that inside such a carouser and debaucher could sit a passion, a naïve "passion for the beautiful."

Tapping a cheap cigarette on his inordinately large and heavy cigarette case (additionally decorated with the diamond-studded coat of arms of the house of Narbut), he said, stuttering and frowning his pockmarked forehead:

"I know I'm taken for a fool. That swine, they say, made off with the harvest, fleeced the peasants and now is drinking it away. He writes poems as a smokescreen, but scratch him and you'll find a slave owner. Mr. Tit Titych, all but an orangutan. But what am I?"

Silence. The intent stare of his sharp, tiny, cold eyes. The usual roguish "Little Russian" grin slides off his face. A sigh.

"And what am I? What kind of a fool am I if I look at a painting by Raphael and cry? Here," he takes out his wallet, which also bears his family coronet, a rumpled postcard. "Here—the Madonna ... from the Sistine Chapel ... I've been abroad. Berlin and such. Zoo, I fed a tiger some caviar—and you know what, he gobbled it away just fine and asked for more, seems like it tastes better than human flesh. Also there was some kind of *Wintergarten*. Well, it's all rubbish, banality. The cognac was horrible, but then it was cheap, cheaper than vodka. We binged on and on, and somehow I wound up in Dresden. While on a binge, obviously, with some drinking buddies of mine. I don't even remember how I got to that, what's it called ... the Pinacoteca ... No, that's in Munich, the Pinacoteca. Well, whatever, we go, we look, well, you know how museums are, pictures, naked women, wild game ... So we go, we shout—you know how we are, one watering hole after another along the way—we dropped into the museum by chance. And suddenly, by some door a guard, an old-looking German, who gives us a sign meaning no shouting is permitted. Surprised as we were, we bit our tongues—maybe in that room some Wilhelm or Bismarck might be viewing the pictures, too ... We enter carefully. There's no one in the room. A so-so little hall. And on the wall that ... the Sistine Madonna ... I must've stood there in front of her for half an hour. I sent away all my scummy friends—what do they understand?—and I'm standing there by myself and my tears keep rolling down. I might've stood there until evening—I forced myself to leave. I've had my fill, it'll keep me going my whole life! Such beauty, such purity, that's the main thing! I gave the doorman twenty-five marks—here you go, I say, I'm giving you this in her honor ... I think he understood..."

Narbut is silent for a moment. His tiny colorless eyes dull over. Two tears appear on the red lids of his lashless eyes.

"Yes, that is beauty, that is art. I stared at her for half an hour, but it'll be enough for a lifetime. For a hundred lifetimes! After that I started drinking wildly—all hell broke loose. We turned all of Dresden upside down. Almost got taken before a judge—we smacked the puss of some Stadtrat, without thinking twice. It turned out all right, though, we bought our way out ... Yes, that's art for you! That and the one by Pushkin:

Evening mist lies upon the hills of Georgia,
The Aragva rumbles before me...[60]

I can't even think calmly about those lines; my heart begins to pound right away. When I was in the Caucasus, I made a special trip to look at that Aragva. It's a nasty, muddy little river by the way ... So here you are! Can I really be an orangutan, when I'm so sensitive to beauty? As to why I carry on like this and why I have no fear of Bryusov, that's because I know that I have nothing to fear from him. Me, him, or the next fellow, we all go for the same price. If one's an orangutan, then everyone's an orangutan. And so far as Pushkin goes, I'd consider it an honor to serve as his lackey. Just listen:

The Aragva rumbles before me ...

Just think, he found this *shashlyk* stand, the Aragva, but what did he turn it into? What a miracle!"

And tears fall from Narbut's eyes, this time one after the other. And he's not even drunk. The two or three small carafes of vodka that he just lapped up don't count.

✳ ✳ ✳

During his respectability phase Narbut decided to publish a journal.

But fussing over the setting up of a journal didn't fit with Narbut's laziness, and it is doubtful that anything would have come from this whim if a certain event had not intervened. After the changing of several publishers and editors the business affairs of the cheap monthly *The New Journal for All* had become extremely woebegone. After the journal had become unprofitable, its last publisher offered it to Narbut. He didn't think about it for long. The deal suited him just fine. There was no need to fuss over anything, everything was ready: the business office, the contract with the printers, paper supplies, and the title. It seems this was in March. The April issue appeared already under the editorship of the new owner.

It is likely that the subscribers to *The New Journal for All* were puzzled when they read the April volume. The journal had a "tendency," it was subscribed to by rural teachers and medical assistants, the so-called "rural intelligentsia." Narbut presented to these readers, who had grown used to Evgeny Chirikov and Victor Muizhel, his own poems in the style of *Hallelujah*, prose by Ivan Rukavishnikov, whereas the sections for articles ranging from politics to agriculture were "taken up" by the dispute about Acmeism in a prolix and confused article by Narbut himself. Right then and there an announcement ran that the prize promised by the former publisher—two volumes of contemporary belles-lettres—was to be replaced by a new one: the compositions of the Ukrainian philosopher Gregory Skovoroda and Charles Baudelaire's poems as translated by Vladimir Narbut.

The subscribers were naturally indignant. The editorial office was inundated with letters expressing bewilderment or outright abuse. In response to them the new editorial board made a "bold gesture." It announced that the title *The New Journal for All* didn't mean "for all dimwits and vulgar simpletons." Those latter, which is to say those demanding Chirikov instead of Skovoroda and Baudelaire, would have their subscription discontinued and offered in satisfaction "pulp of their choosing," such as volumes of *The Messenger of Europe* and the writings of "Semyon Nadson or Razumnik Ivanov-Razumnik."

Immediately, instead of mere reprimands, howls were hurled at Narbut. The words "shame" and "hooliganism" and the like were heard in the press. What surprised Narbut more than anything was that his literary friends, who clearly preferred Baudelaire to Chirikov and knew who this Skovoroda was, were also saying almost the same things. Narbut did not expect that—he was counting on their encouragement and support. And having gotten only trouble instead of the laurels he had expected, he decided to get rid of the journal. But it was easier said than done. Close it down? In that case not only would invested money be lost, but on top of that it would be necessary to return their subscription fee to quite numerous "dimwits and vulgar simpletons." That Narbut did not want to do. Sell it? But who would buy it?

A buyer turned up. Narbut, getting sloshed somewhere, became acquainted by chance with someone, and told somebody about his desire to sell the journal. Right there in the smoke and fumes of binging (after his failure at editing, Narbut began drinking "all out") a buyer materialized on his own—a respectable-looking, plump gentleman of a mercantile appearance, articulate and not particularly tight-fisted. At night in some dive, to the accompaniment of Gypsy howling and the popping of corks, they shook hands on it, not forgetting to drink to eternal friendship. The next morning, groggy and rumpled Narbut was at the notary's office to legalize the deal. The buyer was in a big hurry.

All hell broke loose about two weeks later—when everyone somehow suddenly found out that the "decadent Narbut" had managed to sell what used to be known as "an idealist and democracy-minded" journal to Alexander Garyazin, a member of the Union of the Russian People and a friend of Alexander Dubrovin.

※ ※ ※

After the Garyazin affair Narbut disappeared from Petersburg. Where did he go? For how long? No one knew. About three months passed before he showed up again.

Here's how he showed up. A short, but effective telegram arrived at all the Petersburg editorial offices:

"Abyssinia. Djibouti. Poet Vladimir Narbut engaged to daughter of Menelik, Ruler of Abyssinia."

Soon after a letter arrived bearing Abyssinian seals and stamps. Embossed in lily-colored sealing wax with gold sparkles, the coat of arms of the House of Narbut appeared prominently in the center. Under the seal "Grand Hôtel Djibouti" it said:

"Dear Friends (if you are still my friends), I send regards from Djibouti and envy you because it's better in Petersburg. I came here to shoot lions and to hide from my shame. But there are no lions, and I've now decided there's no shame either: how was I to know he's a Black Hundred? I'm not Semyon Vengerov to know everything. It's beyond misery here. How the hell have I ended up here? Anyway, I'll be coming soon and I'll tell you everything myself.

... My marriage to the daughter of Menelik fell apart, because she's not his daughter. Apart from that there's a rumor about Menelik himself, that he died seven years ago..."

Narbut came back from Africa looking jaundiced and drained. At the "reception" he hastily threw together, he willingly answered questions about Abyssinia put forward by the curious—judging by his stories it turned out that "golden Africa, country of titans" was something like a Russian backwater: mud, boredom, and drunkenness. Someone even expressed doubt that he'd been there at all.

Narbut contemptuously looked at the doubter from head to toe.

"Well, when Gumilyov arrives, let him test me."

... Gumilyov was lost in thought for a moment: "How can I test you? You don't know the languages, you're not interested in anything ... All right then, what is 'tekeli'?"

"One third rum, one third cognac, soda water, and lemon," Narbut answered quickly. "Only I drank it without lemon."

"How about..." Gumilyov said another indigenous word.

"Roasted piglet."

"Not a piglet, but pork in general. Well, all right, tell me if you go to Djibouti and turn to the right of the railway station, what do you see?"

"A garden."

"Correct. And what's behind the garden?"

"A watchtower."

"It's not a watchtower but the ruins of an ancient turret. And what do you see if you turn still more to the right, past the turret and past the corner?"

Narbut's pockmarked, browless face spread into a scabrous smile:

"Not in front of the ladies..."

"He's not lying!" Gumilyov clapped him on the shoulder. "He was in Djibouti. I can attest to it."

It soon turned out that not only had Narbut brought certain knowledge with him from Africa, but also a fever. That was why he arrived looking so yellow. To his chagrin it transpired that the fever was not exotic at all. "You caught it in Pinsk, didn't you?" The doctor asked him.

At first Narbut went away to the country to recuperate, then some place in the south. He was in Petersburg for a short time in 1916. His ensign's greatcoat sat on him like a sack, one arm was in a sling, and he looked morose. Then a rumor went around that Narbut had been killed. But no—in 1920 I caught sight of a thin little volume in a bookstore, published by one of the provincial branches of Gosizdat: Vladimir Narbut, *The Red Tolling* or something like that. I opened it. Rhymes like "capital" and "revolt" hit me right in the eye. I threw the book back on the counter . . .

XIII

Sometimes memories are like dreams. Sometimes dreams are like memories. When you think about the past "so recent and so infinitely long ago," you cannot tell sometimes where memories end and dreams begin.

Well, all right—there was "the last winter before the war," and then the war happened. There was February and there was October . . . And all that followed October happened as well. But if you look more intently— the past becomes entangled, it slips away, and changes.

. . . Bridges are suspended over the wide river in the glassy fog; palaces rise above the granite embankment and two slender golden spires gleam weakly . . . Some people walk on the street and some events are taking place. Here is an Imperial parade on the Field of Mars . . . and here is a red flag above the Winter Palace. The young Alexander Blok reads his poems . . . and here they're burying the "incinerated" Blok. Rasputin was killed last night. And that person giving a speech (his words can't be heard, only a muffled roar of approval)—he's called Lenin . . .

Memories? Dreams?

Some faces, encounters, and conversations arise in one's memory momentarily, unconnected, countless. Now they are vague, now with photographic sharpness ... And again—the glassy haze and through that haze the Neva and the palaces; people walk past and the snow is falling. The chimes ring out "How Glorious Is Our God in Zion..."

No, the chimes are playing "L'Internationale."

Snow is falling. After the train car's warmth, the damp chill of thaw is piercing; it steals into your sleeves and under your collar. What kind of an idea was that to go in the middle of the night to Tsarskoye Selo? But there's nothing we can do now—we're here and there's no train back.

Streetlamps glow dimly. Branches covered in hoarfrost. Stars.

"Hey there, cabby!"

The sleigh flies softly over the loose melting snow.

Gorodetsky gallantly grabs me by the waist on the turns. Mandelstam is sitting in our lap. Gumilyov and Akhmatova are in the first sleigh, showing the way—it was their idea to come to Tsarskoye Selo with night coming on. It's nothing for these Tsarskoye natives. "But what's in it for us, all of us?" It's silly no matter how you look at it. After some literary dinner where quite enough alcohol was consumed, we went somewhere else "to drink coffee." After that, somewhere else. Then after midnight we found ourselves at the Tsarskoye Selo railway station. Our heads were spinning from the "coffee" drunk here, there, and everywhere.

"Let's go to Tsarskoye ... We'll look at the bench where Innokenty Annensky liked to sit."

"Let's go, let's go..."

Indeed, why didn't we think of that earlier? We couldn't have come up with a better idea, could we? At night, over the snow to go to some remote nook of the Tsarskoye Selo park to look at a bench. And for that pleasure to wait until seven in the morning for the first train back to Petersburg.

But the "coffee" was working, our heads were spinning.

"Let's go, let's go…"

No sooner said than done—we've arrived. The warmth of the train car made everyone sleepy. The thawing chill made us limp. How silly, really. Why have we come, where have we come?

Gumilyov and Akhmatova, being Tsarskoye natives, are in front showing the way. Mandelstam is beginning to freeze in Gorodetsky's and my lap; he has grown as heavy as a sack and is silent. Behind us in the third cab are two more "Acmeists" trying not to fall behind—they don't have money to pay for the ride, so if they fall behind they perish.

We stop near some cast-iron gate. We trudge somewhere up to our knees in snow. Tree branches covered in frost crackle. Stars shine weakly. We're still in the same order, Gorodetsky and I hold on to Mandelstam who is becoming heavier and heavier. The snowdrifts become deeper and deeper, the cold more biting. O God…

Gumilyov turns around.

"We've arrived! This is it, Annensky's favorite place. And here's the bench."

Snow, trees, the bench. A man is sitting on the bench like a hump-backed shadow. He reads some poems in a quiet monotone…

… A person in the night in a remote corner of the Tsarskoye Selo park, sits on a snow-covered bench looking at the stars and reading poems. At night, reading poems, on "that very bench." It becomes terrifying for a moment—what if…

No, it is not Annensky's ghost. The person sitting there turns his head in response to our footsteps. Gumilyov approaches him and looks closely…

"Vasily Alekseyevich, is that you? I didn't recognize you for a moment. Gentlemen, let me to introduce you. Here is the Poets' Guild: Gorodetsky, Mandelstam, Georgy Ivanov." The person on the bench gets up heavily and shakes our hands. He introduces himself:

"Komarovsky."

He has a low, hoarse voice, a bit stiff and monotone. His handshake is also stiff, as if he were an automaton. He seems not at all surprised by our meeting.

"You came to look at the bench. Yes, quite right, it's the one. I sit here often … when I'm well. It's nice, quiet, out of the way. It is rare for anyone to come, even during the day. A gymnasium boy shot himself here not long ago—they couldn't find him until the next day. It is a quiet place…"

"Did he shoot himself on this bench?"

"Yes, this one. It's the second such incident. For some reason they pick this one. It must be because of its seclusion."

I interject myself into the conversation:

"Aren't you afraid to sit here all alone at night?"

Komarovsky turns toward me and smiles. The light of the street lamp falls on his face. It is round, an "ordinary" face, the kind of face that a middle-class German merchant might have. His cheeks are all rosy. There's something wooden in his face and in his smile.

"No, when I'm well, I'm not afraid of anything. Save for the thought that my illness might return."

Several times during our conversation he repeats: "my illness," "when I am well," "when I was ill." What kind of illness does he have, this broad-shouldered, red-cheeked man?"

"The illness might return?" I mechanically repeat the end of his phrase.

"Yes," he says, "the illness. It's madness. Nikolay Stepanovich here knows. I'm having a "moment of clarity" right now, and so I am able to walk around. But for the most part I live in the hospital."

And he continues without changing his voice:

"If you are not in a hurry, gentlemen, here is my house. We'll have some tea and read some poetry."

… In the big dining room, below a shiny chandelier, we drink Tokaji wine from light-yellow liquor glasses. Glass doors are open into the winter garden; the fireplace is burning hot. And on top of that, there is a blinding light. All the chandeliers, candelabras, and lamps in the dining room and neighboring rooms are lit as if for a ball. But our host finds there is not enough light. He calls over the lackey.

"Light up the girandoles."

"Certainly, Your Excellency."

Four more tall crystal candelabras flare up with hundreds of candles in the corners.

The oval reddish face of our host smiles woodenly:

"I don't like darkness in the house…"

Komarovsky listens carefully to our poems. Then he reads his own.

His legs set wide apart, he sits in a deep armchair wearing thick American boots. His sparse hair is neatly combed. He has the round reddish face of a German burgher raised on beefsteaks and beer. His face expresses contentment and satisfaction. His eyes look out clear and sleepy.

… He is an utterly sick person. He is so sick that his doctors are at a loss to explain why he is still alive. His heart is so weak that the slightest disturbance might prove fatal. Komarovsky falls into a faint at an unexpected noise, on seeing blood, from any trifle. And quite often when he faints, "it" comes back. He is fated to die soon, and he knows it. Crossing the street is an adventure for him. A trip to Petersburg is a heroic undertaking.

His most passionate desire is to spend some time in Italy, which is as unattainable for him as a voyage to Mars. So he comforts himself by reading guidebooks and descriptions for whole days at a time so that they have long ago become committed to memory. And he writes:

I walk along at a slow pace
And put a small rock in my pocket—
There, where over a new find
The happy Winckelmann cried.[61]

For two or three months he lives "peacefully." He dreams of Italy. He writes poems. At night he trudges to the god-forsaken "suicides' bench" in the snow-covered park.

… When I'm healthy, I'm not afraid of anything. Save for the thought that my illness might return.

… Light up the girandoles. I don't like darkness in the house …

Two or three months pass. Then one night he awakens surrounded by some sort of fiery lions, he screams, and tries to fight them off. Then the hospital, a sack filled with ice, a straightjacket … After long months, a new short-lived moment of lucidity …

Komarovsky was released from the hospital not long ago. This attack had been very serious. They thought he wouldn't survive. But he did. He reads the poems he began writing "there" in an even more wooden voice. What does someone lying on a cot in a psychiatric hospital dream about?

About Rome, glory, and Caesar ...

The lamps glow, it is difficult to breathe from the smell of flowers and the heat of the fireplace. And the steady voice reads in a monotone:

... Into the breaks between the clouds, into that radiant fissure,
Following a slow-moving golden eagle,
Enflamed legions are marching...[62]

His poetry is brilliant and cold. It may well be that they are the most scintillating and most "icy" of all Russian poems. Compared to them, Valery Bryusov's "Parnassus" is childish babble. But as in Komarovsky's voice and smile, there is something wooden in their scintillation. And something unpleasantly stupefying, like this room—overheated, too well lit, too crammed with flowers.

... We listen to poems, drink Tokaji, and converse about something or other. Finally we say our goodbyes. How pleasant it is to breathe in deeply after the fragrant stuffiness of that house. The stuffiness and something else wafting there, among the Smyrna rugs and Sèvres vases ...

It had become frosty. The sky has turned blue before sunrise. The train arrives in half an hour. Oh, how good will it be to get in bed after this sleepless, strange night.

It's 1914, February or March. Komarovsky was talking about his plans for the autumn. The doctors hope ... If I don't have an attack ... A trip to Italy ...

He opened the newspaper, read that war had been declared, and collapsed. At first they thought he had fainted. No, it turned out he did not faint but died.

❋ ❋ ❋

It's a long walk from the House of Writers on Basseyny Street to my place on Kamennostrovsky Boulevard. At Troitsky Bridge I put down my sack of grain for which I had traveled so far, and put my elbows on the railing to rest.

The sky was red with sunset. A wind came from the sea—warm, moist, and "fragrant." The snow on the Neva has softened and compacted; along the bank large yellowish cracks have opened in the ice. If the weather does not change, it won't be possible to walk to Kronstadt over the ice. Then the ice will start to drift and Kronstadt will become impregnable. And then …

The warm wind softly yet insistently strikes one's face. Cannon fire—muffled from the forts, sharp from some battleship that has remained "loyal to the Revolution." Red sky, melting snow … There is not a soul about. "Strolling along the streets" is allowed up to six in the evening, and it's now 5:00 pm, a few minutes past. But everyone has already left work, and it's unlikely that someone will take it into their head to go for a stroll. Better to stay home, really. If the weather doesn't change, though … The ice will start drifting, Kronstadt will become impregnable. Then …

Time for me to go home too. I heave my sack over my shoulder and pick up my pace. Of course, you are allowed to walk in the city until six, and my route will take about fifteen minutes, but still it's better to hurry along …

A man approaches me slowly along an empty bridge. He walks quietly, patting the railing with his palm, clearly not in a hurry. Now he stops, lights up, and throws the match onto the ice. It's as if the siege curfew and "everything that goes along with it" has nothing to do with him. Perhaps that's the way it is. In that case this will be an unpleasant encounter. "Strolling" is permitted until six, my proof of employment is in order … But all the same.

A grayish lock of hair slips free from under his astrakhan hat. He has distinct "bags" under his eyes; still more distinct are the deep wrinkles etched at the corners of his mouth. His broad shoulders slouch. His freezing hands are shoved into his pockets. He has an indifferent, cold, and "vacant" look in his eyes.

This is not a Cheka agent to verify my documents. This is Alexander Blok.

For a minute we stand under the red sky on the empty bridge listening to the cannon fire. The muffled ones come from the forts; the thunderous ones—from the battleship.

"Got your millet?" asks Blok. "Ten pounds? This is good. If you boil it well and add sugar..."

He doesn't finish his sentence. As if he's remembered something pleasant, he takes me by the elbow and smiles.

"They're shooting," he says. "Can you believe it? I don't. Remember Tyutchev?

> In blood to our heels, we fight with corpses,
> Resurrected for new funerals...[63]

The dead are firing at the dead. Whoever wins—it's all the same."

"By the way," he smiles again, "Aren't you afraid? I'm not afraid either. Not at all. And that is perfectly normal. The only ones who will have reason to be afraid later on will be the survivors."

* * *

Sometime in the winter of 1913 my servant woke me quite early by Petersburg standards. "There's a gentleman to see you. Something to do with literature he says." I rubbed my eyes and looked at his business card. Mikhail Aleksandrovich Kovalyov? I didn't have an acquaintance by that name. Who could he be? Could he be a publisher captivated by my poems in *Apollo* or the *Hyperborean* who has come to buy my collected works? Why the hell not? Quite excitedly I asked that the guest be shown into the drawing room while I got dressed. But I didn't get the chance to put on my clothes—my guest was already entering my room.

"Don't be in a hurry to get up," he began speaking in a rapid whispery voice, not rolling his "r's." "Don't be in a hurry to get up, I only came for a moment. What? May I sit here? What? I'll be leaving soon, and you can go back to sleep. Your place is so cold. What? You sleep with your window ajar? Ah, so charming, but I can't do it. You could catch cold, come down with consumption, and die. What? I've got weak lungs..."

Suddenly he assumed a pose, as if he were a ballerina getting ready to make a leap. His head tilted a bit to one side, his fingers spread out, he put his feet in the third position. Speaking rapidly and with a lisp, he recited in a singsong voice:

> He said, shyly smiling—
> As we walked side by side, shoulder to shoulder—
> "You know, I have consumption,
> I've been treating it for a long time…"[64]

And then he added, smiling prissily: "I'm the poet Ryurik Ivnev. This is my poetry."

While he was busy with all that, I took a moment to look him over, astonished as I was.

Thin, "puny" build. His pale, "birdlike," face somehow twitched, his bluish eyes myopically squinted. He is deliberately yet sloppily dressed: his suit is nice, but wrinkled, dusty, and with a thread stuck to the coattail. His shoes are not polished, his foppish tie is askew. And that confused smile of his, that confused twitching, that confused "What? What?" after each word …

"I'm the poet Ryurik Ivnev. This is my poetry. What?"

He read some more, and then again switched to his rapid lisp:

"How did I find your address? N. told me … You know … the one … he sometimes comes around"—here his "birdlike" little face takes on a sophisticated air—"to my uncle X.'s house, the state comptroller. What? That N. read me your poems, and I fell in love with them. What? I even memorized them. Wait, how does that go? Right:"

> It was a quiet night, the night of the ball,
> A summer ball among ancient linden trees,
> There, where the river formed
> Its most sweeping bend.[65]

"And I fell in love with that 'formed,'" he said, stretching his words. "And I've come to tell you that. Now I'll be on my way, and you can go back to sleep … What?"

I thanked him for his courtesy and hastened to clear up a little misunderstanding: the poems just read were not mine. They were by Victor

Hofmann and known to everyone, constantly reprinted in various calendars and recited by performers. In view of that ...

Ivnev was a little surprised.

"Not yours? Hofmann's? How strange. But it makes no difference, they fit you so well..."

I suggested he wait for me in the adjacent room.

"I'll get dressed now and we'll drink some coffee..."

Little bird face frowned haughtily. "Coffee? Thank you, I've already had my morning's hot chocolate. What's the time, anyway? Goodness, 10:15. I'm breakfasting at princess C.'s at twelve. I've got to go home and change. The princess is such a lovely woman ... Have you met? What? I'll make sure to introduce you ... Oh my, it's so late..."

He nodded and ran off, twitching as he went. A glove forgotten by him was left lying on an armchair. It was a foppish thing of bright-yellow suede with a silk lining. It would be of little use in the January weather, however, especially with stitching torn along the fingers ...

At a certain point Ryurik Ivnev became a Stray Dog regular.

For nights on end he sits in a niche by the red fireplace, alone and silent for hours at a time. His little bird face seems even paler than usual; his near-sighted, clear eyes squint at the flames. A cup of black coffee grows cold in front of him "on the low table": he doesn't drink wine.

When asked, he'd rather not read his poems: "another time, I don't remember..." But sometimes, when morning approaches, he might go up on stage: "I will read some..." His poems are muddled, choking, unhinged. For the most part, they're pitifully helpless. And then suddenly some kind of hysterical upsurge:

> From blood the hanky was scarlet.
> Our ship circled the cape.
> Little Dove, our Little Dove,
> Our Little Dove was perishing.[66]

He would read, twitch, and smile confusedly at the halfhearted drunken clapping then dash back to his corner to sit there until morning, squinting his near-sighted eyes at the burning embers ...

"Listen, Ryurik, really why do you spend your nights sitting here? You know it's bad for you..."

"Bad."

"And wearying..."

"Wearying."

"Then why are you sitting here?"

He raised his eyes. Something heavy, some "streak of insanity," flashed in their watery blueness ...

"Why do I sit ... You see ... In everyday life I am exhausted from the consciousness of my own irreality. But here, in these ghostly and absurd surroundings, I don't feel it ... I am an apparition surrounded by apparitions ... And I enjoy it..."

And immediately, as if he got frightened, a prissy smile spreads across his face:

"On the other hand, you are right, you are right—it is harmful, it must come to an end." He primps himself like a sparrow. "Oh, I'm so absentminded." He assumes a dignified sparrow-like air. "At a party at my uncle's ... Princess Drutskaya ... What? Will you be at the opening reception tomorrow? What?"

He's chirping away as if it was not he who half an hour ago was screeching like a madman:

From this sobriety, from this vileness,
Where can one go?
Must one slit one's throat with a razor?[67]

✳ ✳ ✳

The Head of His Imperial Majesty's Chancellery who accepted pleas in the Sovereign's name may have had a chance to get used to some of the most unexpected requests, but even he must have been perplexed to read the one submitted to him by the "Titular Counselor Mikhail Aleksandrovich Kovalyov."

"Prostrate at the Tsar's feet," "Titular Counselor Kovalyov," who expressed himself in the language of "utter subservience" that nonetheless contrived to remain firm, declared (this was in 1915): he refused to perform military service.

Then and there it was clarified that he, Kovalyov, strictly speaking, was not subject to the draft, certainly not in the immediate future. So the declaration he was making came not from personal considerations, but by way of duty to "Your Majesty and Russia." That duty of his he understood as follows: to lay down arms and to welcome the victor with the ringing of bells "in joyful redemption."

It is easy to imagine what kind of "reception" his petition would have been given, had they not made inquiries and ascertained that the petitioner was not simply a "Titular Counselor," but also his uncle's nephew.

That being established, this circumstance was "taken into account": instead of ringing the security services, they dialed the state control bureau. Instead of the gendarmes Ivnev was expecting (having submitted his petition, he became ill from anxiety and anticipation, and took to his bed), his tearful aunty came rushing in and carried him off not to Siberia, but ... to Imatra.

✳ ✳ ✳

Two small rooms so narrow, so low and crammed that they don't even resemble rooms but some sort of cases. And, just like in a case, nothing rigid is to be found inside: throw-covered divans, seamed armchairs, down pillows, pieces of cloth and rugs. There's one stove for two rooms, but it is huge and round, and so stoked that it is difficult to breathe. There are geraniums in wicker flower-stand jardinières, an icon case full of icons is in a corner, and if you turn aside the muslin curtain, a tall fence studded with nails along the top can be seen outside, along with deep snowdrifts and a big, shaggy dog walking about on a chain. Where is this? Siberia? On the Volga? No, it's in Petersburg. Ivnev has found an apartment to his taste: after the petition affair and his return from Finland, he settled in a place of his own.

On Friday evenings about twenty to twenty-five people gather in those tiny rooms. They all fit somehow. They drink tea with Beren's petits fours, but half of those present take their tea from a saucer: the company that congregates here is not exactly usual.

... A rosy-cheeked, towheaded and cassocked boy, a novice from the local branch of Sergiyevsky Monastery. Next to him another "man of the cloth"—a bald, morbidly obese deacon defrocked for his involvement with sectarians. Lost in a fervent discourse with him is a middle-aged man wearing a *poddyovka* and wide jackboots; he speaks in a peasant dialect and has intelligent, cold eyes. This is the poet Nikolay Klyuyev—"of peasant stock," as he describes himself. This "man of peasant stock" is powder-puffed, rouged, and perfumed with *La Rose Jacqueminot* ...

Another rouged poet "of peasant stock" is the blue-eyed Sergey Yesenin. Mixed in with them are some students of the Imperial School of Jurisprudence and the Imperial Lyceum, some kind of former vice-governor who has spent time in exile, some inventor of "a heart magnet" alleged to be the most efficacious means of luring the hearts of apostates to the bosom of the Old Belief. Some sip their tea from saucers, others according to all the rules of English upbringing, but they all spend hours on end conducting strange conversations concerning the *Golubinaya kniga*, the heart magnet, and the New Jerusalem that will arise "in Rus" when the war is over and "The Tsardom of Christ" has come ...

"Soon, oh so soon, my darling children, streams of fire will burst forth, birds of paradise will raise a hue and cry, the font of tears will open, and God's truth will be revealed."

"Amen, amen..."

"*Que Dieu nous bénisse.*"

A confused smile appears on the face of the host, who squints and sniffs English salts.

That was in 1915–1916. Slowly but surely the mix of the visitors alters. In 1917, in the armchair where Klyuyev preached about the "Font of Tears," Anatoly Vasilyevich Lunacharsky sweetly and smoothly holds forth about Marxism. Same or similar Lyceum students politely listen, and just the same the host twitches, smiles, and sniffs English salts. And throughout those same crammed overheated boxy rooms spreads the suffocating and soporific smell of incense, perfume, Rasputin, and Zimmerwald ...

✳ ✳ ✳

In 1918 Ryurik Ivnev made me a proposal when he ran into me on the street: "Do you want to work for us? You don't? But why? Soviet power is Christ's power."

And with a confused smile on his face:

"You know, I'm not proposing that you do revolutionary service, not in the Cheka"—at that point he began twitching and that familiar "streak of insanity" flashed in his eyes—"Although all the work we perform is clean, even in the Cheka, yes, even in the Cheka. But that's not what I'm proposing to you: we need people everywhere—right now the positions of Director of the Imperial Theaters and Director of the Public Library are vacant. Eh? Why don't you want to?"

I looked at that "mighty-of-this-world" fellow, who so easily dispensed directorial positions, looked at his little face, his twitching cheek, his torn shirt, wrinkled suit, and what I felt was an inexplicable, sharp, penetrating pity, almost tenderness. So the service for the Cheka is clean service? Well, all right. Blessed are the poor in spirit ...

"You don't want to?" He twitched like a sparrow and assumed a dignified air. "Too bad. But ... maybe you think that God only knows what kind of riff-raff does service for us? *C'est plein de gens du monde!*"

XIV

Right before the Bolshevik coup d'état I for some reason needed to see the writer Victor Muizhel.

Does anyone still remember that name? The name, possibly, but most likely no one remembers his writings. Muizhel was one of those so-called "writers with convictions" who depicted scenes "from the life of the people" in an appropriately "authentic" language. Writers of this sort stayed away from literature of the "decadent and unprincipled kind." They had their own readers, their own Sainte-Bueves—Vladimir Friche and Vladimir Bonch-Bruevich—their own "poets with convictions," like a certain Cheremnov, a snippet of whose poem I quite clearly remember to this day:

To feast in a burning house, sleep by jaw of crocodile,
To dance a wild jig on a raging volcano—
That thought, of course, never came to anyone,
For everyone can foresee the unavoidable outcome.

Further on, in verses just as penetrating, it was made clear that the Tsarist regime sleeps next to crocodile jaws and dances on a volcano.

Now I don't remember what it was I needed from Muizhel, a man of an entirely different literary circle from the one to which I belonged. I hardly knew him. I don't think I had run into his lanky, depressing figure even once during three years of war. But suddenly I needed something. I was given the address of some sort of military institution—some headquarters or administrative office. I asked for Muizhel. After a minute a foppish-looking ensign came out to see me.

"Have you come to see the commander of the X Division? He's not here. He's at the front."

"No, not really. I've come to see Muizhel, the writer."

"Quite right. Yes, that would be him. Only right now he's at the front. However, if it's urgent I can relay it via a direct line…"

" … Yes, that would be him…" Muizhel, Friche's blue-eyed boy? The one and only, with his cape, convictions, galoshes, with the dandruff on his jacket collar?

It was then when I felt for the first time with inexpressible clarity that "things aren't going at all well." "Things" were going poorly indeed: this conversation took place only a month before the joyful event the tenth anniversary of which has been celebrated not so long ago—

In our workers-and-peasants' country,
In our far-off Russia …

The fact that in 1917 Muizhel could have become a "general" shocked and astonished me. But we get used to anything, don't we? When in 1919 on Nevsky Prospect I met a twenty-two-year-old beauty, all perfumed and dressed up, and was told by her—"Stop by our place. The Admiralty, main entrance. You know, I'm (with a charming smile) the *comarsi* there"—I was not surprised.

That *comarsi* meant: "Commander of the Naval Forces."

Her gray eyes glitter, her painted lips smile ... A smart blue fur coat, a lilac dress, a kid glove that gives off Guerlain's *Vol Aroma* ...

And in addition to all that—*comarsi* ...

And—I was hardly surprised. What was all this? There used to be a young lady, Larisa Reisner, who wrote poems about marquises. The young lady had no shortage of admirers; her poems provoked laughter. And now this young lady is a *comarsi* who at any moment can give orders for the Baltic Fleet to bombard Finland ... And so what, it's just one of those things. Few things surprised people in 1919. It had to be something truly colossal. A side of ham, for example.

I kissed the hand of the Navy Commander wearing a smart blue fur coat and promised her I would stop by some day.

"You must, you must surely come ... The Admiralty, main entrance..."

A woman is always a woman: Larisa Reisner's saying that she was the *comarsi* was a slight embellishment—strictly speaking, the *comarsi* was her husband the midshipman Fyodor Raskolnikov. She herself merely held the title of "Deputy Commissar for Naval Affairs"—or as they said "Deputy Commander for Mug-Punching" (not a petty rank either: something like "Vice Minister" in bourgeois speak).

∗ ∗ ∗

I became acquainted with Larisa Reisner a little earlier than she began to appear in literary salons and her poems about marquises in middlebrow magazines. If I'm not mistaken, I made her acquaintance in the spring of 1913.

Among the numerous highly reputable professors whose paths I chanced to cross in Petersburg, there were several who were not as highly reputable as befitted a learned and gray-haired professor. They did not do anything untoward—they were most varied people, possessed various appearances, a variety of tastes, and a variety of specialties, yet there was something that united them all, something elusive and at the same time evident, some kind of "disreputable" odor that emanated from all those pensive bald pates, respectable spectacles, and "fragrant gray locks" that seemed no different from other gray locks and bald pates that constituted the pride of Petersburg's academic community. But all the same there was something elusive that distinguished them. I was not alone in having that impression. It was Larisa Reisner's father that once invited Gumilyov's jocular remark:

"You know what, I look at him and feel tempted to take him to one side: 'Professor, a couple of words with you,' and say in an icy tone, eye to eye: 'Sir, I know everything about you.'"

"Well?"

"He'll tremble, turn pale, and beg for mercy."

"So what is it that you know?"

"Nothing at all. But I'm sure he'll get embarrassed. I've no doubt he's got some kind of dirt on his conscience."

These days, by the way, that elusive something that not I alone but others sensed in those people, so different yet so mysteriously united, has taken on a more realistic form that can be sensed not only by unprovable "intuition": the majority of the professors and assistant professors with that mystical "odor" now make up the flower of the "Marxist" professoriate ...

It was (it seems) the year 1913, and it was (probably) spring. Along Kamennoostrovsky Boulevard the blessed freshness of Petersburg April wafted from the islands. I walked slowly: it was very nice to do a bit of walking, especially since the goal of my stroll was quite tedious. On assignment from a certain editorial office where I briefly and quite unsuccessfully fulfilled the duties of secretary, I was on my way to discuss with Professor Reisner a number of changes and abridgments in some article of his.

I climbed the wide staircase of an ultramodern house up to the third floor. A varnished door, a brass plate reading "Professor Michael Reisner." But no one would open at my ring. I rang again, same result. Maybe there's something wrong with the bell? I wanted to knock and gave the door a push. It opened without a sound.

From the entryway directly across from me I could see a white room with a piano and flowers—the drawing room, most likely. Its window was of the oriel kind, a large undraped plate-glass looked out to the garden and the rosy evening sky.

With that window as background there stood a girl of about fifteen and a boy, a naval cadet. They did not hear me come in. They probably didn't hear much else: they were kissing.

They stood leaning away from each other. She, putting her hands on his shoulder straps, and he, cautiously holding her by the waist, exactly the way a "first kiss" is depicted in naïve English prints.

First kiss or not, it was very long. What was there for me to do? I coughed. The naval cadet unclenched his hands and quickly turned away to the window. The girl gave a weak "ah," shook her blond head, and walked over toward me. Her face burned, her eyes shone. I must admit that when she got nearer, I envied the naval cadet, who was tapping his fingers on his sleeve with an indifferent air, that's how lovely his girlfriend was. She was an absolute beauty.

The professor, together with his daughter, must have cursed me. I disturbed his after-dinner rest: his sharp little face looked sleepy and rumpled. But he received me with exaggerated, all but stupefying, cordiality. After the napping his pince-nez hadn't yet balanced on his nose and a cheek glowed rosy from the pillow, but he already offered me a cigar, regaled me with port and spoke, and spoke—sweetly, ingratiatingly, "soulfully." He spoke about the young, about holy art, about freedom, ideals, about the bright future of mankind and about many other elevated and deep subjects, which he probably didn't have to discuss with me, an editorial office secretary on a business errand.

Professor Reisner's voice was surprisingly soft, surprisingly "captivating." I recall this voice sounding every bit as softly, "soulfully," at some official gathering of his hungry and emaciated "dear colleagues" at the House of Academics. Those present had failed to become "red stars" due to the absence in their nature of the aforementioned "odor," so now they modestly eked out an existence for themselves when they were not preoccupied with selling off their draperies and surviving on their "academic" rations. Soulfully, captivatingly, the Professor spoke of "holy science," and, along the way, touched upon his service in its cause:

"Suffice it to say that among my students I count three academics with European reputations, ten Red Army commanders, and four"—a particularly velvety modulation here—"chairmen of the Cheka."

"Yes, yes, into exile, by prisoner convoy, to Siberia, to the gallows, to burn at the stake."

She opens her coat wide and throws back her head. What a magnificent "proud human face!" Two years ago, over there by the window I imagined I saw Psyche in her half-childish silhouette. By now that beauty has grown heavy somehow. No, not Psyche. More like a Valkyrie ...

Sleighs fly along the loose snow, along the ice, across the Neva. A yellow winter dawn slowly spreads across the sky. After a sleepless night, one's head is spinning. And that astonishing face, those gray, radiant, wide-open eyes, those fluttering words "dolorous and impassioned."

"Yes, into exile, to burn at the stake. I cannot live like this. I do not want to live like this."

Since that time when I first saw Larisa Reisner, about three years have passed. I run into her often, here and there in various literary settings. There is no special friendship between us: I find her poems extremely distasteful, same goes for the way she carries herself. She does it in "the Moscow style": she acts both as a "decadent" and a blue stocking, both a "comrade" and a heartbreaker. To my "Petersburg" way of seeing things, it's all rather tasteless. In a word, I long ago stopped envying that naval cadet. But ...

But right now, with that pale sky above the deserted Neva, looking at her astonishing face, listening to her voice, I somehow forget all that and experience something like fear, as if I'm standing before a being from a different world. Valkyrie? Perhaps it really is a Valkyrie. To Siberia? To burn at the stake? Perhaps she can really go to Siberia and is not afraid of being burned at the stake ...

At this point "saving irony" comes to my aid. I recall that this Valkyrie is simply a young lady with provincial mannerisms, who writes bad poems, whom I am taking home from a "ball" at Yury Slyozkin's, where a lot of champagne was served (in view of it being war time, it had "the Don" on its label).

And "having recalled," I say in the appropriate tone:

"You have *vin triste*, Larisa Mikhailovna."

But she is not listening. She is looking at the sky with her wide-open, sad gray eyes, a sky just as gray and just as sad.

And, having been silent for a moment, she speaks quietly, as if to herself:

"No, there's nothing I want, there's nothing I can do. In the fairy tale there's a heart of stone. Stone? That's nothing. But if it's dead, dead?"

The resplendent Admiralty chambers are brightly lit and intensely heated. Having grown unaccustomed to so much heat and glitter (it's the winter of 1920), the guests tread awkwardly on the sparkling parquet, awkwardly pick out fragrant tea and caviar sandwiches from trays carried around by foppish Baltic Fleet sailors.

Larisa Reisner is holding a reception for her old bohemian acquaintances. Many have come, some because they heard about the caviar, and some simply out of curiosity. Well, if you forget about the "special circumstances," then this is a reception like any other: the gentlemen click their heels, the ladies twitter, and the hostess smiles sweetly to the right and to the left.

She takes several by the arm and leads them into a small, dark red salon, where not just tea but liqueurs are being consumed. This place is for the chosen. The pleasure of downing a shot of Benedictine is somewhat spoiled by having to do it in the company of Mama Reisner, Daddy Reisner, and a handsome, insolent-courteous young man, Raskolnikov "himself."

The company, what more can be said, is highly placed. That is why they call it: "The Revolutionary Family."

I, alas, fall in among "the chosen." Leading me through the Ministry hallways, Larisa Reisner lets drop the following in the tone of Lady Asquith:

"What a horror, all that gilding, plastering. It's in the taste of our predecessor, Admiral Grigorovich. Everything will have to be redone from the start, everything…"

✳ ✳ ✳

The last time I saw Larisa Reisner was at the ball in the House of the Arts. She must have been very happy—she was laughing and dancing the whole time. Her blue, ample, lustrous, semi-masquerade dress suited her very well. Wearing it, she seemed younger, slenderer, lighter, and once again resembled that girl from the naïve picture—more of Psyche, and not Valkyrie…

Later I only heard about her. I heard various things. About death sentences that she, that's what they say, signed. I heard about Captain Shchastny whom she had over for breakfast and entertained with sweet chatter while the last preparations were being made for his "trial" and shooting. Already abroad, I found out that Raskolnikov had dumped her. Then in some Soviet newspaper I read her obituary, stupid and pompous like all Soviet obituaries.

XV

"Brick in a frockcoat"—Vasily Rozanov's nickname for Fyodor Sologub.

In appearance he didn't look like a man—really, a stone. His movements were slow, strained, and angular. A bald, huge skull; tiny, icy, bore-right-through-you little eyes. A pale, immobile, smoothly shaved face. Even the large wart on his face seemed made of stone.

And a voice to match:

You poured and poured and poured and rocked
Two corporeal-scarlet sheets of glass.
Whiter than a lily, more scarlet than a ruby,
You were white and scarlet…[68]

Sologub reads, and it seems like it isn't a man reading, but a hammer hammering out those even, measured, meaningless words on the wall.

His "treatment" of others was of a corresponding kind.

A young poet, a recognized "rising star," calls Sologub on the telephone:

"Fyodor Kuzmich, is that you?"

"Me."

"This is X. speaking. I'd like to come and see you..."

"What for?"

"To read you my poems."

"I've already read them in *Apollo*."

"To find out your opinion..."

"I have no opinion about them."

Sologub is supervisor of some school on Vasilyevsky Island. And what a supervisor he is!

"Fyodor Kuzmich is coming!" And the wildest of hellions immediately calm down—they know that the supervisor doesn't like to joke around...

This, however, concerned not schoolboys alone. When I was presented for the first time to Sologub in 1911, and he bore in on me with his colorless, icy little eyes and, unhurriedly, extended his palm to me (true, I was only seventeen), my teeth slightly clattered—such was the "chill" that emanated from him.

This, by the way, is what the famous poet said to the beginner at their first meeting:

"I haven't read your poems. Now, whatever they may be, you'd be better off quitting. Not yours, nor mine, no one's poems are needed anywhere by anyone. The writing of poems is a stupid indulgence and a waste of time..."

Sologub himself began to engage in this "stupid indulgence" late, when he was about thirty-five.

And what was he doing before that? The same thing.

An empty, poorly furnished, state-provided apartment; "Fs" for schoolboys; slow strolls along the empty Vasilyevsky Island "lines" taken in his "stony" gate. Lonely evenings under a hanging kerosene lamp, bent over either "written assignments" or, when those have been marked, his favorite book, "stony" as himself and everything surrounding him—*The Critique of Pure Reason*.

"Brick in a frockcoat." Some sort of automaton, created to instill fear in schoolboys and boredom in himself. And no one even guesses that under that frockcoat, in that "brick" there is a heart. How could anyone have guessed, "who would have thought it"? Only when he approached thirty-five was it revealed that he had a heart under that frockcoat.

A heart ready to burst from sadness and tenderness, despair and pity.

✳ ✳ ✳

Once, in a moment of candor, Sologub admitted (in a conversation with Alexander Blok):

"I'd like to keep a diary. A real diary, for myself. But I can't, I'm afraid. What if suddenly, by accident, someone peaks into it? Or suppose I die suddenly and don't manage to burn it. That thought stops me. But you know, sometimes I want to do so much, it gives me the shudders. But then, suddenly, the thought 'it might get read' comes to me—and I can't. I can't write about the main thing."

"About the main thing?"

"Yes. About my terror in the face of life."

And parallel to that conversation is another slip of the tongue by Sologub:

"Art is one of the forms of lying. That's the only thing that makes it magnificent. Truthful art is either an empty bourgeois commonplace or a nightmare. And nightmares are the last thing that people need. They've got enough nightmares as it is."

Well I remember the "stony" smile with which this was said. That was in 1914 at a "glittering" literary salon, where the aesthete-coxcombs would repeat with pleasure and memorize the "pointed paradox" of the *maître*, who was miserly in such matters. Much like those coxcombs, I memorized it, but then forgot it. But it fell to me to recall it all over again . . .

Sologub's wife, Anastasiya Nikolayevna Chebotarevskaya, was small, swarthy, and anxious. Anxious more than anything else. In the calmest of times she was always anxious. About what? About everything. During the Menahem Mendel Beilis trial, in the aesthetic circles where everyone was indifferent to Beilis and to everything else in the world, she would grab the hands of the ladies she didn't know, or take some Imperial Lyceum students stuffed to the gills with Oscar Wilde into a corner and, blinking her wide-open, "restless" gray eyes, would ask in a racing voice: "Listen, do you really think they'll convict him? Do you really think they'll dare?"

"Yes ... What a disgrace..." the Lyceum student would mutter, obligingly bending his torso as he attempted to get away from her as quickly as possible. But she wouldn't let him go. She went on speaking even more quickly, even more heatedly and anxiously. She didn't notice that her interlocutor was stupid and apathetic about everything in the world, except the part in his hair. On the contrary, he said "disgrace," and, of course, he was as outraged as she, and he had the same anxiety. She was already grateful, she already saw in him an ally ...

She was anxious about important things and about trifles. It seemed she didn't notice the difference between the two. Her eternal alarm made her suspicious. She found imaginary friends as easily as imaginary enemies.

"Enemies" naturally tried to pinch, set up, and trip Sologub, whom she deified. They could denounce him to the police (About what? Oh my, an enemy can come up with anything!). They could belittle his popularity, damage his health. And she believed that the new ginger-head yardman was an agent, especially sent to follow Fyodor Kuzmich. X., from a respected thick journal, was a vicious maniac whose every waking thought was about how to find ways to disappoint readers in Sologub. And the Finnish milkmaid surely laced her milk with "vibrio bacterial virus," and on purpose, on purpose ...

That's how it was in "calm" peaceful times. Imagine what it was like in war and then Soviet days?

In 1921, after a prolonged struggle, it seemed that what she had dreamed of, what she had gone on about with her wide-open eyes flickering to the "friends" she ran into on the street, or at a lecture, or in a bread line, would come true. She took great care to hide it (what if we're informed on, what if everything is ruined?) from an improbable number of ever multiplying, particularly vicious "enemies." Departure for abroad.

"To break out of hell"—in the last months of her life this was the focus of all the powers of her soul and of all her "anxiety." She did not talk about or think about anything else. "To break out of hell." And now after a long, enervating, exasperating struggle, the doors of "hell" had opened slightly. In two or three weeks they would be issued their exit passports. This is certain. "Friends" helped, "enemies" retreated.

She could not comprehend that "hell" was inside her, that no Paris with "white rolls and port wine for Fyodor Kuzmich" would change anything. She immersed herself in her struggle, ran about town animated, joyful. She took "friends" she met to one side, and looked about to make sure "enemies" wouldn't hear. Flashing her eyes in agitation, she would whisper:

"In ten days. Certainly. And why don't you go there yourself?"

That "hell" was within her she did not understand. But could it have been that she understood it suddenly, at once, that night when she ran out without a hat into the rain and cold, as if someone had summoned her? Sologub was not home. The woman who was helping in the apartment (there was so much to do before their leaving) asked if the lady would be gone for long. She shook her head: "I don't know." Maybe she really did not know. Maybe she will come right back, have lunch, and leave for Paris in a few days … She ran out into the rain without a hat because suddenly the alarm that had tortured her entire life broke through with terrifying force.

Some sailor saw how a woman threw herself into the Neva from Nikolayevsky Bridge near the chapel. He didn't get there in time to hold her back. It was evening. The street lamps did not function in those days. The sailor could not make out the woman's face, or how she was dressed. Did it seem she was without a hat? It seemed she was wearing a coat and cape affair, like the vanished Chebotarevskaya. The body was never found; perhaps it wasn't even searched for. Who was willing to muck around in that icy water for the wife of some Sologub or other? The Petersburg proletariat had more important things to do. Yes, and a few days later (exactly at the time that their exit passport had been promised, only promised, of course), the Neva froze over.

❋ ❋ ❋

Up to the very instant of her death, Chebotarevskaya still "didn't know." Sologub too, from that autumn evening until spring, when the ice broke and his wife's body was located, he "didn't know" either.

He didn't change anything in his life's routine. When the weather was good, he went out for his stroll—along the ninth line toward the Neva, as far as the chapel by the Nikolayevsky Bridge, and then along the sunny side of the street on his way back. In the evening, under a green lamp in the dining room, he wrote "bergerettes," poems in the style of the eighteenth century, or translated Théophile Gautier or Paul Verlaine for the World Literature publishing enterprise. Whenever he had visitors, he received them with that same cold civility as always. Sometimes in the course of a conversation he would mention Chebotarevskaya in passing in such a tone of voice as if she had stepped out for moment. He joked, willingly recited poetry—pastoral, frivolous bergerettes ...

... The green lamp casts a soft circle of light on the table covered with a varicolored oilcloth. Books and manuscripts arranged neatly on the table. And here is also Anastasiya Nikolayevna's knitting. One needle is stuck in a ball of yarn, the other lies to one side. That is how she left it "that evening." That is how it has remained.

Sologub is reciting poetry. His face as usual is stonily civil, elderly calm. And his voice is the same, without nuances, also "stony."

And the poems are pastoral, frivolous bergerettes:

> ... With Your Honor's permission,
> Colin the shepherd is my beau ...[69]

Once I lingered a little too long. The female servant (the same one who asked when the lady would be returning home), came to set the table.

"Perhaps you will dine with me?" suggested Sologub. "Masha, please be so kind to put out a third setting."

I declined dinner, but I must have done a poor job disguising my surprise. For whom was the second setting if I were to get the third? Most likely the surprise I felt showed.

And stonily civil Sologub clarified:

"*That* setting is for Anastasiya Nikolayevna."

And in spring when Chebotarevskaya's body was found, Sologub locked himself in his apartment, didn't go out anywhere, and didn't receive anyone. Sometimes his female servant came to the World Literature office to collect royalties or to the Public Library to get books. She was a most quiet elderly woman from whom one could not learn a thing, except that "the master, thank God, is quite well, writing all the time, and asks everyone not to worry." Everyone was amazed that the books Sologub took out were all on the subject of calculus.

What did he need them for?

Later Sologub began again to appear here and there, began to receive visitors when they came to see him. He no longer spoke about Anastasiya Nikolayevna as if she were still alive, and a second setting for her was no longer placed on the table. As to the rest, nothing in him or in his life changed in any way.

The reason he needed mathematical books transpired later.

A certain acquaintance who had come to visit him saw on the table a manuscript full of some sort of computations. He asked Sologub what they were.

"Those are differential equations."

"Are you studying mathematics?"

"I wanted to verify whether there is life beyond the grave."

"With the help of differentials?"

Sologub smiled his "stony" smile.

"Yes. And I verified it. Life beyond the grave does exist. And I will meet Anastasiya Nikolayevna once more…"

"*That* setting is for Anastasiya Nikolayevna."

"Yes, I write a lot. These days mostly bergerettes … Here's what I wrote yesterday:

… With Your Honor's permission,
Colin the shepherd is my beau …

His voice is the same. And his smile is the same. And his coat has faded only along the seams. And his poems are pastoral bergerettes. Well, certainly—"That's the only thing that makes art magnificent … And nightmares…"

✳ ✳ ✳

Many springtimes have passed,
And now it's springtime again.
This poor world is intolerable,
And springtime so impoverished.
What will she say to me
About my dreams?
She will show me that same death,
All those very same flowers
That have been before
On this diseased earth,
That released incense into the skies,
And drooped, and bloomed.[70]

Those same flowers, that same death. The key to all of Sologub is in these verses.

Is "art one of the forms of lying"? Did Sologub sincerely believe that? Or, on the contrary, did he fear "to the point of trembling" that someone would "peep" at his "most hidden secret" and out of this fear made up such phrases as "one of the forms of lying"?

I don't know. And it's not important. What is important is something else.

The best of everything created by Sologub, his poetry, is free of such "lying." On the contrary, his poems are some of the most "truthful" in all of Russian poetry.

They are "truthful to the end" from the artistic as well as the human point of view. And they are truthful in their restraint, so alien to everything external and ostentatious, and also in their chastity, their reflection of the "childlike" soul of the poet.

Quite recently, in an answer to a literary questionnaire, Sologub has been called "a great poet." This is an exaggeration, naturally.

In art "great" begins precisely from some "victory" over that "dread before life," that had from the start and forever been victorious over Sologub. But, of course, he was a poet in the true and sublime sense of that word—not a mere man of letters or a versifier, but one of those who are counted in the "Beatitudes of the Blessed."

✳ ✳ ✳

And now Sologub has died. The last time I saw him (I stopped by to say farewell before departing for abroad in the autumn of 1922), he said:

"The only joy left to me is smoking. Yes. Nothing more. So, that's it—I smoke..."

"Somehow" and "someway" he lived for yet another five years. Smoked. Wrote bergerettes, perhaps. Now he has died.

He died in complete solitude, in poverty, forgotten by all, needed by no one. He died of pneumonia, which prevents one from losing consciousness to the last moment, yet smoking is exactly what's not allowed ...

XVI

In 1914, in the summer, a young man journeyed through Italy.

He had just finished the gymnasium—this was his first independent journey. He was seventeen, he was very handsome—dark eyes, slender build, tall—he was carefree and fully secure financially. He had everything—youth, Italy, of which he had been enamored since childhood, money he could spend without counting, time he could dispense with as he pleased. If the whim struck him, he could leave even tomorrow: well, for Norway, for example, or, on the contrary, he could stay another month, year, or two in this slightly old-fashioned, comfortable pension, in this white, high room, its wide window over-woven with climbing roses through which shone the blessed blue of the Bay of Napoli … Youth, freedom, Italy—women vying with each other in falling for him, everyday the pension where he is staying is sent flowers or perfumed notes addressed to "the handsome Russian Signore." Youth, Italy, freedom—his whole life is ahead of him, everything is smiling on him … Paradise, don't you think? He himself would agree— paradise it is. But …

> But why do I hurt so much
> In this most happy paradise of mine?[71]

This is his own perplexed question.

Why, what for, really?

Yes—youth, beauty, Italy, his whole life is ahead of him, everything is smiling on him. But:

> Why this inexplicable burden
> On my quivering heart?[72]

This seventeen-year-old "spoilt child of fortune" demurs, these bitter "why's" and "what for's" are not empty words, not "poetic images." Right there, in Italy, in his white room with its rosy window, Leonid Kannegisser is keeping a diary. And on every line of that diary—the same thing: "Why? What for?"

… I have a room, dinner, books and complete lack of pity for those who do not have those things.

Italy, youth, freedom—"paradise." But in this paradise—it hurts and his heart is weighted down by the "inexplicable burden."

> Why this inexplicable burden
> On my quivering heart?

One line contains a question, the next—the answer: "On my quivering heart…" Yes, life is "smiling" upon this seventeen-year-old boy, yes, paradise is all around him. But his heart has "quivered," and no paradise, however "blessed," can and will bring him rest.

Leonid Kannegisser's childhood poetry strangely echoes the childhood poems of Mikhail Lermontov. Remember:

I began early, I'll end earlier,
My path will accomplish little.
In my breast, as in the sea,
Lies the burden of shattered hopes.[73]

And strange is the way in which the images evoked by these poems echo each other: Lermontov lying "with lead inside my breast," covered by a trench coat, under a pouring rain.[74] Kannegisser with a bullet through the back of his head, lying in a Cheka basement.

Two hearts that "quivered"—found, at last, their rest ...

Around four in the morning at the Stray Dog, I was introduced to a tall, slender, dark-eyed young man. A boy, to be exact. Back then Leonid Kannegisser could hardly have been more than seventeen years of age.

But he had the look of a quite grown man—confident bearing, more-than-average height, foppish tailcoat. "The poet Leonid Kannegisser," commended him the man who introduced us to each other. Kannegisser smiled.

"Well, not that much of a poet, really. I don't consider my poems particularly significant."

"Why is that?"

"I know that in poetry I won't achieve anything great or exceptional."

"Well ... First of all, 'isn't it every soldier's dream to become a general?' ... and then not everyone should become a new Dante, you know. Simply to become a good poet ..."

"Oh, no. Boring and useless."

"I see then—your program is either triumph or death," I joked.

He smiled with his lips alone, the expression in his eyes was as serious as before.

"Something like it..."

"It's only the field for your heroic deed that remains to be chosen, right?"

He smiled again. This time it was a broad smile, with his whole face. The seventeen-year-old boy immediately showed through his tailcoat and adult bearing.

"Right."

... Tobacco smoke floated under the cellar vaults. Glasses clinked, faces appeared green in the bright electric light. Some woman was dancing on the table, the senseless music broke off and then blasted forth again. We sat in a corner, drinking now black coffee, now Riesling, now coffee again. There was a slight ringing in one's ears. I listened to my new acquaintance. Probably because of all that wine he had drunk, he loosened up and kept right on talking. I listened to him with concerned surprise: surely it was for the first time that the walls of the Stray Dog were hearing such an impassioned romantic muddle "about valor, heroic deed, and glory...".[75]

... Yet another surprise was in store for me when I paid a visit to Kannegisser's home.

"Several friends will get together at my place," he wrote to me in his invitation. I painted a vivid imaginary picture for myself: I imagined those guests as loftily and romantically inclined as my nocturnal interlocutor when they get together to discuss "ideals" in a dimly lit room filled with learned tomes and portraits of some kind of "leaders." Heated conversations, flushed faces, cigarette butts, tea with lemon—in a word:

> We argue in the room till morning,
> At dawn one of us
> Steps out toward the rosy sunrise,
> Greeting the golden hour...[76]

I imagined all that and, despite all the sympathy inspired in me by Kannegisser, I got a little bored in advance. But I went anyway.

... In the drawing room hung with silks and furnished with André-Charles Boulle pieces, some twenty-five people were chirping away. A lackey waited on them serving tea and delectable sweets, the Copenhagen lamps emitted a bluish light, while from behind a grand piano Mikhail Kuzmin, that unmelodious nightingale of Petersburg aesthetes, choked on the words of his song:

> ... Were you a heavenly angel,
> Not a tailcoat you'd have on, but a deacon's orarion...[77]

One half of those present were familiar to me. The other, judging by their entire appearance, did not leave any doubt as to what they were all about: Dalcroze-obsessed young ladies puffing away at Egyptian cigarettes in enamel holders bought at Treiman's; poetry-writing and sonata-composing young men with spit-polished parts in their hair wearing lacquered ballroom slippers. Quite a specific kind of crowd, and rather vacuous.

But what about my nocturnal romantic? What does he have to do with all this?

It seemed that he took to that elegant drawing room like a duck to water. His suit was ultrarefined, his conversation languidly affected. Nothing—apart from his beauty—distinguished him from the rest: another aesthetically disposed Petersburg youth ...

> Philosophy we don't need—
> Or silly spats.
> May life be one long delight,
> And sweet nonsense...[78]

His strange eyes sparkling from behind his pince-nez, Kuzmin would turn to the audience to encourage it and went on cooing.

Seeing Kannegisser applauding, I walked up to him and took his the elbow:

"I would never have thought that this might appeal to you."

"How so? Don't you like Mikhail Alekseyevich's singing?"

"I like it all right. But it seems to me this 'sweet nonsense' can't quite fit with your views on life…"

"On the contrary," he bowed sarcastically, "it fits perfectly. Don't be offended, but that time at the Stray Dog I simply pulled your leg. All those heroic deeds, you know…"

And he sang out, imitating Kuzmin:

Two times two—four,
Two plus three—five,
That is all we can do,
All we can know …

* * *

Galas, masquerades, aesthetic tea parties hosted by various artistic ladies, that nocturnal basement where we met, where every midnight various elegant loungers gather to bore themselves until morning, its walls bearing an inscription by their favorite poet, the perfumed, dressed-up Kuzmin, the inscription that goes as follows:

Here many chains have come unbound;
This underground hall will preserve everything—
Including the words uttered in the night
That certain people would not utter in the morning.[79]

Would not utter? Maybe. But "did not utter" does not mean "has forgotten." Far from it. "Something like that" does not simply slip your mind. And even if it does slip your mind (in a crisp morning frost, say, provided that your head had not been completely poisoned by aestheticism and idleness)—if it does slip your mind, then "this underground hall will preserve everything"—whatever slips your mind will come back to you again as soon as at nighttime you step under these low-vaulted ceilings and find yourself surrounded by these gaudily painted walls. Each time you do it, it becomes more difficult to "let anything slip your mind." "Committing it to memory," however, becomes easier. Committing what to memory? Why, this very sensation of unbound chains." Many chains"—almost all of them, really …

The very same faces, the very same conversations at masquerades, galas, five o'clock teas, and mad midnight gatherings. Years—"seasons," actually—go by; jacket cuts and tie patterns change. Nothing else changes. This is the daily grind. It began after 1905; it will end in 1917.

And the end will be horrible.

People of conscience? Bores, all of them. Politics? Vulgar nonsense. Work? God's punishment, which "we" luckily have been spared. The rich have been spared by virtue of having money, the poor by virtue of having the ability to beg for handouts from the rich.

Masquerades, galas, five o'clock teas, mad midnight gatherings. A world of Oscar Wilde-like witticisms, mirror-smooth hair partings, where tie patterns are the only things that change.

It will end horribly. But no one is thinking about the end.

It will end like this. When February 1917 bursts the hothouse mold of a "beautiful and carefree" life, those in whom humanity has not been killed off by that "daily grind," they will rush headlong out into "the fresh air." And the more of that humanity they retain, the more urgent will be their flight, the less of the ability to stay reasonable they will have ...

It's just that sharp temperature fluctuations are a dangerous thing.

1916, winter. It's late—about three in the morning. The drawing room is half-lit and quiet. Plenty of people and much chatter filled it half an hour ago; it resounded with music, singing, laughter. But now the guests have parted, the older ones off to sleep, and only in one corner in the dim yellow lamplight are the young host and a few of his chums "burning the midnight oil." This is a Petersburg drawing room, and these are "Petersburg" young men. Their appearance is aesthetic, and so is their conversation.

One of the interlocutors stands out—he is dressed up like a peasant lad from a ballet. A pink shirt, a golden ribbon for a belt, a comb hangs from it on a thread. However, that entire get-up is much the same "dandyism" even if turned inside out. To top it off, this peasant lad draws out his "o's" as deliberately as the others roll their "r" sounds in the

Parisian fashion. He can't be that old—eighteen, no more. His face is simple and pretty. His last name is Yesenin.

These are all young poets. Conversations concern poems, poems are recited. Now the peasant lad is reading his with a sing-song lilt. His poetry is talented, even very talented ... if only it weren't marred by the same cheap "folksiness" as the comb and the ribbon-belt.

His reading is followed by that of his dark-eyed host:

> O, Heart! No need for this burden!
> Go lightly along your earthly path.
> Like an early swallow from the garden
> Fly into the blue sky...[80]

After the host's performance follows that of some fair-haired adolescent. He's not devoid of talent either, his poetry reads just as smooth and clear; it is just as "light," just as pleasing to the ear, equally failing to touch the heart. Some poems are better, some worse, one image is happy, another isn't, but that is not important. What's important is something else—both the poems in the conversations harbor some a strange vacuity. Pleasing to the ear, yet the heart isn't touched. It's no accident that an hour ago in the same drawing room similar young men with smooth hair partings interrupted each other, requesting Kuzmin to do more and more encores. And the latter, his strange eyes sparkling at the youths surrounding him, sang:

> Philosophy we don't need—
> Or silly spats.
> May life be one long delight,
> And sweet nonsense.

"More, more, Mikhail Alekseyevich..."

> Two times two—four,
> Two plus three—five,
> That is all we can do,

All we can know …

"More, more."

"The peasant lad" in his silk *kosovorotka* follows suit. It's to his taste as well.

"Mikhoil Lekseich, won't you sing the one about the angel…"

… Were you a heavenly angel,
Not a tailcoat you'd have on, but a deacon's orarion …

… 1916. The lack of success at the front becomes more menacing. A revolution is "in the air." Yes, that's all true … But we're mere poets, what can we do? And since we can't do anything, the only thing that's left is:

May life be one long delight,
And sweet nonsense …

Kuzmin is singing. From his tuneless, sweet singing, from his languid, strange gaze, from those naïve little words and simpleminded motifs emanates an imperceptible yet deadly poison. The same one protection from which is sought in the prayer by St. Ephrem the Syrian "The Spirit of Idleness…"

Old poison, true poison. At times it seemed that it had evaporated. No, it did not evaporate, it was as potent as ever. And that is exactly why that tuneless singing was so much to everyone's liking—something everlasting, potent, and overpowering…" The Spirit of Idleness…" Kuzmin has nothing to do with it. Neither do his listeners. He likes it, and they like it, too. This is what they like, and nothing else. Not Blok, nor Sologub, nor Leonid Andreyev—or goodness knows who else. No, right now the power over these human souls, without any doubt, is in these somewhat swarthy hands affectedly pressing the piano keys. Kuzmin has nothing to do with it—if it weren't he then it would be someone else. And his listeners have nothing to do with it either—it's the times.

1916. Disasters at the front. A revolution is closing in—like an underground rumbling. Yes, that's all true … But we're mere poets, what can we do?

And the peasant lad follows suit:

"Mikhoil Lekseich, sing the one about the apple tree…"

After all, notwithstanding his operatic *kosovorotka*, regardless of his golden ribbon for a belt, he really is a country lad. And in order to enter this brilliant drawing room he had to endure a lot, and not in the realm of "betrayed love and early disillusionment," but in most cruel everyday life. He went through everything that all Russian self-made men had to go through as they strove to make their way "from the darkness to the light." It is well known what kind of "drive" is needed not to perish even half or even one-quarter of the way. He had enough of that drive, he endured everything, he did not perish … And there he sits in his silk blouse, with his golden belt, his hair all curled up. As he fought his way toward "the rational, the good, the eternal," he had enough strength to endure everything. And here he is, he's made it. The parquet shines, Egyptian cigarettes trail smoke, and a rouged dandy at the Érard grand piano, goes on cooing and swallowing his "r's," his pince-nez sparkling.

He's sowing seeds …

But are these the seeds of "the rational, the good, the eternal"? Is it what the peasant lad went on dreaming about so sweetly and hungrily a while ago now in a dirty peasant hut as he poured over his grubby book of ABCs by the rushlight?

It is. In 1916, in Petersburg, at the height of the war, on the eve of revolution, in the most refined and select circle, truth is defined as follows:

Philosophy we don't need …

As to whether this is the truth—that is never in doubt. Especially since no one cares to doubt. Everyone likes it the way it is. This and nothing else. And no one is to blame.

The time has come, and the poison is working. The time has come, and there is no resisting the poison …

In 1917 Kannegisser wrote:

And if, reeling from pain,
I'll cling to you, O, Mother,

And in an abandoned field I'll lie,
Shot through the chest—

Then at the Pearly Gates,
In my last and joyous dream,
I will recall—Russia, Freedom,
Kerensky on a white steed...[81]

"About valor, heroic deed, and glory..."—he had dreamed about it for a long time. "A joyous death" for Russia, for freedom, for humanity—it had haunted him for a long time. But what a cruel difference between what had haunted him and the way it turned out to be in reality.

... Russia, Freedom,
Kerensky on a white steed ...

No—a Cheka basement, the dry crack of a revolver.

✳ ✳ ✳

Few know that Moses Uritsky's assassin was a poet.

"A genuine poet?" Yes, a genuine one. If he had simply "dabbled in poetry," like the majority of young people of his age and milieu, his poetry wouldn't be worth mentioning.

But Kannegisser really was a poet. He perished too young "to find his own voice." What remained of his writing are mere experiments, trial runs, premonitions. But that his work is "genuine" can be seen in every line.

So there you have it—Uritsky's assassin was a poet. And what is a poet? First of all that is a being possessing a doubled, tenfold, thousandfold increased sensitivity. The late court physician Karpinsky, psycho-neurologist extraordinaire, used to say:

"Understand that if you cut off a finger from a soldier and from Alexander Blok, both will hurt. It's just that Blok, take my word for it, will hurt five hundred times more."

I don't know about fingers, but in the spiritual realm I'm sure that "a Blok" always hurts more than a "non-Blok," be he a soldier or a banker.

Such is the essence of "poetic nature." Nonpoets shouldn't be offended by it. Although there no pride to take from this either ...

Thus, not a simple "Russian boy" assassinated Uritsky. Uritsky was assassinated by a poet.

... They grabbed him on Millionny Street like a hunted animal. Took him to the Cheka. What did they do to him there, how was he interrogated? They threatened him that his mother, father, his whole family would be shot, had already been shot. Rumor has it they tortured him. Long weeks in prison awaiting execution ... Not a ray of light, no hope ...

They didn't execute Kannegisser for a long time. Why it was necessary—I don't know. Long weeks of such a "life" are hard to imagine. And yet he "lived through" them and apart from the terrible fate he had chosen for himself, he remained the same twenty-year-old, enamored, and proud Lenny Kannegisser ...

When a soldier's finger is getting cut off, he may not "hurt" as much as an "Alexander Blok," yet it hurts horribly, unbearably.

And then there's that infernal "multiplication table":

"Handsome" multiplied by "twenty-year-old" multiplied by "joyful" multiplied by "enamored" multiplied by "proud..." and on top of all that—a poet.

✳ ✳ ✳

Already here, in Paris, I saw the last photograph of Kannegisser, taken two or three days before his execution.

When his relatives were released from prison several months later, it turned out that some half their furniture had been removed from the apartment. It goes without saying that nothing was left of their papers, letters, and photographs—what could anyone expect if even their grand piano was removed as a piece of "material evidence"?

And, having returned home after long months in prison, Kannegisser's parents could not find even a single portrait of their executed son.

"Everything has been destroyed" was the Cheka response to their request to return at least one photograph.

There were several people present in the investigator's office. When Kannegisser's father was already on the street, someone called out to him. It was a leather-jacketed Cheka man, one of those present in the office. He extended his hand with a few photographs.

"Here. They gave copies to all of us. Please take them."

And after a short silence he added:

"Your son died a hero..."

Two small pale imprints, like the ones done for passports.

One in profile was particularly horrific. Could that be Kannegisser? The one we all knew, that handsome, joyful, proud boy?

Yes, it was him. Only neither his beauty, his youth, his joy, nor his poetry remained. The only thing left on that face was pride.

His lips are tightly pressed together. The eyes look out calmly and coldly. The hair is smoothly combed and the cheeks shaven. But there's something in that face, something that will make anyone who glances at that portrait shudder, even without knowing *whose* portrait it is, and *where* it comes from ...

✳ ✳ ✳

Kannegisser was held at Kronstadt Prison. For interrogations he would be escorted to Petersburg in a cutter. And here's a story told by one of the sailors escorting him. Halfway there a storm broke out and the cutter started to take on water. Kannegisser said:

"If we drown, I'll be the only one laughing."

No one who knew Kannegisser would doubt the authenticity of those words. All of him is in that phrase. He would indeed probably laugh if the cutter had overturned. And he was being escorted from prison to a torture-chamber. Behind him were many weeks in anticipation of execution. Ahead—not a sliver of light, no hope ...

The Baltic Sea was smoking
And ripped apart, becoming sunset;
The Baltic sun was setting
Beyond blue, faraway Kronstadt.[82]

XVII

I knew Blok and Gumilyov well. I heard newly completed poems from them, had tea with them, strolled along Petersburg streets with them, breathed the same air with them in August 1921, the month of their mutual—so diverse and equally tragic—deaths ... My remarks about them may be incomplete, but there are only two or three people left in Russia who knew them both as well as I did, and in emigration there is no one ...

Blok and Gumilyov. Antipodes in their poems, tastes, worldviews, political views, appearance—decidedly in everything. The misty radiance of Blok's poetry, and the precision, clarity, measured perfection of Gumilyov's. Blok, the Left Socialist Revolutionary who in *The Twelve* glorified October 1917—"to bring woe to all bourgeois, we will set the world on fire"—and the "White Guardsman," the "monarchist" Gumilyov. Blok who was sickened by war, and Gumilyov who volunteered to fight. Blok who considered the world "frightening," life senseless, God cruel or nonexistent, and Gumilyov who with utmost sincerity asserted "a man who loves the world and believes in God encompasses everything within himself."[83] Blok who his whole life envisaged the revolution as a "magnificent inevitability"—Gumilyov who considered revolution a synonym for evil and barbarity. Blok, who despised literary technique, craftsmanship, mastery, the very title of a man of letters, who remarked about someone—

> He was only a modish man of letters,
> Only the creator of blasphemous words—[84]

and Gumilyov, who called the circle of his disciples a *guild* of poets to underscore the importance, the necessity of studying poetry as a craft. And so on, right down to their appearance: a paragon of Nordic beauty with the face of a skald, marvelously flowing hair, the soft white collar of his shirt unbuttoned over a poetic velvet jacket—Blok, and unattractive, tight-set, "vary-eyed,"[85] crop-haired, in a prim and proper coat—Gumilyov...

Opposites in everything, all their short lives Blok and Gumilyov were hostile to each other, now obliquely, now openly. "Concerning the Soul," the last article written by Blok to appear shortly before his death, is a scathing attack on Gumilyov, his poetics and worldview. Gumilyov's response to that article—patently Gumilyovian in its reserve and civility, yet no less caustic in its essence—was published after his execution.[86]

In the autumn of 1909 Georgy Chulkov brought me to meet Blok. I had just turned fifteen. I wore a cadet uniform. Chulkov had read my notebook of poems and became my literary patron.

What's the point in trying to describe the feelings I had when entering Blok's apartment? At that time he lived on Maly Monetny Street on the fifth floor.

A large window with no curtains with a wide view of the roofs, the trees, and Kamennostrovsky Boulevard. Blok always rented apartments high up so that his windows opened on a large vista. Fifty-seven Ofitsersky Street, where he died, was even higher, one could see New Holland, and the view was still broader, still airier … Mahogany furniture in the "Russian Empire" style, a dark carpet, two large bookcases along the walls facing each other. The one with opened curtains is crammed with books. The glass of the other is completely covered with green silk. Later I found out that instead of books this bookcase held bottles of wine, Nuits Vintage 22, from Yeliseyev's grocery store. Full ones on top, empty ones below. Right there he had a corkscrew, several glasses, and a towel. As Blok works, from time to time he walks over to this bookcase, pours himself some wine, empties it in one gulp, and then sits down at his writing desk again. An hour later he walks over to the bookcase again. "Without it" he cannot work.

Each time Blok pours wine into a new glass. At first he carefully wipes it with the towel then holds it to the light—is there a speck of dust? Blok, the most seraphic, the most "unearthly" of poets, is neat and fastidious to the point of oddity. For example, if Blok locks himself in his study, everyone in the house goes about on tiptoe; the phone receiver (until this very day I remember Blok's telephone number—612-00!) is off its hook—all this, however, does not mean that he is writing poems or an article. Much more often he answers letters. Blok receives voluminous correspondence, often from strangers, often nonsensical or crazy. Whoever the correspondent may be, Blok is sure to answer without fail. Every letter is numbered and awaits its turn. But that isn't all. Blok registers every letter in a special notebook. Thick, with gold edging and bound in olive-colored leather, it occupies a prominent place on his most neatly arranged—not a speck of dust on it—writing desk. The pages of the notebook are ruled: Letter number. Sender. Date received. Brief summary. Brief summary of answer and date ...

Blok's handwriting is regular, beautiful, clear. He writers unhurriedly, confidently, firmly. An excellent pen (Blok uses the finest writing implements) glides gracefully along a thick sheet of paper. Rubbed clean to a shine, his windows open on a broad view. The apartment is silent. In the bookcase behind the green curtains stands a row of bottles, a corkscrew, glasses ...

Completely unable to get accustomed to this Blokian fastidiousness, Chulkov once queried:

"How come you have this in you, Sasha? Is this your German blood or what?" This is Blok's surprising answer as reported by Chulkov:

"German blood? I don't think so. Rather self-defense against chaos."

✳ ✳ ✳

As someone close to Blok, Chulkov shook his thick mane as he casually entered the poet's study; with a smile on his shaven actor's face, he poked his finger at my cadet uniform. "Look, I've brought you a military man— even though you don't like the army, be nice to him..." Following Chulkov, I timidly stepped in, my feet hardly obeying me because of my timidity.

What astonished me the most was the way Blok began speaking to me. It was as if I were someone who has been acquainted with him for a long time, as if I were an adult and as if he were continuing an interrupted conversation. The way he began speaking to me was such that my nervousness didn't just go away—I simply forgot about it. It came back to me with renewed force afterwards, two hours or so later, as I was going down the stairs carrying with me the gift Blok had given me, a copy of the first edition of *Verses about the Beautiful Lady* inscribed "A memento of our conversation."

As time passed, I accumulated several such books, all bearing the same inscription, differing only by dates. What were those conversations about? I also had a batch of Blok's letters—from his Shakhmatovo to our estate in Vilna province where I spent my vacations. The letters were long. What did Blok write to me about? The same things we discussed during our personal meetings, the same things as in his poems. The meaning of life, the mystery of love, the stars rushing through infinite space ... Always hazy, always enthralling ... Beautiful, clear handwriting. Characters separate from each other. Crunchy paper made of English linen. Envelopes with a crimson lining. Hazy words that formed brittle, flickering phrases ...

Why did Blok write long letters to me or conduct long conversations with me, a wet-behind-the-ears adolescent with endless questions about poetic technique ready to roll off his tongue? From time to time one of those questions did roll off my tongue.

"Aleksandr Aleksandrovich, does a sonnet need a coda?" I asked him once. To my amazement, Blok, that famous *"maître,"* had absolutely no idea what a coda was ...

An entry from Blok's diary for 1909: "Spoke with Georgy Ivanov about Plato. He left me a changed person." This entry may well contain an explanation of those letters and conversations. It must be that Blok did not notice my age and did not listen to my naïve comments. It must be that he spoke not so much with me as with himself. An accident—I was in front of him, in his orbit—and he would send me his hazy rays, all but oblivious of me.

Not that many people would wind up in that Blokian orbit, but those who did seemed to have done so by accident. Blok did not have any genuine friends who would by any measure be his equal. The ties of his youth either got severed or, as happened in his relationship with Andrey Bely, mutated into a torturously complex, unresolvable muddle. Blok shied away from the usual literary environment. As for those close to him, those who would visit his place casually, those who accompanied him on his long matinal strolls and frequent nocturnal drinking bouts, they all were some kind of eccentrics.

Chulkov was the only normal person among them—and, in addition to that, he was a writer, even if a second-rate one. But what was it that connected Blok with this sweet, superficially talented inventor of "mystical anarchism," in which nobody, Chulkov himself including, seriously believed?

Incomprehensible is his friendship with Vladimir Pyast, still more incomprehensible those with Evgeny Ivanov and Wilhelm Sorgenfrei, to whom, by the way, are dedicated these masterpieces of Blokian poetry: the former gets "At the foot of a railroad embankment, on the uncut grass of a hollow" and the latter the astonishing "Steps of the Commendatore."[87]

Pyast was a dilettante poet and amateur linguist; he cut a strange figure with those perpetual checkered trousers of his and a *canotier* he would still have on in December. He was constantly obsessed with some sort of "idea": now setting up a colony of linguists on Ezel Island, now calculating accents in nightingale trilling and the versification reform that would be based on those calculations. With a maniac's persistence he could only talk of his current "idea"—for as long as he was obsessed with it ... Evgeny Ivanov—"Zhenya the Gingerhead," ginger from beard to eyeballs—who cooked his dinner on a portable stove out of fear that his maidservant would suddenly get angry about something and "on a whim throw in some arsenic." In contrast with the chatty Pyast, "Zhenya the Gingerhead" could remain silent for hours on end but then out of sudden utter some profound word: "God" or "death" or "fate"—only to fall silent again. Why God? What about death? But "Zhenya the Gingerhead" oddly stares with those odd ginger eyes of his, "bares his white small teeth as if wants to bite," and does not answer. Sorgenfrei—a common denominator of Pyast and Ivanov—speaks in a completely comprehensible and logical manner. The only thing is that most of the time he steers the conversation toward the topic of ritual murders, his hobbyhorse. He is quite an authority on the problem—he has studied the Kabbalah and corresponds with the famous priest Justinas Pranaitis. As if to taunt him, nature has given him a characteristically Jewish appearance, although he is Baltic German on his father's side, and Georgian on his mother's …

Why are these people close to Blok? What brings them close to him? Most likely he doesn't notice them. They have been drawn into his orbit—interacting with them, he sees only his own self, his solitude in the "Terrible World."[88] And he has grown accustomed to their faces, their voices, and even their oddities in the same way as to the glasses he carefully wipes with a towel, to the lined "received-answered" notebook with gilded edging, to the methodical order on his writing desk. It's that same "self-defense against chaos" all over again …

These four—Sorgenfrei, Ivanov, Pyast, and Chulkov—are Blok's constant drinking pals when from time to time he has to indulge in tavern debauchery. "Tavern" is the key word here. Cosseted, gracious, fastidious Blok loves the dirtiest, spit-splattered and smoke-drenched "dives": the Elephant on Razyezzhy Street, the Yar on Bolshoy Prospect. First, it's the Elephant or the Yar; next—off to the Gypsies …

… Stale air, dirty tablecloths, bottles, snacks. "The Machine" hoarsely churns out "O, take pity on me, my darling" or "On the Hills of Manchuria." Drunks are everywhere. Blok's companions are tipsy too. "God!" unexpectedly blurts out Ivanov and falls silent, grinning and looking about with his ginger pupils. Sorgenfrei drones on about Beilis. Pyast, beginning to nod off, mumbles something about Lope de Vega …

Blok is the same as always, as he is on his matinal strolls, as he is in his well-lit study. Calm, handsome, pensive. He too has been drinking a lot, but it doesn't show.

A prostitute walks up to him. "What's on your mind, interesting man? Won't you treat me to a glass of port?" She sits on Blok's knees. He doesn't chase her away. He pours her wine, strokes her gently on the head as he would a child, and talks to her about something. About what? Well, it's the same thing, as always. About the terrible world, about the meaninglessness of life. About love's nonexistence. About how love, like a ray of light, reflects itself in everything, even in these cigarette butts trampled on the tavern's floor …

"Sasha, you are an inspired poet!" shouts out Chulkov, who has attained a state of drunken ecstasy and wants to kiss, spilling his drink all over. Blok regards him as lucidly, soberly, and pensively as always. As if

191

weighing his answer unhurriedly, he responds in the same sober, some-what lusterless voice:

"No. Inspired poet I'm not. Inspired poets burn up and perish in their poems. But I drink wine and publish my poems in *Grainfield*. Half-a-ruble per line. I do the same thing as Gumilyov, only without his sense of the virtuousness of his calling."

Blok is one of the most astounding phenomena in the entire existence of Russian poetry—now no one would debate it, and those who would don't count. "The door of poetry has been shut on them forever," to use Zinaida Hippius's expression. But around the creator of that poetry, its source— Alexander Blok the man—conflicting interpretations will go on for a long time. If they have subsided for now, it is only because no one is around to hold these debates ... *There* Blok has been forgotten according to a Polit-buro edict proclaiming him "disconsonant with our epoch"; *here*—due to the ever-growing weariness and indifference to everything apart from the sad approach of life's end ... But one day the disputes about Blok's person-ality will flare up with renewed force. It is unavoidable, if Russia remains Russia and Russian people remain Russians. The Russian reader has never been and, God willing, will never be a cold aesthete, an indifferent "connoisseur of the beautiful," who cannot be bothered with a poet's personality. When we love poems, we by the same token love their creator—strive to understand, to divine, if need be—and to vindicate him.

It seems that Blok's is exactly the case in need of vindication. *The Twelve* is one of the pinnacles of his poetry, and specifically because it is one of its pinnacles, it casts a sinister shadow of blasphemy with regards to Russia and Christ on his name and on everything he has written. The poems by true poets in general, and the masterpieces of their poetry espe-cially, are inseparable from the personality of the poet. And since Blok wrote *The Twelve*, it means that ...

Further on I will tell about how Blok died. His deathbed delirium alone is enough, in my opinion, for this "it means that" to lose its meaning. But before I proceed to showing how he himself, as he lay dying, regarded his splendid and revolting poem, I want to try to explain why Blok is not responsible for the creation of *The Twelve*, unstained, innocent.

First—pure people are not capable of dirty deeds. Second—the purest of people can make mistakes, sometimes terrible, irreparable ones. Blok the man possessed an exceptionally pure soul. He and baseness are mutually exclusive concepts. To use his own verses, he can be described as—

... a pure child of goodness and light,
a pure triumph of freedom.[89]

Yet it was he who wrote *The Twelve*, who placed Christ "in a snowy garland of roses" at the head of the Red Army guards headed to finish off Russia with their bayonets! How can one combine light, freedom, goodness with that? If Blok was indeed a "child of goodness and light," how could he have blessed crime and filth?

The explanation is that Blok only seemed a man of letters, grownup, proprietor of the Shakhmatovo estate, "apartment tenant," member of some kind of union ... All that was spectral. In the surreal reality where he dwelt and wrote poems, Blok was a child lost in a "Terrible World," afraid of life and not understanding it ...

Endowed with a magical gift, kind, magnanimous, unfailingly scrupulous with regards to life, people, and himself, Blok came to this world with his "skin stripped raw," with a morbid sensitivity to injustice, suffering, evil. As a counterweight to the "Terrible World" and its "worldly claptrap," from his youth on he created a dream of Revolution-Redemption and believed in it as though it were reality. The February Revolution, after the headiness of its first days, disenchanted Blok. The Pre-Parliament, cabinet ministers, election campaign for the Constituent Assembly seemed a profanation to him, and the slogan "War to a Victorious End!" drove him to indignation ...

And so Blok deluded himself into discerning love for mankind and Christian truth in the speech-defect-ridden, coercive shrieking of that misanthrope and atheist Lenin ...

Blok's unfailing sincerity and spiritual honesty are indubitable. And since this is the case, the blasphemous poem *The Twelve*, with its glorification of the October coup d'état, was not only created by him in the name of "goodness and light," but it is, in essence, a manifestation of light and goodness that turned out to be a terrible mistake.

> I will not forgive. Your soul is innocent.
> For it, I will not forgive her, ever—[90]

wrote Zinaida Hippius after reading *The Twelve*. These lines of hers confirm my words. That they contain a contradiction is merely an appearance. In their essence, they are—like everything by Hippius—very precise and clear. Hippius knew Blok closely and loved him very much. That in her irreconcilability she so harshly refuses to forgive Blok, only strengthens the force of her admission-assertion: "your soul is innocent."

For the creation of *The Twelve* Blok paid with his life. This is not a pretty phrase, it is the truth. Blok came to understand the mistake of *The Twelve*, and its irreparability horrified him. Like a sleepwalker suddenly awakened, he fell from high above and crashed. In the exact sense of the word, he died of *The Twelve*, as others die of pneumonia or a heart attack.

Here's a short inventory of the facts. The doctors who treated Blok could never determine the exact nature of his illness. First they tried to fortify his strength as it rapidly depleted for no apparent reason; next, as he suffered unbearably from a cause unknown, they would inject him with morphine ... But what did he die of, after all? "The poet dies when he no longer has air to breathe."[91] Those words, spoken by Blok not long before his death at an evening dedicated to Pushkin, may be the sole correct diagnosis of his illness. Several days before his death a rumor went around Petersburg: "Blok has gone mad!" This rumor definitely spread from Bolshevized literary circles. Subsequently Soviet journals discussed various interpretations of Blok's deathbed "insanity." But no one mentioned one particularly significant detail: as he lay dying, Blok was visited by an "enlightened bigwig"—I think it was Ilya Ionov, the head of the Petrograd State Literary Publishing House, he has been successfully purged by now. Blok was already unconscious. His delirium was unrelenting. He ravings concerned one and only one thing: have all the copies of *The Twelve* been destroyed? Could there have been a single one left somewhere? "Lyuba, go look for it carefully everywhere, and burn, burn them all." Lyubov Dmitriyevna, Blok's wife, patiently repeated that they had all been destroyed, that not a single one remained. Blok would calm down for a while, only to start again: he made his wife swear that she was telling him the truth as he recalled that he had mailed a copy to Valery Bryusov and demanded that he would be taken to Moscow. "I'll force him to give it back, I'll kill him..." And Ionov, head of the Petrograd State Literary Publishing House, was there to listen to these ravings of a dying man ...

Bryusov, that erstwhile "madman," "magician," "theurgist," who during the war began to lean sharply toward the Union of the Russian People, now held a number of governmental posts: he headed commissariats, chaired committees, organized requisitions of private libraries "for the benefit of the Proletariat." As always, he produced a multitude of poems that glorified the Proletariat and its leaders, naturally. As he glorified the living and breathing Lenin, perhaps in accordance with the "theurgic" custom of peeking into the future, he was composing an ode on his death—to have something ready when the occasion arose:

Here he lies—Lenin, Lenin—
Here he lies, sorrowfully putrefied...[92]

Boris Pilnyak would treat those who cared to listen to an anecdote how on the second or third day after Ionov's visit to Blok, at the Poets' Café in Moscow Bryusov went on explaining—details and scientific terms included—the character of Blok's "insanity" along with its causes. The erstwhile "madman" had already taken the Party edict as his command.

✳ ✳ ✳

In the days when Blok lay dying, Gumilyov wrote to his wife from prison: "Don't worry about me. I am healthy, I write poems and play chess." Not long before his arrest Gumilyov had returned to Petersburg from a trip to the Crimea. He traveled to the Crimea on the train of the Tsarist Admiral Alexander Nyomits, who had become an admiral with the Reds. I don't know who exactly, was it Nyomits himself or someone else from his closest circle, who took part in the same Vladimir Tagantsev conspiracy as Gumilyov, and, while traveling on a special train under the protection of Communist sailors, that "glory and pride of the Revolution," Gumilyov and his co-conspirator established links with the surviving officers and members of the intelligentsia in Crimean ports, supplied the right people with the weapons and anti-Soviet propaganda leaflets they had brought along from Petersburg on the Admiral's train. That the Nyomits circle had been infiltrated by a Cheka agent, a provocateur who was tracking him, Gumilyov had no idea. Gumilyov was generally very trusting, especially toward young people who happened to be members of the military to boot. It was as if the provocateur had been custom-made to sway Gumilyov's opinion in his favor.

He was tall, slender, with a cheerful look in his eyes and an open boyish face. He carried the name of a well-known seafaring family and himself was a sailor—he had been promoted to midshipman not long before the Revolution. In addition to those attractive qualities, this young man, "pleasant in all respects," wrote poems imitating Gumilyov's quite convincingly ...

Upon his return to Petersburg Gumilyov sported a tan, looked rested, and was full of plans and hopes. He was satisfied with his trip, his new poems, and his work with his student-apprentices. This feeling of life's fullness, bloom, maturity, success he experienced in the last days of his life, made itself known, by the way, in the title he then thought up for his "future" book: *In the Middle of Our Earthly Wandering*. He had less than a month left to him to "wander" the earth, or rather await execution in the prison cell on Shpalerny Street ...

On the day of his arrest Gumilyov came home about two in the morning. He had spent that last evening in a circle of young people who devotedly adored him. After Gumilyov's lecture there was, as always, the reading of new poems followed by their analysis in accordance with all the rules of Acmeism, "subordinate clauses" required, that is, with a justification for one's opinion: "I like it or I don't like it because … ," "Not good, since…." A strict discipline reigned during the lecture and the discussions of the poems, but when the lessons stopped, Gumilyov would cease to be the *maître* and became a good friend. Later on the participants in his studio recounted that he was very animated and in a good mood that night, and this is why he had lingered for such a long time, later than usual. Several young ladies and men accompanied Gumilyov on his way home. At the entryway to the House of Arts on the Moyka where Gumilyov lived, there was a motorcar waiting. No one paid it any attention—it was during NEP, and motorcars stopped being, as they had during the recent times of War Communism, both a marvel and a monster. They took their time bidding him farewell, joked and made plans "for tomorrow." The people who had arrived in the motorcar parked by the entryway came along with a Cheka-issued search and arrest warrant and were waiting for Gumilyov in his apartment.

On 27 August 1921, aged thirty-five and in the prime of life and talent, Gumilyov was shot dead. Is this a horrible, senseless way to perish? No. Horrible, but profoundly significant. Gumilyov could not have wished a better death for himself. What is more, it was exactly the kind of death that he had predicted for himself, with prescience bordering on clairvoyance:

> … I will not die in bed,
> A notary and a doctor by my side.[93]

✳ ✳ ✳

Having run into Mikhail Lozinsky soon after Gumilyov's execution, Sergey Bobrov—the author of *The Lyre of Lyres*, editor-in-chief of the Centrifuge Press, a snob, a Futurist, and a cocaine addict with Cheka links and most certainly a Cheka man himself—said, as if mentioning an amusing trifle, in passing, carelessly, a twitch distorting the fine-featured, nasty grimace of an aesthete-criminal:

"Right … That Gumilyov of yours … We, Bolsheviks, find it laughable. But you know what, he died with a flair. I heard this from those who were there. Smiled, finished a cigarette ... Sheer braggadocio, of course. But made an impression even on the boys from the Special Division. Empty immature posturing, but a strong type all the same. Few die like that. Well, serves him right for being such a fool. Instead of getting mixed up with the counterrevolutionary lot, he should have gone over to us, he would've had quite a career. We can use people like that..."

This horrible prattle supplements the story of the way Gumilyov conducted himself during interrogations that I personally heard not from a half-Cheka man like Bobrov, but from one Dzerzhibashev, a genuine Chekist, an investigator from the Petersburg Cheka, albeit from the anti-profiteering unit. Strange as it may seem, both the tone and the personality of this storyteller contrasted favorably with the tone and personality of Bobrov. Dzerzhibashev spoke of Gumilyov with unfeigned sadness, referring to his execution as a "terrible misunderstanding." That Dzerzhibashev man was familiar to many people in the Petersburg literary circles of the day. And many, including Gumilyov—absurd as it may sound—treated him with ... sympathy. At the same time Dzerzhibashev was an enigmatic fellow. It may well be that that investigator's position of his was a mask. This would explain, then, both the inexplicable sympathy that he engendered and the unexpected, "individual" execution in 1924.

Gumilyov's interrogations were more like disputations concerning the most divergent of topics—from Machiavelli's *The Prince* to "the beauty of Orthodoxy." Evgeny Jakobson, the investigator in charge of the Tagantsev plot, was, in Dzerzhibashev's words, a real Inquisitor, who combined intellect and a brilliant education with the determination of a maniac. It would not have been possible to choose a more dangerous investigator to lure Gumilyov to his execution. Had the investigator attempted to test Gumilyov's valor or honor, needless to say he would have gotten nowhere. But Jakobson enchanted and flattered Gumilyov. He called him the best Russian poet, recited his poems by heart, deviously engaged Gumilyov in debates only to give ground, surrender, or pretend to surrender before his opponent's intellectual superiority ...

I have already mentioned that Gumilyov was extremely credulous. If to this we add his partiality toward any manifestation of intelligence, erudition, intellectual inventiveness—and, finally, that he was not immune to flattery—it is easy to imagine how Gumilyov without knowing walked into the trap set out for him by Jakobson. How unwittingly Gumilyov, in the course of an abstract debate concerning the principles of monarchy, confessed to being a confirmed monarchist. How easy it was for Jakobson after a debate about revolution "in general," to establish and document Gumilyov's confessing to being an unrelenting enemy of the October Revolution. It is unlikely that Gumilyov's reticence would have changed his fate. For the Petersburg Cheka the Tagantsev trial was an excuse to demonstrate its independence and irreplaceability to the all-Russian Cheka. At that very moment the question was raised about the consolidation of power and right to carry out executions in the hands of the Moscow Cheka collegium. That was reason for Jakobson's thoroughness and haste. But who knows! Had Gumilyov pretended to be a man of the arts indifferent to politics who had become embroiled in the conspiracy accidently, perhaps the prestige of his name—in those days it still meant something to the Bolsheviks—would have outweighed the accusation? Perhaps in that case the reasons presented by Maxim Gorky, who made a special trip to Moscow on Gumilyov's behalf, would have had an effect on Lenin ...

... The seven-year old Gumilyov fainted because another boy outran him when they were competing in a race. At eleven he attempted suicide: he mounted a horse awkwardly, and household members and guests laughed. A year later he fell in love with an unknown girl attending a nearby gymnasium. He followed her, traipsed after her in the streets, and, finally, approached her and confessed, choking on his words: "I love you." The girl replied "Idiot" and ran away. Gumilyov was devastated. He felt as if he had gone blind and deaf. He couldn't sleep at night thinking about how to take revenge: burn down the house where she lives? Abduct her? Challenge her brother to a duel? The insult inflicted on the twelve-year-old Gumilyov was so deep he recollected it thirty years later with a laugh, but with a touch of bitterness ...

As an adolescent Gumilyov would fall asleep dreaming about one thing: how to become famous. Dreaming of fame, he would get up in the morning, drink his tea, and go to the Tsarskoye Selo gymnasium. Wandering around the park for hours on end, he would imagine a thousand ways to make his dream come true. Become a military commander? A scholar? Invent the *perpetuum mobile*? It doesn't matter what, so long as people repeated the name "Gumilyov," wrote books about him, were astounded by and envious of him.

Little by little those childish dreams congealed into a harmonious worldview to which Gumilyov remained loyal his entire life. He firmly believed that the right to call oneself a poet belongs to him who not only in his poems but in life always strives to be the best, first, ahead of others. The only one deserving to be a poet, according to his convictions, is he who, leading by his personal example in matters important and petty alike, overcomes "the old Adam" by force of will while remaining fully cognizant of human frailties, egoism, insignificance, and the fear of death. And naturally a meek, shy, sickly person, Gumilyov "ordered" himself to become a lion hunter, an uhlan who voluntarily went to war and earned two St. George crosses, and a conspirator. What he did in his personal life he brought to bear on his poetry. Dreamy, dolorous lyricist, he strove to return to poetry its former significance; risking to lose his clean, authentic, but quiet voice, he would choose complex forms, "thunderous" words and take on difficult epic themes. Gumilyov's motto in life and in poetry was "always the path of greatest resistance." That worldview of his made him lonely in the literary circle contemporary to him; surrounded as he was by admirers and imitators, recognized as a *maître*, as a poet he was misunderstood all the same. Not long before his death—half a year, to be exact—Gumilyov said to me: "You know, today I watched a brick stove being made, and I felt envious— and guess of whom?—the bricks. They lay them down so firmly, so tightly, and calk every chink to boot. Brick to brick, one next to another, all together, one for all and all for one. Loneliness is the most difficult thing in life. And I am so lonely…"

* * *

All his short life Gumilyov—an acclaimed poet, he was becoming famous—was surrounded by misunderstanding and hostility. Acutely aware of this, he directed his irony at those around him and himself.

> I am polite with modern life,
> But between us there's a barrier—
> Everything that amuses it, the haughty one,
> Is my one and only joy.
>
> Victory, glory, exploit—pale
> Words, now abandoned,
> They resound in my soul like bronze thunder,
> Like the voice of the Lord in the desert.
>
> Oh no, no tragic actor I,
> I am more ironic and dry.
> Like a metallic idol, I seethe with anger,
> Among porcelain toys.
>
> He remembers curly heads,
> Bent toward his pedestal,
> Majestic prayers of pagan priests,
> Forests a-tremble.
>
> But now he sees, a bitter smile on his face,
> A rocking swing, forever still,
> Where a shepherd plays his pipe
> To a lady with a prominent breast.[94]

Contrary to the modernity so foreign to him, with its lack of desire to acknowledge exploits, glory, and victories, both in his poems and life Gumilyov strove to do everything to remind people of "the divine nature of the poet's calling," to remind them that:

... In the Gospel of St. John,
It is stated that the Word is God.[95]

With all the means available to him, all his life, starting with naming his first adolescent collection of poems *The Path of the Conquistador* and down to his last cigarette, which he calmly finished before his execution, Gumilyov sought to prove this assertion. And when people say that he died for Russia, it is necessary to add—"and for poetry."

✻ ✻ ✻

Blok and Gumilyov departed this life divided by mutual incomprehension. Blok considered Gumilyov's poetry artificial, the Acmeist doctrine false, and the work with young poets in literary studios that was so close to Gumilyov's heart damaging. As a poet and a person, Gumilyov provoked Blok's rejection and dull irritation. Gumilyov's censure of Blok's *The Twelve* was particularly harsh. I remember a phrase uttered by Gumilyov not long before their coincident deaths, and I remember the cold, cruel expression on his face when he said with conviction: "By writing *The Twelve*, he (i.e., Blok) has crucified Christ and executed the Emperor for the second time."

I objected that regardless of its content, poetically *The Twelve* is close to being a work of genius. "All the worse if it is a work of genius. All the worse for poetry and for the poet himself. Mark my words, the Devil is also a genius—all the worse for the Devil, and for us..."

Now that so many years have passed since the day of their death, when both "Aleksandr Aleksandrovich" and "Nikolay Stepanovich," both the Left Socialist Revolutionary and "the White Guardsman," both the hater of war, medals, and epaulets and "the Hussar of Death," who took pride in "our storied regiment" and intended to write its history, are no more; now when all that remains is "Blok and Gumilyov"—a sad consolation for us, who have survived them—what has become clear is that there was something they themselves did not understand.

That their enmity was a misunderstanding, since both as poets and as Russians they did not exclude, but rather complement each other. That which separated them was evanescent and inconsequential, while that which essentially was equally dear to both brought them into a brotherly accord that neither of them appreciated.

They both lived and breathed poetry—outside of poetry there was no life for either of them. Both loved Russia selflessly, torturously. Both detested falsehood, mendacity, pretense, unscrupulousness—in both art and life they were exceedingly honest. Finally, in the name of that "metaphysical honor"—the highest responsibility of the poet before God and himself—both were ready to do anything, including facing death, and this readiness of theirs they proved by their terrifying personal examples.

XVIII

On December 27, 1925, Sergey Yesenin committed suicide in the Hôtel Angleterre, an older, modestly grand hotel on St. Isaac's Square familiar to all Petersburgers.

The windows of that hotel look out on—to the right, beyond St. Isaac's Square—a black-marble palace, the home of the Zubovs; to the left, on the other side of the Moyka—the Government Control building stands tall. In prerevolutionary years the pulse of Petersburg's literary-artistic life throbbed in those buildings, they both were frequented by Yesenin ...

It is likely that Yesenin more than once looked through the mirrored windows of Count Valentin Zubov's study at the two-storied Angleterre nestled on the other side of the square. Looked as he recited poems, flaunting coquettishly, as he always did, the incomprehensible coarseness of his deliberately peasant-style words:

> ... The smell of ruddy egg pies,
> A keg of kvass stands by the threshold;
> Above carved stoves
> Cockroaches crawl into a crevice...[96]

"Charming ... Charming..." Applause, obliging smiles. "Sergey Aleksandrovich, Seryozha ... Why don't you read some more, or better still, sing to us. The way you sing those—what are they called now?—*chastushki*—is so lovely."

The rustling of silk, the odor of perfumes, the blend of a Russo-Parisian chatter. Tall lackeys in liveries and white stockings wait on the guests offering tea with cherry brandy and sweets. And amid all this Yesenin's ringing voice resounds, like a warning from another world, like a gust of icy wind in a fragrant hot house:

> … One hidden dream I cherish:
> Pure at heart as I am,
> One day I too will slit someone's throat—
> As I whistle in the fall![97]

To the left of St. Isaac's, on the other side of the Moyka, the ground floor of the State Control building houses parlors that are less lavish, and the furniture there is not as fine as at the Zubovs. But the company is practically the same. This apartment belongs to the well-known courtier X.

X. himself, however, never shows his face at these gatherings. The guests are acquaintances of his nephew Mikhail Aleksandrovich Kovalyov, the poet Ryurik Ivnev. Ryurik Ivnev is Yesenin's closest friend and insepa-rable companion. Frail constitution, a pale birdlike face, a feminine tortoise-shell lorgnette held up to colorless squinting eyes. The way he is dressed is refined in its sloppiness. On his expensive suit—a spot. The elegant tie is askew. The heels of his polished dress shoes are worn down. Ryurik Ivnev constantly twitches, fidgets about, and looks over his shoulder. And to just about every word he utters he adds, half in question, half in bewilderment: "What? What?" "Sergey Yesenin? What? What? His poems are magic. What? Look at his hair. It's the color of ripe rye—what?"

The company is practically the same as at the Zubov palace, but not exactly. Here, among glittering suits pop up cassocks, bowl haircuts, and jackboots.

Yesenin is seated in the place of honor. Speaking with a singsong accent, a middle-aged fellow dressed "à la coachman" converses with him—or, rather, lectures him. A sugary smile spreads across the fellow's face, but his gray eyes are clever and cold. This is Nikolay Klyuyev—a peasant poet, too—or "the *gusli* strummer from Olonets province," as he recommends himself.

Klyuyev is cooing:

"Soon, oh so soon, Seryozha darling, streams of fire will burst forth, birds of paradise will raise a hue and cry, the font of tears will open, and God's truth will be revealed."

Yesenin listens deferentially, but in the depths of his eyes hides a sly little spark. He is very much in love with Klyuyev and finds himself under his great influence. As to the "streams of fire," Yesenin doesn't appear to believe in those that much ...

"What? What?" Ryurik Ivnev's lisp can be heard nearby. "Me? I'm a confirmed pacifist! What? It would be even more accurate to say a defeatist. Russia's only chance is to throw the front line open and greet the victors with the ringing of church bells. The only chance to survive. What?"

By the way, both of them, Klyuyev and Ivnev, will play a fatal role in Yesenin's life. Through them he will make acquaintances that will subsequently bring him closer to the Bolsheviks. The fates of these two men are as different as they are. The last piece of news concerning Ivnev that reached me late in the 1920's–early in the 1930's was his rumored appointment as ... the Soviet plenipotentiary either to Persia or Afghanistan ... Klyuyev, during dekulakization, was sent to Siberia. From Siberia he appealed to Stalin with a pathetic versified request, the ending of which read: "Let me live—or permit me to die!" "The Father of the Peoples" magnanimously permitted Klyuyev to die ...

It was Klyuyev and no one else to whom Yesenin unexpectedly came late at night on the day of his suicide. Their relationship had gone sour long ago, and they had almost stopped seeing each other ... Yesenin looked horrific. Aghast with fright, Klyuyev mumbled like an old man: "Go away, go away, Seryozha darling, I'm afraid of you..." Klyuyev hastened to see off his former friend into the Petersburg December night. From Klyuyev Yesenin went straight to the Angleterre.

Yesenin killed himself at dawn. Unsuccessful at first, he attempted to open his veins, then hanged himself, twice wrapping the strap from his foreign-made suitcase—a memento from his honeymoon with Isadora

Duncan—around his neck. Before his death he created an incredible chaos in the room. Chairs were overturned, the mattress and sheets were ripped from the bed onto the floor, the mirror was shattered, everything around was splattered with blood. With that same blood from an unsuccessfully opened vein, Yesenin wrote his suicide note, an eight-line poem beginning with the words:

Goodbye, my friend, goodbye...[98]

All his short, romantic, wild life Yesenin inspired in those around him tempestuous and contradictory passions while being torn apart by equally tempestuous and contradictory passions himself. They were his life and doom. Perhaps because those passions did not find a full outlet either in his poetry or in his life cut short by the convulsion of suicide, Yesenin's posthumous fate has been the subject of a magical strangeness. He has been dead a quarter-century already, but it is as if everything associated with him has been excluded from the general law of dying, pacification, and oblivion, and continues to live. Not only do his poems continue to live, but so does everything "Yeseninesque," Yesenin "in general," to coin a phrase. Everything that surrounded, affected, tormented, elated him, everything that came into some kind of contact with him, until this very moment continues to draw the vibrant breath of today's living day ...

The way I experience it is more or less as follows. If, for example, somewhere out there Yesenin's hat and coat are preserved hanging on their pegs, they are hanging like the hat and coat of a living person who has just taken them off. They still preserve his warmth, emit his being. Unclear? Unprovable? Agreed. I won't venture either to clarify or prove it. I'm convinced, however, that I'm not the only person among those who continue to hold Yesenin dear experiencing this unprovably irrefutable vitality of everything "Yeseninesque"—right down to his old hat. And this same singular trait endows all Yesenin poems, even the most weak and unsuccessful of them, with a special force and significance. And at once, beforehand, deprives our evaluations of them of any objectivity. A dispassionate appraisal of Yesenin's art will be made by those on whom its charm will have ceased to have an effect. It is possible, even probable, that their appraisal will be much more reserved than ours. Only that will not happen any time soon. It will happen no sooner than Russia liberates herself, recuperates both physically and spiritually. In this lies the singularity—I would even say "genius"—of Yesenin's fate. As long as the Motherland he loved so much is fated to suffer, he is assured not infamous "immortality," but rather *in-transitory*—like Russia's suffering, and like this suffering protracted—*life*.

I first heard Yesenin's name in the autumn or winter of 1913. At the *New Life* editorial offices Fyodor Sologub, with that customary haughty-peevish expression on his clean-shaven white "stony" face—"brick in a frockcoat," Vasily Rozanov's nickname for him—told about a young peasant poet who had come by to introduce himself to him.

"... Such a pretty face, so blue-eyed, so humble..." was Sologub's disapproving description of Yesenin. "Oozes deference, perches on the edge of his chair, ready to jump up at any moment. Shamelessly kisses up: 'Ah, Fyodor Kuzmich! Oh, Fyodor Kuzmich!' And all this is pretense of the first water! As he flatters you, he thinks to himself: 'I'll be sweet to the old cur, and he'll help me get published.' Well, you won't pull the wool over my eyes—I saw through that Ryazan calf right away. I made him confess that not only had he not read my poems and had already gone to kiss up to Blok and Merezhkovsky, but also that that one about the rushlight he used to learn his ABCs is all a pack of lies. Turns out he is a teachers school graduate. In a word, I got right under that phony velvet hide of his and found his real essence underneath: one hell of a self-confidence and the desire to get famous at any cost. I found all that out, ruffled his feathers, gave him a good spanking—this old cur he won't forget!"

And, right then and there, without dropping that haughty-peevish tone of his, Sologub handed the editor in chief Nikolay Arkhipov a notebook of Yesenin's poems.

"Here you are. These poems of his aren't bad at all. They've got a spark. I recommend them for publication—they'll add color to the magazine. And I suggest you give him an advance. After all, the lad is straight from the village; he's probably got about five kopecks in his pocket. But then he's got potential, a will to succeed, passion, hot blood. Head and shoulders above our *Apollo* nursemaids."

People from all sides started talking about Yesenin then. Soon we became acquainted and began to meet each other constantly here, there, and everywhere. The beginning of Yesenin's career happened before my eyes. But after the February Revolution, having allied himself with the Imaginists, he found his way to Moscow, and, save for one chance encounter in Berlin, I did not see him anymore.

Over the three or three-and-a-half years of Petersburg life, Yesenin became a well-known poet. He became surrounded by female admirers and friends. Many of the traits Sologub had found out under that "velvet hide" of his came to the fore. He became impertinent, self-assured, boastful. But strangely enough, that hide of his didn't go anywhere. Naïveté, credulity, some kind of childish tenderness coexisted in Yesenin with naughtiness verging on hooliganism and conceit bordering on insolence. All those contradictions held a certain special charm. And Yesenin was admired. People would forgive Yesenin much they would not have forgiven others. Yesenin got his way with people, especially in leftist-liberal literary circles.

The Petersburg period of Yesenin's career came to a close completely unexpectedly. In the late autumn of 1916 a "monstrous rumor" suddenly went around and then was confirmed: "our" Yesenin, Yesenin the "sweetheart," Yesenin the "charming boy" had presented himself to Aleksandra Fyodorovna in the Tsarskoye Selo Palace, he read her his poems, requested, and was granted the Empress's permission to dedicate an entire cycle of poems to her in his new book!

Today it is difficult even to imagine the level of indignation that took hold of "progressive circles" when Yesenin's "vile deed" was proven to have been not fiction, not "a Black Hundred slander," but an indisputable fact. People came running to Yesenin for an explanation. At first he kept his silence. Then he admitted it. Then took back his admission. Then he disappeared somewhere, some said to the front, some to his Ryazan village ...

Indignation with yesterday's favorite was enormous. At times it took on comic forms. Thus, Sofya Chatskina, a very rich and still more "progressive" lady, who in all seriousness referred to the *Northern Annals* magazine she published as "the artistic battering ram against Tsarism," at a sumptuous reception in her hospitable apartment hysterically tore up Yesenin's manuscripts and letters with the screech: "We've been nursing a snake in our bosoms! New Rasputin! Second Protopopov!" In vain did her more reserved spouse Jacob Saker try to dissuade the furious patroness of the arts from ruining her health "over some renegade."

Yesenin's collection *Goluben* came out already after the February Revolution. He had managed to remove the dedication to the Empress. Some Petersburg and Moscow rare books dealers, however, were able to obtain several *Goluben* galley proofs bearing the fatal: "I reverentially dedicate..." The rare books catalogue at Solovyov's store on Liteyny Boulevard listed one such copy with the "extremely odd" remark next to it. Another one passed through Vladislav Khodasevich's hands.

Had it not been for the Revolution, the doors of the majority of Russian publishers, especially the most rich and influential, would have been closed to Yesenin forever. Liberal circles did not forgive a Russian writer such "crimes" as monarchist sentiments. Yesenin could not have misunderstood that and, in all likelihood, deliberately sought to break away. The goals and hopes that compelled him to take such a bold step are unknown. But, of course, Yesenin would not have taken such a risk for nothing. The Revolution, having destroyed those mysterious calculations on Yesenin's part, in a funny way freed him from unavoidable liberal repressions. An amusing metamorphosis occurred: the all-powerful opposition, having overthrown the monarchy, went on from being the opposition to becoming the new power, and unexpectedly became powerless. "The salt of the Russian earth" suddenly lost its taste ... Before the Revolution, "Daddy" Milyukov could get any "apostate" "expelled from literature" by placing two or three phone calls from the editorial offices of *Speech*. From there the machine of "public opinion" would work on its own—automatically and mercilessly. But as to Milyukov the Minister, along with all those erstwhile makers of literary fates turned grandees of "the great and bloodless Republic," Yesenin, as the saying goes, didn't give a hoot about them. He knew full well that "the real guys" sat not in the Provisional Government ministries, but at the Durnovo dacha, in Kschessinska's mansion, and in the "Workers, Peasants, and Soldiers Council…" Connections in that sphere opened all doors, obliterated the consequences of not mere foolhardy acts, but of any crime. Through Ryurik Ivnev, Klyuyev, Maxim Gorky, Razumnik Ivanov-Razumnik, and Vladimir Bonch-Bruyevich, Yesenin's connections branched out upward and rose to the very "heights"—to Mamont Dalsky, Anatoly Lunacharsky, Trotsky … to Lenin himself …

✳ ✳ ✳

Immediately after the October coup Yesenin found himself if not in the Party—he never became a member of the All-Russian Communist Party—then in close proximity to the "Soviet top brass." There was nothing strange about that. On the contrary, it would have been surprising if it did not happen.

To imagine Yesenin with Anton Denikin or Alexander Kolchak, or, even more so, among the members of the old emigration is psychologically impossible. From his origins to his spiritual makeup, everything predisposed him to turn away from "Kerensky's Russia" and in all honesty lend his support to the "Russia of peasants and workers."

First of all, for Yesenin closeness to the Bolsheviks was devoid of the sinister shadow of *betrayal* inescapable for any member of the Russian intelligentsia. On the contrary, according to the convictions he held at the time, it was the Provisional Government that betrayed the Tsar and the people, and it was Lenin who by wresting power from Kerensky fulfilled the will of the people. That's how he, the peasant that he was, instinctively grasped the events. That was the reasoning shared by the friends he kept at that time: Klyuyev, Pimen Karpov, Sergey Klychkov.

On the contrary, the future "February power," the Constitutional-Democratic and Socialist-Revolutionary circles where Yesenin moved before the Revolution, was naturally foreign to him. There was a time when they indulged and loved him, and he allowed them to indulge and love him. That was the extent of that relationship. The Empress incident had already revealed the depth of mutual misunderstanding between Yesenin and his intelligentsia patrons. As far Lenin & Co. were concerned, that "vile deed" of his was simply a "silly trifle." "So the lad sneaks to the Empress's chamber through the backdoor hoping to get something out of her. What's the big deal! Now that he's with us and has talent, we can use him, and that's it." "Who are you for? For us or against us? If 'against,' then you'll be put to the wall. If 'for,' come over to us and make yourself useful." Those words of Lenin's, uttered by him already in 1905, remained in full force in 1918. Yesenin was "for." And the value of that "for" was additionally increased by his sincerity.

"Sincerity" indeed. The majority of the members of the intelligentsia who joined the Bolsheviks were rogues and swindlers. Yesenin joined the Bolsheviks on "ideological" grounds, so to speak. He wasn't a rogue and wasn't putting himself up for sale. He was brought to Smolny Institute by the same hopes he was harboring when he entered Tsarskoye Selo Palace a year and a half before. He probably was hoping to get from Lenin more or less the same thing as from the Empress. He was expecting the fulfillment of a dream—a dream that like a red line runs through all of his early poems, a genuinely Russian dream that grew in the souls of simple people for centuries—a dream of a fair, perfect, holy peasant kingdom, the establishment of which is being prevented by the "masters."

Klyuyev, who influenced Yesenin more than anyone else, called that dream either "The New City" or "The Forest Truth." Yesenin called it "Inoniya." A narrative poem of 1918 bearing this title is the key to understanding Yesenin's War Communism period. As poetry it is probably the most perfect creation of his entire life. As document, it is the most eloquent testimony to the sincerity of his atheistic and revolutionary feelings.

Scrubbed clean of stylistic embellishments and poetic allegories, the most general terms of that "peasant dream" of Yesenin and Klyuyev could be summarized as follows. An ideal "Forest Kingdom" will come into being in Holy Russia when everything inorganic, artificial, alien to simple people—it can be called "empire," "culture," "the intelligentsia," "the legal order," and so on—is destroyed. For all this to burn to the ground, the "red rooster" needs to be let loose first. It is then that a "New City " will rise from the ashes, like Kitezh from the bottom of the lake. Where the red rooster is going to be let loose from—be it from the right or the left—whatever helps the "Forest Truth" to become reality in Rus—be it the baton carried by the members of the Union of the Archangel Michael or the dynamite vests and bombs carried by the terrorists, it does not make that much of difference ...

Shortly after the Bolshevik power grab Klyuyev expressed all this in a remarkable poem. Unfortunately, I remember only a few lines of it, but even they are sufficiently expressive:

> In Smolny you can find the darkness of slums,
> A taste of pine needles and bramble,
> There lies the rough-hewn coffin
> With the remains of Great Rus.
> In Lenin, you can find the spirit of the Kerzhenets,
> In his decrees, an echo of an Old Believer hegumen's shout ...[99]

That "Great Rus" lies in Smolny in a coffin is in no way an expression of grief on Klyuyev's part on account of her death or indignation at her Smolny-based murderers. Quite the opposite. More likely it is joy—something long-awaited has begun to be realized. The former Rus may have been "great," but it belonged to the masters, members of the intelligentsia, "ours" it was not. It has finally died, and all the better for it. And Lenin—today's murderer of that bygone Rus—is the appropriate builder of a future one. These lines highlight Lenin's traits that Klyuyev finds admirable: the Kerzhenets—which is to say national, peasant-like—spirit; the hegumen-like—which is to say simultaneously bossy and monastically ecclesiastical—"shout" discernible in the wording of Lenin's decrees. One thing is clear: Lenin is a worthy fellow, he fits right in, he is one of the people. And to support him is "the right thing," every peasant's duty.

> God save Freedom—
> The Commune's Red Tsar![100]

Klyuyev exclaimed at that same time. And in those days to him, to Yesenin and those close to them in spirit, of which there were many, such words did not have the absurd sound they have today, sounding more like the words of a solemn "Now Thou dost dismiss..."[101]

✳ ✳ ✳

In the USSR Yesenin has long been dethroned and debunked. Literature textbooks deal with him in a few lines the goal of which is to inculcate into Soviet children that Yesenin is not worthy of their love and still less worthy of their reading: as a poet he is second-rate, "petit-bourgeois," discordant with their epoch ...

Yesenin's name is never mentioned either in the press or on the radio. His books have been pulled from the libraries. In a word, officially Yesenin is forgotten and has been consigned to the archives forever ...

Yet in the meantime Yesenin's popularity keeps growing. Handwritten copies of his poems travel to all corners of Russia. People learn them by heart, sing them as songs. Despite the disapproval of the authorities, circles of his female admirers bearing the romantic name "Yesenin's fiancées" keep springing up. Under the condition of relative freedom found in the displaced persons' camps, their inhabitants reprint his poems. And these sloppily produced and costly books sell like hot cakes not only in the camps, but among older émigrés, who, as is well known, are people exceptionally indifferent to poetry.

What exactly is the secret of Yesenin's ever-growing appeal?

It is indisputable that Yesenin is a very talented poet. But what is equally indisputable is that his gift may not be called first-class. Not only is he no Pushkin, but he is not a Nikolay Nekrasov or Afanasy Fet either. In addition to that an entire series of circumstances—from a too easily and quickly gained fame to a lack of culture—interfered with the harmonious development of his gift. And his literary legacy comprises more failures and mistakes than glorious finds and successes ...

But somehow, on its own, it has come about that in relation to Yesenin a formalist evaluation seems an unnecessary exercise. Of course,

Yesenin's poems, like all other poems, consist of various "paeons," "pyrrhic feet," "anacruses…" Of course, they too may be weighed and analyzed from this angle. But that is a generally boring occupation, and it is especially boring when you have Yesenin's book in your hands. The chemical composition of vernal air could be researched and determined as well, but … how much more natural and simple it is to inhale a full breath of it …

And in the same way one doesn't want to approach Yesenin's biography and personality with the usual standards: moral—immoral, permissible—impermissible, White—Red. With regards to Yesenin, it is neither important nor useful.

Something else is important. For example, this amazing yet irrefutable fact: love for Yesenin brings together a sixteen-year-old "Yesenin fiancée," member of the Young Communist League, and a fifty-year-old "White Guardsman" who has preserved his irreconcilability one hundred percent intact. Two poles of Russian consciousness, deformed and fractured by the Revolution and seemingly having nothing in common, come together in Yesenin—that is, come together in Russian poetry. That is, in poetry as such. That is, in that which Vasily Zhukovsky defined so well once upon a time:

Poetry is God in Earth's holy dreams…[102]

"God in holy dreams…"—that is, an antidote against godlessness, dialectical materialism, slavery of the body, corruption of the soul … , that is, all in all, anti-Bolshevism.

The widespread explanation of Yesenin's fall from grace, which attributes it to his being a peasant poet, is unsatisfactory. Had Yesenin, like Klyuyev, lived to see collectivization, most likely he too would have had to answer for his "kulak tendencies." But Yesenin has been dead for a long time. And we know that Bolshevism, merciless as it is to the living, is extraordinarily forgiving of the dead, especially famous ones. This is understandable: the trappings of "Great October" that may be preserved without presenting a danger for the current regime are growing fewer and fewer in number. Lenin's mummy alone, no matter how hard you try, is not enough. It is this shortfall that gets successfully filled with sundry glorious cadavers, sundry "Gorky cities," "Mayakovsky Squares," and so on. I have no doubt that for Yesenin a square and the rest could have been found, if only all he had to his name were the sins he committed in his lifetime ... But in the eyes of Soviet power Yesenin is guilty of another unforgivable sin—a *posthumous* one. From the grave Yesenin succeeds in doing something that no one of the living has succeeded in doing in the course of thirty years: he unites Russians by the sound of a Russian song in which the consciousness of *a common guilt and common brotherhood merge into a common hope of liberation ...*

And this is precisely why the Bolsheviks try so hard to inveigle into Soviet citizens the idea that Yesenin is not worthy of their love. And this is precisely why he has been proclaimed "discordant with our epoch..."

At the end of 1921, chasing her fading glory, Isadora Duncan arrived in Moscow.

Already quite far from being young, she had let herself go and put on weight. Of "the divine barefoot dancer," "a statue come to life," there remained little. Duncan could hardly dance. But that did not prevent her at all from enjoying the ovations of the jam-packed Bolshoy Theater. Isadora Duncan, breathing loudly, ran out onto the stage with a red flag in her hand. For those who had seen the former Duncan, it was a rather sad spectacle. But all the same she was Isadora, a world-renowned celebrity, and the main thing was that she was dancing in the "Red capital" that had yet to be over-indulged by the attention of distinguished foreigners. And to top it off, she was dancing with a red flag! The enthusiastic applause was unceasing. Surrounded by members of the Council of People's Commissars, Lenin himself signaled the start of that applause from the "Tsar's Box."

At the banquet given in her honor after her first performance, the famous dancer noticed Yesenin. Wound up by her success, she felt as magnificent as she once was. And, as was her custom, she looked at those participating in the banquet, searching among them for someone worthy of "partaking" in the triumph of her day ...

Duncan approached Yesenin with her signature "gliding" gait and, without thinking for long, embraced and kissed him on the lips. She had no doubt that her kiss would make this "modest simpleton" happy. But Yesenin, who had already managed to get drunk, became enraged by Isadora's kiss. He pushed her away—"Back off, you bitch!" Not understanding him, she kissed Yesenin even harder. Then he took a swing and gave the world-renowned celebrity a resounding slap. After a cry, Isadora burst into tears, wailing like a peasant woman.

Immediately sobering up, Yesenin rushed to kiss her hands, to comfort her, to beg forgiveness. That is how their love began. Isadora forgave. Right then and there, using the diamond of her ring, on a window-pane she scratched:

> Yesenin is a hooligan,
> Yesenin is an angel!

"Yesenin is a hooligan, Yesenin is an angel!" Quite soon the romance between the dancer and the "peasant poet" who could pass for her son led to a "legal marriage." Isadora and Yesenin, having registered their union at the Moscow Civil Registry Office, left for abroad—for Europe, America, and from America back to Europe. The marriage turned out to be short-lived and unhappy ...

In the spring of 1923 I was at Förster's Restaurant on Berlin's Möenchstraße. After finishing dinner, I headed for the exit. Suddenly someone called to me in Russian from a table where sat a large and loud party. I turned around and saw Yesenin. I was not surprised. Some days ago I had already heard from Maxim Gorky that Yesenin was in Berlin with his Isadora.

I had not seen Yesenin for several years. At first glance it appeared that he had hardly changed. Those same cornflower blue eyes and blond hair, that same boyish look. He jumped up lightly as if on springs, extending his hand to me.

"Hello there! Long time no see. Are you just passing through or have you turned into an émigré? If you're not in a rush, join us, we'll have a little drink. You don't want to? Well, why don't I see you off then…"

The porter handed him a very broad, short, black overcoat and a top hat. Catching my surprised look, he grinned.

"I like extremes, you know. Either peasant bast shoes or all the way up to a top hat and a Palmerston…" He nimbly plunked the top hat on his curls. Do you remember how back in the day I performed at Gorodetsky's in velveteen pants with a golden ribbon for a belt? You haven't forgotten?"

"Remember?" Yesenin is laughing. "It was a riot! The way I dressed up in those days! Like a village Christmas caroler!"

A caroler indeed. Even now in Berlin in this overcoat that he for some reason calls a "Palmerston" and in this top hat, he also has the appearance of a caroler. Of course, I don't say this to him.

We are walking along the quiet streets of Westen. After a silence, Yesenin says: "Admit it, I repulsed you Petersburgers, didn't I? You, Gumilyov, and that wasp Akhmatova. *Apollo* never got round to publishing me. But Blok, he saw my worth right away. And a piece of advice he gave me, it was excellent: 'Swing harder on life's swings.' And did I ever swing hard! And just you watch me swing even harder! I wonder what Aleksandr Aleksandrovich would say if he saw me swinging this hard, I really do."

I keep my silence, but it is as if Yesenin is not expecting an answer from me. He continues to speak about Blok: "Oh, did I love Aleksandr Aleksandrovich. I was in love with him. Considered him first among poets. But nowadays"—Yesenin pauses—"Nowadays many people—that man Lunacharsky with many others to boot—they all write that I'm number one. You must've heard, right? Not Blok, but me. What do you make of that? They're lying, don't you think? Through their teeth, right?"

Suddenly he stops: "You know what, why don't we head for our place at the Adlon? We'll get Isadora out of bed. She'll be glad to see you. She'll make us some Turkish coffee. Why don't we, really? And it'll be easier for me if you come along—none of those apologies or explanations … The reason I was dining alone was that I had another row with her. We fight often. It's awful, I know that myself. Gets me all riled up, she does. But what a dame she is, a celebrity, and a smart one, too—and yet she doesn't seem to have something, the most important thing. The thing that we Russians call the soul…"

"We should really go to the Adlon. You don't want to? Well, some other time then. You really ought to meet her all the same. See her dancing with that scarf of hers. Remarkable. That scarf, it really comes to life in her hands. Grabs it by the tail, she does, and off she goes dancing. And you look at it, and it doesn't seem like a scarf anymore—it's as if it's some hooligan in her arms. As if it's not she alone, but the two of them are dancing away. I don't believe my eyes, such—whatchamacallit?—expressivity is coming out of it … Now the hooligan embraces her, now he roughs her up, now chokes her … And then suddenly—all at once!—the scarf is under her feet. Tore it off, she did, trampled it—and it's all over and done for! The hooligan is all gone, it's just a crumpled rag thrown on the floor … Amazing how she does it. My heart sinks. Can't watch it calmly. As if it's me who's thrown under her feet. As if it's me who's done for."

I'm in a hurry, people are waiting for me. The description of the dance with the scarf leaves me cold. I imagine a panting Duncan heavily jumping about the stage of the Bolshoy Theater in Moscow with a red flag. The agitation with which Yesenin speaks does not affect me. I will experience agitation later, when I read that Yesenin had hanged himself with the strap of one of those very same suitcases that right now are resting in his room at the Adlon, Berlin's most chic hotel. And then again later, after about two more years, when I learn that in Nice, at the Promenade des Anglais, Isadora Duncan has been choked to death by her own scarf…

True—

Every once in a while
Poets become uncanny prophets…[103]

It's hard to disagree—do they ever …

I stop in front of the entryway to the house where people are waiting for me. "What? Already?" Yesenin is surprised. "And here I am, only just starting to bare my soul to you. 'Too bad, too bad,' as the Hare says in

Afanasyev's fairytales. Oh well, if that's how it has to be. That's the way it always happens with me. As soon as I start baring my soul, something always pops up and gags me. In both life and in poetry—always. And is it ever boring. So many envy me, but what's there to envy, I'm so bored. And my hooliganism and debauchery, it all stems from this boredom. Once I put it very well when talking to myself:

> The spring day danced and cried away,
> The storm died down.
> I'm so bored, Sergey Yesenin,
> To raise my eyes together with you.[104]

"Oh, it's so, so boring! Boring as hell. Well … see you later … I'll go find some nook for myself out of this boredom. Will go raise some hell. Have one hard swing."

A wave of a top hat, a flash of a wide Palmerston tail in the closing taxi doors …

✳ ✳ ✳

After that last encounter of ours Yesenin had a little more than two years to live. But what he would experience and live through during that time would be enough for an entire—long, stormy, and very unhappy—life. Until November 23, 1925, many, so many "things" were to happen to him.

There would be his breakup with Isadora and a lonely return to Moscow. There would be a new marriage and a new breakup. Along the way, there would be many other romantic encounters and partings. There would be a voyage to Persia and a "compulsory repose" … at a medical facility for the mentally ill. There would be the last, very sad, trip to his village where everything would disenchant the poet. There would finally be new bouts and brawls that would stand out from previous ones in that they would invariably end with anti-Soviet and anti-Semitic stunts. Almost every night a drunken Yesenin would holler in a packed restau-rant—or even in the middle of Red Square—"Kill the Communists and save Russia," and so on in the same vein. Had it been anyone but Yesenin, he, of course, would have been executed. But the confounded authorities did not know how to handle "peasant poet number one." Attempts to appeal to his conscience were fruitless. They tried frightening Yesenin by subjecting him to "a public opinion court" in the House of Publishing— that didn't help either. Finally, strange as it may seem, the Bolsheviks backed off. The Moscow city police received an order: if they were to catch Yesenin in the act of making a drunken scene, he should be taken to a local police station to sober up, without "a further investigation of the matter." Soon all Moscow policemen knew Yesenin by sight ...

Yesenin is a typical representative of his people and his time. Behind Yesenin stand millions of identical to him, if nameless, "Yesenins"—his brothers in spirit, "accomplice-victims" of the Revolution. Identical to him, they all got their heads spun out of control by the revolutionary whirlwind, blinded by it; they all lost the criterion of good and evil, truth and lie; they all imagined themselves flying up to the stars only to crash face down in the mud. Having traded God for "dialectical materialism," Russia for "L'Internationale," eventually they all had to come out of their frenzy to face the rubble left in the Revolution's wake. Yesenin's fate is their fate; the sounds of their voices are heard in his voice. That is exactly the reason why Yesenin's poetry strikes Russian hearts with such an "unprecedented force," the reason why for the Russia of our day his name has begun to shine with a Pushkinian radiance, has acquired a Pushkinian indispensability.

I underscore: *for the Russia of our day.* That is to say for whatever has remained of Great Russia after thirty-two years of a new Tartar Yoke.

Even Paul Valéry, a cold snob not given to praise, in his diary listed that former Russia as "one of the three miracles of world history": Hellas, the Italian Renaissance, and nineteenth-century Russia.

Let's be honest: bitter as it is, in today's USSR not much more has been preserved of that "miracle of world history" than of Phidias's Hellas ... in contemporary Greece. Dostoyevsky said: "Pushkin is our everything."[105] And it was not possible to define more precisely, more truthfully the interrelationship of Pushkin and prerevolutionary Russia. "Our everything" meant that Pushkin's magnitude was equal to the magnitude of the culture that had engendered him, that the names "Pushkin" and "Russia" are almost synonymous.

Alas! Far from being synonymous, as entities Pushkin and the USSR simply cannot be compared. It is hardly possible to sink lower in comparison to the level of his divine moral and artistic harmony, to sink lower than "the land of proletarian culture," that unfortunate Motherland of ours, has sunk.

Acquiring the right to call Pushkin "our everything" anew, ascending to his level—that is a lengthy and arduous undertaking, one that Russia will not accomplish any time soon.

Yesenin's significance lies precisely in that he attained the level of the Russian people's consciousness during "Russia's terrifying years," overlapped with it completely, became synonymous with both Russia's downfall and her longing for resurrection.[106] Here lies that Pushkinian indispensability of Yesenin's, one that transforms his sinful life and imperfect poems into a source of light and good. And this is why one may say about Yesenin without exaggerating that he is Pushkin's heir in our day.

Notes

It is profoundly ironic that the first annotator of Georgy Ivanov's writings should have been none other than Vladimir Nabokov. After encountering Ivanov's poem "I conjure it all in a blessed mist" ("Vse predstavliaiu v blazhennom tumane ia," 1952) in the émigré almanac *Opyty* and discovering its closing lines, Nabokov indignantly urged his friend and the almanac's editor Roman Greenberg to denounce Ivanov's appropriative citation technique publicly: "Georgy Ivanov has always been and will remain a swindler ... The first of his poems [in the *Opyty* selection] ends in the phrase '*Poor Folk*—an example of tautology, / Who said that? Perhaps it was me.' In reality it was the late writer and philosopher Grigory Landau" (see "Drebezzhanie moikh rzhavykh russkikh strun..." Iz perepiski Vladimira i Very Nabokovykh i Romana Grinberga [1940– 1967]," published, prefaced, and annotated by Rashit Iangirov, in *In memoriam: istoricheskii sbornik pamiati A.I. Dobkina* [St. Petersburg-Paris: Feniks-Atheneum, 2000], p. 385). Greenberg published no such denunciation, but Nabokov never forgave or forgot. When his interpretative annotations to Alexander Pushkin's *Eugene Onegin* appeared in close proximity to a selection of Ivanov's poems in the same *Opyty* in 1957, Nabokov made sure to include in his notes on Pushkin's nineteenth-century novel in verse the following digression:

> By the way: every time I encounter the title cited above [*Poor Folk*], I immediately recall (such is the tenacity of certain associations) a thought once formulated by the subtle philosopher Grigory Landau (he was seized and tormented to death by the Bolsheviks around 1940) in his book "Epigraphs" (Berlin, around 1925): "An example of a tautology: poor folk."
>
> (see Vladimir Nabokov-Sirin, "Zametki perevodchika II," in *Opyty* 8 [1957], p. 45)

By inviting his readers to discover the irony contained in the familiar title of Fyodor Dostoevsky's debut novel of 1846 (traditionally rendered in English as "poor folk," the phrase literally means "poor people"), Grigorii Adol'fovich Landau (1877–1941) pointed out that it accidentally contained an indication of the tragic essence of the human condition. In accordance with the fundamental tenet of his mature "citatitional" poetics (Vladimir Markov's term), Ivanov integrated Landau's phrase into his poetic stream of consciousness. By doing so in a poem composed in 1952, Ivanov was merely making use of the intertextual technique he had inaugurated and tested in *Disintegration of the Atom* of 1937. From that point onward, Ivanov was to use this appropriative technique liberally by encrusting his creative writing with a plethora of open or hidden citations, allusions, references, and echoes to the works of his predecessors or contemporaries. Since *Disintegration of the Atom* marks the beginning of Ivanov's deliberate employment of this technique, it is important that readers seeking to form an educated opinion of this "lyric poem in prose" are able to locate the sources of Ivanov's major references. Following in the wake of Vladimir Nabokov, students of Ivanov's poetry have made strides in uncovering many intertextual links connecting his poems with their multiple sources (in this respect particularly helpful are the contemporary editions of Ivanov's poems prepared by Nikolay Bogomolov and Andrei Arieff). *Disintegration of the Atom*, while no longer the forgotten literary gem it once was, has not yet received a matching amount of scholarly scrutiny.

In his seminal analysis of Ivanov's intertextuality of 1967, Vladimir Markov laid the foundation for all subsequent attempts to annotate and decipher Ivanov's allusions by not only identifying and tracing them to their points of origin, but also by providing a conceptual framework for all future attempts in this area. While Peter G. Rossbacher (1928–2007), the first translator and annotator of *Disintegration of the Atom* into English (see Georgy Ivanov, "The Breakup [Disintegration of an Atom]," translated, annotated, and with an afterword by Peter Rossbacher, in *Russian Literature Triquarterly* 11 [1975], pp. 7–27), appears to have been unaware of Markov's advances, he was able to create the first, if understandably cursory, commentary to Ivanov's "lyric poem in prose." Even though

Georgy Moseshvili's commentary of 1994 did not take into account Rossbacher's annotations, it certainly became a major step forward in our understanding of *Disintegration of the Atom* in general and its intertextuality in particular. Alexei Lalo, who published his English translation of this work in 2013 under the title *The Decay of the Atom*, added a few valuable hypothetical identifications of the sources of Ivanov's allusions to the store of the already familiar facts (see *The Birth of the Body: Russian Erotic Prose of the First Half of the Twentieth Century*, translated and annotated by Alexei Lalo [Leiden: Brill, 2013], pp. 85–108).

As editors, translators, and annotators of *Disintegration of the Atom*, we have striven to break the vicious circle of miscommunication that has been such a bane for the scholarship devoted to this significant literary artifact. Apart from our original research, the following notes to *Disintegration of the Atom* have been informed by the work of our predecessors Markov, Rossbacher, Moseshvili, and Lalo. Since the appearance of a critically sound scholarly annotated edition of *Disintegration of the Atom* in its original Russian is a question of time, we would like to express our hope that such an edition will incorporate the results of our attempt to integrate the work of the generations of students of Ivanov's "lyric poem in prose" by taking their work into account.

Disintegration of the Atom

1 *"Versinke denn! ich könnt'auch sagen: steige! / 's ist einerlei"* ("Descend, then! I could also have said: Ascend! / 'tis one and the same"). Goethe's Mephistopheles says this while sending Faust into Nothingness and Oblivion in the Realm of Mothers, as he pursues his illusory visions of Helena and Paris (see *Faust* II, l. 6275). In all likelihood Ivanov was familiar with this fiendish assertion of universal relativity via Dmitry Merezhkovsky's interpretation of it in his book of essays *Eternal Companions: Portraits from World Literature* (Vechnye sputniki: portrety iz vsemirnoi literatury; Merezhkovsky's essay "Goethe" [1913] was included in the second, expanded edition of 1914). Here is the relevant fragment of Merezhkovsky's essay: "'It is convenient to compare truth to a diamond the rays of which disperse not in one, but in multiple directions,' says Goethe. No one else had his rays of truth to disperse, to multiply in the same way as he. Hence—that untraceability, incomprehensibility of his, much like that of nature. When we think to say something about him, we do not say anything. 'It is useless to talk about Shakespeare: nothing will be enough,' he observed once. Sometimes it seems that for the same reason it is impossible to speak of Goethe himself. The critics' soundings, no matter how deep down they go into that sea, cannot reach the bottom. What if there is no bottom at all? Neither bottom nor top, neither depth nor height. Bottomlessness, shorelessness, as in that terrifying Realm of the Mothers, into which Mephistopheles invites Faust: 'Descend, then! I could also have said: Ascend! / 'tis one and the same'" (see D. S. Merezhkovskii, *Vechnye sputniki: portrety iz vsemirnoi literatury*, ed. E. A. Andrushchenko [St. Petersburg: Nauka, 2007], pp. 316–317). Ivanov was a prominent and active member of Merezhkovsky's and his wife Zinaida Gippius's "literary-philosophical society" "The Green Lamp" (Paris, 1927–1939).

2   *"I think about the cross I wore around my neck since childhood as some-
one would carry a gun in his pocket—in case of danger it should protect,
save."* The Russian wording of this sentence is ambiguous: the past
tense of the verb "to wear" (*nosit'*) may be interpreted as an indication
that the protagonist *used to wear* a cross from his early childhood on,
but does not have it around his neck anymore. Accidentally or not,
Ivanov chooses not to employ the Russian equivalent of the phrase
"… the cross I have been wearing around my neck since childhood."
The choice of the past tense of the verb "to wear" carries a strong indi-
cation that the protagonist no longer wears his cross, which in its turn
may lead to the conclusion that he no longer considers himself a child-
ish-naïve follower of the belief in a forgiving, merciful Christian god
in concert with the dominant tonality of *Disintegration of the Atom*.

3   *"O, this Russian, this vacillating, glimmering, musical, masturbatory
consciousness. Eternally circling around the impossible, like gnats
around a candle … An inexhaustible source of superiority, weakness,
inspired failures. O, those strange varieties of our lot who to this day
dawdle around the world like lost souls: Anglophiles, Tolstoyans, Russian
snobs—the vilest snobs in the world—and various Russian boys, sticky
leaves."* Ivanov's protagonist may be referring to Leo Tolstoy by name,
yet his evocation of a Russian "sense of superiority," "Russian boys,"
and especially of "sticky leaves" makes it clear that what he has to say
here summons the spirit of another major writer and thinker, Fyodor
Dostoevsky. It is, of course, Ivan Karamazov who speaks of "sticky
leaves" in the third chapter from Book 2 of *The Brothers Karamazov*
(1880), when, in the best of Dostoevskian traditions, he "bares his
soul" to his brother Alyosha: "'On the contrary, you've struck me with
a coincidence!' Ivan cried gaily and ardently. 'Would you believe that
after our meeting today at her place, I have been thinking to myself
just that, my twenty-three-year-old greenness, and suddenly you
guessed it exactly, and began with that very thing. I've been sitting
here now, and do you know what I was saying to myself? If I did not
believe in life, if I were to lose faith in the woman I love, if I were to
lose faith in the order of things, even if I were to become convinced, on
the contrary, that everything is disorderly, damned, and perhaps

devilish chaos, if I were struck even by all the horrors of human disillusionment—still I would want to live, and as long as I have bent to this cup, I will not tear myself from it until I've drunk it all! However, by the age of thirty, I will probably drop the cup, even if I haven't emptied it, and walk away ... I don't know where. But until my thirtieth year, I know this for certain, my youth will overcome everything—all disillusionment, all aversion to life. I've asked myself many times: is there such despair in the world as could overcome this wild and perhaps indecent thirst for life in me, and have decided that apparently there is not—that is, once again, until my thirtieth year, after which I myself shall want no more, so it seems to me. Some snotty-nosed, consumptive moralists, poets especially, often call this thirst for life base. True, it's a feature of the Karamazovs, to some extent, this thirst for life despite all; it must be sitting in you, too; but why is it base? There is still an awful lot of centripetal force on our planet, Alyosha. I want to live, and I do live, even if it be against logic. Though I do not believe in the order of things, still the sticky little leaves that come out in the spring are dear to me, the blue sky is dear to me, some people are dear to me, whom one loves sometimes, would you believe it, without even knowing why; some human deeds are dear to me, which one has perhaps long ceased believing in, but still honors with one's heart, out of old habit ... I want to go to Europe, Alyosha, I'll go straight from here. Of course I know that I will only be going to a graveyard, but to the most, the most precious graveyard, that's the thing! The precious dead lie there, each stone over them speaks of such ardent past life, of such passionate faith in their deeds, their truth, their struggle, and their science, that I—this I know beforehand—will fall to the ground and kiss those stones and weep over them—being wholeheartedly convinced, at the same time, that it has all long been a graveyard and nothing more. And I will not weep from despair, but simply because I will be happy in my shed tears. I will be drunk with my own tenderness. Sticky spring leaves, the blue sky—I love them, that's all! Such things you love not with your mind, not with logic, but with your insides, your guts, you love your first young strength..."" (see Fyodor Dostoevsky, *The Brothers Karamazov*, trans. Richard Pevear and

Larissa Volokhonsky [New York, Farrar, Straus, and Giroux, 1990], pp. 229–230). By evoking Ivan's soliloquy, Ivanov invites his readers to recognize in his abandoned, disillusioned, and faithless protagonist a latter-day incarnation of a Dostoevskian "Russian boy," an Ivan Karamazov who inadvertently fulfilled his dream of coming to Europe, if, ironically, not of his own volition, but compelled by the forces of chaotic, merciless history.

4 *"and that storied Russian type, a knight of the glorious order of the intelligentsia, a scoundrel with a morbidly exaggerated sense of responsibility."* Alluded to here is Ivanov's repeated theme of the fate of Russia's intellectuals abroad. The intelligentsia, primarily a product of nineteenth-century idealistic thinking with deep roots in Hegel and, eventually, Marx, is associated by Ivanov with all that went wrong with Russia, and especially Petersburg, in the twentieth century. For Ivanov the Bolsheviks and the Communists in Soviet Russia "ferreting out injustice everywhere," as well as "mournful, astral, funereal" émigré Russia are two sides of the same apocalyptic coin. This type of socio-cultural relativity represents yet another manifestation of universal relativity, or "universal hideousness" first signaled in the Mephistophelian epigraph to *Disintegration of the Atom*.

5 *"But when that child was still alive."* Ivanov's protagonist cites the opening line from the second quatrain of the poem "A Little Coffin" ("Grobok," 1850) by Nikolai Alekseevich Nekrasov (1821–1877). Closer examination of this short poem in its entirety in the context of *Disintegration of the Atom* leaves no doubt as to its constituting a full-fledged literary reference. Written in a folk idiom that is one of Nekrasov's signature stylistic media, this poem is a part of a poetic cycle titled "On the Street" ("Na ulitse"), the themes of which are echoed and transformed in *Disintegration of the Atom*: much like similar episodes in Ivanov's narrative, each poem in Nekrasov's cycle represents a "snapshot" of a given street impression fixed for posterity by the observant first-person narrator-protagonist (both Nekrasov's and Ivanov's protagonists are fixated on the tragic aspect of life and reveal less-than-flattering aspects of their inner worlds). Apart from representing a rich intertextual parallel, Nekrasov's "Little Coffin" also serves as an intratextual reference: the image of a dead child

correlates with what might be termed the pedo-/necrophiliac imagery that runs through *Disintegration of the Atom*. Likewise, it echoes a further reference to another variation on a similar theme: a citation from and an allusion to Goethe's "Erlkönig," Charlie Chaplin's failed marriage to a former child-actress Lita Gray, and the evocations of the tragic fate of Charles Augustus Lindbergh, Jr. (see below). Below Nekrasov's poem is given in a literal translation:

> A soldier comes along. Under his arm
> He carries a child's coffin, the poor wretch.
> Bitter woe has squeezed tears
> From his stern eyes.
>
> But when that child was still alive,
> He would always say of it:
> "Won't you drop dead, damn you!
> Why were you born, anyway?"

6   *"O, that abyss of nostalgia where the wind alone blows, bringing back from over there the terrible 'International,' and from here to over there—a pitiful, astral, as if singing last rites at Russia's funeral, 'Lord, bring back the Tsar…'"* While in the West "The International" (French "L'Internationale," 1871) is widely acknowledged to be the anthem of the political left, post-1917 Soviet Russia and the Soviet Union used the song as its official anthem until 1944. To the extent that the USSR may be considered the successor of the Russian Empire, in this capacity "The International" replaced "God Save the Tsar," the country's national anthem from 1833 to 1917. The closing phrase of this fragment sarcastically paraphrases the title and the refrain of the imperial Russian national anthem, thus mocking dreams for a restoration of the monarchy after a hypothetic fall of the Bolshevik regime. Contemplation of Russia's future, the question of the country's ability to retain its historic cultural identity is a constant concern of Ivanov's creative output (see such poems as "Russia, the Russia of the workers and peasants" ["Rossiia, Rossiaia 'raboche-krest'ianskaia,'" 1930, *Roses*, 1931]; "They won't destroy you now" ["Teper' tebia ne unichtozhat," *A Portrait Without Likeness*, 1950], etc.).

7 *Along the ocean's blue waves.* Ivanov's protagonist cites the opening line of Mikhail Lermontov's adaptation of the ballad "Das Geisterschiff" (1832) by Joseph Christian Freiherr von Zedlitz (1790–1862), renamed in Lermontov's Russian version "The Aerial Vessel. From Zedlitz" ("Vozdushnyi korabl'. Iz Tsedlitsa," March 1840; see Mikhail Lermontov, *Sochineniia*, 6 vols. [Moscow: Izdatel'stvo AN SSSR, 1954–1957], vol. 2, pp. 151–152). Below the poem is reproduced in a literal English version:

> Along the ocean's blue waves,
> As only the stars twinkle in the sky,
> A solitary vessel rushes,
> Rushes all sails unfurled.
>
> Its tall masts do not bend,
> On their tops weathervanes make no sound,
> And cast-iron cannons silently
> Peer out from their open gunports.
>
> No captain is heard on it,
> No sailors are to be seen on it,
> Yet cliffs, treacherous shoals,
> And storms can do it no harm.
>
> In that ocean there is an island—
> All deserted and desolate granite.
> On that island there is a grave,
> And in it an Emperor interred.
>
> He is interred without military honors
> By his enemies, into quicksand.
> On top of him lies a heavy stone,
> So that he could not arise from his grave.
>
> And at the hour of his sad demise
> At midnight, as the year comes to a close,

At the high shore quietly
An aerial vessel moors.

Then the Emperor, having come to his senses,
Suddenly appears from his grave—
He wears a tricorne hat
And a gray campaign frock coat.

Having crossed his mighty arms,
And having lowered his head onto his chest
He walks up to the helm
And quickly sets out.

He rushes toward his dear France,
Where he left his glory and his throne,
Where he left his son and heir,
And his old royal guards.

And as soon as he makes out his native land
Amid the nocturnal murk,
His heart trembles again
And his eyes blaze with fire.

Toward the shore, taking wide steps,
He walks, bold and straight.
He loudly summons his allies
And sternly calls his marshals.

But the mustachioed grenadiers
Are asleep in that plane where the Elba rumbles,
Under the snows of frigid Russia,
Under the sultry sands of the Pyramids.

And the marshals do not heed his call:
Some have perished in battle,

Others have betrayed him
And sold their sword.

And, having stomped his foot in anger,
He paces back and forth
Along the quite shore,
And calls out again:

He calls out his beloved son,
His support against adverse fate;
He promises him half the world,
But France—to himself alone.

Yet his regal son
Has faded in the bloom of hope and power,
And for a long time, waiting for him,
Stands the Emperor alone—

He stands and sighs heavily
Until sunrise lights in the east,
And bitter tears drop
From his eyes on the cold sand,

Afterwards on his magic vessel
His head lowered onto his chest,
He goes and, having waved his hand,
He sets out on the return journey.

The motifs of exile and imaginary journey to the exile's homeland
(along with those of bitter disappointment and despair) form a mean-
ingful parallel to the predicament of Ivanov's protagonist. Equally
significant are the French substratum of Lermontov's ballad and its
reflection on Napoleon's "greatness" (see the Napoleonic motif that
runs through the narrative and the narrator's sardonic admission that
"he was no Caesar") since in *Disintegration of the Atom* these motifs

undergo an ironic reversal. Ivanov frequently references this poem by Lermontov: see, for example, "The radiance. At midnight every night" ("Siiane v dvenadtsat' chasov po nocham," 1932, from *Embarkation for the Island of Cythera*, 1937), in *On the Border of Snow and Melt: Selected Poems of Georgy Ivanov*, introduction by Stanislav Shvabrin, trans., ed., and annotated by Jerome Katsell and Stanislav Shvabrin [Santa Monica: Perceval Press, 2011], pp. 126–127, 510).

8   *"O last belated love, thou art."* Ivanov's protagonist cites the penultimate line from the poem "Last Love" ("Posledniaia liubov," ca. 1852–1854) by Fedor Ivanovich Tiutchev (1803–1873). Vladimir Nabokov's literary English version of it captures the lofty and antiquated idiom in which Tiutchev's lyrical "I" addresses the themes of love and mortality:

> Love at the closing of our days
> is apprehensive and very tender.
> Glow brighter, brighter, farewell rays
> of one last love in its evening splendor.
>
> Blue shade takes half the world away:
> through western clouds alone some light is slanted.
> O tarry, O tarry, declining days,
> enchantment, let me stay enchanted.
>
> The blood runs thinner, yet the heart
> remains as ever deep and tender.
> O last belated love, thou art
> a blend of joy and of hopeless surrender.

(see *Verses and Versions: Three Centuries of Russian Poetry Selected and Translated by Vladimir Nabokov*, ed. and annotated by Brian Boyd and Stanislav Shvabrin [Orlando: Harcourt Houghton Mifflin, 2008], p. 257). In a more literal English version "Last Love" may read:

> O, how at the sloping of our years
> We love more tenderly and superstitiously ...

Shine on, shine on, [you] farewell light,
Of last love, of evening dawn!

Shadow has embraced half the sky,
Only there, in the west a radiance is trembling,
Tarry, tarry, [you] evening day,
Extend, extend, [you] enchantment!

Let the blood run thin in the veins,
But tenderness in the heart does not run thin ...
O you, last love!
You are both bliss and hopelessness.

In line with the de-poeticized treatment the same themes receive in *Disintegration of the Atom*, this evocation of Tiutchev's lofty rhetoric may be intended to underscore the drastic contrast between the antiquated language used to express them in the nineteenth century and the new direct idiom employed to the same end by Ivanov's protagonist.

9   *"Copulation with a dead girl-child."* In a letter written in 1955, Ivanov claimed that he "'borrowed' many 'images'—the dead girl-child, etc.— from the immortal Aleksandr Ivanovich Tinyakov" (see Ar'ev, *Zhizn' Georgiia Ivanova*, p. 415). Aleksandr Ivanovich Tiniakov (pseudonym Odinokii ["Lonely"], 1886–1934) is featured in *Petersburg Winters*, Chapter IX.

10 *"One cannot believe in the appearance of a new Werther, whose example will suddenly set off the crackle of enthusiastic gunshots of enchanted, enthralled suicides all over Europe."* Young love, idealistic frothings, great spiritual despair, and suicide are the stuff of Goethe's groundbreaking epistolary novel, *The Sorrows of Young Werther* (Die Leiden des jungen Werthers, 1774), which had stupendous success throughout Europe. Similar thematic strains are mocked and distorted in the crooked-mirror reflection of them that is Ivanov's *Disintegration of the Atom*.

11 *"Blessed are the sleeping, blessed are the dead. Blessed is the expert before a painting by Rembrandt, piously convinced that the play of shadows and*

light on the face of an old woman is a universal rapture before which the old woman herself is a nonentity, a speck of dust, a zero. Blessed are the aesthetes. Blessed are the balletomanes. Blessed are Stravinsky's listeners and Stravinsky himself. Blessed are the shadows of the departing world, those seeing its last, sweet, mendacious dreams that for so long have been lulling mankind to sleep. In departing this life, having already departed it, they carry away with them an enormous imaginary richness. What will we be left with?" Ivanov's protagonist sarcastically and blasphemously comments on the "Beatitudes of the Blessed" from the Sermon on the Mount and Sermon on the Plain as pronounced by Jesus (see Matthew 5: 3–11 and Luke 6: 17–49). The new "blessed," the modern world and its representatives—Stravinsky, for example—as referenced by Ivanov, are man's "last, sweet, fake dreams," the final dashing of all hope in art and idealism. "The Beatitudes of the Blessed" are echoed elsewhere in *Disintegration of the Atom*; without any ironic connotations they are also evoked in *Petersburg Winters* (see Chapter XV).

12 *"In seinen Armen das Kind war tot."* In the original Ivanov's protagonist cites the concluding line of Goethe's ballad "Erlkönig" (1782) in a Russian version by Vasilii Andreevich Zhukovskii (1783–1852) made in 1818. In both Goethe's original and Zhukovsky's version of it a demonic Elf King (or Erlkönig [Alder King] in Goethe's German or Forest King in Zhukovsky's Russian) appears to a boy-child in a vision as his father attempts to take him to safety on horseback; the child fears that Elf-King is going to snatch him away from his father as Elf-King tells the child of his attraction to him; despite the father's attempts to comfort his son, the boy dies as soon as they reach a shelter. The last line of the poem cited by Ivanov's protagonist, however, does not specify the gender of the child, which in the context of *Disintegration of the Atom* echoes the earlier reference to Nikolai Nekrasov's "Little Coffin" and also the protagonist's description of his copulation with "a dead girl-child." Much like after reading Goethe's "Erlkönig," the reader of *Disintegration of the Atom* is forced to debate whether the contents of his description are actual or imaginary. This motif is developed further with the aid of references to contemporary mass-culture events.

13 *"Once I lost my way in the Berlin Polizeipräsidium building and acci-dentally found myself in that corridor."* Ivanov's protagonist recounts an experience familiar to each and every Russian émigré living in Berlin (Ivanov stayed in Berlin from 1922 to 1923 before moving to France): foreigners residing in Germany were required to register and then reg-ularly renew their registration with the German authorities; to do so they would have to come to the Polizeipräsidium (Police Headquarters) building on Alexanderplatz, which housed the Museum of Crime. The same museum is featured in Vladimir Nabokov's novel *King, Queen, Knave* (1928).

14 *"Evening mist lay upon the hills of Georgia."* See our introduction for a literal translation of the poem by Alexander Pushkin, the opening line of which is misquoted here by Ivanov's protagonist.

15 *"dyr bu shchyl ubeshchur."* Distorted quotation from the "transrational" (*zaum*) poem by Aleksei Eliseevich Kruchenykh (1886–1968), a lead-ing participant of Russian Futurism. Language, in theory at least, even if beyond sense or system, could convey meaning and truth even with-out making rational sense. The poem reads in full:

> dyr bul shchyl
> ubeshshchur
> skum
> vy so bu
> r l èz

First published in Kruchyonykh's *Pomade* ("Pomada," 1913). The echoes of this phrase reverberate throughout *Disintegration of the Atom* (see below). It is important to remember that Futurism claimed to be able to rejuvenate art; the pathos of Ivanov's confessional soliloquy directly contradicts and challenges such optimism.

16 *"This appeared to me in the midst of a noisy ball—with champagne, music, laughter, the rustle of silk, the smell of perfumes."* The first part of this phrase contains a quotation from the poem "In the midst of a noisy ball, by chance" ("Sred' shumnogo bala, sluchaino," 1851) by Aleksey Konstantinovich Tolstoy (1817–1875; set to music by Pyotr

Tchaikovsky, 1878). The motif of randomness expressed in Tolstoy's poem echo Ivanov's protagonist's reflection on the random nature of human existence, of humans being mere debris rotating in the vortex of "universal hideousness." In a literal English rendition the poem reads as follows (for the original, see Aleksei Konstantinovich Tolstoi, *Sochineniia*, 2 vols. [Moscow: Khudozhestvennaia literatura, 1981], vol. 1, p. 156):

> In the midst of a noisy ball, by chance,
> Among the disquiet of worldly clamor,
> I caught sight of you, but mystery
> Shrouded your features.
>
> Only your eyes looked on sadly,
> Yet your voice sounded so enchantingly,
> Like the ring of a distant reed pipe,
> Like a playful wave of the sea.
>
> I liked your slender frame
> And your entire pensive look,
> But it is your laughter, both sad and sonorous,
> That since then has been resounding in my heart.
>
> In the lonely hours of the night,
> I like to lie down when I'm tired—
> I see your mournful eyes,
> I hear your gay talk;
>
> And I grow sad and thus fall asleep,
> And drift in unknowable reveries ...
> Whether I love you—I don't know,
> But it seems to me that I do!

17 "*Anyone who has a heart*" *knows this.* The phrase between quotation marks comes to Ivanov's protagonist from Osip Mandelstam's poem "Twilight of Freedom" ("Sumerki svobody," 1918).

Let us, brothers, glorify the twilight of freedom,
The great twilight year!
Into the roiling nocturnal waters
The heavy timber of snares is lowered.
During the muted years you arise—
O, sun, arbiter, people.

Let us glorify the fatal burden.
The one that the national leader assumes in tears.
Let us glorify the twilight burden of power,
Its unbearable yoke.
Anyone who has a heart—he must hear, O Time,
How your vessel sinks to the bottom.

Into battle-ready legions
We have bound swallows—and now
The sun is invisible; the entire element
Twitters, moves, lives;
Through the nets—dense twilights they are—
One cannot make out the sun, and the earth is afloat.

Well now, let us give it a try: an enormous, unwieldy,
Creaky turn of the rudder.
The earth is afloat. Man up, men!
As we split the ocean, as if with a plough,
Even in a Lethean blizzard we will remember
That to us the earth was worth ten heavens.

Mandelstam's difficult poem contains a number of images running parallel to *Disintegration of the Atom*, not least of them being the motifs of doom and a guess that the earthly existence may well be much dearer to mortals than the afterlife.

18 *"Razmakhaychik Green Eyes ... Golubchik ... Zhukhla ... Freuhstuck ... Kitaychik ... Tsutik ... Khamka ... Von Klopp."* While it is easy to dismiss the "Australian language" invented by Ivanov's protagonist as

another step in his descent toward nothingness and sheer nonsense, it is important to remember that it represents a mocking echo of Aleksei Kruchyonykh's "transrational" language referred to earlier. In addition to that, the ridiculous, seemingly nonsensical names of the little creatures are full of so-called diminutive suffixes ("Von Klopp" being the only exception; "klop" in Russian means "bedbug"), which in the original convey feelings of tenderness and affection. Ivanov's protagonist indicates that his emotional range includes such feelings as well. The designation of this nonsense language as "Australian" corresponds to the motif of universal relativity declared in the Goethean epigraph ("Descend, then! I could also have said: Ascend! / 'tis one and the same").

19 *"That doesn't consume us."* Play on words: the Russian phrase "eto nas ne kusaetsia" (literally "this doesn't bite us") contains an easily recognizable punning echo of the bureaucratic or legalistic turn of speech equivalent to the English phrase "this doesn't concern us."

20 *"The little foot taps along, the golden ringlet tosses."* Ivanov's protagonist cites the closing lines from the poem "The resplendent city, the poor city" ("Gorod pyshnyi, gorod bednyi," 1828) by Alexander Pushkin, reproduced below in a literal translation:

> The resplendent city, the poor city,
> The spirit of captivity, upright appearance,
> The dome of the sky greenish-pale,
> Boredom, frost, and granite—
>
> All the same, I do have a little pity for you,
> Because it is here where from time to time
> The little foot taps along,
> The golden ringlet tosses.

The poem opens with an expression of Pushkin's attitude toward Petersburg, then the capital of the Russian Empire, and closes with an expression of the poet's admiration for Anna Olenina (1808–1888). In addition to containing obvious parallels to the protagonist's complex relationship with Paris and his beloved, in the context of *Disintegration of the Atom* Pushkin's poem carries a number of verbal echoes to the poem by Aleksei Eisner (see below).

21 *"not a Lindbergh."* In the context of *Disintegration of the Atom* the name of the pioneering aviator Charles Lindbergh (1902–1974) acquires palpably sinister associations as it becomes integrated into the "violated dead child" motif with its intra- and intertextual (Goethean, Nekrasovian) associations: like every literate European of his time, Ivanov would have been aware of the sensationalist global coverage of the "Lindbergh baby" case that revolved around the kidnapping of Charles Augustus Lindbergh, Jr. (1930–1932), the world-famous aviator's son.

22 *"not a Chaplin."* Once again, the appearance of the great comic actor Charlie Chaplin (1889–1977) in *Disintegration of the Atom* is hardly accidental: both Ivanov and his protagonist would have been aware of Chaplin's much-publicized divorce from his second wife, Lita Gray (Lillita Louise MacMurray, 1908–1995). In a mass-culture prefiguration of some of the aspects of the morbid romantic intrigue at the center of *Disintegration of the Atom*, Chaplin was thirty-five when he married sixteen-year-old Gray, a former child-actress; their divorce trial was unprecedented for the light it shed on the comedian's private affairs and intimate predilections.

23 *"not a Montherlant."* Henri de Montherlant (1895–1972) was a French novelist and essayist, author of *Les Célibataires* (The Bachelors, 1934) and, still more relevant to *Disintegration of the Atom*, *Les Jeunes filles* (The Young Girls, 1936–1939). In the 1930s, Montherlant gained notoriety for his alleged antifeminist or misogynistic bias, a sentiment echoed in *Disintegration of the Atom*.

24 *"'A human being begins from sorrow,' as some poet has put it."* The protagonist recalls the refrain from the poem "Autumn is setting in. Bushes turn yellow" ("Nadvigaietsia osen'. Zhelteiut kusty," 1932) by Aleksei Vladimirovich Eisner (1905–1984). A sarcastic reproach addressed by the male protagonist to his beloved, this poem forms an important source of inspiration for *Disintegration of the Atom*:

> Autumn is setting in. Bushes turn yellow.
> And once again the heart breaks apart.

A human being begins from sorrow. But you
Simple-heartedly preserve your moth-size happiness.

A human being begins from sorrow. See
How in it hothouse roses suffocate.
And from distant tracks, as they await the dawn,
At nighttime locomotives wail of parting.

A human being begins ... No. Wait.
No words will be of help with anything.
Outside the window rains have started to pour heavily,
And you, like a bird before flight, are ready to be on your way.

And in the forest our footprints wash away,
And our pale passions wash away from memory—
All those poor tempests in teapots.
And once again the heart breaks apart.

A human being begins ... Tersely. Abruptly.
Goodbye. Enough. A huge period.
Sky, wind, and sea. And seagulls' screams.
And someone from the stern waves a handkerchief, pitifully.

Sail away. Only circles of black smoke.
The distance already measures a century.
Hold on to your motley happiness—
Because you too will become a human being some day.

The sky-blue world will burst forth ringing and crumble,
Your snow-white throat, like a turtledove, will begin to moan,
And a polar night will float above you,
And like the *Titanic*, your pillow will drown in tears ...

Yet, already drowning in the Arctic ice,
Your hot hands grow cold forever.

And the steamship made of oak casts off
And, as it rocks, it sets its course for the Pole of Parting.

The wet handkerchief tosses, and the wake foams,
As it happened back then … But you, I see, have forgotten everything.
Across thousands of miles and for thousands of year to come,
Hopelessly and pitifully twangs the thurible.

And that's all. Only obscure hearsay about a paradise …
The Mediterranean rumbles on indifferently.
It's grown dark. All right then. Sail away. Die away.
A human being begins from sorrow.

Ivanov would have been familiar with this poem's first publication in the most authoritative and prestigious "thick journal" of the diaspora *Contemporary Annals* in 1932 (see Aleksei Eisner, "Stikhotvoreniie," *Sovremennye zapiski* 49 [1932], pp. 211–212). Apart from its direct relevance to *Disintegration of the Atom*, Eisner's poem contains numerous semantic overlaps with the constant themes and images found in Ivanov's verse.

25 *"The Volga flows into the Caspian Sea."* Here Ivanov's protagonist trots out a phrase that in Russian signifies the quintessence of suffocating banality. Perhaps the best-known example of the use of this kind of clichéd phrase appears in Chekhov's story "The Teacher of Literature" (1889, 1894), where the teacher of geography, Ippolit Ippolitich ("he was either silent or only spoke about that which everyone already had long known"), roommate of the story's protagonist Nikitin, delivers himself of such immortal phrases as: "It's May, soon it will be real summer. And summer is not the same as winter. In winter you have to heat the stove, but in summer it's warm without stoves." The succession of phrases "A human being begins from sorrow. Tomorrow life begins. The Volga flows into the Caspian Sea. Dyr bu shchyl ubeshchur" represents an example of the "disintegration of the atom" in action: from a highly meaningful observation to what Ivanov considered to be a pseudoliterary, grotesque mockery of poetry by way of a platitude.

26 *"Sunset over Le Temple. Sunset over Lubyanka."* Ivanov's protagonist mentions two city squares linked by their associations with bloody events of historic significance: the Square du Temple, the former site of Le Temple, the medieval fortress in Paris associated with the imprisonment and execution of the French royal family at the time of the Revolution, and Lubyanka Square in Moscow, eponymous with the headquarters of the Soviet secret police (or Extraordinary Commission [Russian Chrezvychainaia komissiia, commonly abbreviated as "Cheka"]). That the sun orderly sets over the two infamous crime scenes underscores the motif of nature's indifference to human suffering and God's absence from the world of "universal hideousness" over which soulless relativity holds sway (cf. this motif with the Mephistophelian epigraph to *Disintegration of the Atom*).

27 *"Sunset on the day the war was declared and on Armistice Day: everyone danced, everyone got drunk, no one heard how the voice said: 'Woe to the Victors.'"* Here Ivanov's protagonist has reversed the traditional Latin of "Vae victis," or "Woe to the Conquered!" that referred to the defeat of Rome by an army of Gauls in 390 B.C.E. In 1938, when *Disintegration of the Atom* was published, the former conquered—that is, the forces of Germany in World War I—were on the rise and threatening to destroy the previously victorious countries of Europe. This fragment in its entirety revisits the motif of universal relativity first formulated in the epigraph and continuously developed throughout *Disintegration of the Atom*: revolutionary, military victories mark both the high and low points of historic events, as was the case with the French and Russian revolutions before they descended into bloody terror and the "triumphant" resolution of World War I that paved way for still greater calamities and carnage, the arrival of which Ivanov's protagonist anticipates.

28 *"Akaky Akakiyevich trudges home from his job to Obukhov bridge."* Akakii Akakievich Bashmachkin is the lowly, downtrodden, and frustrated scrivener-protagonist from the novella "The Overcoat" ("Shinel," 1842) by Nikolai Gogol.

29 *"'He was a Titular Counselor—she a general's daughter,' ingratiatingly, tenderly sighs the velvety guitar."* The protagonist cites the opening lines from the humorous poem "On byl tituliarnyi sovetnik" (1859) by Petr

Isaevich Veinberg (1831–1908), written as a parody of a wave of hackneyed Russian imitations of the early lyrical poetry by Heinrich Heine. Set to music by Aleksandr Sergeevich Dargomyzhskii (1813–1869), the poem became a popular romance song.

> He was a titular counselor,
> She—a general's daughter;
> He meekly confessed his love,
> She kicked him out.

> So the Titular Counselor went out
> And drank all night long from grief,
> And the general's daughter
> Whirled before him in the wine-induced mist.

According to the imperial "table of ranks," the title of "titular counselor" was the lowest of bureaucratic ranks, much below that of a general (and the reflected glory of his daughter). The motif of greatness and insignificance runs throughout *Disintegration of the Atom*.

30 *"With his head clouded by the boredom of life and beer, to the insinuating murmur of a guitar, Akaky Akakiyevich abandons vanity and surface and descends into the essence of things. Secret longings envelop the image of Psyche and little by little his greedy thought transforms into her desired flesh. Obstacles, so insurmountable in daytime, fall by themselves. He slides soundlessly across the empty sleeping city; unnoticed by anyone he enters His Excellency's dark chambers; like an inaudible shadow, between statues and mirrors, along parquet and carpets, he steals to the cute little angel's very bedroom. He opens the door, stops at the threshold, and sees "a paradise of the kind which does not exist even in heaven." He sees her white little undergarment casually spread on the armchair, sees her sleepy little face on a pillow; sees the little bench onto which she places her little foot of a morning as she pulls her white-as-snow stocking over that little foot. He was a Titular Counselor—she a general's daughter. And now... Nothing, nothing, silence."* Cf. with the following fragment from Nikolai Gogol's "Diary of a Madman"

("Zapiski sumasshedshego," 1834): "November 11. Today I sat in our director's study and sharpened twenty-three pens for him, and for her, aie, aie! ... four pens for Her Excellency. He likes very much having more pens. Oh, what a head that must be! Quite silent, but in his head, I think, he ponders everything. I wish I knew what he thinks about most; what's cooking in that head? I'd like to have a closer look at these gentlemen's lives, at all these equivocations and courtly tricks—how they are, what they do in their circle—that's what I'd like to find out! I've meant several times to strike up a conversation with His Excellency only, devil take it, my tongue wouldn't obey me: I'd just say it was cold or warm outside, and he decidedly unable to say anything else. I'd like to peek into the drawing room, where you sometimes see only an open door into yet another room beyond the drawing room. Ah, such rich furnishings! Such mirrors and chine! I'd like to peek in there, into that half, Her Excellency's—that's what I'd like! Into the boudoir, with all those little jars and vials standing there, such flowers that you're afraid to breathe on them; with her dress thrown down there, more like an air than a dress. I'd like to peek into her bedroom ... there, I think, there are wonders; there, I think, there is paradise, such as is not even to be found in heaven. To look at the little stool she puts her little foot on when she gets out of bed, at how a snow-white stocking is being put on that foot ... aie! aie! aie! [nothing, nothing] ... silence" (see Nikolai Gogol, *The Collected Tales*, trans. Richard Pevear and Larissa Volokhonsky with an introduction by Richard Pevear [New York: Alfred A. Knopf, 1999] pp. 278–279). By merging the two Gogolian protagonists, Akaky Akakievich Bashmachkin ("The Overcoat") and Avksentii Ivanovich Poprishchin ("The Diary of a Madman"), Ivanov's narrator creates a composite portrait of a lowly man burdened by his frustrated desires. Having been transplanted from "The Diary of a Madman" verbatim, in *Disintegration of the Atom* the phrases "a paradise of the kind which does not exist even in heaven" and "nothing, nothing, silence" emerge as additional references and leitmotif-refrains (see below).

31 *"'Show all your splendor, Peter's city, and stand erect,' Pushkin exclaims impishly, in defiance of premonition, and who is not to be found on his*

Don Juan's list. 'Nothing, nothing, silence,' mumbles Gogol, his eyes upturned into the void as he masturbates under his cold bed sheet." By taking a verse from Pushkin's "Petersburg tale" "The Bronze Horseman" ("Mednyi vsadnik," 1833) out of its context, Ivanov's protagonist continues his deliberately irreverent assault on the lofty rhetoric of the Golden Age of Russian poetry in general and on Pushkin's amorous poetry in particular. The following reference to Pushkin's so-called "Don Juan's list" (an actual list of the women with whom the poet was intimate or infatuated prior to 1829) is meant to highlight the chasm that separates the poet's chivalrous treatment of women in his famous love lyrics of which "Evening mist lies upon the hills of Georgia" is but one example and the same man's less than respectful listing of all the objects of his desire and their inevitable objectification. Pushkin's Renaissance bawdiness is also contrasted to Nikolai Gogol's torturous, suppressed sexuality (subject of much speculation) that in the context of *Disintegration of the Atom* appears to be much more akin to that of the protagonist. Pushkinian priapism is therefore revealed to be self-centered, shallow, and essentially mendacious (compare with bitter rhetorical reproaches that will be addressed to Pushkin later in the text), whereas the torturous sexuality of the composite Gogolian protagonist is shown to be genuine in spite of—or thanks to—all its baseness and ignominy. The premonition which Ivanov's protagonist appears to be attributing to Pushkin presumably refers to the doubts the poet must have had as to St. Petersburg's ability to overcome the curse cast upon it by Peter the Great's first wife, Tsarina Evdokiia Lopukhina (1669–1731). After being forcibly estranged by her husband, Lopukhina allegedly predicted that Peter's pet project, Petersburg, "will be empty [i.e., devoid of inhabitants]." Pushkin's "Bronze Horseman" recounts the events of a disastrous 1824 flood that once again reminded the new capital's dwellers of Lopukhina's prediction. The following scenes of the desecration of Petersburg's holy sites echo the motifs of Pushkin's premonition and Lopukhina's famous curse.

32 *"A man who in a dream sees himself playing a game of tennis in a white shirt and swimming in the Crimea as he is eaten alive by lice in Solovki."* Whereas the Crimean Peninsula has always been associated with

relaxation as the most desired Russian resort destination in the south, by the second half of the 1930s the distant northern Solovki archipelago and the former monastery of the same name had already acquired infamy as the most brutal Soviet extermination camp. Declared in the epigraph, the motif of universal relativity, of overlapping joy and suffering, is nearing its crescendo.

33 *"Ost Honored Mister Commissar ... With astonishing, irresistible clarity I understand this now. But—once again switching to the Australian language—'This does not consume you, Your High-Chinned Excellency.'"* The nonsensical sound of the closing paragraph is amplified by a deliberate mixture of pronouncedly non-Soviet and Soviet ways of addressing someone in a position of power: with its political incongruity, the phrase "Mister Commissar" represents a specific reference to the state of historical, political, and geographical suspense in which the protagonist finds himself. Writing to a correspondent in 1955, Ivanov stated; *"Atom* should have had a different ending: 'Heil Hitler, Long Live the Father of the Peoples Comrade Stalin; Britons never, never shall be slaves!' I dropped [this ending], but now regret it" (see Ar'ev, *Zhizn' Georgiia Ivanova*, p. 415). Additionally, the protagonist's punning appeal to "His Excellency" is redolent of Poprishchin's obsequious way of addressing his superior in Gogol's "Diary of a Madman."

Petersburg Winters

Tempting as it is to follow the lead of certain interpreters of *Petersburg Winters* and treat Ivanov's memoir as a purely literary work, this memoir-ist's insistence on being true not only to the spirit of the events and people he portrays, but to the facts of the matter (cf. "my remarks about [Blok and Gumilyov] may be incomplete, but there are only two or three people left in Russia who knew them both as well as I did, and in emigration there is no one," "this is not a pretty phrase, it is the truth," "here's a short inventory of the facts") considerably complicates the veracity of such interpretations. First and foremost, Ivanov should be seen as a memoirist with a well-defined individual ideological (antiliberal) agenda, a writer who is fully aware of his ability to affect his readers' notion of the people and facts he presents in *Petersburg Winters*. This tendentiousness of his becomes particularly apparent in his highly distortive and damaging interpretation of the lives and creative legacy of Alexander Blok and Nikolay Gumilyov. Apart from disseminating his widely popular memoirs, Ivanov had a hand in the editorial work on Gumilyov's unpublished writings and did not shy away from instilling his reproductions of the late poet's work with his biased personal vision.

Petersburg Winters represents a discreet stage in the development of Ivanov's "citational" technique. Whereas in *Disintegration of the Atom* it remains part and parcel of his fictional style, in *Petersburg Winters* Ivanovian "citationality" serves the needs of his biased ideological agenda as he frequently "adjusts" the material he cites to support his interpretations. Readers interested in a detailed commentary to *Petersburg Winters* should consult both Nikolay Bogomolov's notes to the memoir (see Georgii Ivanov, *Stikhotvoreniia. Tretii Rim. Peterburgskie zimy* [Moscow: Kniga, 1989], pp. 541–565) as well as those by Georgii Moseshvili found in the third volume of the three-volume edition of Ivanov's works (see Georgii Ivanov, *Sobranie sochinenii*, 3 vols. [Moscow: Soglasie, 1994], pp. 638–675).

The following notes have been compiled with the aim of assisting our Anglophone readers in locating the sources of the majority of Ivanov's "citational" references. Notwithstanding the major advances in our understanding of the aims and results of the subtle and not so subtle adjustments made by Ivanov in the works of the authors he cites, this process is far from complete.

1 *"One citizen calls out to another citizen ... / I traded my soul for kerosene."* Ivanov cites the poem "Over the Neva" ("Nad Nevoi," 1920) by Vilgel'm (Wilhelm) Aleksandrovich Zorgenfrei (Sorgenfrei, 1882–1938). A distorted avatar of Sorgenfrei is featured in Chapter XVII.

2 *"Golden sparks above checkpoint fires ... / Seeks out your poor heart."* Distorted quotation from Anna Akhmatova's poem "I wasn't being dishonest with you, my angel" ("Ia s toboi, moi angel, ne lukavil," 1921).

3 *"I have no need of a night pass, / I have no fear of sentries"* An imprecise quotation from the poem "In Petersburg we shall come together again" ("V Peterburge my soidemsia snova," 1920).

4 *"Into the yellow fog of Petersburg winter, / Into the yellow snow clinging to the flagstones."* The opening lines of the poem "Petersburg" ("Peterburg," published posthumously in 1910) by Innokenty Annensky (Innokentii Fedorovich Annenskii, 1855–1909). This poem, rich in apocalyptic predictions concerning the imminent demise of both Petersburg and the Russian Empire, may be said to set the tone for the entire memoir; it also provides *Petersburg Winters* with one of its leitmotifs.

5 *"I'm going to bring Lerner to meet him—let them have a little talk."* Like many members of St. Petersburg intelligentsia including Gumilyov, the Pushkin scholar Nikolai Osipovich Lerner (1877–1934) took part in Maxim Gorky's editorial project "World Literature."

6 *"I love you, Peter's creation, / Its embankment of granite."* The famous apostrophe comes from Aleksandr Pushkin's "Petersburg tale," *The Bronze Horseman* (1833).

7 *"A year later, to the thunderous accompaniment of Kronstadt cannons, I was walking down Kamennostrovsky Boulevard."* Kronstadt is a

fortified island and a Russian Baltic Fleet naval base in the Gulf of Finland; Kronstadt has guarded approaches to Petersburg-Petrograd since its founding in 1703 by Peter I. During the Bolshevik coup d'état of 1917 (the so-called October Revolution), sailors from Kronstadt participated in the overthrow of the Kerensky regime, later joining with the Bolsheviks during the Civil War, only to revolt against them in 1921. It is the suppression of this Kronstadt rebellion by the Bolsheviks that Ivanov expects his reader to have in mind as he evokes "the thunderous accompaniment of Kronstadt cannons" here. Many people believed that Nikolay Gumilyov was executed by the Bolsheviks for his connection to the mutineers; the version of Gumilyov's last days presented in Ivanov's *Petersburg Winters* only strengthened this belief.

8 *"O, Rus! O, rus!"* The ironic invocation that juxtaposes the ancient—Kievan, pre-Muscovite—denomination of the country that is now known as Russia (Rus) and the Latin word for "coutryside" (*rus*) is famously used by Pushkin as the epigraph for the second chapter of his *Eugene Onegin*.

9 *"And suddenly he grew a mane, / He demonstrated the art of touching."* A comically distorted quotation from the poem "The thickets were filled with sound" ("Byli napolneny zvukom trushchoby," 1910) by Velimir Khlebnikov (Viktor Vladimirovich Khlebnikov, 1885–1922).

10 *"Or those subsequently famous 'Laughaniks'—'o, laugh laughingly, laughaniks, laughers ho, laughing so ... '"* Ivanov evokes Khlebnikov's poem "Incantation by Laughter" ("Zakliatie smekhom," 1908–1909), which he misquotes.

11 *"How I love pregnant men, / When they gather at Pushkin's monument."* Distorted quotation from the poem "The Fecund Ones" ("Plodonosiashchie," 1915) by David Davidovich Burliuk (1882–1967).

12 *"It is customarily assumed that Igor Severyanin's all-Russian fame began with Tolstoy's famous quip concerning the worthlessness of Russian poetry."* According to witness testimony, not long before his death in 1910 in a private conversation Leo Tolstoy singled out Severyanin as an example of particularly pernicious modern poetry.

13 *"On a business card tacked to the apartment door stood a signature with a grand flourish above the first 'e': 'Igor Severyanin.'"* The flourish Ivanov mentions appeared above a character made obsolete by the reform of Russian orthography of 1917–1918.

14 *"Thus one time a certain Pyotr Larionov—this possessor of the strange position of the head of the Tsarskoselsky Poultry Farm was seduced by Futurism at the age of forty-five—walked out of Ignatyev's place with a half-shaven head (he had sported a full head of poetic hair), face painted like that of a Red Indian, and sporting an ace of diamonds on his back."* In prerevolutionary Russia a yellow mark in the shape of the ace of diamonds was sown on the clothes of convicts serving hard labor for serious crimes to make them easily identifiable in case they escaped.

15 *"we won't trade anything for this magnificent, / These black solemn gardens."* Distorted quotation from the poem "Surely somewhere simple life and light exist" ("Ved' gde-to est' prostaia zhian' i svet," 1915) by Anna Akhmatova.

16 *"Walls are painted gray, / A green sign: 'Tailor.'"* Quotation from the poem "This house completely ordinary" ("Etot dom sovsem obykno-vennyi," 1922) by Ivanov's wife, Irina Odoyevtseva.

17 *"The police chief must have read a little too much of Kurbatov."* In 1915 Vladimir Iakovlevich Kurbatov (1878–1957) published a popular and accessible study of St. Petersburg history and culture.

18 In terms of easiness of reproduction and memorability the melody of "Chizhik" ("Little Siskin") is the perfect Russian counterpart to the English "Baa, Baa, Black Sheep."

19 *"All vanishes—and there remains only / Space, the stars, and the singer."* Quotation from the poem "Poisoned is the bread and emptied the air" ("Otravlen khleb i vozdukh vypit," 1913) by Osip Mandelstam.

20 *"In the Comedians' Repose stands . . . / Never, really?"* Here and else-where Ivanov integrates into the text of his memoir a quotation from his own poem "Thaw. It looks like" ("Ottepel'. Pokhozhe," published 1916).

21 *"O Phaedra, a pseudoclassical shawl / Slides down from your shoulders."* Ivanov transposes lines from the poem "Akhmatova" (1913) by Osip Mandelstam.

22 *"And for whom will these pale lips . . . / Peers out cunningly."* Quotation from Akhmatova's poem "Old Portrait" ("Staryi portret," 1910).

23 *"My breast turned helplessly cold … / The glove from my left hand."* Quotation from Akhmatova's poem "A Song of the Last Encounter" ("Pesnia poslednei vstrechi," 1911).

24 *"in the ocean of primordial gloom … / And sinister metallic ringing."* Distorted quotation from "Sick Man" ("Bolnoi," 1916).

25 *"Yes, I loved them, those nocturnal gatherings … / And a friend's first glance, helpless and terrifying."* Ivanov cites the opening poem of Akhmatova's tripartite poetic cycle "Three Poems" ("Tri poemy," 1917).

26 *"The little windows boarded shut forever … / What's out there—hoarfrost or storm?"* Quotation from the poem "Here we are all sinners or harlots" ("Vse my greshniki zdes', bludnitsy," 1913); see also note 28.

27 *"Here many chains have come unbound … / That certain people would not utter in the morning."* Separate-standing poem-quatrain by Mikhail Kuzmin ("Zdes' tsepi mnogie razviazany," 1913).

28 *"Here we are all sinners or harlots … / Languish among clouds."* Distorted quotation of the opening lines of the eponymous poem; see also note 26.

29 *"And now I've become a plaything— / Like my rosy friend the cockatoo."* Quotation from Akhmatova's poem "They lead horses along the alley" ("Po allee provodiat loshadok," 1911).

30 *"Sleep my quiet little boy, / Preserve your father."* from Akhmatova's poem "Lullaby" ("Kolybel'naia," 1915).

31 *"Tea Room of the Russian People."* Ivanov's evocation of infamous "tea rooms of the Russian people" seeks to taint Gorodetsky by associating him with the ultranationalist Union of the Russian People that flourished in prerevolutionary Russia. The Union established its "tea rooms" as part of its abstinence campaign aimed at improving the physical and mental health of patriotic, tsar-loving Russian workers and peasants it allegedly represented.

32 *"Everything was very simple, everything was very nice."* Quotation from Igor Severyanin's poem "It happened by the sea" ("Eto bylo u moria," 1910).

33 *"O, Sweet Bird, Bird of Paradise, / Fluffing your golden feathers."* Distorted quotation from the poem "A Song About a Falcon and Three God's Birds" ("Pesnia o sokole i trekh ptitsakh Bozhiikh," 1908).

34 *OSVAG* (abbreviation of OSVedomitel'noe AGentstvo) a propaganda organ of the anti-Bolshevik White Army during the Russian Civil War of 1917–1922/1923.

35 *Speech* (Rech'). Ivanov has in mind the daily newspaper that was the central information outlet of the Constitutional-Democratic Party. Published in St. Petersburg in 1906–1917, it was co-edited by Paul Milyukov and was the main organ of Russian liberals.

36 *"A golden sunset. Snows ... / As it was in days gone by."* Ivanov cites his own poem published in 1916.

37 *"Do not awaken her in the dim morn / Warm her drowsiness with a kiss."* Distorted quotation from the poem "A reseda wafting in a dim railway car" ("Struia resedy v temnom vagone," 1908).

38 *"and naked youths, /Forgetting their shyness, retire to an alcove."* Quotation from the poem "M. A. Kuz'min" by the prominent economist and dilettante poet Vladimir Vladimirovich Sviatlovsky (1869–1927).

39 *"If only I could finish with this burdensome life ... / A quiet death from carbon monoxide."* Quotation from the poem "It's terrifying to live without a samovar" ("Strashno zhit' bez samovara," 1914).

40 *"It's my delight, spit-wad spit that I am, / Pressing up along the slippery side."* Distorted quotation from the poem "Spit-Wad" ("Plevochek," 1912) by Tinyakov; see also note 9 to *Disintegration of the Atom.*

41 *"Your image, tortured and tremulous ... / And an empty cage behind."* Ivanov cites the poem by Mandelstam in its entirety.

42 *"For us—abandoned in space ... / And loyalty!"* Quotation from the poem "Of unprecedented freedom" ("O svobody nebyvaloi," 1915).

43 *"A body given to me—what shall I do with it ... / I'm not lonely in the prison of the world."* Opening lines of the eponymous poem by Mandelstam ("Dano mne telo. Chto mne delat' s nim," 1910).

44 *"My breath and my warmth / Have already lain on the windowpanes of eternity."* Ivanov continues to cite the same poem by Mandelstam.

45 *"Above the yellow of government buildings ... / Breathes in gasoline, and curses his fate."* Ivanov cites the opening lines and the closing quatrain of Mandelstam's poem "Petersburg Stanzas" ("Peterburgskie strophy," 1913).

46 *"If he so desires, a poet finds / Happiness even in wet asphalt."* Quotation from the poem "Dozhdik" ("Rain," 1909) by Innokenty Annensky.

47 *"Don't feel low ... / So Number Eight."* According to Ivanov, Mandelstam improvised this poem in 1913 or 1915.

48 *"I shook such dirty hands, / I agreed to such things."* Distorted quotation from the poem "Iambs" ("Iamby," 1906) by Innokenty Annensky.

49 *"She was silent, and he was silent. / And what is there to talk about, my friend?"* Distorted quotation from the poem "Through a nasty wintry day" ("Skvoz' nenastnyi zimnii denek," 1927) by Vladislav Khodasevich.

50 *"The owners of the café, the Imaginists, persuaded Blumkin to put away his Mauser."* The Imaginists (a title alternatively translated into English as "[Russian] Imagists") were a poetic group characterized by Vladimir Markov as "the last of the individualists in [Soviet] Russian literature" (see his *Russian Imagism 1919–1924* [Giessen, Wilhelm Schmitz Verlag, 1980], p. 65). The group were a loosely organized collective ("Order") where Vadim Shershenevich (1893–1942), Anatolii Mariengof (1897–1962), and Sergei Yesenin (1895–1925) played leading roles. Thanks to their entrepreneurial prowess and connections in the Bolshevik-controlled Kremlin, the Imaginists were able to establish and maintain a string of "literary cafes" even before the Communist authorities relaxed their ban on private businesses as part of their New Economic Policy (NEP, 1921–1928). *Mauser:* In Russia the name of a German firearms manufacturer, Gebrüder Mauser, became synonymous with the volatility of the revolution and civil war periods. The semiautomatic pistol Mauser C96 (produced 1896–1937) was particularly popular with the members of the Soviet secret services, thus becoming one of the most iconic, instantly recognizable visual emblems of that time.

51 Even though Kuzmin's "Concerning Beautiful Clarity (Remarks on Prose)" was not intended to be a manifesto, the title phrase of the essay quickly acquired a life of its own and became associated with Acmeism, a post-Symbolist movement and a brainchild of Gumilyov

and Gorodetsky that sought to break with the Symbolist worship of the ineffable (see Mikhail Kuzmin, *Selected Writings*, trans., ed., annotated, and with an introduction by Michael A. Green and Stanislav A. Shvabrin [Lewisburg: Bucknell University Press, 2005], pp. 225–230, 255–256).

52 Evdokia Nagrodskaia (Evdokiia Apollonovna Nagrodskaia, 1866–1930), author of the novel *The Wrath of Dionysus* (1910; see Evdokia Nagrodskaia, *The Wrath of Dionysus*, trans. and ed. Louise McReynolds [Bloomington: Indiana University Press, 1997]).

53 *"Two times two—four ... / All we can know."* Annotators have not been able to identify the source of this quotation in Kuzmin, it may well have been invented by Ivanov and ascribed to Kuzmin.

54 *"How joyful spring in April ... / We'll go to have our photograph taken at Boason's."* Distorted quotation from the poem "How joyful spring in April" ("Kak radostna vesna v aprele," 1912).

55 *"O, sisters Gravity and Tenderness—your features are identical."* Opening line of the eponymous poem by Mandelstam (1920).

56 *"Darling child, don't reach for a rose in spring, / You can pluck it in summer too."* Quotation from the romance "A Child and a Rose" (1913) by Kuzmin.

57 *"If we had known in our youth ... / Catching bliss here and there."* Once again, the source of Ivanov's quotation has not been identified, and it may well be of his composition.

58 *"Mommy-dear told me ... / An indifferent life at sixteen?"* Distorted quotation from the poem "Consolation for Shepherdesses" ("Uteshenie pastushkam," 1914).

59 *"Where shall I find a style to catch a stroll / Chablis on ice, a crispy toasted roll."* This poem opens not Kuzmin's first verse collection, *Nets* (1908), but rather the cycle "This Summer's Love" (see Kuzmin, *Selected Writings*, p. 35).

60 *"Evening mist lies upon the hills of Georgia, / The Aragva rumbles before me."* See our introduction for a literal translation of this poem. Notably, in *Petersburg Winters* the poem is cited correctly (cf. *Disintegration of the Atom*). In this episode Ivanov's Narbut, however, mistakes the name of the river in Georgia for that of a kebab stand.

61 *"I walk along at a slow pace / The happy Winckelmann cried."* Distorted quotation from the poem "As in the days of yore—toward the hamlets of Anatolia" ("Kak drevle—k selam Anatolii," 1913) by Vasily Komarovsky (Vasilii Alekseevich Komarovskii, 1881–1914).

62 *"Into the breaks between the clouds, into that radiant fissure … / Enflamed legions are marching."* Distorted quotation from the poem "Evening" ("Vecher," 1910) by Komarovsky.

63 *"In blood to our heels, we fight with corpses, / Resurrected for new funerals."* Quotation from the poem "A horrific dream has oppressed us" ("Uzhasnyi son otiagotel nad nami," 1863).

64 *"He said, shyly smiling … / I've been treating it for a long time."* Distorted quotation from "Everything happened as if in conversations" ("Vse bylo, tochno v razgovorakh," published 1915) by Ryurik Ivnev (Riurik Ivnev [real name Mikhail Aleksandrovich Kovalev], 1891–1981).

65 *"It was a quiet night, the night of the ball … / Its most sweeping bend."* Distorted quotation from the poem "A Summer Ball" ("Letnii ball," 1917) by Victor Hofmann (Viktor Viktorovich Gofman [Viktor Balthasar Emil Viktorowitsch Hofmann], 1884–1911).

66 *"From blood the hanky was scarlet / Our Little Dove was perishing."* Quotation from the poem "Wind, holy wind" ("Veterochek, sviatoi veterochek," published 1916) by Ivnev.

67 *"From this sobriety, from this vileness … / Must one slit one's throat with a razor?"* Ivanov adds nonexistent words and transposes lines from the poem "O Lord! O Lord! O Lord! The dark arch of the sky" ("Gospodi! Gospodi! Gospodi! Temnyi svod nebes," published 1917) by Ivnev.

68 *"You poured and poured and poured and rocked … / You were white and scarlet."* Quotation from the poem "Playing with light love" ("Liubov'iu legkoiu igraia," 1901) by Fyodor Sologub (Fedor Kuzmich Teternikov, 1863–1927).

69 *"With Your Honor's permission, / Colin the shepherd is my beau."* Quotation from the poem "From behind the bushes a tremor is audible" ("Za kustami shorokh slyshen," 1921) by Sologub.

70 *"Many springtimes have passed ... / And drooped, and bloomed."* Ivanov cites Sologub's poem "Many springtimes have passed" ("Mnogo bylo vesen," 1904).

71 *"But why do I hurt so much / In this most happy paradise of mine?"* The source of this quotation has not been found.

72 *"Why this inexplicable burden / On my quivering heart?"* The source of this quotation has also not been found.

73 *"I began early, I'll end earlier ... / Lies the burden of shattered hopes."* Distorted quotation from the poem "No, I am not another Byron, I am different" ("Net, ia ne Bairon, ia drugoi," 1832) by Mikhail Lermontov.

74 *"Lermontov lying 'with lead inside my breast,' covered by a trench coat, under a pouring rain."* Ivanov cites the uncannily prophetic lines from Lermontov's poem "The Dream" ("Son," 1841).

75 *"about valor, heroic deed, and glory."* Distorted quotation from the poem "About valorous honors, heroic deeds, and glory" ("O doblestiakh, o podvigakh, o slave," 1908) by Alexander Blok.

76 *"We argue in the room till morning ... / Greeting the golden hour."* Distorted quotation from the poem "Matutinal" ("Utrenniaia," 1904).

77 *"Were you a heavenly angel, / Not a tailcoat you'd have on, but a deacon's orarion."* Distorted quotation from the eponymous poem "Were you a heavenly angel" ("Esli by ty byl nebesnyi angel," 1906) by Kuzmin.

78 *"Philosophy we don't need ... / And sweet nonsense."* While the source of this quotation has not been found, other memoirists recorded Kuzmin's performing it (see, for example, Nikolai Chukovskii, *Literaturnye vospominaniia* [Moscow: Sovetskii pisatel', 1989], p. 144).

79 *"Here many chains have come unbound."* See note 27.

80 *"O, Heart! No need for this burden! / Fly into the blue sky."* Opening lines from the poem "Serdtse! Bremeni ne nado" (1916) by Leonid Ioakimovich Kannegisser (1897–1918).

81 *"And if, reeling from pain ... / Kerensky on a white steed."* Ivanov cites two closing quatrains from the poem "Parade" ("Smotr," 1917).

82 *"The Baltic Sea was smoking / Beyond blue, faraway Kronstadt."* Ivanov cites the first stanza of the eponymous poem (see *On the Border of*

Snow and Melt: Selected Poems of Georgy Ivanov, pp. 42–43). This seemingly innocuous seascape contains visual references to the Kronstadt rebellion references to which run through *Petersburg Winters*.

83　*"a man who loves the world and believes in God encompasses everything within himself."* Concluding lines from the poem "Fra Beato Andzheliko" ("Fra Beato Angelico," published 1912) by Nikolay Gumilyov.

84　*"He was only a modish man of letters, / Only the creator of blasphemous words—"* From the poem "In the Wake of a Coffin" ("Za grobom," 1908) by Alexander Blok.

85　*"vary-eyed."* Ivanov uses a nonce word (linguistic occasionalism) in reference to Gumilyov's amblyopia (also known as the "lazy eye" condition).

86　*"'Concerning the Soul,' the last article written by Blok to appear shortly before his death, is a scathing attack on Gumilyov, his poetics and worldview. Gumilyov's response to that article—patently Gumilyovian in its reserve and civility, yet no less caustic in its essence—was published after his execution."* Blok wrote no article of such title; Ivanov presumably refers to Blok's "Without Deity, Without Inspiration" (published posthumously in 1925), a critical evaluation of the Acmeist movement and poetics written from a Symbolist point of view. As he was executed in 1921, Gumilyov did not and could not respond to Blok's article in any form or medium.

87　*"Incomprehensible is his friendship with Vladimir Pyast, still more incomprehensible those with Evgeny Ivanov and Wilhelm Sorgenfrei, to whom, by the way, are dedicated these masterpieces of Blokian poetry: the former gets 'At the foot of a railroad embankment, on the uncut grass of a hollow' and the latter the astonishing 'Steps of the Commendatore.'"* As he compounds his tendentious and libelous mischaracterization of Pyast, Sorgenfrei, Evgenii Pavlovich Ivanov (1879–1942), and their friendship with Blok with further inventions, Georgy Ivanov the memoirist continues to demonstrate that his grasp of the basic facts of Blok's life and work was tenuous at best. Blok dedicated his poem "By the Railroad" ("Na zheleznoi doroge," 1910) not to Evgenii Ivanov, but to his sister Maria. A constant point of reference in Georgy Ivanov's own poetry (1910–1912; see Ivanov's poem "How cold it is to roam the world" ["Kholodno brodit' po svetu," *Roses*, 1931] in *On the Border of Snow and Melt: Selected Poems of Georgy Ivanov*, pp. 72–73), Blok's poem "Steps of the Commendatore" is indeed dedicated to Wilhelm Sorgenfrei.

88 *"Terrible World"* is the title of Blok's poetic cycle ("Strashnyi mir," 1910–1916).

89 *"a pure child of goodness and light, / a pure triumph of freedom."* Distorted quotation from the poem "Yes, I long to live madly" ("Da, ia khochu bezumno zhit'," 1914).

90 *"I will not forgive. Your soul is innocent. / For it, I will not forgive her, ever—"* Here Ivanov cites the poem "To Aleksandr Blok" ("A. Bloku," published 1922) by Zinaida Hippius. Hippius's poem articulated her disagreement with what she had perceived as her former friend Blok's justification of the Bolshevik October coup d'état. Throughout the 1920s and 1930s, together with her husband Dmitry Merezhkovsky Zinaida Hippius emerged as a great champion of Ivanov's poetry and prose.

91 *"The poet dies when he no longer has air to breathe."* Distorted quotation from Blok's celebration of Pushkin's memory, a commemorative speech titled "Concerning the Destiny of a Poet" ("O naznachenii poeta," 1921).

92 *"Here he lies—Lenin, Lenin— / Here he lies, sorrowfully putrefied."* Distorted quotation from the poem "Requiem" by Valery Bryusov.

93 *"I will not die in bed, A notary and a doctor by my side."* Quotation from the poem "You and I" ("Ia i Vy," published 1918) by Gumilyov.

94 *"I am polite with modern life … / To a lady with a prominent breast."* Distorted reproduction of the eponymous poem by Gumilyov (published 1916).

95 *"In the Gospel of St. John, / It is stated that the Word is God."* Quotation from the poem "The Word" ("Slovo," published 1921) by Gumilyov.

96 *"The smell of ruddy egg pies … / Cockroaches crawl into a crevice."* Quotation from the poem "In the Hut" ("V khate," 1914) by Yesenin.

97 *"One hidden dream I cherish … / As I whistle in the fall!"* Quotation from the poem "In that corner of the world where the yellow nettles" ("V tom kraiu, gde zheltaia krapiva," 1915).

98 *"Goodbye, my friend, goodbye."* Opening line of the poem "Do svidan'ia, drug moi, do svidan'ia" (1925) by Yesenin.

99 *"In Smolny you can find the darkness of slums / In his decrees, an echo of an Old Believer hegumen's shout."* Distorted quotation from the poem "In Lenin, there is the spirit of the Kerzhenets River" ("Est' v Lenine kerzhenskii dukh," 1918) by Nikolay Klyuyev.

100 *"God save Freedom— / The Commune's Red Tsar!"* Quotation from the poem "The Commune" ("Kommuna," 1918).

101 *"Now Thou dost dismiss."* The opening line of the so-called "Song of Simeon" (known alternatively as "Canticle of Simeon" or the *Nunc dimittis*), a canticle comprising an excerpt from the Gospel of Luke (2:29–32): "Now Thou dost dismiss Thy servant, O Lord, according to Thy word in peace; / Because my eyes have seen Thy salvation, / Which Thou hast prepared before the face of all peoples: / A light to the revelation of the Gentiles, and the glory of Thy people Israel" (in the wording from the Douay-Rheims Bible).

102 *"Poetry is God in Earth's holy dreams."* Quotation from the dramatic verse narrative "Camoens" (1938) by Friedrich Halm (real name Eligius Franz Joseph von Münch-Bellinghausen, 1806–1871), translated into Russian by Vasily Zhukovsky (1839).

103 *"Every once in a while / Poets become uncanny prophets."* Opening lines from the poem "Byvaiut strannymi prorokami" by Mikhail Kuzmin (published in 1914).

104 *"The spring day danced and cried away … / To raise my eyes together with you."* Distorted quotation from the eponymous poem by Yesenin (1917).

105 *"Pushkin is our everything."* The phrase belongs to Apollon Aleksandrovich Grigor'ev (1822–1864).

106 *"Yesenin's significance lies precisely in that he attained the level of the Russian people's consciousness during 'Russia's terrifying years,' overlapped with it completely, became synonymous with both Russia's downfall and her longing for resurrection."* The phrase "Russia's terrifying years" is borrowed from Alexander Blok's poem "Born during the years of oppression" ("Rozhdennye v goda glukhie," 1914).